Praise for David Lagercrantz

and THE GIRL WHO LIVED TWICE

"[Lisbeth Salander] is imbued with a grit and gumption that would make Larsson . . . proud." —*USA Today*

"Masterful. . . . Intricate and ambitious. . . . Salander is an extraordinary heroine whose hacker skills are more relevant than ever in an increasingly high-tech surveillance society." —*The Atlantic*

"Salander is what she's always been: a force to be reckoned with and one of the most memorable series leads in the history of crime fiction." —*Booklist*

"Lisbeth Salander remains, in Lagercrantz's hands, the most enigmatic and fascinating anti-heroine in fiction." —*Financial Times*

"Lagercrantz has more than met the challenge. Larsson's brainchildren are in good hands and may have even come up a bit in the world." —*The Wall Street Journal*

"*The Girl Who Lived Twice* delivers a suspenseful story, offering some welcome escapism." —*The National Book Review*

David Lagercrantz

THE GIRL WHO LIVED TWICE

David Lagercrantz is an acclaimed Swedish author and journalist. He is the author of three books in the Millennium series: *The Girl in the Spider's Web*, *The Girl Who Takes an Eye for an Eye*, and *The Girl Who Lived Twice*. He is the coauthor of numerous biographies (including the internationally best-selling memoir *I Am Zlatan Ibrahimović*) and the acclaimed novel *Fall of Man in Wilmslow*, on the death and life of Alan Turing.

www.davidlagercrantz.com

THE GIRL
WHO LIVED TWICE

THE GIRL
WHO LIVED TWICE

David Lagercrantz

Translated from the Swedish by George Goulding

VINTAGE CRIME/BLACK LIZARD
Vintage Books
A Division of Penguin Random House LLC
New York

FIRST VINTAGE CRIME/BLACK LIZARD EDITION, MAY 2020

Translation copyright © 2019 by George Goulding

All rights reserved. Published in the United States by Vintage Books,
a division of Penguin Random House LLC, New York. Originally published
in Sweden as *Hon som måste dö* by Norstedts, Stockholm, in 2019.
Copyright © 2019 by David Lagercrantz and Moggliden AB. This translation
simultaneously published in Great Britain by MacLehose Press, an imprint
of Quercus Publishing Ltd, London, in 2019, by agreement with Nordstedts
Agency. Published by arrangement with Quercus Publishing PLC (U.K.).
Originally published in hardcover in the United States by Alfred A. Knopf,
a division of Penguin Random House LLC, New York, in 2019.

Vintage Crime/Black Lizard and colophon are trademarks and Vintage is
a registered trademark of Penguin Random House LLC.

This is a work of fiction. Names, characters, places, and incidents
either are the product of the author's imagination or are used fictitiously.
Any resemblance to actual persons, living or dead, events,
or locales is entirely coincidental.

The Cataloging-in-Publication Data is available at the Library of Congress.

Vintage Trade Paperback ISBN: 978-1-101-97417-9
eBook ISBN: 978-0-451-49435-1

www.vintagebooks.com

Printed in the United States of America
10 9 8 7 6 5 4 3 2 1

CONTENTS

CHARACTERS AND ORGANIZATIONS
IN THE MILLENNIUM SERIES

LISBETH SALANDER, an elusive, exceptionally talented hacker and mathematical genius, tattooed and with a troubled past, driven by a need for justice—and vengeance.

MIKAEL BLOMKVIST, a leading investigative journalist at *Millennium* magazine. Salander helped him to research one of the biggest stories of his career, about the disappearance of Harriet Vanger. He later helped to clear Salander of murder and vindicate her in a legal battle over her right to determine her own affairs. Sometimes nicknamed "Kalle Blomkvist," after a boy detective who appears in several novels by Astrid Lindgren.

ALEXANDER ZALACHENKO, also known as Zala, or by his alias, Karl Axel Bodin. A Russian spy who defected to Sweden and was protected for years by a special group within Säpo. He was the head of a criminal empire but also the father of Lisbeth Salander, who tried to kill him for the violent abuse of her mother. Ultimately he was finished off by Säpo.

RONALD NIEDERMANN, Lisbeth Salander's half brother, a blond giant impervious to pain. Salander arranged his murder.

CAMILLA SALANDER, Lisbeth's troublesome twin sister, from whom she is estranged. Linked to criminal gangs and thought to live in Moscow. Known within her networks as Kira.

AGNETA SALANDER, Lisbeth and Camilla's mother, who died in a nursing home at the age of forty-three.

PETER TELEBORIAN, Salander's sadistic child psychiatrist. Chief prosecution witness in Salander's incompetency trial.

HOLGER PALMGREN, Salander's former guardian, a lawyer. One of the few people who knows Salander well and whom she trusts. Recently murdered by associates of Peter Teleborian, for holding documents that shed light on Salander's abuse as a child.

DRAGAN ARMANSKY, Salander's former employer, the head of Milton Security. Another of the few people she trusts.

MIRIAM WU, Salander's friend and occasional lover, also known as "Mimmi."

ERIKA BERGER, editor-in-chief of *Millennium* magazine, a close friend and occasional lover of Blomkvist's.

GREGER BECKMAN, Erika Berger's husband, an architect.

MALIN ERIKSSON, managing editor of *Millennium* magazine.

ANNIKA GIANNINI, Blomkvist's sister, a defence lawyer who has represented Salander.

JURIJ BOGDANOV, star hacker in Camilla Salander's "Spider Society," and erstwhile drug addict and petty criminal.

"ED THE NED," Edwin Needham, a gifted and outspoken computer security technician at the NSA, America's national security agency.

JAN BUBLANSKI, chief inspector with the Stockholm police; headed the team investigating the Salander case. Known as "Officer Bubble."

SONJA MODIG, a police inspector who has for some years worked closely with Bublanski, along with CURT SVENSSON, AMANDA FLOD and JERKER HOLMBERG.

HANS FASTE, a police officer who has clashed with colleagues in the past, and leaked information during an earlier investigation into Salander.

FARAH SHARIF, professor of computer sciences, fiancée to Jan Bublanski.

SÄPO, the Swedish security police, which harboured a secret faction, known as "the Section," dedicated to protecting Zalachenko.

MUST, the Swedish Military Intelligence and Security Service.

MSB, the Swedish Civil Contingencies Agency.

THE GIRL
WHO LIVED TWICE

PROLOGUE

A beggar nobody had seen before appeared in the neighbourhood that summer. No-one knew him by name, nor seemed to care much about him, but to a young couple who passed him every morning he was the "crazy dwarf." He was in fact around five feet tall, but he was certainly erratic, and he would occasionally spring up and grab people by the arm, babbling incoherently.

Most of the day he sat on a piece of cardboard right by the fountain and the statue of Thor in Mariatorget, and there he commanded a measure of respect. With his head held high and his back always straight he looked like a chieftain who had fallen on hard times. That was all the social capital he had left, and it was why some people still tossed him coins or banknotes, as though they could sense a lost greatness. And they were not mistaken. There had indeed been a time when people bowed before him. But all repute, all status, had long since been stripped from him. He was missing several fingers and the dark patches on his cheeks did not improve his appearance. They looked to be a shadow of death itself.

The only thing which stood out was his quilted down jacket, a blue Marmot parka which must have been expensive. It looked so out of place, not just because of all the dirt and stains on it, but also because it was much too wintry a garment to be worn at the height of summer in Stockholm. An oppressive heat lay over the city, and as the sweat trickled down the man's cheeks, passersby studied the jacket with a pained expression, as if the very sight of it made them feel uncomfortably hot themselves. But the beggar was never without it.

He looked lost to the world and seemed unlikely ever to be a threat to anybody, but it was later said that at the beginning of August a more determined expression came over him. On the afternoon of the eleventh he was seen painstakingly writing out a screed on lined A4 paper and, later that same evening, he stuck it up like a newspaper on the bus stop at Södra Station.

It was a rambling account of a storm and referred by name to a member of the government. A young medical intern called Else Sandberg, who was waiting for the number 4 bus, managed to decipher parts of it and could not help being intrigued, professionally. Her best guess at a diagnosis was paranoid schizophrenia.

But when the bus arrived ten minutes later, she forgot all about it, left only with a feeling of unease. It was like the curse of Cassandra: Nobody was going to believe the man because the story he was telling was so wrapped up in madness. Yet somehow his message must have got through, because the very next morning a man in a white shirt got out of a blue Audi and tore the papers down, crumpling the shreds of them and taking them back to his car.

On the night of Friday, August 14, the beggar made his way over to Norra Bantorget to get hold of some moonshine. There he met another drunk, a former industrial worker named Heikki Järvinen, from Österbotten.

"Hey, brother. Are you desperate?" Järvinen said.

There was no answer, not at first. Then a stream of words came pouring out, which to Heikki sounded like a load of bragging, and he hissed "what total bullshit," adding needlessly—he admitted as much himself—that the man looked like a "bloody Chinaman."

"Me Khamba-chen . . . hate China!" the beggar yelled at him.

Then he punched Heikki with his damaged hand and, even though there was no skill or technique there, the blow carried an unexpected authority. Heikki was bleeding from the mouth and swearing profusely in Finnish as he staggered away, down into the tunnelbana at Central Station.

The beggar was next seen back in his familiar neighbourhood, very drunk and clearly feeling ill. Saliva ran from his mouth and he was holding his throat and muttering:

"Very tired . . . Must find Dharamsala, and Ihawa, very good Ihawa . . . Do you know?"

He never waited for an answer but crossed Ringvägen like a sleepwalker, and soon after that he threw an unlabelled bottle onto the ground and disappeared among the trees and bushes of Tantolunden. A light rain fell overnight and in the morning a north wind was blowing. By eight the wind had died down and the skies had cleared, and the man was seen on his knees, leaning up against a birch tree.

On the street, preparations were underway for the Midnattsloppet race that coming night. The neighbourhood was in a festive mood.

The beggar was dead.

No-one cared or knew that this strange man had lived a life of unimaginable hardship and heroism, still less that he had only ever loved one woman, and that she too, in another time, had died in devastating solitude.

PART I

THE UNKNOWN

AUGUST 15–25

Many dead never have a name and some not even a grave.

Others get one white cross among thousands of others, as in the military cemeteries in France.

Some few have a whole monument dedicated to them, like the Tomb of the Unknown Soldier at the Arc de Triomphe in Paris or in the Alexander Garden in Moscow.

CHAPTER 1

August 15

The first person to pluck up the courage to cross the street and go up to the tree, only to discover that the man was dead, was the writer Ingela Dufva. It was half past eleven by then. The smell was terrible. Flies and mosquitoes were buzzing about, and Dufva was not being entirely truthful when she later said there was something deeply moving about the figure.

The man had vomited and suffered from diarrhoea. Instead of empathy, she felt anxiety and contemplated with dread the prospect of her own death. Even Sandra Lindevall and Samir Eman, the police officers who arrived at the scene fifteen minutes later, looked upon their assignment as some sort of punishment.

They photographed the man and examined the immediate surroundings, but their search did not extend to the slope below Zinkens Väg, where a half bottle of alcohol lay with a thin layer of grit in the bottom. Even though neither of them thought the incident had crime "written all over it," they examined his head and chest with care. They found no trace of violence, nor any other sign that pointed to the cause of death, apart from the thick drool which had trailed from his mouth. Having discussed the matter with their superiors, they decided not to cordon off the area.

While waiting for an ambulance to come and take the body away, they went through the pockets of the filthy, shapeless and quite unsuitable down jacket. They found many pieces of the translucent paper in which hot dogs are sold in the street, some coins, a twenty-kronor note and a receipt from an office supplies store on Hornsgatan, but no ID card or other papers that might have allowed them to identify the dead man.

They supposed it would not be difficult to find out who he was. There was no shortage of distinctive features. But like so much else, this proved to be a mistaken assumption. When the autopsy was carried out at the forensic medicine unit in Solna, X-rays were taken of the man's teeth. No match was found for them in any database, nor for the prints from his remaining fingers. Having sent off some samples to the National Forensics Laboratory, Medical Examiner Dr. Fredrika Nyman checked some telephone numbers handwritten on a piece of paper found in one of the man's trouser pockets, though it did not in any way fall within her responsibilities to do so.

One number was that of Mikael Blomkvist at *Millennium* magazine. For a few hours she thought no more about it. But later in the evening, after a particularly upsetting row with one of her teenage daughters, she reminded herself that in the past year alone she had performed autopsies on three bodies which were then buried without being identified, and she swore at that, and at life in general.

She was forty-nine, a single mother of two, and she suffered from back pain and insomnia and the sense that life was meaningless. Without thinking it through she rang Mikael Blomkvist.

The telephone buzzed. It was an unknown number and Blomkvist ignored it. He had just left his apartment and was on his way down Hornsgatan towards Slussen and Gamla Stan with no clue where he was heading. He wandered aimlessly through the lanes until at last he sat down at an open-air café and ordered a Guinness.

It was seven in the evening, but still warm. Laughter and applause could be heard coming from Skeppsholmen and he looked up at the blue sky and felt a mild, pleasant breeze coming off the water. He tried to persuade himself that life was not, after all, so bad. But even after a beer and then a second he wasn't convinced, so he paid and decided to head home to do some work. Or perhaps he would immerse himself in a TV series or a thriller.

Then almost immediately he changed his mind and set off towards Mosebacke and Fiskargatan. Lisbeth Salander lived at Fiskargatan 9. He was not at all confident she would be at home—after the funeral of Holger Palmgren, her former guardian, she had travelled around Europe and only sporadically answered Blomkvist's e-mails and texts—but he would try his luck. He took the steps up from the square and turned to face the building opposite the apartment block. He was amazed. Since he had last been there the entire blank wall had been covered by an enormous work of street art. But he spent no time studying it, even though it was a painting to lose oneself in, full of surreal detail, like a funny little man in tartan trousers standing barefoot on a green tunnelbana carriage.

He keyed in the front-door code, got into the lift and glared at the mirror inside. You would hardly know that the summer had been hot and sunny. He saw himself pale and hollow-eyed and he was weighed down still by the stock market crash which he had been wrestling with all through July. It was an important story, no question. It had been a rout, caused not just by high valuations and over-inflated expectations but also by hacker attacks and disinformation campaigns. By now every investigative journalist worth his salt was digging into it, and even though he had uncovered a great deal—among other things he had discovered which troll factory in Russia had chiefly been spreading the lies—it felt as if the world was managing just fine without his efforts. He should probably take some time off, get some much-needed exercise, and maybe take better care of his colleague Erika, who was in the throes of getting a divorce from Greger.

The lift came to a halt and he pushed open the wrought-iron gate and got out, already convinced that his visit would be a waste of time. Salander was almost certainly away, and was definitely ignoring him. But then he saw that the door to her apartment was wide open, and remembered how frightened he had been all summer that her enemies would go after her. He rushed in over the threshold. "Hello . . . hello!"

he shouted, and was met by the smell of fresh paint and cleaning products.

He heard footsteps behind him. Someone was snorting like a bull on the stairs and he spun around and found himself confronting two stocky men in blue overalls. They were carrying something large, and he was so agitated that he was unable to grasp this perfectly normal scene.

"What are you doing?" he said.

"What does it look like?"

It looked like two removal men lugging a blue sofa, a stylish new piece of designer furniture, and Lisbeth—he of all people knew—was not one for stylish interiors. He was about to say something when he heard a voice from inside the apartment. For an instant he thought it was Lisbeth's and he brightened. But this was only wishful thinking. It didn't sound remotely like her.

"A distinguished visitor. To what do I owe this honour?"

He turned and saw a tall black woman standing on the threshold, contemplating him with a mocking look. She was wearing jeans and an elegant grey blouse. Her hair was in braids and her almond eyes sparkled, and he became even more confused. Did he know her?

"No, no," he managed. "I just . . ."

"You just . . ."

"Got the wrong floor."

"Or didn't know the young lady had sold her apartment?"

He did not. And now he felt uncomfortable, especially since the woman kept smiling at him. He was almost relieved when she turned to the removal men to make sure the sofa didn't bang against the doorframe, and then vanished into the apartment again. He wanted to get away, to digest the news. He wanted to drink more Guinness. But he stood there as if frozen to the spot, and glanced at the mailbox. The name there was no longer v. KULLA, but LINDER. Who the hell was Linder? He searched the name on his mobile and up came an image of the woman.

Kadi Linder, psychologist and non-executive member of various boards. It didn't give him much to go on and he was intrigued. But most of all he thought about Lisbeth, and he had only just managed to compose himself when Kadi Linder reappeared in the doorway. Now she was not only teasing, but curious too. Her eyes flicked back and forth. She was slim, with slender wrists and pronounced collarbones, and there was a waft of perfume in the air.

"Go on, tell me. Did you really come to the wrong place?"

"I'll pass on that one," he said. Not a good answer, he realized at once.

But he understood from her smile that she had seen through his confusion and he wanted to get away, leaving as little as possible behind. Under no circumstances would he reveal that Lisbeth Salander had lived at this address under an assumed name, regardless of what Linder did or did not know.

"That doesn't make me any less curious," she said.

He laughed—as if the whole thing was a silly private matter.

"So you're not here to check me out? I mean, this place wasn't exactly cheap."

"Unless you've cut off a horse's head and left it in someone's bed, I should probably leave you in peace."

"Can't say I remember every detail of the negotiations, but I don't think that came up."

"I'm happy to hear it. In that case I'll wish you all the best," he said with feigned ease. He wanted to leave together with the removal men who were on their way out of the apartment, but Linder evidently hoped to keep the conversation going and was nervously fiddling with her braids. It struck him that what he had construed as an irritating self-confidence might in fact be a cover for something quite different.

"Do you know her?" she said.

"Who?"

"The woman who lived here."

He turned the question around.

"Do you?"

"No," she said. "I don't even know her name. But I still like her."

"Why's that?"

"Despite all the chaos on the stock exchange, the bidding turned out to be pretty crazy. There was no way I was going to keep up, so I dropped out. But I still got the apartment because 'the young lady'—as the lawyer called her—wanted me to have it. Believe it or not, it went through in two weeks!"

"Extraordinary."

"Isn't it?"

"Maybe you'd done something the young lady liked?"

"I'm actually best known in the media for having run-ins with old boys who sit on boards."

"It's possible that she approves of that kind of thing."

"Maybe. If I can tempt you with a moving-in beer, we

could talk about it. I have to say"—she hesitated again—"I loved your story about the twins. It was so touching."

"Thanks," he said. "You're very kind. But I really do have to go."

She nodded and he just managed a "See you." He hardly could have said how he got away, only that he emerged into the summer evening. He didn't notice the two new surveillance cameras over the street entrance, or even the hot-air balloon immediately above. He crossed Mosebacke and continued down towards Urvädersgränd. Only at Götgatan did he slow down, and he felt totally deflated. All that had happened was that Lisbeth had moved, which he should have welcomed. She was safer now. But instead of being glad for her, Blomkvist felt it like a slap in the face. It was absurd.

She was Lisbeth Salander. She was who she was. But he felt hurt all the same. She could have given some indication. He reached for his mobile to send her a text, a question, but no, best let it go. He walked along Hornsgatan and saw that the youngest participants were already running their lap of the Midnattsloppet and he stared in astonishment at the number of parents cheering and clapping from the pavement, as if he simply could not understand their excitement. He had to concentrate to cross the street in a gap between the runners. Up on Bellmansgatan his thoughts continued to meander, and he remembered the last time he had been with Salander.

It was at Kvarnen restaurant on the evening of Holger's funeral, and neither of them had found it easy to talk. Under the circumstances that was hardly surprising. The only thing that stayed with him from their encounter was her answer to his question:

"What are you going to do now?"

"I will be the hunter and not the hunted."

The hunter and not the hunted.

He never managed to get her to explain, and he remembered how she had later disappeared across Medborgarplatsen, wearing a black tailored suit which made her look like an angry boy reluctantly dressed up for some formal occasion. It was in early July, not that long ago, but already it felt like an age. He thought about that and other things as he continued home. When at last he had opened his door and settled into the sofa with a Pilsner Urquell, his mobile rang again.

It was a medical examiner, a doctor by the name of Fredrika Nyman.

CHAPTER 2

August 15

Salander was in a hotel room on Manezhnaya Square in Moscow, her eyes on her laptop, and she watched as Mikael Blomkvist emerged from the building entrance on Fiskargatan. He did not look his usual confident self, instead he seemed lost. She felt a pang of something she did not fully recognize and did not feel minded to probe. She glanced up from her screen at the glass dome in the square outside, glittering with light of all colours.

The city that until recently had held no interest for her now beckoned, and it crossed her mind that she should just drop everything and go out on a binge. But that was idiotic, she had to remain disciplined. She had more or less been living at her laptop recently, sometimes she hardly slept. And yet she looked much neater than she had for a long time. She had had her hair cut short. Her piercings were gone and she was wearing a white shirt and her black suit, just as she had at the funeral, not actually to honour Holger, but because it had become habit and she wanted to blend in better.

She had resolved to strike first, not wait like some cornered prey, and that was why she now found herself in Moscow, and why she had arranged for cameras to be installed at Fiskargatan in Stockholm. But she was paying a higher price than expected. Not only because it brought back her past and kept her awake at night. It was also the fact that her enemies were hiding behind smokescreens and impossible encryptions, and she had to spend hours covering her tracks. She was living like a prisoner on the run. Nothing of what she was searching for came easily to her, and it was only now, after a month's work, that she was nearing her objective. But it was hard to know for certain, and sometimes she wondered if the enemy was, in spite of everything, always one step ahead.

Today, when she had been out on reconnaissance, she had felt she was being watched, and sometimes at night she would listen for footsteps in the hotel corridor, especially those of one man—she was sure it was a man—suffering from dysmetria, an irregularity in his gait, who often slowed down outside her door, and who seemed to be listening too.

She pressed rewind. Again Blomkvist came out of the apartment on Fiskargatan with a hangdog look, and she reflected on that as she drained her glass of whisky. Dark clouds drifted over the State Duma towards Red Square and the Kremlin. A storm was on its way, and that was perhaps just as well. She got up and considered taking a shower or a bath, then settled for changing her shirt, choosing a black one. That seemed appropriate. From a hidden compartment in her suitcase she retrieved her Beretta Cheetah, the pistol she had bought on her second day in Moscow, and slotted it into the holster under her jacket. She sat on the bed and contemplated the room.

She did not like it, nor the hotel for that matter. It was too luxurious, too ostentatious, and it was not just that there were men like her father socializing down in the bar, pompous shits with a sense of unconditional entitlement to their mistresses and subordinates. There were also eyes on her, and word could be passed to the intelligence services or to gangsters. Often she found herself sitting as she was now, fists clenched, ready for a fight.

She went into the bathroom and splashed cold water on her face. It didn't help much. Her forehead was tense from lack of sleep, her head ached. Was it time to go, so soon? Probably just as well. She listened first for sounds from the corridor, then slipped out. Her room was on the twentieth floor, close to the lifts. A man of middle age was already waiting, good-looking with short hair, wearing jeans and a leather jacket and a black shirt just like hers. She knew she had seen him somewhere before. There was something strange about his eyes, they shone with different colours. She ignored him and stared at the floor as they rode down in the lift.

She stepped into the lobby and went straight out into the square. Ahead of her the large glass dome sparkled in the dark. Beneath this revolving map of the world was a four-storey shopping centre. On top, a bronze statue of St. George and the Dragon. St. George was Moscow's patron saint and she ran into him everywhere in the city, with his sword raised. Sometimes she put a hand to her left shoulder blade, a gesture of protection for her own dragon. Or she would caress an old bullet wound in the same shoulder, or her hip, where there was a scar from a knife injury, as if to remind herself of past pain.

Her mind was on conflagrations and disasters, and she thought also of her mother. Yet she was still careful to avoid surveillance cameras. Her movements were therefore tense and irregular as she hurried towards Tverskoy Boulevard, the large, splendid avenue with its parks and gardens, and she did not pause until she reached Versailles, one of the fanciest restaurants in the city.

The building looked like a baroque palace, with columns, gold ornaments and crystal, an entire glittering seventeenth-century pastiche. She wanted nothing more than to get far away. But tonight a party was to be held there, for the city's wealthiest, and from a distance she could observe the preparations. So far the only people there were small groups of beautiful young women, probably call girls hired for the occasion. The staff were also hard at work making the final arrangements.

As she drew closer she caught sight of the host. Vladimir Kuznetsov. He was at the front entrance in a white dinner jacket and patent-leather shoes, and even though he was not old, barely fifty, he looked like Santa Claus with his white hair and beard, and a fat belly at odds with his thin legs. Officially he was something of a success story, a petty criminal fallen on hard times who had turned his life around to become a celebrity chef specializing in bear steak and mushroom sauces. But covertly he ran a string of troll factories that spewed out fake news, often with overtly anti-Semitic content. Kuznetsov had not only caused chaos and influenced political elections. He also had blood on his hands.

He was guilty of fomenting genocide and had turned hatred into big business. The mere sight of him at the entrance gave Salander a boost. She felt the outline of her Beretta in its holster and looked around her. Kuznetsov was tugging nervously at his beard—it was to be his big night.

A string quartet, which Salander knew would be followed by the Russian swing jazz band, was playing inside. A red carpet had been rolled out beneath a broad black awning. It was bounded by rope and bodyguards who stood in serried ranks, kitted out in grey suits and earpieces. All were armed. Kuznetsov studied his watch. Not a single guest had arrived—perhaps it was some kind of game? Nobody wanted to be the first.

But the street was full of people who had come to gawp. Word had clearly got out that VIPs were expected, and that was no bad thing, Salander thought. She would melt into the crowd more easily. Then the rain began to fall, first a drizzle, soon a downpour. There was a flash of lightning in the distance. Thunder rolled. The crowd dispersed, except for a few hardy figures with umbrellas who stayed put. Before long the first limousines and guests arrived. Kuznetsov greeted them one by one with a bow, and a woman beside him ticked off names in a little black book. The restaurant slowly filled up with middle-aged men and even more young women.

Salander heard the hum of voices from within and, more faintly, the music from the string quartet. Every now and then she glimpsed figures she had come across during her research, and she observed how Kuznetsov's expressions and movements varied according to the status of each arrival. All guests received the particular smile and bow he considered they merited, and the really distinguished ones were treated to a little joke too, though most of the laughter came from Kuznetsov himself.

He grinned and chortled like a court jester, and Salander stood frozen and wet, staring at the spectacle. A guard noticed her and nodded at a colleague—she had become too absorbed and that was not good, not good at all. She pretended to walk away but instead hid in a doorway a little way off. She noticed then that her hands were shaking and she did not think it was because of the rain or the cold. Nervous tension had brought her close to breaking point.

She pulled out her mobile to check everything was prepared. The attack had to be perfectly coordinated, or she would be lost. She went through it once, twice, three times. But the minutes were running away from her and she began to have doubts. The rain fell and nothing was happening. It was looking more and more like yet another missed opportunity.

The guests all seemed to have arrived. Even Kuznetsov had gone inside. The party was in full swing, the men were already knocking back shots and groping the girls. She decided to go back to the hotel.

But at that moment another limousine drew up and a woman by the entrance hurried inside to fetch Kuznetsov, who came shambling out of the restaurant with sweat on his forehead and a glass of champagne in his hand. Salander decided to stay after all. This guest was important, that much was obvious from the behaviour of the security guards and the tension in the air, as well as the ridiculous look on Kuznetsov's face. Salander slunk back into her doorway. But nobody emerged from the limousine.

No chauffeur jumped out into the rain to open the door, the car just stood there. Kuznetsov straightened his hair and bow tie, pulled in his stomach and drained his glass. Salander stopped trembling. She picked up something in Kuznetsov's eyes that she recognized only too well, and with no further hesitation she launched her attack.

Then she tucked her mobile into her pocket and let the programme codes do their work while she looked around, noting every detail of her surroundings with photographic precision: the body language of the guards, the proximity of their hands to their weapons, the gaps between their shoulders along the red carpet, the irregularities and puddles on the pavement before her.

Motionless, almost catatonic, she stood watching right up to the moment when the chauffeur got out of the limousine, unfurled an umbrella and opened the back door. Then she moved forward with cat-like steps, her hand on the grip of the pistol inside her jacket.

CHAPTER 3

August 15

Blomkvist was no longer on very good terms with his mobile and should have got himself a private number long ago. But he was reluctant to do so. As a journalist he did not want to make himself inaccessible to members of the public. And yet he suffered from the endless calls he received, and he felt that something had changed in the course of the past year.

The tone had become rougher. People insulted him and shouted at him, or came to him with the craziest tip-offs. He had all but given up answering calls from unknown numbers. He simply let his mobile vibrate and ring, and if he ever did pick up, as now, he often found himself pulling a face without intending to.

"Blomkvist," he said, grabbing another beer from the refrigerator.

"Apologies," said a woman's voice. "Shall I call back later?"

"No, don't bother," he answered in a milder tone. "What's it about?"

"My name is Fredrika Nyman, I'm a doctor at the National Board of Forensic Medicine in Solna."

He was struck by fear.

"What's happened?"

"Nothing's happened, other than the stuff that always happens, and I'm sure that's got nothing to do with you. But we've had a body in—"

"A woman?" he interrupted.

"No, no, very definitely a man. Well, very definitely . . . that's a strange way of putting it, isn't it? But it is a man, maybe in his sixties or a bit younger, who's clearly been to hell and back. I've never seen anything like it."

"Would you mind getting to the point?"

"I'm sorry, I didn't mean to worry you. I don't think it's likely you knew him. He was a down-and-out, and right at the bottom of the pecking order even in those circles."

"So what has he got to do with me?"

"He had your mobile number in his pocket."

"Lots of people do," Blomkvist said, irritated. Immediately he felt he had been tactless.

"I do understand," Fredrika Nyman went on. "You must be bombarded with calls. But this is something I feel strongly about."

"In what way?"

"I believe that even the worst wrecks among us deserve some dignity in death."

"Of course," he said, to make up for his lack of sympathy a moment ago.

"Precisely," she said, "and Sweden has always been a civilized country in that respect. But with each passing year we receive more and more bodies we don't manage to identify, and that really upsets me. Everyone's entitled to an identity in death. To a name, and a history."

"True," he said, but he had already lost his concentration and almost without being aware of it he went over to the laptop on his desk.

"Sometimes I'm sure there have been genuine difficulties," the woman said. "But often it's just down to a lack of resources or time, or worse, a lack of will, and I have a nasty feeling that may be the case with this body."

"What makes you say that?"

"The fact that there have been no hits in any database, and because the man looks like someone without any significance at all. The lowest of the low. The sort we normally look away from and simply forget."

"Very sad," he said.

He searched through the files he had created over the years for Salander.

"With any luck I'm wrong," Fredrika Nyman said. "I've just sent off my samples, and soon we may know more about this man. Now I'm at home, and I thought I could try and speed things up a bit. You live on Bellmansgatan, don't you? It's not that far from where he was found, you might have bumped into each other. Maybe he's even called you?"

"So where was he found?"

"Beside a tree in Tantolunden. You would remember if you'd seen him. His face was dark brown and dirty, with deep furrows. Sparse beard. He's almost certainly been exposed to strong sunshine and severe cold. His body bears the marks of frostbite and he's missing most of his fingers and toes. His muscle attachments show signs of extreme exertion. I would guess that he comes from somewhere in Southeast Asia. He may have been quite handsome once upon a time. His features are clean, even though his face is ravaged. Yellowish skin due to liver damage. There are black patches on his cheeks, signs of necrosis. It's always hard to determine age at this early stage, as I'm sure you know. But I would guess that he was getting on for sixty, as I said, and for a long time he'd been on the verge of dehydrating. He was short, a little under five feet."

"I'm not sure. Doesn't ring any bells," Blomkvist said.

He was searching for messages from Salander among his files, but found none. She didn't even appear to be hacking him these days, and this made him more and more worried. He could almost feel in his bones that she was in danger.

"I'm not done yet," Fredrika Nyman said. "I haven't mentioned the most noticeable thing about him, his down jacket."

"What was so special about that?"

"It was so large and warm that it ought to have been pretty conspicuous in this heat."

"As you say, I would have remembered it."

He closed the computer and looked out over Riddarfjärden. Once again he thought it was probably sensible of Salander to have sold her apartment.

"But you don't, right?"

"No . . ." he said hesitantly. "You don't have a picture you could send me?"

"I don't think that would be ethical."

"How do you think he died?"

He was not fully focused.

"Well, poisoning finished him off, I would guess, self-inflicted no doubt, first and foremost from alcohol, of course. He reeked of it, but that doesn't rule out the possibility that he had something else inside him as well. I'll hear more on that from the forensics lab in a few days. I've requested a drug screening which covers more than eight hundred substances. But the broader picture is of slow and steady organ failure, and an enlarged heart."

Blomkvist sat on the sofa and emptied his beer, and was clearly silent for too long.

"Are you still there?" the medical examiner said.

"Yes, I'm here. I was just thinking . . ."

"Thinking what?"

He was thinking about Lisbeth.

"That it may be a good thing he had my number," he said.

"How do you mean?"

"Maybe he felt he had a story to tell, and I'm sure that'll encourage the police to try harder. Sometimes, when I'm at my best, I can put the wind up them."

She gave a laugh.

"I'm sure you can."

"Sometimes I just annoy them."

Sometimes I annoy myself, he thought.

"Let's hope it's the first of those."

"Yes, let's."

He wanted to end the call. He wanted to be left alone with

his thoughts. But the medical examiner wanted to talk some more and he did not have the heart to hang up on her.

"I mentioned that he was the sort of man one normally just wants to forget, didn't I?" she went on.

"You did."

"But that's not entirely true, not for me. It feels like . . . it feels like his body has a story to tell."

"In what way?"

"He looks as if he's gone through both ice and fire. As I said, I don't think I've seen anything quite like it."

"Tough guy."

"Yes, maybe. He was tattered, and indescribably dirty. He stank. And yet he had a sort of dignity. I think that's what I'm trying to say. Something which gave him some respect, notwithstanding all the humiliation. He had fought the good fight."

"Had he been a soldier?"

"I saw no sign of battle scars, nothing of that sort."

"Or a man from some primitive tribe?"

"Hardly. He'd received dental care and could evidently write. There's a tattoo of a Buddhist wheel on his left wrist."

"I understand."

"You do?"

"I understand that he made you care in some way. I'll check my voicemail and see if he's been in touch."

"Thanks," she said, and they probably talked a little longer, he wasn't sure; he was still a little distracted.

When they had hung up, Blomkvist remained sitting, deep in thought. The sounds of cheering and clapping could be heard from the Midnattsloppet on Hornsgatan and he ran his fingers through his hair. It had to be almost three months since he last had it cut. He needed to get a grip on his life. He even needed to *have* a life, enjoy himself like everyone else and not just work and keep pushing himself to the limits. Maybe also answer his phone and not be so focused on his bloody news stories.

He went into the bathroom, not that that made him feel any better. Clothes were hanging out to dry. There were blobs of toothpaste and shaving foam in the washbasin, and hair in the bathtub. A down jacket, he thought, in the middle of summer? There was something in that, wasn't there? But he found it hard to focus. Too many thoughts were crowding in, and he wiped the washbasin and the mirror, folded the laundry, and picked up his mobile to check his voicemail.

He had thirty-seven unopened ones. Nobody should have thirty-seven unopened voicemails, for Christ's sake, and now, with a pained expression, he listened to every one of them. My God, what was it with people? Admittedly there were many who wanted to give him tip-offs, and others who were courteous and respectful. But most were plain angry. You're lying about immigration, they shouted. Keeping us all in the dark about the Muslims. Protecting the Jews in the financial elite. It was like being sprayed with muck, and he was on the point of ringing off. But he listened on bravely and then finally he heard something which was neither the one nor the other. It was just a moment of confusion.

"Hello . . . hello," said a voice in accented English, breathing heavily, and after a short silence it added: "Come in, over."

It sounded like a call on a walkie-talkie, and was followed by a few more words which Blomkvist could not understand, perhaps in another language? There was desperation and loneliness in the voice. Could it be the beggar? Possible. There was no way of knowing. Blomkvist hung up and went into the kitchen, and considered calling Malin Frode or anyone else who could put him in a better mood. But he resisted the impulse and instead sent off an encrypted text to Salander. What did it matter if she wanted nothing to do with him?

He was and he remained bound to her.

Camilla, or Kira as she called herself these days, was sitting in her limousine on Tverskoy Boulevard, looking admiringly at her long legs. She was wearing a black Dior dress with red Gucci high heels, and a Graff diamond necklace which gleamed with a blueish light just above her neckline.

She was devastatingly beautiful, nobody knew this better than she herself, and often, as now, she would linger in the backseat of her car. She liked to visualize the scene: how the men give a little start when she makes her entrance; how so many of them cannot help staring. She knew from experience that only a few ever have the courage to pay her compliments and meet her gaze. Kira always dreamed of sparkling like nobody else, and now she closed her eyes and listened to the rain drumming against the body of the car. Then she looked out of the tinted glass windows.

There were only a handful of men and women shivering out there under their umbrellas, and they seemed barely interested to see who would be emerging from the car. She cast a bored glance at the restaurant. Throngs of guests were toasting each other, laughing and chattering. A few musicians were standing on a small stage further in. And there was Kuznetsov, dragging himself outside with his piggy eyes and fat belly—what a sight! He really was a clown. She felt like getting out of the car and slapping his face. But she had to keep her composure, her regal aura, and not betray with the slightest expression her recent sense of having fallen into an abyss. They had not yet been able to locate her sister, and she was furious. She had thought it would be easy once they had cracked her address and cover. But they could find no trace of her. Not even Kira's contacts at the GRU—not even Galinov himself—had been able to track her down. They knew that there had been sophisticated hacker attacks against Kuznetsov's troll factories and other targets. They might be linked to her, but it was not certain how much of this could be down to Lisbeth. Whatever, it now had to stop. Kira needed peace at last.

Thunder could be heard in the distance. A police car drove by and she took out a mirror and smiled at herself, as if to bolster her courage. When she looked up she saw Kuznetsov squirming and fiddling with his bow tie and collar. The idiot was nervous and that was a good thing. She wanted him to sweat and tremble, and she didn't want to hear any of his dreadful jokes.

"Now," she said. Sergei got out and opened the back door.

Her bodyguards stepped out but she took her time, waiting for Sergei to open the umbrella. Then she placed one foot on the pavement and expected to hear the usual sigh, the gasp, the "Ooh!" But there was nothing, nothing other than the rain and the string instruments of the musicians in the restaurant, the hum of voices. She would be cold and aloof, she thought, and hold her head high, and she just registered Kuznetsov lighting up with anticipation and anxiety, throwing out his arms in welcome, when she felt something else too: sheer, pure terror, cutting into her.

She could sense something over her right shoulder, a little way along the front of the building, something elusive, and she glanced in that direction. A dark figure seemed to be coming directly towards her with one hand inside its jacket. She wanted to scream at her bodyguards or throw herself onto the pavement, but instead she froze in total concentration, as if realizing that right now, even the slightest movement could cost her her life. Perhaps she knew already who it was, although she could not distinguish anything beyond an outline, a shadow coming closer.

But something in the way the figure moved, the resolute stride, gave Kira a terrible premonition, and before she had time even to grasp its full impact she knew she was lost.

CHAPTER 4

August 15

Had there ever been a chance for the two of them to come together, to be anything other than enemies? Perhaps not altogether inconceivable. After all, there was a time when they shared one vital thing: their hatred of their father, Alexander Zalachenko, and their fear that he would beat their mother Agneta to death.

At the time, the sisters were living in a cubbyhole of a room in an apartment on Lundagatan in Stockholm, and when their father showed up, usually reeking of alcohol and tobacco, and dragged their mother into the bedroom to rape her, they could hear every scream, every blow and gasp. Sometimes Lisbeth and Camilla would seek comfort in an embrace, that was all they had, but at least . . . there was a shared terror, a common vulnerability. Then even that was taken from them.

It escalated when they were twelve. Not only the degree

of violence, but its frequency. Zalachenko began to live with them on and off, and then he would beat Agneta night after night. At the same time a change also crept into the relationship between the sisters, not obvious at first, but it was betrayed by the excited gleam in Camilla's eyes, a fresh spring in her step as she walked to greet her father at the door. And that was the tipping point.

Just as the conflict was about to become lethal, they chose different sides in the war, and after that there was no chance of a reconciliation. Not after Agneta was beaten within an inch of her life on the kitchen floor and suffered irreversible brain damage, and Lisbeth threw a Molotov cocktail at Zalachenko and watched him burn in the front seat of his Mercedes. Ever since then it had been a matter of life and death. Since then, the past had been a bomb waiting to explode, and now, years later, as Salander slipped out of the doorway on Tverskoy Boulevard, those days at Lundagatan flashed by in a series of lightning sequences.

She was in the here and now. She had identified the gap through which she would shoot and knew exactly how she would escape afterwards. But those memories of the past were more present than she realized, and she moved slowly, slowly. It was only when Camilla stepped onto the red carpet in her high heels and black dress that Lisbeth began to move faster, although she was still in a crouch and didn't make a sound.

Laughter and string music and clinking glasses poured through the open door of the restaurant, and all the time the rain fell. A police car drove through the puddles, and she stared at it and at the row of bodyguards, wondering when they would be alert to her again. Before she fired, or after? There was no way of knowing. But so far she was OK. It was dark and misty, and all eyes were on Camilla.

She was as radiant as ever, and Kuznetsov's eyes shone like those of the boys in the school playground so many years ago. Camilla could bring life to a standstill. It was the power she had been born with, and Salander watched as her sister glided forward. She saw Kuznetsov straighten up, open his arms in a nervous but welcoming gesture, and she saw the guests crowding into the doorway to catch a glimpse. But at that exact moment a voice was heard from the street, one that Salander had been expecting: "Там, посмотрите"— "There, look." A guard with a boxer's nose and fair hair had spotted her, and then there was no room for hesitation.

She laid a hand on the Beretta in its holster and felt herself pitched into the same icy cold as when she threw the petrol-filled milk carton at her father. She had time to see Camilla freeze in fear as at least three bodyguards reached for their weapons. She would have to act now, with lightning speed and with no mercy.

Yet she was paralyzed, inexplicably. All she felt was a shadow from her childhood sweep over her once more, and she realized that not only had she missed her chance, she now stood defenceless before a rank of armed enemies. And there was no way out.

Camilla never saw the figure hesitate. There was only her own scream, and the sudden movement of heads and bodies and of weapons being drawn. She had no doubt it was too late, her chest would be ripped open by bullets at any moment. But no assault came and she had time to run towards the entrance and take shelter behind Kuznetsov. For a few seconds all she was aware of was her own heavy breathing and the agitated movements around her.

It was a while before she realized that not only had she escaped unscathed but the situation had now shifted to her advantage. It was no longer she who was in danger of her life. It was that dark figure over there, the one whose face she had not yet seen. The figure bent its head to check something on a mobile. It had to be Lisbeth. With a thirst for blood pounding in her throat, Camilla was desperate to see the figure suffer and die, and, calmer now, she surveyed the chaotic scene.

It looked better than she could have dreamed. While she herself was surrounded by bodyguards in bulletproof vests, Lisbeth stood alone on the pavement with a number of weapons pointed at her. It was fantastic, nothing less. Camilla wanted to prolong the moment, and she could see already that this was a moment she would come back to, over and over again. Lisbeth was finished, she would soon be destroyed, and in case anyone should even think to hesitate, Camilla screamed:

"Shoot! She wants to kill me," and a second later she even thought she could hear the sound of gunfire mixed with the piercing siren of a police car apparently driving directly at her. She could actually feel the noise and the din booming throughout her body, and although Lisbeth was no longer visible—people were milling around in front of her—she imagined her sister dying in a hail of bullets, falling to the street covered in blood.

But no . . . there was something wrong. Those were no pistol shots, they were . . . what? . . . a bomb, an explosion? A deafening racket that swept towards them from the restaurant, and even though Camilla did not want to miss a single second of Lisbeth's humiliation and destruction, she stared at the crowd inside. But she could make no sense of what she was seeing.

The violinists had stopped playing and were gaping in terror at the party crowd in front of them. Many of the guests were rooted to the spot, their hands clapped to their ears. Others were clutching at their chests, or screaming in fear. But most were rushing towards the exit in a state of panic, and only when the doors to the restaurant flew open and the first people came running out into the rain did Camilla understand. This was no bomb. It was music, turned up to such an insane volume that it was barely recognizable as sound. This was more like a high-frequency sonic attack.

An elderly bald man was yelling: "What's going on? What's going on?" A woman in a short, dark-blue dress, barely twenty years old, fell to her knees with her hands over her head, as if afraid the ceiling was about to collapse on her. Kuznetsov, standing right next to her, mouthed something which was drowned out by the cacophony, and in that instant Camilla realized her mistake. She had allowed her concentration to lapse, and furiously she looked back at the street, past the red carpet, past the police car, and her sister was no longer there.

It was as if the earth had swallowed her and Camilla looked about the pandemonium in desperation, at the guests screaming in confusion, and only just had time to let out a roar of frustration when a savage blow to the shoulder knocked her down. She banged an elbow and her head on the pavement. As her forehead throbbed with pain and her lip bled, and as feet were stamping all around her, she heard an icily familiar voice directly above her—"Just wait, sister, I will have my revenge"—and she was much too dazed to react.

By the time she raised her head and could see properly, there was no sign of Lisbeth, only a stream of people stampeding out of the restaurant. Again she shouted: "Kill her," but even she no longer believed it.

Vladimir Kuznetsov did not notice Kira falling to the ground. He was all but oblivious to the madness around him. In the midst of all the racket he had picked up something which terrified him more than everything else, a sequence of words bawled out with a pulsating, staccato rhythm, and at first he refused to believe his ears.

He shook his head and muttered "No, no," trying to dismiss it as a horrible figment of his imagination, a trick played by his fevered fantasy. But it really was that tune— that nightmare tune—and he wanted only to sink into the ground and die.

"It can't be true, it can't be true," he groaned as the chorus blared at him, like the pressure wave from a grenade:

Killing the world with lies.
Giving the leaders
The power to paralyze

Feeding the murderers with hate,
Amputate, devastate, congratulate.
But never, never
Apologize.

No song on earth had petrified him like this one, and compared to that it did not matter that the party he had so been looking forward to had been sabotaged, or that he was likely to be sued by livid oligarchs for bursting their eardrums. All he could think of was the music. That it was being played here, right now, told him that someone had penetrated his darkest secret. He was in danger of being disgraced before the whole world. His chest seized up in panic and he could hardly breathe, but he made every effort to look as if nothing were untoward. When his men finally managed to turn off the racket, he even pretended to breathe a sigh of relief.

"Ladies and gentlemen, I do beg your pardon," he announced above the hubbub. "This just goes to show you should never rely on technology. I apologize profusely. But let's get on with the party. There'll be no shortage of drinks, or other treats for that matter . . ."

He looked around for some lightly clad girls, as if an interlude of feminine beauty might rescue the situation. But the only young girls he saw were backed against the walls, scared to death, and he never finished his sentence. His guests could tell that he was falling apart, and since the musicians had now filed past him and out onto the street, most of them seemed anxious only to hurry home. In fact Kuznetsov was quite thankful for that. He wanted to be left alone with his thoughts and his fear.

Now would be the time to ring his lawyers and his contacts in the Kremlin, in the hope of getting a little comfort. He wanted to be told for certain that he would not be named as a pariah and war criminal in the Western press. Kuznetsov had powerful protectors; he was a big shot who had committed appalling crimes without it troubling his conscience. But he was not a strong person for all that, not when "Killing the World with Lies" was being played at his own ostentatious private party.

When things like that happened, he was back to being a cheap nothing, a second-rate criminal who had, thanks to an amazing stroke of good fortune, ended up in the same Turkish bath as two members of the Duma one afternoon, and told them a few tall tales. Kuznetsov had no other talents— no education and no special skills—but he could spin incredible yarns, and that, it seemed, was all it took. Since then he had worked hard to build up a circle of influential friends and these days he had hundreds of employees, most of them significantly more intelligent than he was himself: mathematicians, strategists, psychologists, consultants from the FSB and the GRU, hackers, computer scientists, engineers, AI and robotics experts. He was rich and powerful and, most important of all, nobody on the outside connected him with the information agencies and the lies.

He had skilfully concealed his responsibility and ownership, and lately he had been thanking his lucky stars for that. Not because of his involvement in the stock market crash, quite the opposite (in fact he considered that a feather in his cap), but rather because of the assignments in Chechnya which had exploded in the media, and led to protests and uproar at the United Nations. Worst of all, they had prompted a hard rock protest song which became a world-wide hit.

The track had been played at every bloody demonstration against the murders, and each time he had been terrified that his own name would be associated with them. Only during these last few weeks, while he had been planning his party, had life returned to normal. He could laugh and joke again, and tell his tall tales, and one important guest after the other had shown up tonight. He had squared his shoulders and had been enjoying the experience, when suddenly that song had started to blare out—and so loudly that his head almost burst.

"Fuck, fuck, *fuck*!"

"I beg your pardon?"

A distinguished older gentleman with a hat and cane—in his confusion he could not place him—looked at him disapprovingly. Even though he would have liked to tell the ancient to take a running jump, he was afraid that he might be more powerful than he was himself. So he answered as politely as he could.

"Apologies for my language, I'm just angry."

"You should check your IT security."

As if I've been doing anything else, he thought. "It's got nothing to do with that," he replied.

"So, what is it then?"

"It was something . . . electrical," he said.

Electrical. Was he totally stupid? Had the wiring simply short-circuited and played "Killing the World with Lies" all by itself? He was embarrassed and looked away, waving pathetically to some of the last guests who were slipping off in taxis. The restaurant was emptying of people and he looked around for Felix, his young chief technician. Where the hell was that useless cretin?

Eventually he found him by the stage, talking into his mobile with his ridiculous goatee and the absurd dinner jacket which hung on him like a sack. He seemed agitated, and so he should be. That moron had promised that nothing could possibly go wrong, and now the sky had fallen on their heads. Kuznetsov gestured at him angrily.

Felix responded with a dismissive wave, which made Kuznetsov want to punch him or bang his head against the wall. Yet when Felix finally ambled over, Kuznetsov reacted quite differently. He sounded helpless.

"Did you hear what song that was?"

"I heard," Felix said.

"So someone on the outside knows."

"I guess so."

"What do you think'll happen?"

"No idea."

"Does it mean we can expect to be blackmailed now?"

Felix did not reply and bit his lip, and Kuznetsov stared blankly out at the street.

"I think we can expect something much worse than that," Felix said.

Don't say that, Kuznetsov thought. *Don't say that.* "Why?" His voice cracked.

"Because Bogdanov just called—"

"Bogdanov?"

"Kira's guy."

Kira, he thought, *gorgeous, odious Kira,* and then he remembered: That was how it had all started, with her beautiful face twisted into a dreadful grimace, and her mouth screaming "Shoot! Kill!" and her eyes fixed on that dark figure further along the wall. Thinking back, all this seemed to be linked to the ensuing cacophony.

"What did Bogdanov say?" he said.

"That he knows who hacked us."

Electrical, he thought. *How the hell could I have said "electrical"?*

"So we've been hacked?"

"That's what it looks like."

"But that was supposed to be impossible. Impossible, you fucking idiot."

"No, but this person—"

"What about this bloody person?"

"She's highly skilled."

"So it's a she?"

"And she doesn't seem to be after any money."

"What is she after, then?"

"Revenge," Felix said. Kuznetsov's whole body shook and he punched Felix on the chin.

Then he walked away and drank himself into a stupor on champagne and vodka.

Salander was calm as she let herself into her hotel room. She poured herself a glass of whisky and drained it in one, and took some nuts from a bowl on the coffee table. Then she took her time to pack, and there was nothing rushed or nervous about her movements.

Only once she had zipped up her bag, ready to go, did she notice that her body was unnaturally tense. Her eyes were casting around for something to smash to pieces—a vase, a painting, the crystal chandelier in the ceiling—but in the end she just went into the bathroom and stared into the mirror, studying every feature in her face. She saw nothing.

In her mind she was back on Tverskoy Boulevard, her hand reaching for her weapon, and the same hand then being withdrawn. She remembered what made it feel easy, and what made it so difficult, and realized that, for the first time all summer, she had no idea what to do. She was . . . well, what was she . . . ? Lost, most likely, and she didn't even get a boost from picking up her mobile and finding out where Camilla lived.

From a Google satellite map she could see a large stone house surrounded by terraces, gardens, pools and statues. She tried to imagine it all burning, just like her father in his Mercedes on Lundagatan, but it made her feel no better. What had seemed like a perfect plan was one big mess, and she realized that her hesitation, both now and all those years ago, was deadly dangerous and a handicap to her. She reached for more whisky.

When she had paid her hotel bill online, she picked up her bag and left, and only once she was several blocks away did she take the pistol, wipe it clean, and throw it into a drain. She took a taxi, booked a flight to Copenhagen for early the following morning using one of her fake passports, and checked in to the Sheraton next to Sheremetyevo airport.

In the early hours of the morning she saw that Blomkvist had sent her a text. He was worried, he told her, and that reminded her of the film sequence from Fiskargatan. She decided to sneak into his computer via her usual back door. She couldn't have said why. Maybe she just needed to turn her thoughts to something other than the images that kept repeating in her mind, and she sat down at the desk.

After a while she found some encrypted documents, and assumed they must be important to him. Yet it seemed as though he wanted her to be able to read them. In the files he had created for her, he had left clues and leads which only she could understand, and having skipped around on his server for half an hour or so, she immersed herself in a long article he'd written about the stock market crash and troll factories. He had managed to unearth a fair amount, but not as much as she had, and after ploughing twice through the article she added something towards the end and inserted a link to various documents and e-mails. By this time she was so tired that she failed to notice she had misspelled Kuznetsov's name, and had also failed to stick to Blomkvist's usual writing style. But she made sure to log out and lay back on the bed without taking off either her suit or her shoes.

When she fell asleep, she dreamed that her father was standing in a sea of fire, telling her that she had become weak and would not stand a chance against Camilla.

CHAPTER 5

August 16

Blomkvist woke at six on Sunday morning. *It must be the heat,* he thought. The air was close, as before a storm, and his sheets and pillows were soaked with sweat. His head was pounding and briefly he wondered if he was falling sick, until the events of the evening before came back to him. He remembered sitting up late and having a few drinks, and he cursed as the morning light now seeped under the curtains. Pulling the covers over his head, he tried to go back to sleep.

But then he made the mistake of checking his mobile to see if Salander had answered his text message. Of course she had not. He began to brood over her again, which was no way to relax, and in the end he sat up in bed.

There was a jumble of books on the bedside table which he had started but never finished, and for a while he contemplated staying in bed and reading, or perhaps working on his article. Instead he went into the kitchen and made himself a cappuccino, then fetched the morning papers and buried himself in the news. Half an hour later he had answered a number of e-mails and had puttered around in his apartment, tidying a little as he went.

At half past nine he got a text message from Sofie Melker, his young colleague who had just moved into the neighbourhood with her husband and two sons. Sofie wanted to discuss an idea for a story, and he didn't feel like it at all. But he was fond of Sofie so he suggested meeting at Kaffebar on St. Paulsgatan in half an hour. He got a thumbs-up in reply. He did not like emojis; language seemed to him perfectly adequate. But he did not want to seem old-fashioned and decided to send some cheerful little image in response.

With his clumsy fingers he sent a red heart instead of a smiley. That could perhaps be misconstrued. But what the hell . . . there had been inflation there too, he thought. These days an emoji heart didn't mean anything, did it? He went to shower and shave, and put on jeans and a summer shirt.

There was a clear blue sky and brilliant sunshine, and he took the stone steps down to Hornsgatan, swung out into Mariatorget and looked around. He was surprised to see so few signs of the previous evening's festivities. Not even a cigarette butt on the gravel paths. The trash cans had been emptied and over to the left, outside the Rival Hotel, a young girl in an orange vest was picking litter off the grass with some elongated tongs. He passed her and then the statue in the middle of the square.

It was a statue he walked past more often than any other in town. Yet he could not have said what it represented, as with so many things in front of our noses. If anyone had asked him, he would probably have guessed at St. George and the Dragon. But it was Thor slaying the sea serpent Jörmungandr. During all these years he had never even read the inscription, and this time too he looked past the statue at a young father pushing his son on a swing in the playground, and at the benches and the grass on which people were sitting with their faces turned to the sun. It looked like any Sunday morning. And yet he sensed that there was something missing. It must be his memory playing tricks, he thought, and he had already set off again, turning into St. Paulsgatan, when it dawned on him.

What was missing was a figure he had not seen for a while now, but who used to sit on a piece of cardboard by the statue, motionless, like a meditating monk. A man with some fingers no more than stumps, with a weather-beaten, ancient face and a bulky, blue down jacket. For a while he had been a part of the scenery of Blomkvist's daily life, although, as so often when his work was intense, only by way of a backdrop.

He had been too wrapped up in himself to really see. But the poor devil had been sitting there all the time, something that he was not even conscious of, and only now that he was gone was he more visible, oddly. Now Blomkvist had no difficulty in conjuring up a number of details about him: the dark patches on his cheeks, the cracked lips and a dignity about his demeanour, in contrast to the suffering that was manifest in his body. And even when the medical examiner had been asking him about the man who had died, he had not made the connection.

How could he have so completely blocked him out? Somehow, he knew the answer.

In the past, a presence like his in the street would have been painfully obvious. But nowadays you could hardly walk more than fifty yards without someone trying to touch you for a few kronor. There were women and men begging everywhere on pavements, outside shops, at recycling centres and on the steps leading down into the tunnelbana. A whole new broken Stockholm had emerged, and in no time at all everyone had got used to it. That was the sad truth.

The number of beggars had grown at around the same time that Stockholmers had stopped carrying cash, and just like everybody else he had learned to look away. Often he did not even feel guilty, and he was overcome by melancholy, not necessarily because of the man or even the plight of beggars in general; it was perhaps rather the transience of time, and how life changes and we barely notice it.

A truck was parked outside Kaffebar, in such a tight spot that he wondered how it would ever be able to get out. As usual he knew far too many people in the café. He was in no mood for chatting, so he gave them only the most perfunctory of greetings before ordering a double espresso and a chanterelle toast, and he sat down at a window table facing St. Paulsgatan and let his thoughts carry him away. A moment later he felt a hand on his back. It was Sofie, who smiled at him cautiously. She ordered tea with milk and a bottle of Perrier, and then held out her mobile with the red heart.

"Flirting? Or just staff motivation?"

"Clumsy fingers," he said.

"Wrong answer."

"In that case, good HR instructions from Erika."

"Still wrong, but better."

"How's the family?" he said.

"The mother thinks that the summer holidays have been way too long. You have to keep those kids entertained the whole time, the little hooligans."

"How long have you been living here now?"

"Almost five months, and you?"

"Oh, a hundred years."

She laughed.

"I sort of mean it," he said. "When you've lived here as long as I have, you end up not seeing anything anymore. You walk around in a kind of daze."

"You do?"

"I do, at least. But when you're new to the area your eyes are probably wide open."

"Maybe."

"Do you remember a beggar sitting in a big quilted jacket in Mariatorget? He had dark patches on his face and was missing most of the fingers on one hand."

She gave a sad smile.

"Oh yes, very well."

"Why do you put it like that?"

"Because he wasn't easy to forget."

"Well, I forgot him."

Sofie looked at him in surprise.

"How do you mean?"

"I must have seen him at least ten times, yet I never really registered it. Only now that he's dead does he seem alive to me."

"He's dead?"

"The medical examiner called me yesterday."

"Why you, of all people?"

"Because my mobile number was in the man's pocket and she was probably hoping I could help identify him."

"But you couldn't?"

"Not at all."

"He probably thought he had some story for you."

"Presumably."

Sofie finished her tea and they sat quietly for a little while.

"He accosted Catrin Lindås a week ago," she said eventually.

"He did?"

"He went berserk when he caught sight of her. I saw it from some way off, on Swedenborgsgatan."

"What did he want from her?"

"He'd probably seen her on TV."

Catrin Lindås did appear on television every now and then. She was a leading writer and columnist, a conservative who often took part in debates about law and order, or on school discipline and teaching standards. She was good-looking in an elegant sort of way. She wore beautifully tailored suits and silk pussy-bow blouses, and never had a hair out of place. Blomkvist thought of her as serious and unimaginative. She had been critical of him in *Svenska Dagbladet*.

"What happened?"

"He grabbed hold of her arm and was shouting."

"Shouting what?"

"I've no idea. But he was waving some sort of stick. It left Catrin in a complete state. I tried to calm her down and helped her remove a grubby mark on her jacket."

"Oh dear, that must have been awful for her."

He had not meant to sound sarcastic, but Sofie was onto him in an instant.

"You've never liked her, have you?"

"Nothing much wrong with her, I guess," he said defensively. "She's just a bit too right-wing and proper for me, that's all."

"Little Miss Perfect, right?"

"I didn't say that."

"No, but you meant it. Do you have any idea how much shit she gets online? She's seen as some sort of upper-class bitch who's been to boarding school at Lundsberg and looks down her nose at ordinary people. But have you any idea what she's been through?"

"No, Sofie, I don't."

He could not understand why she had suddenly got so angry.

"In that case I'll tell you. She grew up in miserable circumstances, in a cracked-out hippie commune in Göteborg. Her parents were doing LSD and heroin, and home was a total mess, with people sitting around stoned out of their minds. Her suits and her tidiness have been her way of surviving. She's a fighter. A rebel, in a way."

"Interesting," he said.

"Exactly so, and I know you think she's a reactionary, but she does an enormous amount of good in her fight against the new age and spiritual crap she grew up with. She's a lot more interesting than people realize."

"Are you friends?"

"We are."

"Thanks, Sofie. In that case I'll try to see her in a different light in the future."

"I don't believe you," she said, laughing apologetically, but the way she mumbled made it clear that this mattered to her.

Then she asked him how he was getting on with his story. He told her that he wasn't exactly progressing in leaps and bounds. He said that the Russian lead had dried up.

"But you've got good sources, haven't you?"

"What my sources don't know, I don't know either."

"Maybe you should head off to Saint Petersburg, find out more about that troll factory. What was its name again?"

"New Agency House?"

"Wasn't it some sort of hub?"

"That looks like a dead end too."

"Am I listening to an unusually pessimistic Blomkvist?"

He could hear it too, but he had no wish to go to Saint Petersburg. The place was already teeming with journalists, and no-one had been able to find out who was behind the factory, or to what extent the intelligence services and the government were involved. He was fed up with it. He was tired of the news in general, tired of all the depressing political developments around the world. He ordered another espresso and asked Sofie about her idea for an article.

She wanted to write about the anti-Semitism in the

disinformation campaign. This was nothing new because the trolls had been unable to resist suggesting that the whole stock market crash was a Jewish conspiracy. It was the same ugly rubbish which had been churned out for centuries, written about and analyzed countless times before, but Sofie had a more specific angle. She wanted to portray how this had affected people in their everyday lives—schoolchildren, teachers, intellectuals—ordinary individuals who had hitherto given hardly a thought to the fact that they were Jewish. "Great, go for it," Blomkvist said. He asked her a few questions and made one or two suggestions, and spoke generally about hate in the community among the populists and extremists. He told her about all the idiots who had left bile on his voicemail. After a while he became fed up with listening to himself and gave Sofie a hug. He apologized—without really knowing why—and said goodbye, and then went home and changed to go for a run.

CHAPTER 6

August 16

Kira was in bed in the large house in Rublyovka to the west of Moscow when she received the message that her chief hacker, Jurij Bogdanov, wanted to talk to her. He would have to wait, she replied. For good measure she threw a hairbrush at her housekeeper Katya, and pulled the duvet over her head. It had been a night from hell. The memory of the commotion at the restaurant, her sister's determined stride and silhouette, would not leave her, and she kept touching her shoulder, still aching from the impact of her fall to the pavement: It was not the pain so much as a presence which she simply could not shake off.

Why could it not end? She had worked so hard and achieved so much. But the past kept coming back, again and again, and each time it seemed in a new guise. There had been nothing good about her childhood, yet there had been parts which in her way she had loved. Now even those were being torn from her, one by one.

As a child, Camilla had longed to get out and away, far from Lundagatan, and away from life with her sister and mother, leaving behind the poverty and vulnerability. From an early age she knew that she deserved better. She had a distant memory of being in the Ljusgården atrium at the NK department store. A woman wearing a fur coat and patterned trousers was laughing, and she was so incredibly beautiful that she seemed to belong to another world entirely. Camilla moved closer until she was standing right by her legs, and then an equally elegant friend arrived and kissed the woman on both cheeks.

"My goodness, is that your daughter?" she said.

The first woman turned and looked down, seeing Camilla for the first time. "I wish it were," she answered in English with a smile.

Camilla did not understand, but she could tell that it was meant to be flattering. As she walked away she heard the woman continue in Swedish: "Such a pretty girl. Shame that her mother doesn't dress her better," and those words left a gash in her. She stared at Agneta—even then she called her mother Agneta—who was looking at the Christmas window display with Lisbeth, and she saw the yawning gulf. These two women were radiant, as if life was laid out for their enjoyment alone, whereas Agneta was stooped and pale, dressed in worn and ugly clothes. A searing sense of injustice flared within her. *I've ended up in the wrong place,* she thought.

There were many such moments in her childhood, times when she felt both elated and damned: elated because people would call her as pretty as a little princess, damned because she was part of a family which lived on the margins, in the shadows.

It was true that she began to steal things to be able to buy clothes and barrettes. It wasn't much, not at all, coins mostly, then a few notes, an old brooch of her grandmother's, the Russian vase on the bookshelf. But it was also true that she was accused of much more than that, and it became clear to her that Agneta and Lisbeth were ganging up against her. She often felt like a stranger in her own home, a changeling who was being kept under supervision, and matters did not improve when Zala came to visit and threw her aside like a mongrel.

At times like those she was the loneliest person in the world. She would dream of running away and finding someone else to look after her, someone who was more deserving of her. But slowly light began to seep in, a false sheen perhaps. But it was all there was. It started with her noticing small things—a golden wristwatch, wads of money in trouser pockets, a commanding tone over the telephone— tiny indications that there was more to Zala than his violence. Gradually she began to see the self-confidence, the authority, the urbane and forceful nature—the power that he radiated.

Above all it was the way that *he* began to look at *her*. He would take his time to look her up and down, and sometimes he would smile and there was no way she could resist that. Usually he never smiled, which made this so powerful, as if a searchlight had been turned on her, and at some point she stopped dreading his visits and even began to fantasize that it was *he* who would take her away from there to a richer, more beautiful place.

One evening, when she was eleven or twelve years old and Agneta and Lisbeth were out, her father was in the kitchen, drinking vodka. She joined him there and he stroked her hair and offered her a drink which he had mixed with juice. "A screwdriver," he said, and he told her how he had grown up in a children's home in Sverdlovsk in the Urals, where he had been beaten every day, but that he had fought his way to power and wealth, to having friends all over the world. It sounded like something out of a fairy tale, and he put his finger to his lips and whispered that it was a secret. She shivered, and it was then that she plucked up the courage to tell him how mean Agneta and Lisbeth were to her.

"They're jealous. Everybody envies people like you and me," he said, and he promised that he would see to it that they were nicer to her. After that life at home changed.

With Zala's visits, the big wide world was also there, and she loved him not only because he was her saviour. It was also that nothing could ruffle him. Not the serious men in grey coats who sometimes visited them, nor even the policemen with broad shoulders who knocked on the door one morning. But *she* could.

She could get him to be gentle and considerate, and for a long time she did not realize the price she was paying, still less that she was fooling herself. She saw it simply as the best time of her life. At last someone was paying attention to her, and she was happy. Her father was visiting more and more often, and furtively giving her presents and money.

But at the very moment when something new, something

great seemed about to be hers, Lisbeth took it all away, and since then she had loathed her sister with a vengeance, with a hatred that had become her most enduring and defining characteristic. Now she wanted to destroy Lisbeth, and she was not about to waver just because her sister happened to be one step ahead.

After the night's rain, the sun was beating down beyond the curtains. She heard the sound of lawn mowers and distant voices, and she closed her eyes and thought about the footsteps in the night, approaching their room on Lundagatan. Then she clenched her right fist, kicked off her duvet and got up.

She was going to retake the initiative.

Jurij Bogdanov had been waiting for an hour. But he had not been idle. He had been hard at work with his laptop on his knees, and only now did he cast a worried look onto the terrace and the large garden outside. He had no good news to share, and he expected only abuse and more hard work, but still, he felt strong and motivated, and he had mobilized his entire network. His mobile rang. Kuznetsov again. Stupid, hysterical, bloody Kuznetsov. He declined the call.

It was 11:10 and the gardeners were having an early lunch outside. Time was racing on and he looked down at his shoes. These days Bogdanov was rich and wore made-to-measure suits and expensive watches. But the gutter never altogether left him. He was an old junkie who had grown up on the streets, and that life had left traces in his demeanour and his movements that would never go away.

He had an angular, pockmarked face, and was tall and lean with narrow lips and amateur tattoos on his arms. But even though Kira would not want to show him off in stylish society, he continued to be invaluable to her, and that gave him strength now as he heard her heels echoing along the marble floor. Here she came, as ethereally lovely as ever, wearing a light-blue suit and a red blouse buttoned all the way up, and she sat down in the armchair next to him.

"So, what have you got?" she said.

"Problems."

"Let's hear them."

"That woman—"

"Lisbeth Salander."

"We don't have confirmation of that yet, but yes, it has to be her, mainly because of the sophistication of the attack. Kuznetsov is so paranoid about his IT systems that he has them checked by experts from every possible angle. He'd been given assurances that they were impossible to penetrate."

"That was clearly wrong."

"It was, and we still don't know how she went about it, but the operation itself—once she was inside—was relatively straightforward. She connected to Spotify, and to the speakers which had been set up for the evening, and put on that rock song."

"But people were driven nearly crazy by it."

"There was an equalizer there too, which unfortunately was both digital and parametric, and connected to the WiFi."

"Use words that I can understand."

"The equalizer adjusts the volume, gets the base and treble just right, and Lisbeth—let's just say it was her— connected her mobile up to that and created the worst kind of sound shock. Horrific, in fact, to the point where it could be felt in the heart. Apparently that's why so many people were clutching their chests. They had no idea it was sound that was doing the damage."

"So her objective was to create chaos."

"Above all she wanted to send a message. The song's called 'Killing the World with Lies,' by the Crazy Sisters. You know, that hard rock protest band."

"Those red-haired whores?"

"The very ones," Bogdanov said, without admitting that he thought the band were pretty cool. "The song was written about the killings of gays in Chechnya, but in fact it's not about the murderers themselves, or even the machinery of state, but about the person who orchestrated the hate campaign on social media which led to the violence."

"Kuznetsov himself, in other words?"

"Exactly, but the thing is—"

"—that nobody on the outside is supposed to know about it."

"No-one's even meant to know that he's behind the information agencies."

"So how did Lisbeth find out?"

"We're looking into that, and trying to reassure all those involved. Kuznetsov is wild. He's wasted and scared witless."

"How come? It's not as if it's the first time he's pitted people against each other."

"No indeed, but it all got out of hand in Chechnya. People were buried alive," he said.

"That's Kuznetsov's own fucking problem."

"It is. But what worries me . . ."

"Well, what?"

"Salander's main target probably isn't Kuznetsov at all. We can't rule out that she knows about our own involvement in the information agencies. Don't you think her vengeance might be directed at you, not him?"

"We should have killed her a long time ago."

"There's one more thing I haven't mentioned."

"What?"

Bogdanov knew that there was no point in putting it off any longer.

"After barging into you last night, she stumbled," he said. "The impact made her lose her balance and she tumbled forward—that's what it looked like anyway. She had to catch herself with her hand against your limousine, just above the rear wheel. At first I thought it looked pretty natural. But then I ran the surveillance footage over and over, and came to the conclusion that it might not have been a fall after all. Rather than steadying herself, she was in fact pressing something against the bodywork. Here it is."

He held up a small rectangular box.

"What is it?"

"A GPS transmitter that followed you all the way here."

"So now she knows where I live?" Camilla forced out the words through clenched teeth and tasted blood in her mouth.

"I'm afraid so," Bogdanov said.

"Idiots," she spat.

"We've taken all precautions," Bogdanov went on, increasingly nervous. "We've stepped up protection, especially of the IT system, obviously."

"So we're on the defensive now, is that what you're saying?"

"No, no, not at all. I'm just telling you."

"Just make sure you find her, then."

"That's not so easy, unfortunately. We've checked all the surveillance cameras in the area. We don't see her anywhere, and we've not been able to trace her via any mobiles or computers."

"Search the hotels then. Report her as missing. Turn everything upside down and inside out, everything you see and hear."

"We're working on it, I'm convinced we'll crush her."

"Just don't underestimate that witch."

"I don't underestimate her for one second. But I think she's missed her chance—the advantage has shifted to us."

"How the hell can you say that when she knows where I live?"

Bogdanov hesitated, fumbling for words.

"You said you thought she would kill you, right?" he said.

"I was certain of it. But she must be planning something worse."

"I think you're wrong there."

"How do you mean?"

"I think she really did want to shoot you. I can't see why

else she would have attacked. Sure, she scared the shit out of Kuznetsov. But apart from that, what did she gain? Nothing. All she did was expose herself."

"So what you're suggesting . . ." She looked out at the garden, and wondered where the hell the gardeners had got to.

"I'm suggesting that she hesitated and couldn't bring herself to do it. That she hasn't got it in her. That she's not so strong after all."

"That's a comforting thought," Kira said.

"I think it's true. Otherwise it doesn't add up."

She suddenly felt a little better.

"And I suppose she has people she cares about," she said.

"She has her girlfriends."

"And she has her Blomkvist. More than anything, she has her Mikael Blomkvist."

CHAPTER 7

August 16

Blomkvist was in Gondolen restaurant at Slussen, dining with Dragan Armansky, the founder of Milton Security. He was slightly regretting it now. His legs and back hurt after his run in Årstaviken, and on top of that he was rather bored. Armansky was droning on about opportunities for developing his business in the East, or maybe it was the West, and then in the middle of it all there was an anecdote about a horse which had managed to get into a festival tent on Djurgården:

". . . and then those idiots pushed the grand piano into the swimming pool."

Blomkvist was not sure if that had anything to do with the horse. But he was not listening all that carefully. Furthest away from them was a group of colleagues from *Dagens Nyheter*, among them Mia Cederlund with whom he had had an unhappy affair, and over there was Mårten Nyström, the Royal Dramatic Theatre actor, who had not been shown

in a flattering light in *Millennium*'s investigation into misuse
of power in the theatre world. None of them looked all that
pleased to see him, and Blomkvist kept his eyes on the table,
drank his wine, and thought of Lisbeth Salander.

She was his and Armansky's only point in common.
Armansky was the only employer she had ever had, and he
had never really got over her, which was perhaps not so surprising. Long ago Armansky had given her a job as some sort
of a social welfare project, and she turned out to be the most
brilliant colleague he had ever had. For a while he may even
have been in love with her.

"Sounds wild," Blomkvist said.

"You can say that again, and the piano—"

"So you had no idea either that she was going to move?"
he interrupted.

Armansky was reluctant to change the subject, and perhaps it upset him that Blomkvist was not more amused by
his story. After all, a grand piano in a swimming pool . . . But
then he quickly became serious.

"I shouldn't really be telling you this," he began.

Blomkvist thought that sounded like a good start and he
leaned forward.

Lisbeth had had a nap and a shower and was sitting at her
computer in her Copenhagen hotel room when Plague—her
closest contact in Hacker Republic—sent an encrypted message. It was only a short, routine question, but it still disturbed her.

<What's up?> he wrote.

It's all fucked up, she thought. She answered:

```
<I'm not in Moscow any longer>
<Why not?>
<I couldn't pull off what I'd planned>
<What couldn't you pull off?>
```

She felt like going out on the town, to forget everything. She wrote:

```
<Finishing it all off>
<What?>
```

Bye bye, Plague, she thought. She wrote:

```
<Nothing>
<Why couldn't you finish off nothing?>
```

"Never you mind," she muttered.

```
<Because I remembered something>
<What?>
```

Footsteps, she thought, her father's whispered voice and her own hesitation, her inability to fully understand, and then the silhouette of her sister getting up from the bed and slipping out of the room with Zala, that pig. She answered:

```
<Shit>
<What sort of shit?>
```

She felt like throwing the computer at the wall. She wrote:

```
<What contacts do we have in Moscow?>
<I'm worried about you, Wasp. Just drop
Russia. Get the hell out>
```

Give me a break, she thought.

```
<What contacts do we have in Moscow?>
<Good ones>
<Who can set up an IMSI-catcher in a
tricky place?>
```

Mobile interception is child's play, but who does he know in situ?

`<Katya Flip, for example>` he wrote.

`<Who she?>`

`<More or less crazy. She used to be in Shaltay Boltay>`

Which means she won't come cheap.

`<Can we trust her?>`

`<Depends how much you're willing to pay>`

`<Send me her details>`

Then she closed her computer and got up to dress. She decided that the black suit would have to do for today too, even though the rain yesterday had crumpled it and there was a grey stain on the right sleeve. And it didn't look any better for having been slept in. But what the hell, and she had no intention of putting on make-up either. She ran her fingers through her hair, left the room and took the lift down to the ground floor, where she ordered a beer in the bar.

The open spaces of Kongens Nytorv lay outside, and there were a few dark clouds in the sky. But Salander noticed none of this. She was stuck in the memory of the hand that had hesitated on Tverskoy Boulevard, and in the film from the past that kept replaying in her head. She was oblivious to everything else, until a voice close to her ear suddenly asked:

"Are you OK?"

This annoyed her. Why was it anyone's business? She did not even look up, and then she saw she had a text from Blomkvist.

. . .

Armansky leaned forward and whispered conspiratorially:

"In the spring Lisbeth called to ask me to speak to the apartment owners' association, and see to it that surveillance cameras were installed outside the entrance to her building on Fiskargatan. I thought that sounded like a good idea."

"So you arranged for it to be done."

"Well, it's not something you can fix just like that, Mikael. You need permission from the county council and one thing and another. But it all worked out this time. I had to point out that the level of threat was considerable and Chief Inspector Bublanski produced a report."

"Hats off to him."

"We pulled out all the stops and at the beginning of July I sent two guys over to install a couple of remote-controlled Netgears. We took the greatest care over the encryption, believe you me. Nobody else was to be able to view the film sequences, and I told my team at the surveillance centre to keep an eye on the monitors. I was worried about Lisbeth. I was afraid they were going to come for her."

"We all were."

"But I wasn't expecting to be proved right so soon. Six days later, at half past one in the morning, the microphones we had mounted there picked up the sound of motorcycles, and our night-shift operator Stene Granlund was on the point of repositioning the cameras when someone got there before him."

"Oops."

"Exactly. Stene didn't even have time to think about it. The bikers were two men in leathers from Svavelsjö Motorcycle Club."

"Bugger."

"Precisely. Lisbeth's address was no longer quite so secret, and Svavelsjö don't usually show up with coffee and buns."

"Not their style."

"Fortunately the guys turned around and left when they saw the cameras, and of course we immediately contacted the police, who were able to identify the men—one of them was called Kovic, I remember. Peter Kovic. But that didn't get rid of the problem, of course, so I rang Lisbeth and asked to meet her right away. She agreed, though rather reluctantly. She came to my office, looking the very image of a perfect daughter-in-law."

"Sounds like a bit of an exaggeration."

"I mean, by her standards. The studs had gone, her hair was cut short, and she looked respectable, and I thought, my God, I've missed this funny person. I couldn't bring myself to tear into her—obviously I realized that she'd hacked our cameras—so I just warned her to be careful. They're out to get you, I told her. 'People have always been out to get me,' was all she said, and that really made me mad. I told her that she needed to look for help, for protection: 'Or they're going to kill you.' But then something happened that scared me."

"What?"

"She looked at the floor and said: 'Not if I keep one step ahead.'"

"What did she mean by that?"

"That's what I asked myself, and then the story of her father came back to me."

"Meaning what?"

"Meaning that she defended herself that time by going on

the attack, and I had a feeling that she was planning something similar now: by getting her retaliation in first, and that made me very frightened, Mikael. I saw her eyes and then it no longer mattered how neat and tidy she looked. What I saw was lethal. Her eyes were jet black."

"I think you're exaggerating. Lisbeth takes no unnecessary risks. She's normally quite rational."

"She is rational—in her own crazy way."

Blomkvist thought about what Salander had said to him at Kvarnen: that she would be the hunter and not the hunted.

"So what happened?"

"Nothing. She just pushed off, and I haven't heard a word from her since. Every day I've been expecting to read somewhere that Svavelsjö's clubhouse has been blown to smithereens or that her sister's been found burned to a crisp in a car in Moscow."

"Camilla is being protected by the Russian mafia. Lisbeth would never start a war with them."

"Do you honestly believe that?"

"I don't know. But I'm certain that she never . . ."

"What?"

"Nothing," he said, and bit his lip. He felt naïve and stupid.

"It's not over till it's over, Mikael. That was the feeling I got. Neither Lisbeth nor Camilla will give up until one of them is lying dead."

"I think you're making too much of this," Blomkvist said.

"You do?"

"I hope so," he corrected himself. He poured them both some more wine and excused himself for a moment.

He picked up his mobile and texted Salander.

To his surprise, he got an answer right away.

`<Chill out, Blomkvist>` it read. `<I'm on holi-
day. Keeping out of harm's way. Not doing anything stupid>`

Holiday was maybe putting it a bit strongly. But Salander's
idea of happiness had to do with relief from pain, and as she
knocked back her beer at the bar of the Hôtel d'Angleterre,
that is precisely what she felt: a form of release, as if she were
only just beginning to register how tense she had been all
summer long—how the hunt for her sister had driven her to
the edge of madness. Not that she really unwound; her childhood memories still went round and round in her brain. But
her field of vision seemed to broaden and she even began to
feel a yearning, not necessarily for anything in particular, but
simply to get away from everything. It was enough to give
her a sense of freedom.

"Are you OK?"

She heard the question again above the noise of the bar,
and she turned to find herself looking straight at a young
woman standing next to her.

"Why do you ask?" she said.

The woman was perhaps thirty years old, dark and
intense, with slanting eyes and long, curly black hair. She
wore jeans with a dark-blue blouse and high-heeled boots.
There was something both hard and probing about her. Her
right arm was bandaged.

"I'm not sure," the woman said. "It's just the sort of thing one says."

"I guess it is."

"But if you don't mind my saying, you looked pretty fucked up."

Salander had heard this many times in her life. People had come up to her and said that she seemed surly, or angry, or precisely that—fucked up—and she always hated it. But for some reason she accepted it now.

"I suppose I have been."

"But it's better now?"

"Well, it's different, in any case."

"I'm Paulina, by the way, and I'm not in great shape myself."

Paulina Müller waited for the young woman to introduce herself. But she said nothing, she didn't even nod. But nor did she tell her to get lost. Paulina had noticed her because of the way she walked, as if she didn't give a damn about the world and would never bother to ingratiate herself to anyone. There was something strangely appealing about that, and Paulina thought that maybe she had once walked like that too, before Thomas took those strides away from her.

Her life had been destroyed so slowly, so gradually, that she had hardly noticed it. Even though the move to Copenhagen had brought home to her the extent of the damage, the presence of this woman made her feel it even more keenly. The mere fact of standing next to her made Paulina aware of her own lack of freedom. She was drawn to the aura of total independence the woman projected.

"Are you local?" she asked tentatively.

"No," the woman said.

"We've just moved here from Munich. My husband's been made head of Scandinavia for Angler, the pharmaceutical company," she continued, and saying it made her feel almost respectable.

"I see."

"But this evening I ran away from him."

"OK," the woman said.

"I was a journalist at *Geo,* you know, the science magazine, but I quit when we moved here."

"I see," the woman said.

"I wrote about medicine and biology, mostly."

"OK."

"I really enjoyed it," she said. "But then my husband got this job, and things turned out the way they did. I've freelanced a bit."

She kept answering questions which had never been asked, and the woman just said "I see," or "OK," until finally she asked what Paulina was drinking. "Anything, whatever," Paulina replied, and she got a whisky, a Tullamore Dew with ice, and a smile, or at least the hint of a smile. The woman was wearing a black suit which could have done with some cleaning and a pressing, and a black shirt, and she wore no make-up at all. She looked haggard, as if she had not slept properly for a long time, and there was a dark, unsettling force in her eyes. Paulina tried to make her laugh.

It was not a great success. Except that the woman came

closer, and Paulina realized that she liked that. Maybe that was why she looked nervously out into the street, even more afraid now that Thomas would appear, and then the woman suggested that they should go for another drink in her room instead.

She said, "No, no, absolutely no way, no chance. My husband really wouldn't like that." Then they kissed and went up to the room and made love, and she could not recall having experienced anything like it before, so full of fury and desire all at once. Then she told the woman about Thomas and the whole tragedy back home, and the woman looked as if she could kill. But Paulina could not tell whether it was Thomas or the whole world she wanted to destroy.

CHAPTER 8

August 20

Blomkvist did not show up at the magazine the following week, nor did he spend any time on his story about troll factories. He tidied up the apartment, went for some runs, read two novels by Elizabeth Strout and had dinner with his sister Annika Giannini, mainly because she was Salander's lawyer. But Annika did not have much to report, except that Salander had been in touch, asking about German lawyers specializing in family law.

Mostly he just whiled away the days. Sometimes he would spend hours lazing around, and talking on the phone to his old friend and colleague Erika Berger about the latest developments in her divorce. There was something strangely cathartic in that, as if they were teenagers again, chattering away about their love lives. But in reality it was a difficult process for her, and on the Thursday she rang again, sounding completely different. She wanted to talk about work and they had a row. He should stop being so self-absorbed, she told him, and she really gave him a piece of her mind.

"It's not that, Ricky," he said. "I'm knackered. I need a holiday."

"But you said the story was basically finished. Send it over and we'll fix it."

"It's just a load of old rubbish."

"I don't believe that for one second."

"Well, it's true, unfortunately. Did you read the *Washington Post* investigation?"

"Certainly not."

"They show me up on every point."

"It doesn't all have to be scoops, Mikael. Just to get your perspective is worth a great deal. You can't always be the one with the breaking news. It's crazy even to think so."

"But the article just isn't good enough. The writing is tired. Let's can it."

"We're not canning anything, Mikael. But OK . . . let's hold it for this issue. I think I've got enough content for this one anyway."

"I'm sure you do."

"What will you do instead?"

"I'll go and spend a few days at Sandhamn."

It was not their happiest conversation, but still he felt as if a burden had been lifted, and he took a suitcase out of the wardrobe and began to pack. It was slow work, as if he didn't want to go there either, and every now and then Salander drifted back into his thoughts. He cursed the fact that he could not get her out of his head; however much she promised not to do anything stupid, he was worried about her, and angry too. In fact he was furious with her for being so uncommunicative, so cryptic. He wanted to hear more about the threats and the surveillance cameras, and about Camilla, and Svavelsjö M.C.

He wanted to turn everything inside out to see if he could do something to help, remembering what she had said at Kvarnen. He could still hear her footsteps disappearing into the evening on Medborgarplatsen. He stopped packing, sauntered into the kitchen and was drinking yoghurt straight from the carton when his mobile rang. Number unknown. But now he was off work, he thought he might as well answer. He could even put on a cheery voice: *Hey, how fucking great of you to call and give me some more abuse.*

Medical Examiner Dr. Fredrika Nyman got to her home in Trångsund outside Stockholm and found her daughters on the living-room sofa, absorbed in their phones. She was no more surprised by that than to see the lake still in its usual position through the window. The girls spent every spare moment on their phones, watching YouTube or whatever it was, and she wanted to snap at them to put them away and read a book instead, or play the piano, or not skip their basketball training again. Or at least to get out into the sunshine.

But she had no energy. It had been an awful day, and she had just been talking to an idiot of a policeman who, like most idiots, thought he was a genius. He had looked into the matter, he said, which meant that he had simply read the Wikipedia entry and was now an expert on Buddhism. *That weirdo was probably sitting around somewhere, feeling enlightened.* It was so disrespectful and stupid that she had not even bothered to answer, and now she found a place next to her daughters on the grey sofa and hoped that one of them would say hello. Neither did. But Josefin did at least reply when Fredrika asked what she was watching.

"A thing," she said.

A thing.

Fredrika wanted to scream, but instead she got to her feet, went into the kitchen and wiped the counter and the table clean. She scrolled through Facebook on her phone to show that she could keep up with the girls, and then daydreamed of going far away. She searched a few things on Google and, without quite knowing how, ended up on a website for holidays to Greece.

She was looking at a photograph of an ancient man sitting at a beachside café when an idea came to her, and she thought immediately of Mikael Blomkvist. She was reluctant to call him again. The last thing she wanted was to be the boring woman who keeps hassling the famous journalist. But he was the only person she could think of who might be interested, so she dialled his number after all.

"Hello there," he said. "How nice of you to call!"

He sounded so cheerful that she felt at once it was the best thing that had happened to her all day, which was not saying much.

"I was thinking—" she said.

"You know what," he interrupted. "It dawned on me that I had actually seen your beggar, at least it must have been him."

"Really?"

"It all fits, the down jacket, the patches on the cheeks, the truncated fingers. It can't have been anyone else."

"So where did you see him?"

"In Mariatorget. In fact, it's astonishing that I'd forgotten him," he went on. "I can hardly believe it. He used to sit totally still on a piece of cardboard by the statue on the square. I must have passed him ten or twenty times."

His enthusiasm was contagious.

"That's amazing. What was your impression of him?"

"Well . . . I'm not really sure," he said. "I never paid him much attention. But I remember him as broken. And proud—the way you described him when he was dead. He'd sit bolt upright with his head high, a bit like a Sioux chieftain in the movies. I don't know how he managed to stay like that for hours on end."

"Did he seem under the influence of alcohol, or drugs?"

"I can't really say. He could have been. But if he'd been out of it he'd hardly have been able to hold that position for so long. Why do you ask?"

"Because this morning I got the results of my drug screening. He had 2.5 micrograms of eszopiclone per gram of femoral blood in his body, and that's an awful lot."

"What's eszopiclone?"

"A substance you find in some sleeping pills, in Lunesta, for example. I'd say that he must have had at least twenty tablets, mixed with alcohol, and on top of that quite a lot of dextropropoxyphene, a painkilling opiate."

"What do the police say?"

"Overdose or suicide."

"On what grounds?"

She snorted.

"On the grounds that it's easiest for them, I'd guess. The person in charge of the investigation seemed to be focusing on doing as little work as possible."

"What's his name?"

"The officer in charge? Hans Faste."

"Oh, brilliant . . ." he said.

"Do you know him?"

Blomkvist knew Faste all too well. He had once convinced himself that Salander belonged to a lesbian satanic hard rock gang, and on the basis of no evidence whatsoever—other than some good old-fashioned misogyny—had her accused of murder. Bublanski used to say that Faste was punishment for the sins of the police force.

"I'm afraid so," he said.

"He called the man 'the weirdo.'"

"Sounds very much like Faste."

"When he got the test results he said right away that the weirdo had got a bit too fond of his pills."

"But you don't seem convinced?"

"An overdose would be the most straightforward explanation, but I find it odd that it should be eszopiclone. You can get hooked on it, of course, but addiction usually involves benzodiazepines, and when I pointed that out and said the man was probably a Buddhist, that really got your policeman going."

"In what way?"

"He called back a few hours later having done some

research. Which involved reading the Wikipedia entry on suicide. Apparently it says Buddhists who consider themselves especially enlightened have the right to take their own lives, and he seemed to find that funny. He said that the man had probably been sitting under a tree, feeling enlightened."

"Jesus."

"It made me furious. But I let it go. I didn't feel like having a row, not today anyway. But then I got home and was feeling generally frustrated, and it occurred to me that it simply made no sense."

"In what way?"

"I kept thinking about his corpse. I've never seen such evidence of hardship. Everything about him, every single sinew and muscle, speaks of a life which has been a terrible struggle. This may sound a bit like pop psychology, but I find it very hard to believe that a person like that suddenly stops fighting and stuffs himself full of pills. I don't think we can rule out that somebody was responsible for his death."

Blomkvist gave a start.

"You'll have to tell them that, of course. They'll need more people working on the investigation, not just Hans Faste."

"And I will. But I wanted to tell you anyhow, as a sort of insurance in case the police don't do their stuff."

"I'm grateful for that," he said and thought of Catrin Lindås, who Sofie had told him about.

He remembered her well-pressed suits and the mark on her jacket, and the hippie commune she had grown up in. He wondered if he should mention her name. Maybe there was something she could tell the police. But then he decided he ought to spare her Hans Faste's attentions for the time being, and instead he said:

"And you still don't know who he is?"

"No, no hits anywhere. No-one with those distinguishing features has been reported missing. But I wasn't expecting that anyway. What I do have is a DNA sequence analysis from the National Forensics Lab, which has just come in. But it's still only shallow, autosomal. I'm going to ask for an analysis of his mitochondrial DNA as well, and his Y chromosome, and then I hope that'll get me further."

"I'm sure there are going to be many others who remember him," he said.

"What do you mean?"

"He was someone you'd notice. It was just me being too self-absorbed this summer. The police ought to have a word with people around Mariatorget, lots of them will have seen him."

"I'll pass that on."

Blomkvist was beginning to find this interesting.

"You know what? If he really was taking those tablets, he's unlikely to have got them on prescription," he said. "He didn't look like someone who makes an appointment with a psychiatrist, and I know from experience that there's a black market for drugs like that. The police are bound to have informants in those circles."

Nyman was silent for a second or two.

"Oh, damn it," she said.

"I'm sorry?"

"I've been an idiot."

"I find that hard to believe."

"No, I have. But listen . . . I'm glad you remember him. It really does mean something to me."

Blomkvist looked at his half-packed suitcase and found that he no longer wanted to go to Sandhamn after all.

Blomkvist had said something appreciative in return, but Fredrika had barely heard it. She ended the call and almost didn't notice Amanda, who was standing next to her asking what was for dinner. Maybe she even apologized for having been so sulky earlier. Fredrika simply told them to order a takeaway.

"What?" they both said.

"Whatever you want. Pizza, Indian, Thai, chips, liquorice sweets . . ."

The girls looked at her as if she had gone off her rocker. She went into her study and closed the door, and e-mailed the forensics lab asking them to run a segmental hair analysis right away, something she should have done at the start.

Not only would that show how much eszopiclone and dextropropoxyphene had been in the man's bloodstream when he died, it would also give her the levels for every week going back several months. In other words, she would know if he had been taking the drugs over a period of time or on only one occasion. It could become an important piece in the jigsaw, and all of that made her forget her daughters, the back pain, the lack of sleep and the feeling that life might be meaningless in the end. That puzzled her. She spent her life investigating suspicious deaths, and nowadays it was rare for her to become so emotionally involved. But she had been fascinated by this character, and perhaps she even hoped that he had had a dramatic death. It was as if his ravaged body deserved more of a story, so much so that she spent many hours looking at images of the corpse, each time noticing new details. Every so often she said to herself:

What have you been through, my old friend?

What hellish trials have you had to suffer?

Blomkvist sat down by his computer and googled Catrin Lindås. She was thirty-seven years old, held a master's degree in economics and political science from Stockholm University, and had now established herself as a conservative commentator and writer. She ran a successful podcast and wrote columns for *Svenska Dagbladet*, *Axess*, *Fokus* and also *Journalisten*.

She had lobbied for begging to be made illegal and often discussed the risks of welfare dependence and the shortcomings of the Swedish educational system. In addition to being a monarchist and an advocate for a robust national defence, she felt strongly about safeguarding the nuclear family, although she did not seem to have one of her own. She claimed to be a feminist, but feminists had often criticized her. She faced a barrage of hatred online from both the Right and the Left and had a disturbingly long comments thread on the Flashback Forum. "We must have standards," she often said. "Standards and responsibilities allow us to grow."

She hated woolliness, she frequently wrote, and superstition, and religious convictions, although she was more cautious on the last. Writing in *Svenska Dagbladet* about constructive journalism—stories which not only describe problematic situations but actually suggest a way out of them—she said that "Mikael Blomkvist claims to want to fight the populists, but then plays into their hands with his pessimistic view of society."

It troubled her, she said, that young journalists looked upon him as an example to follow. She wrote that he had a tendency to see people as victims. And that his default setting was to take sides against the business establishment. He ought to make more of an effort to identify solutions, not only problems. That was more or less what he would have expected her to say.

He'd known worse, for sure, and she might have had a point or two. But in some ridiculous way, she still alarmed him. He could not help feeling as if one look from her would be enough to reveal that he had not done the washing-up or showered or done up his fly. Or that he drank yoghurt straight from the carton. There was something damning about that look, he thought, a cold streak in her, though it only enhanced her severe beauty.

Yet he could not stop thinking about her confrontation with the beggar—the ice queen and the man in tattered rags. In the end he found her number and called. She did not answer, and perhaps that was just as well. There was nothing there. There was no story, and he should be heading out to Sandhamn now, before it got too late. He took some shirts from the wardrobe and a jacket in case he decided to treat himself at Seglarhotellet. Then his mobile rang. It was Catrin Lindås, and she sounded every bit as severe as she looked.

"What is it?" she began, and he considered saying something nice about her column, to get her to relax. But it was more than he could bring himself to do, so he simply asked if he had got her at a bad moment.

"I'm busy," she said.

"OK, let's speak later then."

"We can speak later if you tell me what it's about."

I'm writing a bitchy column about you, he was tempted to say.

"My colleague Sofie Melker told me that recently you had an unpleasant altercation with a homeless man in Mariatorget."

"I have many unpleasant altercations," she said. "It goes with the job."

My God, he thought.

"I'm just curious, I'd like to know what the man said."

"Whatever it was, it was gibberish."

He took another look at the pictures of Lindås on his screen.

"Are you still at work?" he said.

"Why do you ask?"

"I thought I could drop by for a moment, and we could talk about it. You're on Mäster Mikaels Gata, aren't you?"

Reflecting on it afterwards, he could not imagine what had prompted him to suggest such a thing, but he knew that if he was going to find out anything at all, it was not going to happen over the telephone. It was as if there were barbed wire along the line.

"OK, but let's make it quick," she said. "In an hour."

A tram could be heard rattling past the hotel near Náměstí Republiky in Prague. Salander was drinking too much again, and was once more glued to her computer, behind the screens of her Faraday cage. Yes, there had been moments of relief and oblivion, but she had always got there with the help of alcohol and sex, and afterwards the rage and the frustration had returned.

Some sort of madness was overwhelming her, the past was spinning in her head like a centrifuge. *This is no life,* she often thought to herself. *It's not possible to go on like this.* She had to take action. It was no good just waiting and listening out for footsteps in the corridors and streets, or running away. So she had tried to regain the initiative. But it wasn't easy.

The handle Katya Flip, recommended by Plague, was said to be one hell of a badass. To begin with it hadn't felt like that. She kept on asking for more money and said that no-one messes with that branch of the mafia—especially not now that Ivan Galinov was involved.

There was endless talk about Galinov, and Kuznetsov too, and about some notorious acts of vengeance. Only after lengthy conversations on the dark web had Salander persuaded Flip to hide an IMSI-catcher in a rhododendron a hundred yards from Camilla's house in Rublyovka, after which she had picked up tracking numbers—IMEI numbers—from the mobile traffic inside. That was something at least. But it gave no guarantees, nor any respite from the past, which was still throbbing and clamouring inside her. Often she would sit as now, eating room service junk food and emptying the minibar of whisky and vodka, and staring down at Camilla's house via a satellite link she had hacked.

This alone was pure madness. She wouldn't take any exercise or even go outside, and only when there was a knock at the door did she get up and open for Paulina, who was already chattering away about something. But Salander did not hear a word, not until Paulina burst out:

"What's happened?"

"Nothing."

"You look—"

"—fucked up?" Salander said.

"Something along those lines. Is there anything I can do?"

Stay away, she thought. *Stay away.* But instead she went and lay on the bed, and wondered if Paulina would dare to join her.

Blomkvist shook Catrin Lindås's hand. Her grip was firm, but she avoided his eyes. Her white blouse was buttoned to the neck, and she wore a skirt and a light-blue blazer with a tartan shawl and black high-heeled shoes. Her hair was up in a bun, and even though her clothes fitted closely and accentuated her figure, she looked as prim as a teacher at the English School. She was apparently the only person left in the office. On the bulletin board above her desk there was a picture of her onstage with Christine Lagarde, managing director of the International Monetary Fund. They looked like mother and daughter.

"Impressive," he said, pointing at the photograph.

She made no comment, just asked him to take a seat on the sofa and settled into an armchair opposite him, her legs crossed and her back straight. In some absurd way it felt as if a reluctant queen were granting an audience to one of her subjects.

"Good of you to see me," he said.

"Don't mention it."

She eyed him suspiciously, and he felt like asking why she disliked him so much.

"I'm not researching a piece on you, if that's any comfort," he said.

"You can write what you like about me."

"I'll bear that in mind."

He gave a smile. She did not return it.

"In fact I'm on holiday," he continued.

"Aren't you lucky."

He felt an inexplicable urge to needle her.

"I'm curious to hear about that beggar. What did he say to you? He was found dead a few days ago with my telephone number in his pocket."

"OK . . ."

You could at least react to the fact that the guy is dead, he thought.

"He may have had something he wanted to tell me, so I'm curious to find out what he said to you."

"Not much. All he did was shout and wave some sort of stick and frighten the life out of me."

"What was he shouting?"

"The usual rubbish."

"What do you call 'the usual rubbish'?"

"That Johannes Forsell is a dodgy character generally."

"He shouted that?"

"Well, it was something to do with Forsell, but my main concern was to get away. He was pulling at my arm and was violent and unpleasant, so you'll forgive me for not staying and listening patiently to his conspiracy theories."

"I understand. I really do," he said, and he could not help feeling disappointed.

He was fed up with all the garbage being spouted about the Minister of Defence. It was one of the trolls' favourite topics and the story grew more extravagant by the day. It seemed only a matter of time before they had Forsell running a pizzeria for paedophiles, and that was no doubt partly due to his uncompromising attitude towards right-wing extremists and xenophobes and his stated misgivings about Russia's increasingly aggressive policies, but also because of his personality. He was well educated and rich, a marathon runner and a cross-Channel swimmer who could sometimes come across as supercilious. Certainly he'd been known to put people's backs up.

But Blomkvist liked him. Every now and then they would run into each other in Sandhamn and exchange pleasantries. Out of a sense of duty he had followed up the rumours that Forsell had made huge sums from the stock market crash, and might even have been one of the contributing factors. He had not found a shred of evidence to support the claims. Forsell's assets were managed on a discretionary basis and there had been no transactions either before or during the collapse. What is more, the market falls had most decidedly not strengthened his position. But as of now he was the most hated man in the government. His principal achievement was to have got increased funding for Must, the Swedish Military Intelligence and Security Service, and MSB, the Swedish Civil Contingencies Agency, so it was hardly surprising under the circumstances.

"I can't stand all the lies that are being churned out," she said.

"I don't much like them either," he said.

"Then we can agree on one thing, at least."

"I accept that it's not easy to talk to a guy who's shouting and waving a stick," he said.

"That's generous of you."

"But sometimes it's worth listening even though it doesn't seem to make sense. There might still be a grain of truth there."

"And now you're telling me how to do my job?"

Her tone was infuriating.

"Do you know something?" he said. "It can drive you mad when no-one believes you, or listens to you."

"Are you serious?"

"To be ignored year after year? Oh yes, that can destroy you."

"The man became homeless and psychotic because people like me wouldn't listen to him?" she said.

"That's not what I meant."

"It sounded like it."

"In that case, I apologize."

"Thank you."

"You haven't had an easy time of it yourself, from what I've heard," he tried.

"What's that got to do with it?"

"Nothing, I guess."

"Well, then. Thank you for coming by," she said.

"Christ," he muttered. "What's the matter with you?"

"What's the matter with *me*?" she repeated and got to her feet. For a few seconds they glared at each other.

He had the ridiculous feeling that they were duelling, or that they were two boxers in a ring, and without quite understanding how it happened they were suddenly very close to each other. He felt her breath and saw her eyes glow and her chest heave. When she inclined her head to one side he kissed her, and for a moment he thought he had done something unforgivably stupid. But she kissed him back, and for a few seconds they looked at each other in astonishment, as if neither could grasp what had happened.

Then she put a hand around his neck and pulled him to her, and within moments it got completely out of hand. They found themselves on the sofa and on the floor, and in the middle of all the madness Blomkvist realized that he had wanted her ever since he first saw her picture online.

CHAPTER 9

August 24

Fredrika Nyman was sitting in the laboratory at the Forensic Board thinking about her daughters, and wondering what had gone wrong.

"I don't get it," she said to her colleague Mattias Holm-ström.

"What don't you get?"

"How I can be so angry at Josefin and Amanda. It's as if I'm about to explode."

"What is it that's making you so angry?"

"They're so arrogant. They don't even say hello."

"Jesus, Fredrika, they're teenagers. It's normal. Don't you remember how you were at that age?"

Nyman did remember. She had been a model child, good at school and good at the flute, volleyball and choral singing. And at being polite and mannerly. She had been one big smile and had said "Yes, Mamma" and "Of course, Pappa" like a happy little trouper. She must have been unbearable in her own way. But heavens . . . to not even answer when you're spoken to?

She couldn't understand it, nor could she help being in a bad mood all the time, losing her temper and yelling at the girls in the evenings. She was simply too tired. She had to get some sleep, and some peace, and of course the obvious thing would be to prescribe herself some sleeping pills. And why not a controlled substance while she was at it? Since she had been such an exemplary teenager, surely she could go off the rails a bit now and, well, why not mix some red wine with the painkillers too? She laughed to herself and when a few perfunctory words to Mattias elicited a warm smile, she felt like screaming at him too.

Then she began to think about the beggar again. His case was the only one at work that really engaged her, and she decided to ignore the fact that the police could not be bothered with it. She had asked for a carbon-14 dating test on the teeth as a matter of high priority. This would show how old the man had been within a tolerance of two years, and a carbon-13 test would reveal his eating habits in childhood, when his teeth were being formed, and indicate their strontium and oxygen content.

Fredrika had also compared the autosomal DNA results with the internationalgenome.org database, and this indicated that the man came in all probability from the southern parts of Central Asia. She was still waiting for the segmental hair analysis to come back. In the worst case, testing a hair sample can take months, and she had been leaning as hard as possible on the forensics lab. She decided to call her medical secretary yet again.

"Gunilla," she said. "I'm sorry to keep on at you."

"Don't worry, you're the one who nags me least of all. It's only lately that you've upped your game."

"The results of the hair analysis, have they come in yet?"

"For the unidentified man?"

"The very one."

"I'll check with central office."

Nyman drummed her fingers on the table and looked at the clock on the wall. It was 10:20 in the morning and she was already longing for lunch.

"Well I never, *that's* a surprise," Gunilla said after a short pause. "They've speeded up. It's already come in. I'll bring it over to you."

"Just tell me what it says."

"It says . . . wait a moment now."

Nyman was surprised by her impatience.

"It seems he had long hair. We have all three segments, and they are . . . all negative. No trace of opiates. Or benzos."

"So he was no narcoholic."

"Just an honest-to-goodness alcoholic. No, wait . . . here . . . he's taken aripiprazole in the past, that's a neuroleptic, isn't it?"

"Correct, for the treatment of schizophrenia."

"That's all I can see."

Nyman hung up and sat thinking for a while. So the man had not taken any other psychotropic drugs, except for aripiprazole, and that was some time ago. What could that mean? She bit her lip and glared at Mattias, who wore the same silly smile as before. But it was fairly straightforward, wasn't it? Either the man had suddenly—maybe by chance—got hold of a large number of sleeping pills and swallowed them. Or else somebody had wanted to kill him, and had ground them up and put them in his moonshine. Not that she knew what a mixture of alcohol and eszopiclone might taste like. Presumably not very nice. But she guessed that her man was not all that fussy. On the other hand, why would anybody want to kill him? There was no way of knowing, of course, not yet at least. But assuming that scenario, she could already rule out manslaughter. This was no act committed on the spur of the moment. It takes a measure of sophistication to mix pills into a bottle and then to spike it with opiates. With dextropropoxyphene.

With dextropropoxyphene.

Something about that made her suspicious. The dextropropoxyphene made the cocktail just a little too good. As if it had been made up by a pharmacist, or someone who had consulted a doctor. She felt a certain excitement again, and wondered what to do next. She could ring Hans Faste and be treated to yet another lecture on the habits of weirdos. But instead she finished off her report and called Mikael Blomkvist. Since she had already begun to talk out of turn, she might as well continue.

Catrin Lindås was sitting in Blomkvist's cabin out at Sandhamn, trying to put together a short editorial for *Svenska Dagbladet*. It was not going well. She felt uninspired and was fed up with deadlines. She was even tired of having opinions. In fact she was altogether bored with everything except Mikael Blomkvist, and that was the very last thing she needed. But there was nothing she could do about that. She ought to go home and see to her cat and her plants, and demonstrate that she had some independence.

But she stayed put. It was as if she could not tear herself away from him. It was so strange, they had not argued at all, just made love and talked for hours. Maybe it was because she had had a thing for him hundreds of years ago, like every other young female journalist at the time. But it was more likely the fact that she had been taken completely by surprise—the power of the totally unexpected. She had been certain that he despised her and wanted to score points off her, which had made her defensive and arrogant, as she often was under pressure. She had been wanting to get him out of her office when she saw something quite different in his eyes, a hunger, and then it had spiralled out of control. She had become the very antithesis of everything people believed about her, and she didn't even care that one of her colleagues might turn up in her office at any moment. She had thrown herself at him with a passion which surprised her even now, and afterwards they had gone out and had far too much wine. Normally she never had far too much of anything.

They had arrived in Sandhamn by taxi boat late at night and tumbled into his cabin. They spent the next few days in each other's arms in bed, or sitting in the garden, or out in the little motorboat—more of a dinghy with an outboard— he'd bought the year before. They simply watched the days go by. Yet she refused to believe that it was anything serious, and so far she had not said a single word about the one truly permanent feature of her life, the terror that never left her. She kept saying she would go home tomorrow, or maybe even that evening. But she had stayed on, and now it was ten-thirty on Monday morning. There was a wind out on the water and she looked up at the sky. A green kite swooping erratically in the wind. There was a sudden buzz next to her.

It was Blomkvist's mobile. He was out running and she had certainly not offered to look after his phone. Nevertheless she checked the display. Fredrika Nyman. That must be the medical examiner he had been talking about, so she picked up.

"Mikael's mobile?" she said.

"Is he there?"

"He's out running. Can I take a message?"

"Please ask him to call me," the doctor said. "Tell him I've got the results of a test back."

"Is this about the beggar in the down jacket?"

"It is."

"I met him, you know," she said.

"You did?" Catrin heard the curiosity in her voice. "I'm sorry, who are you?"

"I'm Catrin, a friend of Mikael's."

"What happened?"

"He accosted me in Mariatorget one morning, shouted at me."

"What did he want?"

She already regretted having said anything. She recalled the feeling of something bad from the past coming back to hit her, like a chill wind.

"He wanted to talk about Johannes Forsell."

"Forsell, the Minister of Defence?"

"He probably wanted to bad-mouth him, like everyone else does. But I got away from there as quickly as I could."

"Did you get any sense of where he might have come from?"

Catrin thought she had a pretty good idea.

"No, I didn't," she said. "What test results were you talking about?"

"I think I'd better discuss that with Mikael."

"Fine, I'll get him to call you."

She hung up and felt the fear creep back again, and she thought of the beggar; how he had been kneeling by the statue in Mariatorget and her sense of déjà vu, and how it had taken her back to her childhood travels. Maybe she had given him a slightly nervous smile, the kind she always used to give to all the poor broken wretches back then. At any rate the man must have felt he was being acknowledged. He sprang to his feet and grabbed a stick which lay next to him, and came hobbling towards her, shouting:

"Famous lady, famous lady."

She had been surprised to be recognized. But then he came up close and she saw the stumps of his fingers and the dark patches on his yellowish skin. There was desperation in his eyes, and she felt paralyzed. Only when he took hold of her jacket and started to shout about Johannes Forsell did she manage to tug herself free and escape.

"Can't you remember a single thing of what he said?" Blomkvist had asked.

She had said it was the usual rubbish. But maybe it was

more than that, after all. The words came back to her and
now she no longer found them incomprehensible, or thought
they were the sort of thing people always said about Forsell.
Now they suggested something entirely different.

Mikael was nearing home, exhausted and sweaty. He looked
around him, but there was no-one, and again he thought:
I'm just imagining things, this is absurd. In recent days he had
begun to suspect that he was being followed, and felt he was
bumping into a man with a ponytail and beard and tattoos
on his arms rather too often. The man was dressed as a holi-
daymaker, but there was something altogether too watchful
about him. He did not look like a person off duty.

Not that he really believed the man had anything to do
with him, and most of the time he devoted himself to Catrin
and managed to forget the world out there. But every so
often, as now, he felt a stab of anxiety, and then he almost
always thought of Salander. He imagined the most terrible
scenes . . .

Still catching his breath, he looked up. There were no
clouds in the sky. They'd said that the heat wave was to
continue, but that it would turn windy overnight and there
might be a storm. He stopped outside his gate, and his garden with the two currant bushes which he ought to have
pruned. Breathing heavily, he looked out at the water and
the swimmers as he bent forward, his hands on his knees.

Then he went indoors, expecting an enthusiastic reception. Catrin had spoiled him by greeting him like a returning
soldier if he popped out even for ten minutes. But now she

just sat there stiffly on the bed, looking grim, and he was worried. His thoughts immediately went back to the man with the ponytail.

"Has anything happened?"

"What . . . no," she said.

"And no-one's come to visit?"

"Were you expecting someone?" she said, and that reassured him a little. He stroked her hair and asked her how she was feeling.

Catrin said she was fine, but he did not believe her. It was not the first time he had noticed this gloomy streak in her. But it had always vanished as quickly as it appeared, and when she told him that the medical examiner had called, he decided to leave her be and went to ring Nyman to hear about the hair test.

"So what conclusions do you draw?" he asked her.

"To be honest, I've been twisting and turning this every which way. And it still seems suspicious," she said.

Blomkvist looked at Catrin, who was sitting with her arms across her stomach. He smiled and she gave a forced smile in return, and he looked out of the window. There were whitecaps as far out as he could see. His outboard motor was bobbing up and down on the waves. He would have to pull it up properly later.

"What does Faste say now?"

"He doesn't know yet, but I've put it in my report."

"You have to let him know."

"I will. Your friend said that the beggar was talking about Forsell."

"The man's a kind of virus," he said. "Every nutcase has him on the brain."

"I had no idea."

"A little like the Palme assassination back then, which seemed to creep into every little psychosis. I'm inundated with absurd conspiracy theories about Forsell."

"How come?"

He looked at Catrin, who got up and went into the bathroom.

"I don't think you ever know," he said. "Certain public figures just seem to wind up people's imaginations. But in this case it can only have been planted, in revenge for the fact that Forsell identified Russia's involvement in the stock market crash at a very early stage, and generally took an uncompromising line against the Kremlin. There's more than a suspicion that he's been targeted by a disinformation campaign."

"Isn't he also a bit of a risk taker? An adventurer?"

"I think he's OK, actually. I had a good look at his affairs," he said. "Do you still not know where the beggar came from?"

"No more than what the carbon-13 analysis reveals, that he probably grew up in extreme poverty, but I'd already guessed that much. He seems to have eaten mostly vegetables and grains. Perhaps his parents were vegetarians."

He looked towards the bathroom.

"Isn't it all a bit odd?" he said.

"In what way?"

"That the man just pops up one day out of nowhere, and is then found dead with a cocktail of lethal poisons inside him?"

"Yes, it is," she said.

A thought struck him.

"Do you know what? I have a friend on the homicide squad, a chief inspector who's worked with Faste and thinks he's a total idiot," he said.

"A man of sound judgment, clearly."

"I could have a word with him, see if he might be able to take a look at the case. That way we can maybe speed up the process."

"That would be good."

"Thanks for the call," he said. "I'll get back to you."

He hung up, happy to have a reason to call Bublanski. He and the chief inspector had known each other for a long time, even if their relationship had not always been entirely cordial. But in later years they had become friends and it was always comforting to talk to him. The mere fact that Bublanski always thought so carefully about everything helped Blomkvist to see things in perspective and to disconnect from the constant flow of news about the world which was his life, but which sometimes made him feel as if he were drowning in sensationalism and madness.

The last time he and Bublanski had met was at Holger Palmgren's funeral and they had talked about Salander and her eulogy in the church, and what she had said about dragons. They had agreed to see each other again soon. But nothing had come of it, as so often happens, and now Blomkvist reached for his mobile to call him. Yet he hesitated, and instead knocked on the bathroom door.

"Are you all right in there?"

. . .

Catrin did not feel like answering, but she knew she had to say something, so she mumbled "just a moment" and got up from the toilet seat. She tried to make her eyes look a little less red by splashing water on her face, but it made little difference. Then she came out and sat on the bed, and did not feel entirely comfortable when Mikael came close to her and caressed her hair.

"How did you get on with the article?"

"It's a disaster."

"I know the feeling. But there's something else, isn't there?" he said.

"That beggar . . ." she began.

"What about him?"

"He made me hysterical."

"I've gathered that."

"But you don't know why."

"Not really, I guess," he said. She hesitated for a while, but then she began to speak, her eyes fixed on her hands.

"When I was nine my parents told me I wasn't going to go to school for a year. My mother persuaded the school that she and Pappa would teach me themselves, and I suppose they must have been given a stack of materials and learning assignments. Not that I ever saw them. Then we flew to India, to Goa, and it was probably quite cool to begin with. We slept on the beach or in hammocks, and I ran around with other kids and learned how to make jewellery and carve things out of wood. We played football and volleyball, and in the evenings we danced and lit fires. Pappa played the guitar and Mamma sang. For a while we ran a café in Arambol. I waited on tables and made a lentil soup with coconut milk which we called Catrin's soup. But slowly it all fell apart. People came to the café naked, many of them with needle marks on their arms. Others were stoned, and some of them groped me or tried to frighten me by doing crazy things."

"That sounds horrible."

"One night I woke up and saw Mamma's eyes glowing in the dark. She was shooting up. Pappa was standing a little way off, swaying and moaning in a barely conscious voice, and not long after that we began to have problems for real. Pappa's demons, we talked about them all the time. 'What's the matter with Pappa?' I'd ask. 'It's just his demons,' Mamma always said. Pappa's demons. Soon afterwards we moved, as if we were hoping to escape the demons too, and I remember we walked for hours and days and weeks, pulling a cart with rotting old wooden wheels, piled high with shawls and clothes and knickknacks which Mamma tried to sell. Then we must have got rid of everything because from one day to the next we had hardly any baggage at all. We went by train and hitchhiked instead. We went to Benares, and finally ended up in Kathmandu where we lived on Freak Street, the old hippie street, and that was when I realized we had a completely different line of business. Mamma and Pappa weren't just doing heroin, they were selling it too. People came to our home and begged us 'please, please,' and sometimes we got chased by men in the street. Many were missing fingers, sometimes even an arm or a leg. They were dressed in rags, and had yellowy skin and blotches on their faces. I still see them in my dreams."

"And the beggar reminded you of them."

"All of that came back to me."

"I'm sorry," he said.

"That's just the way it is. I've lived with it for a long time."

"I don't know if this makes it any easier for you, but that man was no drug addict. It seems he didn't take pills at all."

"He still looked like them," she said. "He was just as desperate."

"The medical examiner thinks he was killed," Blomkvist went on in a new tone, as if he had already forgotten her story, and maybe this upset her. Or else she was just tired of herself. She told him she needed to get out for a while, and even though he made a half-hearted attempt to stop her, his mind was evidently on other things.

Turning in the doorway she saw that he was dialling a number on his mobile. It occurred to her that she did not have to tell him everything; she could just as well follow it up herself, after all.

CHAPTER 10

August 24–25

Chief Inspector Jan Bublanski was permanently beset by doubt, and right now he was not even sure whether or not he deserved lunch. Maybe just a sandwich from the machine in the corridor and keep on working, although on second thought a sandwich was no good either. He ought to have a salad or nothing at all. He and his fiancée Farah Sharif had been on holiday in Tel Aviv, and he'd certainly put on a bit of weight. He seemed to have lost a little more hair from the crown of his head too. But that was normal, not something to get worked up about. He got his teeth into some work instead, and became absorbed in a report of a cross-examination—badly written—and a forensic analysis from Huddinge—another slipshod piece of work. That could have been why his mind began to wander, because when Mikael Blomkvist called he answered quite truthfully:

"It's a funny thing, Mikael, not ten minutes ago I was thinking about you."

Although he may in fact have been thinking about Lisbeth Salander, or perhaps that was just a feeling he had.

"How are you?"

"Good, all things considered," Blomkvist said.

"I'm glad you qualified that. I'm starting to find uncomplicated cheerfulness hard to cope with. Have you had any holiday?"

"I'm doing my best right now."

"If you're calling me, you're not trying very hard. It's about your girl, I guess?"

"She's never been my girl," Blomkvist said.

"I know, I know. No-one's less like someone's girl than she is. She's a bit like the fallen angel in paradise, isn't she? She serves nobody, belongs to nobody."

"It beats me that you're a policeman, Jan."

"My rabbi says I ought to retire. But, seriously, have you heard from her?"

"She tells me she's keeping out of the way and not doing anything stupid. And for the moment I actually believe her."

"I'm pleased to hear it. I don't like the fact that Svavelsjö are nosing around after her," Bublanski said.

"No-one likes it."

"I suppose you know we've offered her protection."

"I heard."

"And did you also hear that she refused, and hasn't been contactable since?"

"Well, yes . . ."

"Although . . ."

"Although nothing," Blomkvist went on. "Except I do take comfort from the fact that nobody knows as much about keeping under the radar as she does."

"You mean from electronic surveillance and stuff like that," Bublanski said.

"It's not as though she can be traced via any base station or IP address."

"That's something, at least. We'll just have to wait and see, then."

"We will. Can I ask you about something completely different?"

"Fire away."

"Your man Faste's been saddled with an investigation which he doesn't seem in the least interested in."

"Often it's better that way. Sometimes when he can be bothered to make an effort . . ."

"Hmm, maybe so. It's to do with a beggar who was found dead in the street. Fredrika Nyman, a medical examiner, thinks he may have been murdered."

Blomkvist told him the story, and afterwards Bublanski left his office, got himself two plastic-wrapped cheese sandwiches and one chocolate wafer from the machine, and called his colleague, Inspector Sonja Modig.

Catrin put on a gardening glove that she found lying in the grass, and tugged away at the nettles that had grown under Blomkvist's currant bushes. When she looked up, she saw a man with a ponytail and a broad, slightly menacing back hurrying away along the shoreline. But she put him out of her mind and went back to the confused thoughts that had occupied her in the cabin.

It was probably true that the beggar in Mariatorget was not really like the junkies on Freak Street. But she was convinced that he came from the same part of the world and had been treated by the same careless breed of doctor. She remembered his mutilated fingers and his distinctive way of walking, as if he were missing a centre of gravity beneath his feet. She recalled his powerful grip and the words:

"I know something very bad about Johannes Forsell."

She was expecting more of the sort of abuse that she saw on the internet every day, along with the hate mail addressed to her, and she was afraid that he would become violent. But just as she was about to panic he let go of her arm, and continued in a more sorrowful tone:

"I took Forsell. And I left Mamsabiv . . . terrible, so terrible."

Or perhaps he did not say "Mamsabiv," but it was something similar, a long word with the stress on the first syllable. The word had rung in her ears as she ran away from him and bumped into Sofie Melker on Swedenborgsgatan. She had somehow forgotten it, and now, out at the cabin, the conversation with the medical examiner had brought it all back, and she wondered what it might mean. It needed looking into after all.

She took off the gardening glove and keyed in several versions of the word, but her search yielded nothing that made sense in any language. Google only asked if she meant Mats Sabin, and maybe she did, Matssabin pronounced in one breath. It couldn't be ruled out, especially when she discovered that Mats Sabin had been an officer in Kustartilleriet, the coastal artillery, and later a military historian at Försvarshögskolan, the Swedish Defence University. He could very easily have had dealings with Forsell, a former intelligence officer and an authority on Russia.

Catrin put both names into her browser, on the off-chance, and got an immediate hit which revealed that not only had they met, they had been enemies, or at least had public disagreements. She considered going inside and telling Mikael. But no, it felt too far-fetched, so she stayed in the garden and got back to work on the weeds, occasionally looking up to contemplate the waterfront, her mind full of conflicting thoughts.

Salander was still at the Kings Court Hotel in Prague, sitting at the desk near the window and staring once again at images on her screen of Camilla's large house in Rublyovka. But she was no longer doing so compulsively, or as part of her routine to imprint things on her memory. The house seemed increasingly like a fortress, a command centre. People came and went all the time, even big shots like Kuznetsov, and everybody was frisked. Every day there were more and more guards, and IT security was certainly being checked over and over again.

Thanks to the base station which Katya Flip had put in position and taken away after a few days, Lisbeth was able to follow Camilla step by step, relying on the tracking signals from her sister's mobile. But she hadn't yet been able to hack the IT system and so was reduced to guessing what was happening inside the house. She knew only that the level of activity had increased.

The house was pulsating with the sort of nervous energy which precedes a major operation, and yesterday Camilla had been driven to the Aquarium, as it was known, the headquarters of the GRU, the military intelligence service in Khodinka, outside Moscow. That was not a good sign. It looked as if she was calling in all the help she could muster.

It seemed that she had no idea where Lisbeth was, however, and to some extent this was reassuring. So long as her sister remained in the house in Rublyovka, Lisbeth and Paulina ought not to be in any danger. But there was no certainty of anything.

Salander closed down the satellite image and instead checked in to see what Paulina's husband Thomas was up to. Nothing, or so it would seem. He was just staring into the webcam, looking his usual aggrieved self.

Salander had not been especially communicative of late. But at least in the evenings she had been spending hours listening to Paulina. She knew more than enough about her life, and by now she had even heard about the incident with the iron. Thomas, who was just then blowing his nose in front of the webcam, had always taken his shirts to the laundry when they were living in Germany. In Copenhagen he had Paulina iron them—"to give her something to do during the day." But then one day she just forgot about the ironing, and the washing-up too, and walked around in her knickers and one of his unironed shirts, drinking red wine and then whisky.

Paulina had been beaten up the evening before. She had a split lip, and she hoped to get drunk enough to dare either to end the relationship or to bring matters to a head. Things went from bad to worse. She broke a vase by accident. Then some glasses and plates—not quite so accidentally—and somehow she also managed to spill red wine on the shirt, and whisky on the bedclothes and the carpet. In the end she fell asleep, drunk and defiant, and with a feeling that at last she would have the courage to tell him to go to hell.

She woke up to find Thomas sitting on her arms, hitting her repeatedly in the face. Then he dragged her to the ironing board and ironed his shirt himself. Paulina remembered nothing after that, except for the smell of burned skin and an indescribable pain, and her own steps racing towards the front door. Every so often Salander would think about this, and even though she sometimes stared straight into Thomas's eyes, as now, his face often merged with that of her father.

When she was tired, everything flowed into one—Camilla, Thomas Müller, her childhood, Zala, everything—and tightened like a restraint belt across her chest and forehead, and she would gasp for air. Music could be heard from outside, a guitar being tuned. She craned her neck to look out of the window. The street was full of people, streaming into and out of the Palladium shopping centre. On a huge white stage over to the right, preparations were being made for a concert. Perhaps it was Saturday again, or a public holiday—it was all the same to her. And where was Paulina? She must be out on one of her never-ending walks around town. In an attempt to dispel her thoughts, Salander checked her inbox.

Hacker Republic had not come back to her as she had

hoped, and there was no answer to the questions she had asked during the day. But she had received some encrypted documents from Blomkvist, and that did bring a little smile to her face. *So you've finally got around to reading your own article,* she thought. But no, the files had nothing to do with Kuznetsov and his lies. Instead they were . . . well, what were they, actually?

Endless rows with masses of numbers and letters, XY, 11, 12, 13, 19. It was clearly a DNA sequence—but whose? She scanned through the documents and an attached autopsy report, and saw that they related to a man who was between fifty-four and fifty-six years old, according to a carbon-14 test. He came from somewhere in southern Central Asia. Several of his fingers and toes had been amputated and he had been in a very bad way, also an alcoholic. The autopsy concluded that he had died of poisoning by eszopiclone and dextropropoxyphene.

Blomkvist wrote:

<If you really are taking some holiday and aren't up to anything stupid, perhaps you could have a go at working out who this is. The police have no name, nothing. A capable medical examiner called Fredrika Nyman thinks the man may have been murdered.

He was found beside a tree in Tantolunden on August 15. I'm sending a DNA analysis—autosomal—and some other stuff, the results of a carbon-13 test and a hair analysis together with a photograph of a piece of

```
paper with the man's handwriting. (Yes,
that's my number.)
    M.>
```

"The hell I will," she muttered. "I'm going to go out and find Paulina, and get pissed again. I'm definitely not poring over someone's DNA results, and I'm not talking to any pathologists."

But she didn't leave the hotel room this time either, because just then she heard Paulina's footsteps in the corridor. She took two small bottles of champagne from the minibar and threw her arms wide, in a brave attempt not to look fucked up.

It was a crazy plan. But Blomkvist had been feeling lonely and dejected ever since Catrin Lindås said she had to go home to feed her cat and water her plants—he was particularly unhappy to lose out to the plants—and having waved her off at the harbour he had gone home and called Nyman again.

He had claimed to know a prominent woman geneticist who might be able to make some progress on the DNA analyses. Nyman was keen to know who this was and exactly what field she worked in. He said only that she was a very determined person, a professor in London who specialized in tracing genealogy. Salander was indeed brilliant at DNA analyses. She had gone to great lengths to try to find out why her family all had such extreme genetic features. It was not just her highly intelligent and odious father, Zalachenko. There was her half brother too, Ronald Niedermann, with his exceptional strength and his lack of sensitivity to pain. There was Lisbeth herself, with her photographic memory. There were a number of people among her blood relations with exceptional characteristics, and although Blomkvist had no idea what she had discovered, he did know that Salander had taught herself the scientific methodology in no time at all. After a lengthy exchange with Fredrika Nyman, he eventually got the material she had been sent.

Then he forwarded it all to Salander. He was not optimistic. Perhaps it was no more than an excuse to get in touch. Whatever. He looked out to sea. The wind was getting up and the last bathers were packing away their things. He became absorbed in his thoughts.

What had got into Catrin? In just a few days they had become so close that he had thought . . . well, he wasn't sure what he thought. That they really belonged together? That was plain silly, they were like night and day . . . he should leave it for now, and ring Erika instead. He ought to make up for the fact that he had put his article on hold. He picked up his mobile and rang . . . Catrin. That was just how it went, and at first the conversation continued more or less as it had ended, stiff and hesitant. Then she said:

"I'm sorry."

"For what?"

"For leaving."

"No plant should ever have to die because of me."

She gave a sad laugh.

"What are you going to do now?" he said.

"Not sure. Well, maybe I'll force myself to sit down and try and write something."

"Doesn't sound like much fun."

"No," she said.

"But you needed to get away, was that it?"

"I think so."

"I watched you through the window when you were weeding. You looked worried."

"Yes, perhaps I am."

"Did something happen?"

"Not really."

"But something did, right?"

"I was thinking about the beggar."

"What about him?"

"That I hadn't told you what he was shouting about Forsell."

"You said it was the usual stuff."

"But it may have been more than that."

"Why are you telling me this now?"

"Because it started to come back to me more clearly when that doctor called."

"So what *was* he saying?"

"Something along the lines of: 'I took Forsell. I left Mamsabiv, terrible, terrible.' Something like that."

"What do you think it means?"

"I don't know. But when I checked Mamsabiv, Mansabin, all sorts of words like that, I got Mats Sabin, that was the closest I found."

"The military historian?"

"Do you know him?"

"Years ago I was one of those people who read everything about the Second World War."

"Do you also know that Sabin died four years ago, during a mountain hike in Abisko National Park? He froze to death by a lake. People think he had a stroke and couldn't get to a shelter out of the cold."

"I didn't know that," he said.

"Not that I think it's got anything to do with Forsell . . ."

"But . . ." he said to encourage her.

"But I couldn't resist doing a search against the two of them together and I saw that Forsell and Sabin had a falling-out in the media. About Russia."

"Explain?"

"After he retired, Sabin changed his opinion and went from being a hawk to having a more Russia-friendly outlook, and in several pieces—in *Expressen*, among others—he wrote that everyone in Sweden suffered from a terror of Russia, a paranoia, and that we should be taking a more sympathetic view. Forsell countered by writing that Sabin's words simply replicated Russian propaganda and implied that he was a paid lackey. After that all hell broke loose. There was talk of libel suits and other legal action, but in the end Forsell backed down and apologized."

"Where does the beggar come into this?"

"No idea. Although . . . he did say 'I left Mansabin,' or something similar, and that might fit. Sabin was alone and abandoned when he died."

"It's a lead," he said.

"Probably nonsensical."

"Can't you come back so we can talk it through, and also touch on the meaning of life and everything else while we're at it?"

"Next time, Mikael. Next time."

He wanted to persuade her, he wanted to beg and plead. But he felt pathetic, so he just wished her a nice evening and hung up. He got up and took a beer from the fridge and wondered what to do with himself. The sensible thing would be to stop thinking about both Catrin and the beggar. None of that was going to get him anywhere. He should go back to his article about troll factories and the stock market crash or, better still, actually take a proper holiday.

But he was as he was: obstinate, and perhaps a little dumb too. He could not let go of things, and when he'd done the dishes and tidied up the kitchen corner, and stood for a few moments gazing at the ever-changing sea, he looked up Mats Sabin and found himself reading a lengthy obituary in *Norrländska Socialdemokraten*.

Sabin grew up in Luleå and became an officer in the coastal artillery—he was involved in the hunt for foreign submarines in the '80s—but alongside that he also studied history and took leave for a while from the military in order to get a doctorate from Uppsala University. His thesis was on Hitler's invasion of the Soviet Union. He became a lecturer at Försvarshögskolan, but, as Blomkvist knew, he also published popular histories about the Second World War. He was a long-time advocate of Swedish membership of NATO. He was certain that what he had been chasing in the Baltic were none other than Russian submarines. Yet in his final years he became a friend of Russia and defended their intervention in Ukraine and the Crimea. He had also applauded Russia as a force for peace in Syria.

It was never clear why he had altered his point of view, though he had been quoted as saying that "opinions are there to be changed as we grow older and wiser." Mats Sabin was reputed to have been a good cross-country runner and a diver. Soon after his wife died, he walked the classic trail between Abisko and Nikkaluokta, and according to the obituary he was "in good shape." It was the beginning of May and the forecast had been good, yet the weather turned to freezing towards the evening of the third. The temperature dropped to minus eight degrees, and Sabin seemed to have suffered a stroke and collapsed not far from the Abiskojåkka River. He never reached any of the mountain huts dotted along the track. He was found dead on the morning of the fourth by a group of hikers from Sundbyberg. There was no suggestion of suspicious circumstances, nor any sign of violence. He was sixty-seven years old.

Blomkvist tried to find out where Johannes Forsell—another keen outdoor sportsman—would have been at the time, but the internet yielded nothing here. This was May 2016, almost one and a half years before Forsell became Minister of Defence, and not even the press at his home in Östersund was monitoring his movements. But Blomkvist did manage to establish that Forsell had business interests in the area. It was not inconceivable that he might have been in Abisko at the time.

Yet it was all far too uncertain and speculative. Blomkvist got up and browsed his bookshelf in the bedroom. Most of the books there were detective novels, and he had read them all, so he tried to call Pernilla, his daughter, and Erika, without reaching either of them. Increasingly restless now, he set off to have dinner at Seglarhotellet by the harbour. When he came home late that evening, he felt completely deflated.

Paulina was asleep. Salander was staring at the ceiling. It was the usual state of affairs; either that, or both of them lying awake. Neither was getting enough rest, and they did not feel particularly well. But that evening they had managed to comfort each other quite satisfactorily with champagne and beer and sex, and had quickly fallen asleep, although that provided little solace when Salander woke with a start a while later, with the memories and questions from Lundagatan and her childhood sweeping over her like an icy wind. What was wrong with them all?

Even before Salander began to take an interest in science, she would say there was a genetic flaw in her family. For a long time she meant simply that many of them had extreme traits in one way or another, and were evil. But a year or so ago she resolved to get to the bottom of her hypothesis, and by accessing a sequence of computer servers, she got hold of Zalachenko's Y chromosome from the Laboratory of Forensic Genetics in Linköping.

She spent long nights learning how to analyze it, and read up on everything she could find on haplogroups. Small mutations have occurred in all lines of descent. The haplogroups show which mutational branch of humanity each individual belongs to and it had not surprised her in the least that her father's group was extremely unusual. When she researched it she found an over-representation not only of high intelligence, but also of psychopathy, and that made her no happier, nor any wiser.

But it had taught her how to work with DNA techniques. Now that it was past two in the morning and she was only reliving the past, shuddering at the memories and staring up at the smoke detector which blinked like an evil red eye in the ceiling, she wondered if she might not after all take a look at the material Blomkvist had sent her. It would at least shift her mind onto other things.

So she got up carefully from the bed, sat at the desk and opened the files. "Let's see, now," she muttered. "Let's see . . . What's this?" It was the result of a preliminary autosomal DNA test, with a number of selected so-called STR markers—short tandem repeats—so she opened her BAM Viewer from the Broad Institute, which would help her analyze them. It was a while before she applied her full attention to the task—she was easily distracted by the satellite images of Camilla's house—but there was something in the material which began to slowly fascinate her, perhaps the realization that the man had no ancestors or kin in the Nordic region.

He came from somewhere a long way away. Having read through the autopsy report again, above all the carbon-13 analysis and the descriptions of the injuries and amputations, she was struck by a surprising thought and sat there for a long time, immobile and leaning forward with a hand pressed against the bullet wound in her shoulder.

Swiftly she ran a series of searches. Could it really be true? She found it hard to believe, and was preparing to hack into the medical examiner's server when she had the outlandish idea of trying first by conventional means. She sent off an e-mail and then helped herself to what was left in the minibar, a Coca-Cola and a miniature of brandy, and let the hours drift by until morning came, sometimes dozing off in her chair. At about the time Paulina opened her eyes and sounds could be heard outside in the corridor, she received a signal on her mobile and connected to the satellite images again. At first she only peered at them with tired eyes, but then she was suddenly wide awake.

Her screen showed her sister and three men—one of them unusually tall—leaving the house in Rublyovka and getting into a limousine. Salander followed them all the way to the international airport at Domodedovo, outside Moscow.

CHAPTER 11

August 25

Fredrika Nyman tossed and turned through the small hours and finally looked at the alarm clock. She hoped it would be 5:30 at least. It was twenty past four and she swore out loud. She had had no more than five hours' sleep, but she could tell—the way an insomniac knows—that she would sleep no more now, so she got up and made a pot of green tea. The morning newspapers had not yet arrived. She settled at the kitchen table with her mobile and listened to the birds. She missed the city. She missed having a man around, or anyone at all who was not a teenager.

"I didn't sleep last night either, and I have a headache and my back hurts," she would have said, and she said it anyway, but to nobody other than herself. And then she also had to respond: "Poor you, Fredrika."

The surface of the lake was smooth after the night's squalls, and she could just glimpse the two resident swans a little way off. They were gliding along, close to each other. Sometimes she envied them, not because she wanted to be a swan, but because there were two of them. They could have bad nights together. Complain to each other in swan language . . . The lack of sleep was getting to her. She checked her e-mails and found one from somebody who called themselves "Wasp":

```
<Got the STR markers and the autopsy reports
from Blomkvist. Have an idea about the man's
origins. Interesting carbon-13. But I need
whole   genome   sequencing.   Guess   it'll   be
quickest with UGC. Get them to hurry up.
Don't have time to wait.>
```

Bloody insolent tone. And not even a sign-off. Why don't you go sequence yourself, she thought. She could not stand that type of charmless, geeky researcher. Her husband had been the same, utterly hopeless now that she thought about it. Then she read the e-mail again and calmed down. It was rude and bossy, but it was exactly what she had been thinking, and she had in fact sent a blood sample to Uppsala Genome Center a few days earlier and asked them for exactly that, for the whole genetic make-up to be sequenced.

She had pressed them hard and urged the bioinformaticians to flag any unusual mutations and variations. She was expecting an answer any time now, so she wrote to them rather than the pushy researcher, having decided to adopt the same sort of tone herself while she was at it:

```
<I need the sequencing now>
```
she wrote.

She hoped they would also be favourably impressed by the hour of writing. It was not yet five in the morning and even the swans on the lake looked to be out of sorts. And not so bloody smug about being a couple, after all.

Kurt Widmark Electronics on Hornsgatan had not yet opened. But Inspector Sonja Modig saw an elderly, stooped gentleman inside and knocked on the door, and he shuffled over wearing a forced smile.

"You're early. But do come on in anyway," he said.

Modig introduced herself and explained why she had come, whereupon the man stiffened and looked irritated, and huffed and grumbled for a while. He was pale, had a slightly crooked face and a long comb-over across his bald pate. There was a hint of bitterness around his mouth.

"Things are bad enough as it is in my line of business," he said. "Competition from online companies and department stores."

Modig smiled and tried to appear sympathetic. She had spent the early part of the morning walking around at random, making enquiries, and a young man in the hairdressers next door had told her that the beggar Bublanski had been talking about had quite often stood at the window of the electrical shop, glaring at the television screens inside.

"When did you first see him?" she said.

"He came marching in here a few weeks ago and stood in front of one of my sets," Kurt Widmark said.

"What was on?"

"The news, and a rather tough interview with Johannes Forsell about the stock market crash and total defence."

"Why do you think the beggar would have been interested in that?"

"How the hell should I know? I was mostly trying to get him out of the shop. I wasn't being unfriendly. I don't care what people look like, but I did tell him that he was alarming my customers."

"In what way?"

"He stood there muttering to himself, and he smelled pretty bad. He seemed to me to have a screw loose."

"Did you hear what he was saying?"

"Oh yes, he asked me very clearly in English if Forsell was a famous man now. I was somewhat taken aback, but I told him yes, he certainly is. He's the Minister of Defence—and he's very rich."

"Did it seem as though he knew of Forsell before he became famous?"

"I couldn't say. But I do remember him saying, 'Problem, now he has problem?' He put the question as if he wanted the answer to be yes."

"And what did you say?"

"I told him yes, absolutely, he has big problems. He's been up to all sorts of hanky-panky and tricks with his shares, and he's pulled off some palace coups behind the scenes."

"But surely those are no more than idle rumours?"

"Well, the stories have been doing the rounds."

"And what happened to the beggar then?" Modig said.

"He started shouting and kicking up a fuss, so I took him by the arm and tried to lead him outside. But he was strong and pointed at his face. 'Look at me,' he shouted. 'See what happened to me! And I took him. And I took him.' Or something like that. He looked absolutely desperate, so I let him stay there for a while, and after the Forsell interview there was a piece about schools in Sweden, and that prim little upper-class witch came on and pontificated."

Modig felt a growing irritation.

"Which 'upper-class witch' would that be?"

"The Lindås woman. Talk about snooty. But that beggar stared at her as if he'd seen an angel, and he mumbled, 'Very, very beautiful woman. Is she critical to Forsell also?' and I tried to say that the one thing had nothing to do with the other. But he didn't seem to understand. He was beside himself. But soon after that he took himself off."

"And then he came back?"

"He came back every day at the same time, shortly before closing, for about a week. He would stand outside, staring in through the window, and ask my customers about journalists, people he could call. In the end I got so annoyed that I rang the police, but of course no-one there could be bothered with it."

"So you got no name, and no other information about the man?"

"He said he was called Sardar."

"Sardar?"

"'My name is Sardar' is what he said when I tried to get him to clear off one evening."

"Well, that's something," Modig said, and she thanked Widmark and left.

In the tunnelbana on her way to Fridhelmsplan and

police headquarters, she googled "Sardar." It was an old Persian word referring to princes and aristocrats, or leaders of a group or tribe in general. It was used in the Middle East and in Central and Southeast Asia. You could also spell it Sirdar, Sardaar or Serdar. *A prince,* Modig thought. *A prince in beggar's clothing. That would be something. But real life is never the way it is in fairy tales.*

It had taken them a while to get away, and not only because they had failed to pick up a single trace of Lisbeth Salander. Ivan Galinov, the old GRU agent, had been busy with other things too, and Camilla was determined to have him along. He was sixty-three, a man of great education with years of experience in intelligence work and infiltration.

He was a polyglot; he spoke eleven languages fluently and could switch between different dialects. In Britain, France or Germany he could even have passed for a native. He was tall and slim and carried himself well, and was without doubt a handsome man, with grey hair and white sideburns, even though there was something bird-like about his features. Face-to-face he was invariably polite and gallant, nevertheless he frightened people; there were rumours about events in his life which added substance to this aspect of his character, and said more about the person he really was.

One of the stories concerned the loss of an eye during the war in Chechnya. He had had it replaced with an enamel prosthesis, said to be the best available on the market. According to the anecdote—which was inspired by an old joke about a loan officer at a bank—nobody could work out which was the real eye and which the false one, until a subordinate of Galinov hit on the simple truth: "The eye with the faint gleam of humanity is the enamel one."

Another account involved the crematorium on the second basement level of the GRU's headquarters in Khodinka. Galinov had allegedly taken a colleague there and cremated him alive for having sold classified material to the British. It was said that his movements became slower and his eyes stopped blinking when he was torturing his enemies. Probably just talk, most of this, exaggerations becoming myth, and even though Camilla herself used the power of those stories to get what she wanted, it was not what she most valued in him.

Galinov had been close to her father; like her he had loved and admired him, and just like her he had been let down. That experience had given them a crucial bond. In Galinov she found understanding rather than cruelty, and fatherly concern, and she never had any trouble in seeing which eye was the real one. Galinov had taught her to soldier on, and quite recently, when it became clear to her what a crushing blow it had been for him all those years ago when Zalachenko defected to Sweden, she had asked:

"How did you survive?"

"The same way you did, Kira."

"And how was that?"

"You survived by becoming like him."

They were words she had taken to heart. Words which both scared her and gave her strength and often, as now, with the past hot on her heels, she wanted to have Galinov close by. In his presence she was not afraid to be a little girl again. He was the only person in recent years who had seen her cry and now, heading for Arlanda airport and Stockholm in her private jet, she sought his smile.

"Thanks for coming along," she said.

"We'll catch her, my love. We'll get her," he replied, tenderly patting her hand.

Salander must have slept after seeing Camilla and her entourage driving off towards the airport, because she woke up and discovered a note on the bedside table to say that Paulina had gone down to breakfast. But now it was ten past eleven and the dining room must be closed. Salander stayed up in the room and cursed to herself when she remembered she had eaten the last of the snacks in the minibar. She drank water from the tap and then showered and put on jeans and a black T-shirt, and sat at the desk to check her e-mails. She had received two files of more than ten gigabytes, together with a message from Medical Examiner Dr. Fredrika Nyman:

```
<Hi, I'm not an idiot. Obviously I'd already
requested full sequencing. I got it this
morning. Don't know how thorough the guys
have been, but they've highlighted some
anomalies. I've got my own specialists of
course, but it won't do any harm if you have
a look too. I'm sending both a worked file
```

```
with annotations and a FastQ with raw data,
in case you prefer to work directly with
that. I'd appreciate prompt feedback.
     F.N.>
```

The anger between the lines passed Salander by, and in any case she was swiftly distracted. She could see that Camilla was now in Sweden, on the E4 from Arlanda heading for Stockholm. She clenched her fists and briefly wondered whether she should go there now too. But she stayed at the desk and pulled up the files the Nyman woman had sent, letting the pages scroll past her eyes like a flickering microfilm. Why was she even doing this, could she really be bothered?

For now she resolved to concentrate and take a look, at least while she decided what to do next. She knew that this was where she always excelled.

Salander was capable of grasping within a very short time the content of even the most voluminous documents, and that is why she preferred, as Nyman had suspected, to work directly with raw data. This way she could avoid being influenced by the opinions and annotations of other people. She used the SAMtools programme to convert the information into a so-called BAM file, a document containing the entire genome, and that in itself was no small feat.

In a way it was like a gigantic cryptogram, with four letters: A, C, G and T, the nitrogenous bases adenine, cytosine, guanine and thymine. At first glance it looked like one big incomprehensible mass. But in fact it was code for an entire life.

To begin with Lisbeth looked for deviations, any deviations, by trawling indices and studying graphs. Then she turned to her BAM Viewer, her IGV, and compared specific and random segments with the DNA sequences of other people she had found in the 1,000 Genomes Project— genetic information collected from all over the world—and it was then that she discovered an anomaly in the rs4954 frequency in what is known as the *EPAS1* gene, which regulates the body's haemoglobin production.

There was something so sensationally different there that she immediately ran a search in the PubMed database, and not long after she suddenly exclaimed aloud and shook her head. Was it really possible? She had had an inkling it might be something like that, but she had not expected to see it in black and white quite so soon. Now utterly focused, she forgot all about her sister in Stockholm and even failed to notice that Paulina had come in and greeted her before going into the bathroom.

Now Salander was entirely concentrated on learning more about this variant of the *EPAS1* gene. Not only was it extremely unusual, it also had a spectacular background, traceable all the way back to the Denisova hominins, a subspecies of Homo sapiens which had died out forty thousand years ago.

For a long time the Denisovans were unknown to scientists, but their existence had been recognized ever since Russian archaeologists discovered a bone fragment and the tooth of a woman in the Denisova cave in the Altai Mountains of Siberia in 2008. It seemed that in the course of history the Denisovans interbred with Homo sapiens in South

Asia and passed on some of their genes to contemporary humans, among others this variant of *EPAS1*.

Thanks to the variant, the body can assimilate even small volumes of oxygen. It makes the blood thinner and helps it to circulate faster, and this lowers the risk of blood clotting and edema. It is especially advantageous for people living and working at high altitudes, where oxygen levels are lower, and that matched Salander's initial assumptions, based on the beggar's injuries and amputations and his carbon-13 analysis.

But even though she now had such an obvious indication, she could not be certain. The variant was unusual but still found in various parts of the world, so she investigated the man's Y chromosome and mitochondrial DNA and saw that he belonged to haplogroup C4a3b1, and once she had checked that her remaining doubts disappeared.

That group was found only among people who live high up on the slopes of the Himalayas in Nepal and Tibet, who often work as porters or guides on high-altitude expeditions.

The man was a Sherpa.

PART II

THE MOUNTAIN PEOPLE

AUGUST 25–27

The Sherpas are an ethnic group in the Himalayan region of Nepal. Many of them work as guides or porters on high-altitude expeditions.

The majority are adherents of Nyingma, an ancient school of Buddhism, and believe that gods and spirits inhabit the mountains. The deities must be respected and revered in accordance with religious rituals.

A *Lhawa,* a shaman, is thought to be able to help a Sherpa who is ill or suffers an accident.

CHAPTER 12

August 25

There were dark clouds out at sea and Blomkvist, in his cabin in Sandhamn, was searching aimlessly online. He kept being drawn to information about Johannes Forsell. Occasionally he bumped into him at the grocer's or down at the harbour, but he had also interviewed him when he became Minister of Defence three years ago, in October 2017. He remembered waiting in a big room with maps on the walls and Forsell putting his head round the door like a cheerful little boy arriving at a party.

"Mikael Blomkvist," he said. "My God, how wonderful."

Blomkvist was not used to being greeted in that way by politicians, and perhaps he should have dismissed it as an attempt to butter him up. But there was something genuinely enthusiastic about Forsell, and he recalled how stimulating their conversation had been. Forsell was quick-witted and on top of his subjects, and he gave real answers, as if he were truly interested in the questions and not engaging in party politics. Even so, Blomkvist's clearest memory was of the Danish pastries. On the table there was a plate laden with them, and Forsell most definitely did not look like a man who ate Danish pastries.

He was tall and fit, a fine figure of a man. He ran three miles and did two hundred push-ups every morning, he said, and displayed no signs of lightheartedness whatsoever. Maybe the pastries were an effort to show a common touch, an elitist trying to appear normal, just like the time he told *Aftonbladet* that he had always loved the annual Melodifestivalen song competition, without then being able to answer a single question about it.

Blomkvist and he were the same age, they realized, even though Forsell surely looked younger, and would score better in any health check. He was bursting with energy and optimism. "The world looks a dark place, but we're making progress. There are fewer and fewer wars, let's not forget that," he said, giving Blomkvist a book by Steven Pinker which was lying around somewhere, still unread.

Forsell had been born in Östersund to a family with a small business consisting of a guest house and a holiday village in Åre. He stood out at school from an early age, was a promising cross-country skier and went to a special high school in Sollefteå for talented young winter sportsmen. After an assessment when he was called up for his military service, he was admitted to the Swedish Armed Forces Interpreters' School, where he learned Russian and became an officer at the Swedish Military Intelligence and Security Service. For obvious reasons, his years in Must were the least known part of his life. He may, however, have been keeping the GRU's activities in Sweden under observation; that much transpired from information leaked to the *Guardian* when Forsell was deported from Russia, where he had been attached to the Swedish Embassy, in late autumn 2008.

The following year, in February, his father died. He resigned from his post and took over the family business, and in no time at all turned it into a major enterprise. He built hotels in Åre, Sälen, Vemdalen and Järvsö, and also in Geilo and Lillehammer in Norway. In 2015 he was able to sell the business to a German travel group for almost two hundred million kronor. He did, however, hold on to some minor interests in Åre and Abisko.

That same year he joined the Social Democrats and, without any real political experience, was elected to the town council in Östersund and soon became popular, gaining a reputation for getting things done and for his unconditional attachment to the local football team. He moved swiftly through various posts and before long found himself Minister of Defence. For a time it looked like a PR coup for the government.

He was spoken of as a hero and an adventurer because of two major achievements alongside his career: swimming the English Channel in the summer of 2002 and climbing Mount Everest six years later, in May 2008. But the tide soon turned, and that could probably be dated back to his uncompromising statement that Russia had been supporting the xenophobic Sweden Democrats during the election campaign.

He was subjected to attacks which became increasingly

savage. But they were nothing compared to what was to follow. After the stock market crash in June, there was a flood of
fake news about him, and it was not hard to sympathize with
his Norwegian wife, Rebecka, who, in an interview in *Dagens
Nyheter,* called the lies shameless and added that even their
two children now needed bodyguards. The mood was ran-
corous and frenzied, and the bombardment was constantly
being stepped up.

Recent press pictures showed Forsell no longer as a man
who had inexhaustible reserves of energy. He looked gaunt,
and the previous Friday he had apparently taken an unexpected week's holiday. There was even talk of a breakdown.
From whichever angle he viewed it, Blomkvist could not but
feel sorry for Forsell. Which might be just the wrong attitude,
now that he had to investigate whether he had any connection with the beggar and perhaps even with Mats Sabin, the
military historian.

Was it still sensible to assume that Forsell was all decency
and enthusiasm? According to the smear campaign, he was
said to have hitched a ride on the rowing boat which accompanied his cross-Channel swim, and there were suggestions
that he had never reached the summit of Everest, as he said
he had. But Blomkvist found no evidence to support any of
these accusations, beyond the fact that the expedition on
Everest had been a monumental disaster, a Greek tragedy of
sorts, where nothing could be established with any certainty.

Forsell himself was not the focus of the story. He had
been far from the epicentre of the turmoil, in which the
spectacularly wealthy American woman Klara Engelman
had died together with her guide Viktor Grankin at twenty-

seven thousand feet. Blomkvist did not research it in any greater depth, and concentrated instead on learning more about Forsell's career as an officer.

The fact of his having been an intelligence agent should have been classified, but it had leaked out in connection with his deportation from Russia, and even though the most absurd rumours were being bandied about in the ongoing hate campaign, the army's commander-in-chief, Lars Granath, several times described Forsell's role in Moscow as having been "nothing but honourable."

There was precious little else in the way of hard facts, and eventually Blomkvist let go of it and simply noted that Johannes and Rebecka had two sons, Samuel and Jonathan, who were eleven and nine years old. The family lived in Stocksund, outside Stockholm, but also owned a place in the country not far away, on the southeastern shore of Sandön island. Is that where they were right now?

Blomkvist had Forsell's private number. "Call me if you have any questions," he had said in his inimitably unstuffy way. But Blomkvist saw no reason to disturb him just now. He ought to forget about all this and have a nap. He was incredibly tired. But he wasn't bloody well going to rest just because of that. He called Chief Inspector Bublanski and talked about Salander again, and reported what the beggar might have said about Mats Sabin, although he did add:

"I'm sure it's nothing."

Paulina Müller came out of the bathroom in a white bathrobe and saw that Salander was still engrossed with her laptop. She rested a careful hand on her shoulder. Salander was no longer staring at the big house outside Moscow, the way she usually did. She was reading an article, and as usual Paulina could not keep up. She had never met a person who read so fast. The sentences flashed by on the screen. But she did catch the words ". . . Denisovan genome and that of certain South Asian . . ." and then she immediately became interested. At *Geo* she had done some pieces on the origins of Homo sapiens and the species' kinship with the Neanderthals and the Denisovan hominids.

"I've written about that," she said.

Salander did not answer, and that made Paulina furious. Salander took care of everything, and protected her, it was true, but she often felt alone and excluded. She could not bear Salander's silence or her endless hours in front of the computer. Especially at night, that drove her mad, and the nights were bad enough as it was. That was when all the awful things Thomas had done raged inside her, and she dreamed of revenge and retribution. Those were the hours when she really needed Lisbeth.

But Salander was dealing with her own private hell. Sometimes her body was so tense that Paulina did not dare to press up close, and how was it possible for someone to sleep so little? Whenever Paulina woke up, Salander was lying next to her with her eyes open, listening for sounds in the corridor, or she was sitting at the desk looking at footage from surveillance cameras and satellite images. Paulina felt that she could no longer bear to be kept out of it all, not when they were living so closely together, and she wanted to scream: *Who's out to get you? What are you up to?*

"What are you doing?" she said.

There was no answer this time either. But Salander did at least turn and give her a look, and it felt a little like an outstretched hand. There was a new, softer light in her eyes.

"What are you doing?" she said again.

"I'm trying to discover the identity of a man," Salander said.

"A man?"

"A Sherpa, a little over fifty years old, dead now, probably from the Khumbu Valley in northeastern Nepal, and although he could also be from Sikkim or Darjeeling in India, the signs mostly point to Nepal, and the area around Namche Bazaar. His family originates from eastern Tibet. As a child he seems to have had a fat-deficient diet." Coming from Lisbeth that was like an entire lecture, and Paulina's face lit up as she sat down on a chair beside her.

"Anything else?"

"I have his DNA and an autopsy report. With the injuries he has, I'm pretty sure he was a porter or guide on high-altitude climbing expeditions. He must have been very good at it."

"What makes you say so?"

"He was unusually well endowed with type 1 muscle fibres and was probably able to carry heavy loads without consuming very much energy. But the main reason is the gene in his body which regulated the haemoglobin in his blood. He must have possessed great strength and endurance in low-oxygen environments. I suspect that he had some terrible experiences. He suffered severe frostbite and torn muscles. Several of his toes and fingers had been amputated."

"Do you have his Y data?"

"I've got the whole of his genome."

"Shouldn't you check with YFull in that case?"

YFull was a Russian company—Paulina had written about them only a year or so ago—which was run by a team of mathematicians, biologists and programmers who collected Y chromosome DNA from people all over the world. It came either from subjects who had enrolled in academic studies or from people who had taken their own DNA samples to find out more about their origins.

"I was thinking of checking with Familytree and Ancestry, but YFull, you say?"

"I think they're the best. The company's run by people like you, a bunch of out-and-out nerds."

"OK," Salander said. "But I think it'll be difficult."

"Why do you say that?"

"My guess is the man belongs to a group that doesn't have its DNA analyzed all that often."

"There might be material from relatives of his in scientific reports? I happen to know there's been a fair amount of research into why Sherpas are such effective climbers at high altitude," Paulina said, proud to be actually involved.

"That's true," Salander said, no longer quite there.

"And it's a pretty small population, isn't it?"

"There are only a little over twenty thousand Sherpas in the entire world."

"Well, then?" she said, perhaps hoping that they could have a go at it together.

But Salander opened another link on her laptop instead: a map of Stockholm.

"Why's it so important to you?"

"It's not important."

Salander's eyes darkened and Paulina got to her feet, feeling awkward, and dressed in silence. She left the room and the hotel and walked up towards Prague Castle.

CHAPTER 13

August 25

Rebecka Forsell, then Rebecka Loew, had fallen in love with Johannes's strength and good humour. She had been the doctor on Viktor Grankin's Everest expedition, and had long had misgivings about her assignment. Nor had she been insensitive to the criticism that was directed at them. The commercialization of Everest was a hot topic in those years.

There was talk of clients who bought themselves a place on the summit, just as others buy a Porsche. Not only were they considered to be sullying the very purity of the mountaineering ideal, they were also accused of increasing the risk to others on the mountain. Rebecka worried that too many in their group simply did not have enough experience, and perhaps Johannes especially, since he had never been above sixteen thousand feet.

But once they reached Base Camp and the others began to suffer from coughs and headaches, and had doubts about the whole undertaking, Johannes was the least of her worries. He literally bounded along on the moraine, and made buddies with everyone, even the local population, perhaps because his attitude towards them was completely natural and always respectful. He joked with them, just as with everyone else, and told his amusing stories.

He was his own man and was regarded as genuine. But Rebecka was not sure if this was entirely true. In her opinion he was an intellectual who had consciously decided to see the world in a positive light, which only made him more attractive. Often all she wanted to do was take off with him and embrace life to the full.

It was true that he went through a deep crisis after Klara and Viktor died. For some reason the tragedy affected him more deeply than it did all the others. He fell into a severe depression, and it was a while before he was his happy and energetic self again. After that he took her to Paris and Barcelona, and in April the following year—just a few months after his father died—they were married in Östersund, and she said goodbye to her home in Bergen in Norway without ever looking back.

She liked Östersund and Åre and all the skiing, and she loved Johannes. She was not in the least surprised that his business flourished and people were drawn to him, or even that he became rich and was so swiftly made a cabinet minister. He was a phenomenon. He seemed to be running non-stop yet at the same time was able to reflect, and maybe that was the reason why she rarely got cross with him. He never quit, and he firmly believed that any problem could be solved merely by rolling up one's sleeves and trying a little harder. The flip side was that he pushed their boys too much.

"You can do better," he was forever saying, and even though he never failed to encourage her, he seldom had time to take her concerns seriously.

He would kiss her and say, "You can do it, Becka, you can do it." He became busier and busier, especially after being made a government minister, and he often worked into the small hours, yet he was up early and doing his three miles and his Navy SEALs, as he called them, his bodyweight training. The pace was inhuman. But he liked it that way, she thought, and he did not seem to care that the tide had turned, and that he who had been so admired was now the object of so much abuse.

She was the one who suffered more. Last thing at night and first thing in the morning she would google his name compulsively, and find the most dreadful threads and accusations, and sometimes, in her darkest hours, she thought it was all her fault—she blamed her Jewish roots. Even Johannes, who was a fine Aryan specimen, fell victim to those anti-Semitic hate campaigns, yet for a long time he just shrugged it off and remained optimistic.

"It will make us strong, Becka, and soon everything will change."

But in the end the lies must have got to him too. Not that he complained or grumbled for one second. He was a person whose enthusiasm ran on autopilot, and last Friday he took a week's holiday—without a word of warning or explanation—which must have caused his staff a headache or

two. That was why they were now on Sandön, in their house
by the water, while the boys were with his mother. They had
come out accompanied by the inevitable bodyguards, which
meant she had to talk to them and look after them. Johannes
had gone to ground in his study on the top floor. Yesterday
she had heard him shouting into the telephone. This morning he had not even worked out. He had eaten his breakfast
in silence and gone into hiding upstairs again. Something
was seriously wrong. She could feel it.

Outside, the wind was getting up. She was in the kitchen
making a beetroot salad with feta and pine nuts. It was time
for lunch, but she could hardly bring herself to let him know.

She did go up in the end, and even though she should
have known better she walked into the room without knocking to find him hurriedly putting away some papers. If he
had not been acting so suspiciously, she wouldn't even have
noticed them. But now she could see that it was a psychiatric
medical file. That was strange. Perhaps a security check on
some colleague? She tried to smile her usual smile.

"What's the matter?" he said.

"It's lunchtime."

"I'm not hungry."

You're always hungry for Christ's sake, she wanted to shout.

"What's wrong?" she said. "Tell me."

"Nothing."

"Come on, I can see there is."

She could feel the anger pounding inside.

"I told you, nothing."

"Are you ill or something?" she said.

"What do you mean?"

"I can see you're reading medical records, so obviously I'm interested," she snapped back, and that was a mistake.

She realized it at once. He looked at her with eyes filled with anxiety, and that scared her. She muttered an apology, and as she left the room she noticed that her legs could hardly carry her.

What's wrong? she thought. *We used to be so happy.*

Salander knew that Camilla was now in an apartment on Strandvägen in Stockholm. She knew that Camilla's hacker, Jurij Bogdanov, and the former GRU agent and gangster Ivan Galinov were there with her, and she realized that she had to act. But how? Instead she carried on looking into the case of Blomkvist's Sherpa. Perhaps it was a form of escapism. With her BAM Viewer she found sixty-seven distinctive markers in the DNA segment, so she went through them one by one and eventually identified a haplogroup, even a patrilineal one.

It was called DM174, and it too was highly unusual, which could be either a good or a bad thing, and she entered the group into the YFull search engine—the Moscow DNA-sequencing company Paulina had recommended—and waited.

"What a crap site, this is unbelievably slow."

She was not hoping for anything much, and wondered why she was even bothering. She should forget the whole thing and concentrate on Camilla. But then she got an answer, and she whistled. There had been 212 hits, spread

over 156 family names. That was much more than she had
been expecting. She closed her eyes and took a deep breath,
and then went through all the material, going into more
depth with unusual variants in the segment. One name kept
cropping up. It felt absurdly wrong. But it came up over and
over again: Robert Carson in Denver, Colorado.

He did indeed look a little Asian. But apart from that,
he was American through and through, a marathon runner,
downhill skier and geologist at the city's university, forty-
two years old, father of three, a politically active Democrat
and fierce opponent of the National Rifle Association, ever
since his oldest son had been caught up in a school shooting
in Seattle.

Robert Carson was also a keen amateur genealogist. Two
years earlier he had had his large Y chromosome analyzed,
which revealed that he had the same *EPAS1* mutation as the
beggar.

"I have the supergene," he had written in a piece on the
rootsweb.com ancestry website, to which he added a picture
of himself posing in high spirits by a stream in the Rocky
Mountains, showing off his biceps, wearing overalls and a
Colorado Avalanche ice-hockey team cap.

He recounted that his paternal grandfather, Dawa Dorje,
had lived in southern Tibet, not far from Mount Everest,
but that he had fled the country in 1951 during the Chi-
nese occupation and settled with relatives in the Khumbu
Valley, near the Tengboche Buddhist monastery in Nepal.
Online there was a picture of his grandfather together with
Sir Edmund Hillary at the inauguration of the hospital in
the village of Kunde. He had had six children, among them

Lobsang, "a madcap and good-looker and, believe it or not, a Rolling Stones nut," Robert wrote. "I never got to meet him, but Mom has told me he was the strongest climber in the expedition and the most handsome and charismatic by a stretch. (Then again Mom was not exactly objective, and neither was I.)"

Lobsang Dorje had apparently taken part in a British expedition in September 1976, to climb Everest via the West Ridge. The group included an American woman, Christine Carson. She was an ornithologist and, during the approach march, studied the bird life—"a profusion of passerines," she wrote. At the time, Christine was forty years old, unmarried and childless, and a professor at the University of Michigan. At Base Camp she was struck by severe nausea and head-aches, and decided to go back down to Namche Bazaar for medical treatment. On September 9 she learned that six members of the expedition, among them Lobsang Dorje, had died not far from the summit.

When she returned home she discovered she was expect-ing Lobsang Dorje's baby. It was a delicate situation. Lob-sang had been only nineteen and engaged to a girl in the Khumbu Valley. But Christine gave birth to Robert in April 1977, in Ann Arbor, Michigan. Even though it was not pos-sible to say for certain—there is always an element of ran-domness in genetic selection—Robert and the beggar were probably third or fourth cousins. They would have had a common ancestor some time during the nineteenth cen-tury, which was not all that close, but Salander guessed that Blomkvist would be able to fill in the gaps, especially since Carson appeared to be actively interested in these questions himself, and seemed a talkative and bright sort of person. Salander found pictures of him meeting his father's family in the Khumbu Valley the previous year.

She wrote to Blomkvist:

```
<Your guy is a Sherpa. He's probably been
a porter or guide on high-altitude expedi-
tions in Nepal, for example on Lhotse, Ever-
est or Kangchenjunga. He has a relative in
Denver. I've attached information about all
this. Aren't you going to check your article
on troll factories?>
```

She deleted the last sentence. It was his own bloody business how he did his job. Then she pressed send and went out to look for Paulina.

Bublanski was strolling along Norr Mälarstrand with Inspector Modig. It was one of his newfangled ideas to hold meetings while walking. "It seems to make it easier to think," he explained. But it was also an attempt to lose some weight and improve his fitness.

These days he was out of breath at the slightest exertion, and it was not at all easy for him to keep up with Modig. They had talked about everything imaginable and had now got on to the case that had prompted Blomkvist's call. Modig described her visit to the electrical shop on Hornsgatan, and at that he heaved a sigh. Why did everyone have this thing about Forsell? People seemed to want to blame him for all the ills in society. Bublanski hoped to God that it did not have anything to do with Forsell's Jewish wife.

"I see," he said.

"Well, yes, it does seem pretty crazy."

"Any other motives you can think of?"

"Envy, maybe."

"What could anyone have envied in that poor man?"

"There's envy even on the lowest rung of the ladder. I spoke to a woman from Romania, Mirela her name is," Sonja said. "She told me that the man pulled in more money than all the other beggars in the neighbourhood. There was something about him that made people generous, and I know that caused some resentment among those who had been in the area for a while."

"Doesn't sound to me like something you'd kill for."

"Maybe not. But the man seemed to have a relatively large amount of money at his disposal. He was a regular at the hot dog stand below Bysistorget and at McDonald's on Hornsgatan, and of course also at the Systembolaget liquor store on Rosenlundsgatan, where he bought vodka and beer. And a few times it seems he was also spotted in the early hours further up towards Wollmar Yxkullsgatan in Södermalm, where he bought moonshine."

"Did he now?"

Bublanski thought it over.

"I can guess what you're thinking," Modig said. "We ought to have a word with the people who sell that stuff."

"Quite right," he said, taking a deep breath so he could make it up the hill to Hantverkargatan, and his thoughts turned again to Forsell and his wife, Rebecka, a charming woman whom he had met at the Jewish Community Centre.

She was tall, certainly more than six feet, fine-limbed with light, elegant steps and large, dark eyes which shone with warmth and vitality. He could understand why this couple attracted so much animosity.

Of course people resented those who exude such boundless energy. They make the rest of us feel small and feeble in comparison.

CHAPTER 14

August 25

Blomkvist read Salander's message and got up from his desk to look out across the water. It was five in the afternoon, and it was becoming increasingly windy out there. A yacht was racing along in the storm further out in the bay. A Sherpa, he thought, a Sherpa. There must be something to that, surely?

Not that he had really believed it was anything to do with the Minister of Defence. But still . . . one could not ignore the fact that Forsell had climbed Mount Everest in 2008. Blomkvist resolved to get to the bottom of the story. There was no shortage of material about the drama, and that, as he had already concluded, was chiefly down to Klara Engelman.

Engelman was glamour personified, God's gift to gossip columnists, with her dyed-blond hair and surgically enhanced lips and breasts. She was married to a notorious tycoon, Stan Engelman, who owned hotels and other properties in New York, Moscow and Saint Petersburg. Klara was not a society girl but rather a Hungarian former model who had travelled to the United States in her youth and won a Miss Bikini contest in Las Vegas. There she met Stan, a member of the judges' panel—a detail the tabloids loved.

But in 2008 she was thirty-six years old and mother to the couple's then twelve-year-old daughter, Juliette. She had a degree in Public Relations from St. Joseph's College in New York and seemed to want to show that she could accomplish something on her own. Today, more than ten years after the tragedy, it was difficult to understand the indignation she aroused at Base Camp. Her blog for *Vogue* admittedly featured a number of ridiculously styled photographs of her wearing the latest fashions. But with the benefit of hindsight it was clear that the coverage she got was patronizing and sexist. The reporters made her out to be nothing more than a bimbo, and held her up as the very antithesis to the mountains and an affront to the local population. She was the vulgarity of the wealthy West contrasted with the purity of the mountain's wide-open spaces.

Klara Engelman was on the same expedition as Johannes Forsell and his friend Svante Lindberg, who was now his parliamentary undersecretary. All three had paid seventy-five thousand dollars to be guided to the summit, and that of course added insult to injury. Everest was said to have become a haunt for the rich, who were there only to boost their egos. The leader of the expedition and owner of the guiding company was Viktor Grankin, a Russian, and in addition to him there were three guides, a Base Camp manager, a doctor and fourteen Sherpas—and the ten clients. This many people were needed to get them to the top.

Could the beggar have been one of those Sherpas? The thought had occurred to Blomkvist right away, and before he looked into the tragedy any further he tried to find out more about them. Was it possible that one of them had ended up in Sweden, or had a special relationship with Forsell? For many of them he drew a complete blank, but for a young Sherpa, Jangbu Chiri, there seemed to be a connection.

He and Forsell met again in Chamonix three years later, and had a beer together. It was perfectly possible that they could have become sworn enemies after that. But in the picture online, they were giving a thumbs-up and looked absurdly happy. As far as Blomkvist could discover, none of the Sherpas on the expedition had a bad word to say about Forsell. There were anonymous accusations—these had surfaced in the current disinformation campaign—that Forsell had contributed to Klara Engelman's death by delaying or holding back the group on the mountain. But according to many eyewitness accounts, the opposite was the case: It was Engelman herself who slowed the expedition down, and by the time disaster struck, Forsell and Svante Lindberg had already left the others behind and gone on to the summit on their own.

No, Blomkvist did not believe it. Or perhaps he simply didn't want to. He was always—it was the way he did his job—on his guard against the pitfalls of wishful thinking in his journalistic research, and in this case he found it hard to imagine that the man whom the cyber trolls loved to hate should have been involved in poisoning a poor down-and-out in Stockholm. And yet . . . what the hell?

He read Lisbeth's message again, and then documents she had attached about the presumed relative in Colorado, Robert Carson. Although his opinion may have been influenced by the research, Carson struck him as a cheerful and energetic man, not unlike Forsell himself, and without really giving it much thought he dialled the number Salander had supplied.

"Bob speaking," a voice answered.

Blomkvist introduced himself, and was then unsure how to explain what the call was about. He began with flattery.

"I read online that you have a supergene."

Carson laughed. "Impressive, don't you think?"

"Very. I hope I'm not disturbing you."

"Not at all, I'm reading a boring paper, so I'd much rather talk about my DNA. Is it a science publication you work for?"

"Not exactly. I'm investigating a suspicious death."

"Oh, I'm sorry."

"It's a homeless man, between fifty-four and fifty-six years old, with several fingers and toes amputated. He was found dead in Stockholm just over a week ago. He had the same variant in his *EPAS1* gene as you do. In all likelihood, you and he are third or fourth cousins."

"I'm sorry to hear that, but incredible that you've made the connection. What's his name?"

"That's just the thing. We don't know. All we've been able to establish is that you and he are related."

"So how can I help?"

"I don't honestly know. But my colleague thinks the man may have been a skilled porter on high-altitude expeditions, and that he was involved in some major incident. That would explain how he got his injuries. Are there any Sherpas in your family who fit that description?"

"My God, I should think there are any number of them if we look at the extended family. I think it's fair to say that we're pretty extreme."

"Do you have anything more specific?"

"Give me some time to think about it, then I'll probably find something. I've written up a whole family tree that includes biographical data. Do you have any more details you could send me?"

Blomkvist thought for a moment. Then he said:

"If you promise to treat them confidentially, I can send over the autopsy report and the DNA analysis."

"I give you my word."

"I'll get them to you right away. I'd be very grateful if you could take an urgent look at them."

Carson was silent for a while.

"Do you know," he said, "it would be an honour. It feels good to have had a relative in Sweden, although I'm sorry that he had such a hard time."

"That does seem to have been the case. A friend of mine met him."

"What happened?"

"He was very agitated and gabbled something about Johannes Forsell, our current Minister of Defence. He was on an Everest expedition in May 2008."

"May 2008, you say?"

"Yes."

"Wasn't that when Klara Engelman died?"

"Exactly."

"That's funny."

"In what way?"

"I did actually have a relative who was on that expedition, a bit of a legend in fact. But he died three, maybe four years ago."

"Then he could hardly have turned up in Stockholm."

"No."

"I can send over lists of the Sherpas I know were on the mountain then—that might give you some clues."

"That would be helpful."

"Not that I actually think this has anything to do with Everest," Blomkvist said, more to himself than to Carson. "There's quite some distance separating this man from the Minister of Defence."

"You want me to tackle this with an open mind?"

"I guess so. I was fascinated to read your life story."

"Thanks," Carson said. "Send the stuff over and I'll be in touch."

Blomkvist hung up and thought for a while, and then wrote a thank-you to Salander, telling her about Forsell and Everest, and Mats Sabin, and everything else. She might as well have the whole picture.

Lisbeth saw the e-mail at ten in the evening, but she did not read it. She had other things on her mind. Besides, she was in the middle of a row.

"Can't you stop staring at your bloody laptop?" Paulina snapped.

Salander stopped staring at her bloody laptop and looked up at Paulina instead. She was standing right by the desk with her long, curly hair loose, and her slanting, expressive eyes full of tears and anger.

"Thomas is going to kill me."

"But you said you could go to your parents in Munich."

"He'll follow me there and soon have them wrapped around his little finger. They love him, don't ask me why. Or at least they think they do."

Salander nodded and tried to think clearly. Would it after all be better to wait? No, she decided, no. She could not hold back any longer, and she definitely couldn't take Paulina with her to Stockholm. She had to go there at once—and by herself. She could not afford to remain passive, stuck in the past. She now had to follow the chase at closer quarters. If not, others would suffer, especially with people like Galinov on the scene.

"Shall I have a word with them?" she said.

"With my parents?"

"Yes."

"Not on your life."

"Why not?"

"Because you're a social freak, Lisbeth, don't you see that?" Paulina barked at her. Then she grabbed her handbag and marched out, slamming the door behind her.

Salander weighed up whether or not to run after her, but she remained frozen to the spot by her computer. She decided to try hacking the surveillance cameras around the apartment on Strandvägen, where Camilla apparently still

was. But it was slow work. And she was distracted by so much else. Not just Paulina's outburst, but all sorts of things. Including Blomkvist's e-mail, although in the circumstances that seemed to be the lowest of her priorities.
It said:

<Don't know how you do it. Whoop whoop! Hats off. Should perhaps say that the beggar was going on about Defence Minister Johannes Forsell. "I took him. I left Mamsabin," he said. Or something like that. (Maybe "Mats Sabin"?) Not clear. But Forsell did climb Everest in May 2008, and for a while looked like he was close to copping it too. I'm sending over a list of the Sherpas who were on the south side of the mountain at the time. Perhaps you'll be able to spot something in there too. I've spoken to Robert Carson, who's going to try to help me.
Take care and a big thanks to you.
M.
P.S. There was a Mats Sabin, formerly an officer in the coastal artillery and a military historian at the Defence University. He died in Abisko a few years ago. We know he had a huge row with Forsell.>

"Is that so?" she mumbled. "Is that so?" She closed the e-mail and kept working on the surveillance cameras. But her fingers had a life of their own. Within half an hour she had looked up Forsell and Everest and become engrossed in endless reports about a woman called Klara Engelman.

Engelman looked a bit like Camilla, she thought, a cheaper version of her sister with the same charisma—someone who also took it for granted that she was the centre of attention—and Salander was certainly not going to waste any time on her. She had better things to do. She did, however, go on reading, even though her mind was not really on it at all. She sent a message to Plague about the cameras, and called Paulina, who didn't pick up, but little by little she still managed to piece together a fuller picture, above all of Johannes Forsell's ascent.

He and his friend Lindberg had reached the summit at one in the afternoon of May 13, 2008. The sky was still clear and they stayed up there for a while, admiring the view. They took photographs and reported back down to Base Camp. But not long after, in the narrow rock passage known as the Hillary Step, on the way down to the South Summit, they started to have problems and time began to run away from them.

At half past three—by which time they had only got as far as the so-called Balcony at 27,500 feet—they began to worry that they would run out of oxygen and would not make it down to Camp IV. Visibility had worsened too, and even though Forsell had no idea what was happening around them, he suspected that something serious had occurred.

He heard desperate voices on his radio. But by then he was too exhausted to fully grasp the situation, as he said later.

He just staggered through the void, his legs barely holding him upright.

Soon after that the storm hit the mountain and everything turned into a lashing chaos. The cold was extreme, close to minus seventy-six degrees Fahrenheit, and the two of them were freezing and hardly able to distinguish up from down. It was understandable that neither of them could give a detailed account of how they made it down to the tents on the Southeast Ridge.

But if there was a time that was unaccounted for in all the reports of that day, then it was between seven and eleven in the evening. Even if that was not much to be going on, Salander did spot some discrepancies in their stories, especially with regard to Forsell's condition and how bad it had really been.

It was as if his crisis had been made to appear less and less serious over time. Personally, she did not think it was all that remarkable, not compared to the real drama that was unfolding on another part of the mountain, where Klara Engelman and her guide Viktor Grankin died that afternoon. It was not so surprising that endless column inches had been devoted to that. Why, of all people, was it the prestige client who lost her life, when there were so many others on the mountain that day? Why did she have to die, she, the subject of so much gossip and vilification?

For a while there was talk that it was all down to envy and class hatred and misogyny. But once the initial furor had died down, it was clear that no effort had been spared to save Engelman, and that right from the start she had been beyond rescue—ever since she collapsed very suddenly in the snow. The assistant guide, Robin Hamill, even said:

"It wasn't that too little was done to save Klara, but too much. She was considered so important to Viktor and the expedition that we risked the lives of many others in our endeavours," and that sounded plausible, Salander thought.

Engelman was such a major celebrity that nobody had dared to send her down while there was still time. The whole expedition was held up as she dragged herself along, and after she tore off her oxygen mask in confusion and desperation, just before one in the afternoon, she only became weaker.

She collapsed on her knees and toppled forward onto the snow. Panic broke out and Grankin, who was clearly not his usual robust self that day, shouted at everybody to stop. Significant efforts were made to bring her down at that point. But not long afterwards the weather deteriorated, and the snowstorm slammed into them. Many others in the group—in particular Mads Larsen, a Dane, and Charlotte Richter, a German—found themselves in a critical condition, and for a few hours it looked as if they were heading for a full-scale catastrophe.

But the expedition Sherpas, above all their Sirdar, Nima Rita, worked ceaselessly in the storm and led people down on ropes or steadied them as they descended. By evening, all had been rescued, all except for Klara Engelman and Viktor Grankin. He had refused to leave Engelman, rather like a captain staying on his sinking ship.

In the weeks and months that followed there was an extensive investigation of the drama, and by now most of the questions seemed to have been answered. The only thing that was never fully explained—although it was assumed to have been caused by the powerful jet stream at those altitudes—was that Engelman was found half a mile further down, even though all witnesses said that she and Grankin had died together, side by side in the snow.

Salander thought about this, and about all the other bodies left up there on the slopes, year after year, without anybody being able to bring them down and bury them. As the hours went by she scrutinized the various accounts until it seemed that there was perhaps something not quite right with the story after all. She even read about Mats Sabin — Blomkvist had mentioned him—and then drifted into the gossip threads on the internet. At some point an entirely different thought struck her, but that was as far as she got.

The door flew open and Paulina came in, quite drunk, and tore into her for being a total monster. Salander gave as good as she got, until they threw themselves over each other and made frenzied love, united in a feeling of despair and loneliness.

CHAPTER 15

August 26

Mikael ran a full six miles along the water's edge and back that morning, and when he got home to the cabin the telephone was ringing. It was Erika Berger. The next issue of *Millennium* was going to press the following day. She was not altogether happy with it, but she was not unhappy either.

"We're back to normal," she said, and asked him what he was up to.

He said he was breathing some fresh air and had started running again, but also that he was doing some research into the Minister of Defence and the campaign against him, which Berger said was funny.

"Why funny?"

"Sofie has that in her story."

"In what way?"

"She's written about the aggression shown towards Forsell's kids, and the policemen having to patrol outside the Jewish school."

"I read about that."

"You know . . ."

He was disturbed to hear the pensive tone in her voice. That was how she always sounded when she had an idea for a story.

"If you really don't want to pursue your report about the stock market crash, maybe you can do a profile on Forsell instead, and show him in a more sympathetic light. I remember that you got on well together."

His eyes scanned the water.

"I think we probably did."

"So what do you say? You could also help our readers by doing a spot of fact-checking."

"Not such a bad idea," he said.

He was thinking about the Sherpa and the Everest expedition.

"I've just been told that Forsell has taken an extra week's holiday himself. Doesn't he have a place near you?"

"On the other side of the island."

"Well, then," she said.

"I'll think about it."

"You used not to think so much. You used to just get on with it."

"I'm on holiday too, you know," he said.

"You're never on holiday. You're way too much of a guilt-ridden old workaholic to get the whole holiday thing."

"So there's no point in even trying, you mean?"

"No," she said, and laughed, and then he felt he had to

laugh too. He was relieved that she hadn't suggested coming out to see him.

He did not want to complicate things with Catrin, so he said good luck and goodbye to Erika. He was thoughtful as he watched the storm whipping up the waves. What should he do? Show her that he did get the whole holiday thing after all? Or keep working?

He came to the conclusion that a meeting with Forsell was a good idea, but first he would have to read his way through more of the filth that had been written about him, and after moaning and grumbling to himself and taking a long shower, he got down to work. At the beginning it was depressing and nauseating, as if he had climbed back down into the same quagmire as when he was investigating the troll factories.

But slowly he became absorbed, and he put a great deal of effort into tracing the original sources of all the allegations and mapping out how they had spread and been distorted. He was gradually getting closer to the events on Everest once more when his mobile rang, startling him. This time it was Bob Carson from Denver.

Carson sounded excited.

Charlie Nilsson was sitting with a furrowed brow on a bench outside the Prima Maria Addiction Centre, or the Spin Dryer, as he called it. He did not like talking to the police, and he especially did not want his friends seeing him do it. But the woman, whose name was Moody or something, frightened him, and he did not want any grief.

"Gimme a break, will you?" he said. "I'd never sell a bottle that's been messed with."

"Oh, you wouldn't, would you? So you taste everything first?"

"Very funny."

"Funny?" Modig said. "I couldn't be less funny if I tried."

"Just lay off," he said. "Anyone could have given him that booze, couldn't they? You know what they call this place?"

"No, Charlie, I don't."

"The Bermuda Triangle. People go from the Spin Dryer to Systembolaget and the beer joint over there and back again, and they just vanish."

"Meaning what, exactly?"

"That there's a whole lot of shady stuff going on around here. Some fucking weird creatures come along, pushing dodgy booze and funky pills. But those of us who run a serious business, who stand here in the wind and rain, night after night, we can't afford to pull stunts like that. Unless we deliver quality goods so we can look people in the eye, the next day, we're fucked."

"I don't believe a word of that," Modig said. "I'm pretty sure you're not all that fussy. And I'd say you're in deep shit right now. Do you see the guys in police uniforms over there?"

Charlie had had his eyes on them all along and could feel them glaring at him.

"If you don't tell us all you know, we're pulling you in here and now. You said you'd sold to the man," Modig said.

"I sold to him all right. But I thought he was scary, so I kept as far away as I could."

"Scary in what way?"

"He had scary eyes, and he had stumps instead of fingers and bloody patches on his face. He was going on about the moon. 'Luna, luna,' he kept saying. That's moon, right?"

"As far as I know."

"At least he did once. He appeared from Krukmakargatan, limping, and was beating his chest and saying that Luna was alone and calling for him, she and someone whose name was Mam Sabib or whatever the fuck it was, and it frightened me. He was a complete psycho, and I gave him the stuff even though he didn't have the right money. It didn't surprise me at all that he turned violent later."

"In what way violent?"

Shit shit shit, Nilsson thought. He had promised not to say anything. But it was too late now, he would have to go with it.

"Not with me."

"With whom?"

"Heikki Järvinen."

"And who's that?"

"A customer, one of my customers who actually has a bit of style. Heikki met the bloke in Norra Bantorget in the middle of the night. At least it must have been him. Heikki described a little Chinaman with fingers missing wearing a huge fucking down jacket. He was going on about having been up in the clouds, and when Heikki wouldn't believe him he got himself a punch which made his head swim. The Chinaman was as strong as an ox, he said."

"Where can we find this Heikki Järvinen?"

"Järvinen comes and goes, so you never really know."

The policewoman made notes and nodded, and asked a few more questions. Then she left him, along with the uniforms, and Nilsson gave a sigh of relief. He had been sure that there was something very odd about the Chinaman, and he took himself off to call Heikki Järvinen before the police got hold of him.

Blomkvist heard at once that Carson's voice had changed, as if he had been up all night or had come down with a cold.

"It's a civilized time of day at your end, isn't it?" he said.

"Very much so."

"Not here. My head feels as if it's about to blow apart. You remember I told you I had a relative who was on the mountain in 2008? And you remember I said he was dead?"

"Absolutely."

"Well, he was. Or at least presumed dead. But I should take it from the top. I called my uncle in Khumbu. He functions as a sort of local information exchange, and we went through the whole list you sent. The only relative we found there was this one person, and I was about to give up. If he was dead then he was dead and couldn't very well show up in Stockholm and die all over again. But my uncle told me that no body had ever been found. I looked into it all more closely, and I saw that the age was right, and so was the height."

"What's his name?"

"Nima Rita."

"He was one of the leaders, wasn't he?"

"He was the Sirdar, the head of the group of Sherpas, and the one who worked hardest on the mountain that day."

"I know, I know, I read about him...He saved Mads Larsen, and Charlotte somebody."

"That's right, and if it hadn't been for him, there would have been an even worse catastrophe. But he paid a high price. He raced up and down like a galley slave, and afterwards he had bad frost damage to his face and chest. He had to have some of his fingers and toes amputated."

"So you really do think it's him?"

"It has to be. He had a tattoo of a Buddhist wheel on his wrist."

"My God," Blomkvist said.

"Exactly, it's all falling into place. Nima Rita is my third cousin, as they call it, so it's perfectly reasonable to assume that he and I shared that special mutation in the Y chromosome that your researcher colleague pointed out."

"Can you see any explanation for his having ended up in Sweden?"

"No, I can't. But there's a follow-up which is interesting."

"Tell me. I haven't had time to acquaint myself with all the details yet."

"At first the assistant guides, Robin Hamill and Martin Norris, were praised for their rescue efforts, to the extent there was any praise going since Engelman and Grankin were dead," Carson said. "But with the issuing of the more comprehensive reports, it was clear that the decisive role in the drama had been played by Nima Rita and his Sherpas. But I don't know if that did Nima much good."

"Why not?"

"Because by then he was going through hell already. He had fourth-degree frostbite, which is indescribably painful,

and the doctors waited as long as they could before ampu-
tating. They knew that his livelihood depended on his being
able to climb. For a native of the Khumbu Valley, Nima
Rita had earned a lot—although still not much by Euro-
pean standards—but money just ran through his fingers. He
drank heavily and had no savings at all. But, worse still, his
name was being dragged through the mud. He was plagued
by his own demons."

"In what way?"

"It turned out that he had been paid by Engelman to take
special care of Klara—he had of course failed to do that—
and afterwards was accused of having worked against her
interests. I don't believe that. Nima Rita was by all accounts
an incredibly loyal person. But like many other Sherpas, he
was extremely superstitious, and thought of Everest as a living being which punishes climbers for their sins, and Klara
Engelman . . . well, I guess you've read about her?"

"I saw the reports at the time."

"Many of the Sherpas were upset by her. At Base Camp
they were complaining that she could jinx the expedition and
she must have irritated Nima, too. He certainly went through
the tortures of hell afterwards. Apparently he suffered from
hallucinations, and that may have been partly neurological.
He had sustained brain damage from all the time he'd spent
above twenty-six thousand feet, and he became increasingly
bitter and behaved strangely. He had lost a number of his
friends. No-one wanted anything to do with him. No-one
except his wife, Luna."

"Luna Rita, I presume. And where is she now?"

"That's just the point. Luna took care of Nima after his

operations. She baked bread and grew potatoes, and sometimes went over to Tibet to buy wool and salt which she sold
in Nepal. But in the end it wasn't enough, so she started
working on climbing expeditions. She was much younger
than Nima, and she was strong. She quickly rose from
kitchen help to become a climbing Sherpani. But in 2013
she was part of the Dutch attempt on Cho Oyu, the world's
sixth highest mountain, and she fell into a crevasse at high
altitude. The expedition turned into total chaos. There was
an avalanche, a blizzard was blowing, and the climbers had
to get off the mountain in a hurry. They left Luna to die in
the crevasse. Nima was driven mad with grief, and he took it
for an act of racism. He shouted that if it had happened to a
Sahib, they would have got him out straightaway."

"But she was just a poor local woman."

"I have no idea if that made any difference. I doubt it
did. Generally, I have a high opinion of people in the climbing world. But Nima was determined, and he tried to get an
expedition going to recover her body from up there and give
her a decent burial. There was not one single volunteer so in
the end he set off on his own, far too old and apparently not
sober either."

"Jesus."

"If you speak to my relatives in Khumbu, that was his
greatest achievement, more so than all his ascents of Everest.
He got up there and saw Luna down in the crevasse, pre-
served forever in the ice, and he decided to climb down and
lie next to her so they could be reborn together. But then . . .
the mountain goddess whispered to him that he should go
out into the world instead and tell her story."

"Sounds . . ."

". . . totally crazy, oh yes," Carson said. "And although he really did go out into the world, or at least to Kathmandu, and told the tale, nobody could make out what he was talking about. He became more and more incoherent, and was sometimes seen crying beneath the flags at the Boudhanath Stupa. Every so often he would go to the shopping districts in Thamel to nail up papers in poor English and even worse handwriting. He was still going on about Klara Engelman."

"What did he say?"

"By this point he was suffering from severe mental disorder, don't forget, and it was probably all one big muddle in his head, Luna and Klara and everything else. He was completely shot, and after he launched a diatribe against a British tourist and was locked up for a day, his relatives got him into the Jeetjung Marg mental health centre in Kathmandu. He stayed there on and off until the end of September 2017, and then one day he goes off to get himself some beer and vodka. He was apparently suspicious about the drugs the doctors were giving him and said that the only thing that silenced the voices in his head was alcohol. I think the staff reluctantly let it happen. They allowed him to abscond because they knew he would always come back. But this time he didn't come back, and they grew concerned at the hospital. They knew he was expecting a visit that he was very excited about."

"What kind of visit?"

"I don't know. But it might have been from a journalist. To mark the tenth anniversary of Klara Engelman's and Viktor Grankin's deaths, a number of articles and documentaries were being prepared. Nima was apparently very happy that at last somebody wanted to listen to him."

"But you don't know anything more about what he wanted to get off his chest?"

"Only that it was all but impenetrable, full of ghosts and spirits."

"And nothing about Forsell, our Minister of Defence?"

"I don't know, all I have is hearsay and I don't think the centre is going to release its records any time soon."

"What happened when he didn't return?"

"They searched for him, of course, in all the places he would usually hang out. But they found no trace at all, except for various reports that his corpse had been seen not far from the Bagmati River, where the dead are cremated. But no body was ever identified as his, and after a year the investigation was wound up. They abandoned hope, and in the end his family held a little memorial ceremony in Namche Bazaar, or maybe more of a . . . how shall I put it? . . . a moment of prayer for him. It was very beautiful, apparently. He hadn't been so well regarded those last years. But that restored his reputation. Nima Rita had been on the summit of Everest eleven times without oxygen. Eleven times! And his climb up Cho Oyu, that was . . ."

Carson went on animatedly, but Blomkvist was no longer listening quite so intently. He was looking up Nima Rita, and even though quite a lot had been written—there were Wikipedia entries in both English and German—he found only two photographs. In one, Nima Rita was standing with the Austrian star climber Hans Mosel, after their ascent of the North Face of Everest in 2001. In the other, more recent, he was shown in profile in front of a stone house in the village of Pangboche in Khumbu. Like the first picture, it had been taken from a bit too far away—certainly too far for any face-recognition software to be effective. But Blomkvist was in no doubt. He recognized the eyes and the hair, and the patches on the cheeks.

"Are you still there?" Carson said.

"I'm just a bit shocked."

"I'm not surprised. That's some mystery you've got on your hands now."

"You can say that again. But honestly, Bob . . . I can tell that you've got supergenes. You've been fantastic."

"My supergenes are for high-altitude climbing, not detective work."

"I think you should check out your detective genes too."

Carson gave a tired laugh.

"Can I ask you to be discreet about this for the time being?" Blomkvist said. "It would be bad if anything got out before we know more."

"I've already told my wife."

"Please keep it in the family, then."

"I promise."

Afterwards, Blomkvist wrote to Nyman and Bublanski to tell them what he had learned. Then he went on reading the Forsell material, and later in the morning he rang him to see if he could set up an interview.

Forsell had a fire going in the stove. Rebecka could smell it from downstairs in the kitchen, and she heard him pacing back and forth. She did not like the sound of his footsteps and she could not bear his silence and his glassy look. She would have done anything to see him smile again.

Something is wrong, she thought again, *just wrong.* She was on the point of going upstairs to demand to speak to him when he came down the winding staircase. She was happy at first. He was wearing his training gear and his Nike running shoes, and that should have been a sign that he was getting his spirits back. But there was something about his posture that frightened her. She met him halfway up the stairs and stroked his cheek.

"I love you," she said.

He gave her such a disconsolate look that she flinched, and there was nothing soothing in his reply:

"I love *you.*"

It sounded like a farewell and she kissed him. But he shook himself free and asked where the bodyguards were. She took a moment before answering. They had two terraces, and the guards were sitting out on the western one, facing the water. They would have to change and accompany him if he was going on a run, and as usual they would struggle to keep up. Sometimes he would run back and forth a bit so as not to exhaust them.

"On the west terrace," she said, and he hesitated.

He seemed to want to say something. His chest heaved. His shoulders were unnaturally tense, and there were red patches on his throat which she had never seen before.

"What is it?" she said.

"I tried to write you a letter. But I couldn't."

"Why on earth would you write me a letter? I'm standing right here."

"But I . . ."

"But you?"

She was about to break down, but vowed not to give in before he had told her exactly what was going on. She took hold of his hands and looked into his eyes. But then the worst thing imaginable happened.

He tore himself loose, said "I'm sorry," and then ran off, not towards the bodyguards but instead across the terrace which faced the forest. In no time at all he was out of sight, so she screamed for her life. When the guards rushed in she was distraught.

"He's run away from me, he's run away from me."

CHAPTER 16

August 26

Forsell ran so fast that his temples were pounding and his mind was filled with the clamour of an entire life. But there was nothing remotely uplifting about it—not even the happiest moments. He tried to think about Becka and their sons. All he could picture was the disappointment and shame in their eyes, and when he heard birdsong in the far distance, as if from another world, he could make no sense of it. How could anyone be singing? How could they want to live?

His whole existence was black and hopeless. Yet he had no idea what he wanted to do. In town, he would have thrown himself in front of a long-distance truck or a tunnelbana train. Here there was only the sea and, although he felt it beckoning, he knew that he was far too good a swimmer, and that amid his despair there was an untameable will to live which he was not certain he could suppress.

So he kept on running, not in his usual way but as if he

were trying to run from life itself. It was incomprehensible that it had come to this. He had thought he could cope with anything. He had thought he was as strong as a bear. But he had made a mistake and been drawn into something he knew he could not live with. At first, he had really wanted to hit back, to fight. But they had him. They knew they had him, and here he now was. Birds flew up all around, and further on a startled roe deer leaped into the trees. *Nima, Nima.* That it should be him of all people. There was no logic in it.

He had loved Nima, although that was of course the wrong word, but still . . . there had been a bond between them, an alliance. Nima had been the first to pick up on the fact that Johannes was stealing into Rebecka's tent at night at Base Camp, and it had upset him. His Everest goddess was offended by sex on her sacred slopes.

"Makes mountain very angry," he said, and in the end Johannes could not help pulling his leg. Even though everybody warned him—*That man can't handle a joke!*—Nima had taken it well and laughed, and the fact that Rebecka and Johannes were both single no doubt helped.

Grankin and Engelman's case was more problematic because both were married to other people. It was difficult in all sorts of ways, and he remembered Luna, wonderful brave Luna, who sometimes came up with fresh bread, goat's cheese and yak butter in the mornings, and he recalled his decision to help them, yes, that was probably where it all began. Johannes gave them money—as if paying off a debt that he did not yet know he had.

He kept on running and was drawn inexorably towards the water. Once on the beach he pulled off his shoes and

socks and his running shirt and waded into the sea. He
began to swim, just as he had been running, wildly and furiously. He noticed that there were white crests on the waves
and that the water out here was colder than he had expected.
The current was strong, but instead of slowing down, he
ploughed on.

He was going to swim and forget.

The bodyguards had sent for backup and, without knowing what else she could do, Rebecka went up to Johannes's
office. She was hoping it might help her understand what
had happened. But she found no clues, only that paper had
been burned in the stove, and as she leaned on the desk there
was a sudden buzz next to her. For an instant she thought it
was something she had done.

But it was Johannes's mobile, with the name Mikael
Blomkvist on the display. She let it ring. The last person she
wanted to talk to was a journalist. They had poisoned her
and Johannes's lives, and she wanted to scream: *Come back,
you old fool. We love you . . .* She had no idea what happened
next, her legs must have given way.

She sat on the floor and prayed, though she had not
prayed since she was a little girl, and when the phone buzzed
again, she got up on her unsteady legs. Blomkvist again.
Blomkvist, she tried to remember, surely he had been on
their side? Maybe he knew something. It was not impossible,
so on the spur of the moment she picked up and heard the
despair in her own voice:

"Johannes's phone, Rebecka speaking."

. . .

Blomkvist realized at once that something was amiss, but he could have no idea how serious it was. Some kind of row between husband and wife? It could have been anything . . .

"Is this a bad time?" he said.

"Yes . . . actually, no."

He could tell that she was overwrought.

"Shall I call back?"

"He just took off," she burst out. "Just ran away from his bodyguards. What's going on?"

"Are you on Sandön?"

"What . . . ? Yes," she mumbled.

"Have you any idea what's got into him?"

"I'm terrified that he's gone and done something stupid," she said, at which he made some comforting remark about how things would surely sort themselves out.

Then he ran down to the jetty to his boat. It was not a powerful boat, and Sandön was a sizeable island, 133 acres. The Forsell house was a good way off and it would take time to get there. The wind was blowing hard and the boat felt small and light. Water sprayed into his face. What the hell did he think he was doing? He had no answer to that, but this was his way of tackling a crisis: He took action. He pushed the throttle forward and soon heard the rattling sound of a helicopter overhead.

It was likely to be something to do with Forsell and once again he thought about the wife. It had sounded as if she were shouting at everyone and no-one: *What's going on?* He had been shaken by the shrill anxiety in her voice.

He kept his eyes on the water ahead and for the time
being had the wind at his back, which helped a little. Now he
was approaching the southern tip of the island. A speedboat
was being driven recklessly towards him, and as it passed,
his small boat was pitched from side to side in its wake. He
had to struggle not to turn and scream at those testosterone-
fuelled kids, but he kept going and scanned the shoreline.
There weren't all that many people about, and no swimmers
in the water either. He was considering heading for land and
searching the forest when he spotted a tiny dot far out in the
channel, bobbing up and down in the waves. He turned the
boat towards it and yelled:

"Hey there! Hey!"

The wind had drowned out all noise and Forsell was alone in
the world. The punishing muscle strain and the cramp building up in his arms felt almost liberating. His only focus was
to forge ahead until he could let go and sink down through
the water, away from life. But it was not that simple. He did
not want to live. Yet he was not sure he wanted to die either.
He knew only that all hope was gone. What remained was
shame, and the towering rage which was now an imploding
force, a sword thrust inwards, and it was too much. He could
take it no longer.

He thought about his sons Samuel and Jonathan. And
then it became clear that he could not face the choice that
confronted him. To fail them by dying. Or to live and have
them see him as a man disgraced. So he swam on, as if the

sea would provide an answer. He heard a helicopter overhead and swallowed a mouthful of water. He thought he had
been overwhelmed by a wave. But it was his strength ebbing
away.

He was struggling to keep his head above the surface and
switched to breaststroke. But his legs dragged him down,
and in an instant, without knowing quite how, he was under
the water. Gripped by panic, he began to flail with his arms.
One thing was absolutely certain: Even if he did want to die,
he did not want it to be like this. He fought his way up, gasping for breath, then turned towards shore and swam some
five or ten yards before sinking again.

Now fear really seized him. He held his breath, but within
seconds he swallowed more water and his throat spasmed.
He could not breathe at all. His body protected him for as
long as it could until his galloping fear of death caused him
to hyperventilate. His chest and head were bursting with
pain and fear. He lost consciousness briefly, then came to.
But he was sinking to the bottom, and to the extent that he
could think at all he thought of his family, and of everything
and nothing.

The head out there in the waves vanished, then reappeared,
and Blomkvist shouted: "Wait for me, I'm coming." But his
boat was too slow and when he looked again, he saw nothing
but the sea and a seagull diving, and further off a blue sailing boat. He tried to work out where he had last spotted the
figure. Was it there . . . or there? He had to hope for the best,

and in the end he shut off the engine and stared down into the water. It was murky. He had read that this was caused by a combination of rain, flowering algae, chemicals and soil particles. He waved at the helicopter above him—but what good would that do? He took off his shoes and socks and stood for a while in the boat as it rocked in the wind. And then he jumped in.

It was shockingly cold. He swam down below the surface and looked around, but he could not see anything at all. It was hopeless, and after a minute he went back up to the surface and caught his breath. He saw that his boat had already drifted far away, but there was nothing he could do to stop it. He dived again, in the opposite direction this time, and caught sight of a body some way off, apparently lifeless and sinking like a pillar. He swam towards it and grabbed the man under his arms. He was as heavy as lead, unwieldy. Blomkvist gave it all he had and kicked hard as he tried to swim, and slowly, inch by inch, he bore the man up. But he had got the physics wrong.

If he could only get the body to the surface, he had thought, everything would be easier. But it felt as if he were carrying a tree trunk. The man was in a bad way and even heavier above water. He was showing no signs of life at all, and Blomkvist realized how far out in the bay he was. He would never make it back to shore with the body. But he couldn't give up. A long time ago, in his youth, he had been on a life-saving course. He kept trying to change the way he held on to the man, to get a better grip.

But he just felt heavier and heavier, and Blomkvist was

struggling hard, beginning to inhale water. His muscles were cramping. That was it. He would have to let the man go, or he himself would be dragged into the depths. One moment he was going to give up, and the next he felt he could not. He struggled on until everything went black.

CHAPTER 17

August 26

It was late and Bublanski was still in his office at police head-quarters, surfing the news sites. Defence Minister Forsell was in a coma in intensive care at the Karolinska hospital, having nearly drowned. His condition was described as critical. Even if he were to regain consciousness, there was a risk he had suffered brain damage. There was talk of that, and of cardiac arrest, osmotic pulmonary edema and hypothermia, as well as arrhythmia. Things were not looking good.

The serious media were suggesting that it could have been a suicide attempt, which must have been leaked by some insider. It was widely known that Forsell was an excellent swimmer, in which case the most reasonable explanation would be that he had overestimated his capabilities, gone too far out and got caught in the freezing currents. But it was impossible to know for sure. There were reports that he had been saved by a man with a motorboat, and then picked up by a boat from the Sea Rescue Society. He had been taken to hospital by helicopter.

Beneath these stories were articles praising Forsell as a "strong and enterprising minister who had stood up for fundamental human values." They sounded like obituaries. He had, they said, "battled intolerance and destructive nationalism" and been an "incurable optimist who had always sought out the middle ground." The articles mentioned that he had been the victim of a "deeply unjust hate campaign," which could be traced back to troll factories in Russia.

"About time someone said that," Bublanski muttered, and nodded in agreement while reading a column by Catrin Lindås in *Svenska Dagbladet,* in which she argued that this was a logical consequence of the "mood in a society that encourages witch hunts and the demonization of people."

Then he turned to Inspector Modig, who was sitting in the worn armchair next to him, her laptop on her knee.

"Well, Sonja," he said. "Are we getting anywhere with our story?"

Modig looked up at him, somewhat at a loss.

"I can't say we are, really. We haven't found Heikki Järvinen yet, but I've been speaking to one of the doctors who took care of Nima Rita in the mental health clinic in Kathmandu, the one Blomkvist mentioned."

"And what did he say?"

"*She* said that Nima Rita had developed severe psychosis and was hearing voices and cries for help. He was desperate because he couldn't do anything about them. Her impression was that he was constantly reliving something."

"What sort of thing, could she say?"

"Things he had experienced on the mountain, times when he'd felt inadequate. She said that they tried to medicate him and give him electroconvulsive therapy, but it was hard."

"Did you ask if he'd talked about Forsell?"

"She recognized the name, but that's all. He had mostly spoken about his wife and Stan Engelman, of whom he was frightened. I think that's something we should follow up. Apparently this Engelman's pretty unscrupulous. But I heard something else that's interesting too."

"What's that?"

"After the drama on Everest in 2008, the journalists all wanted to speak to Nima Rita. But that interest soon petered out. It became known that he was sick and confused and he was more or less forgotten. But as the tenth anniversary approached he was contacted by someone called Lilian Henderson, a journalist with *The Atlantic,* who was writing a book about the drama. Lilian tried to interview Nima at the hospital, by telephone."

"What did she find out?"

"Actually nothing, from what I understand. But she and Nima Rita agreed to meet up since she was coming to Nepal to do some research. Except that, by the time she got there, he was already gone, and at the end of the day no book ever materialized. The publishers were afraid of being sued."

"By whom?"

"By Engelman."

"What was he so scared of?"

"That's what I think we ought to find out."

"So are we absolutely certain that the beggar and this Nima Rita are one and the same person?" Bublanski said.

"I'd say so. Far too many things match up, and apparently there's a genuine physical likeness."

"How did Blomkvist find this out?"

"All I know is what he wrote to you. I've tried to reach him. But no-one seems to know where he is, not even Erika Berger. She says she's worried. They'd just been talking about doing a profile on Forsell, and ever since the accident she's been frantically trying to get hold of him."

"Doesn't he have a place out on Sandön as well?"

"Yes, at Sandhamn."

"Could Must or Säpo have got their hands on him? The whole thing seems very hush-hush."

"It is. We've informed military high command, but they haven't got back to us. And we don't know either if Blomkvist's told us everything. Maybe he really did find a connection between the Sherpa and Forsell."

"Don't you find this whole story distasteful?" Bublanski said.

"How do you mean?"

"Forsell criticizes Russia and accuses them of interfering with the Swedish electoral process and suddenly he's hated by everybody and up to his neck in lies, and driven to the depths of despair. Then, hey presto, a dead Sherpa appears from nowhere and the finger points straight at Forsell. I have the feeling someone's trying to set him up."

"It doesn't sound great when you put it like that."

"No," he said. "Do we still not know how the beggar got into the country?"

"The Migration Agency has reiterated that he's not in any of their records."

"Odd."

"He should have cropped up in our databases."

"Maybe the intelligence services have put a lid on that too," he muttered.

"Wouldn't surprise me."

"Are we not allowed to talk to Forsell's wife either?"

Modig shook her head.

"We'll need to question her soon, I'm sure they understand that. They can't stop us doing our job," he said.

"I have a bad feeling that's precisely what they think they can do."

"Are they scared of something too?"

"Almost seems like it."

"Well, we'll just have to accept it, and make do with what we have. But what a mess," Bublanski said, and he couldn't stop himself from having another look at the news sites.

Johannes Forsell's condition remained critical.

Thomas Müller was late home from work, back in his large loft apartment on Østerbrogade in Copenhagen. He took a beer from the refrigerator and saw that the sink was dirty and the breakfast dishes had not been put in the dishwasher. He walked through all the rooms. None of them had been cleaned.

The cleaners had simply not bothered. As if he didn't have enough trouble already. Nothing but grief and moaning at work. His secretary was brain-dead. Today he had yelled at

her so much that it had given him a headache, and then, of
course, right in the middle of everything else, there was Paulina. He had had enough of it now. How could she! After all
he had done. She had been a little nothing when they first
met, a worthless journalist on a local paper. He had given
her everything—everything apart from a signed prenuptial
agreement, which had been a big mistake. Bloody dyke.

When she came back to him like a wet rag, he would
pretend to be nice. Then he'd let her have it. No way would
he ever forgive her, especially not after that message. <I've
left you> it had said. <I've met a woman. I'm in
love> That was all, and he had smashed his mobile to bits,
and a crystal vase . . . No, he didn't want to think about it.

He took off his jacket, settled onto the sofa with his beer
and wondered whether to ring Fredrike, his mistress. But he
was bored with her too. He turned on the TV and heard that
the Swedish Minister of Defence was hovering between life
and death. He could not have cared less. That buffoon was
a PC idiot, everyone knew that, and a hypocrite and a cheat
too. He switched over to Bloomberg and the financial news
and let his thoughts wander, and he must have flipped chan-
nels at least a dozen times when the doorbell rang. Fuck.
Who the hell turns up at ten at night? He was tempted to
ignore it.

Then it struck him that it could be Paulina, so he hauled
himself to his feet and yanked open the door. But it was not
his wife. A stroppy-looking, black-haired girl in jeans and a
hoodie was standing in the corridor, holding a bag and looking down at the hall floor.

"I don't need anything," he said.

"It's about the cleaning," she said.

"You can tell your boss from me that she can go to hell," he said. "I have no time for people who don't do their job properly."

"It's not the cleaning company's fault," the woman said.

"What are you talking about?"

"I'm the one who cancelled the service."

"You did *what*?"

"I cancelled it, and I'll take care of things myself."

"Don't you get it? I don't want any more cleaning. Piss off," he spat, slamming the door.

But the woman put her foot in the way and stepped over the threshold, and only then did he notice that there was something odd about her. She walked in a funny way, without moving her arms or upper body and with her head slightly tilted to one side, as if she were looking at a remote point over by the windows. Perhaps she was a criminal or had some mental problem. Her eyes were icy and expressionless, as if she were not entirely present, and he said with all the authority he could muster:

"If you don't fuck off right away, I'll call the police."

She did not answer. She did not even appear to have heard. She bent to get some rope and a roll of duct tape out of her bag, and for a moment he could not think of anything to say. Then he yelled "Out!" and grabbed her by the hand.

But somehow she managed to take hold of his wrist and drag him over to the dining table. He was both furious and frightened, and he tore himself loose, meaning to hit her or ram her against the wall, but she rushed at him so that he toppled onto his back on the table. In a matter of seconds she was on top of him with those same icy, blank eyes, and quick as a flash she had him tied down. In her monotone she said:

"Now I'm going to iron your shirt for you."

Then she put tape over his mouth and eyed him the way a wild beast eyes its prey. Thomas Müller had never felt so terrified in all his life.

Blomkvist had suffered badly in the cold currents and had swallowed a lot of water. He and Forsell had been winched up and flown away in the same helicopter. For a while he had been more or less unconscious. But he had recovered fairly quickly and now, late in the evening, after the ward round and three interrogation sessions by military intelligence, he was given back his belongings, including his mobile which had been retrieved from his dinghy. A young family in a sailing boat had towed it in from the bay. He was given permission to go home, but the doctors recommended he stay in hospital overnight. He was also informed that a prosecutor by the name of Matson had placed a gag order on him. He needed to call his sister Annika, the lawyer.

He knew very well that the legal basis for silencing journalists was shaky, and in any case he resented the autocratic behaviour of the men from the intelligence service. But he let it lie. He was not going to write one word until he had got to the bottom of the story anyway, so he stayed sitting on the bed, gathering his thoughts. He was not left in peace for long.

There was another knock at the door and a tall woman

with dark-blond hair and bloodshot eyes appeared in the room. For some reason—perhaps because he was just staring at all the missed calls on his mobile—it was a while before he realized it was Rebecka Forsell. Her hands were shaking, and she said she really wanted to thank him before he left.

"Is he better?" Blomkvist asked.

"The worst is over, thank God. But we don't yet know if he's suffered any brain damage. It's too early to tell."

He asked her to take a seat in the chair next to him.

"They say that you too had a close shave," she said.

"That's a bit of an exaggeration."

"But still . . . do you realize what you've done—for us? Do you get that? It's immense."

"Thanks," he said. "I'm touched."

"Is there anything we can do for you?" she said.

Tell me everything you know about Nima Rita, he thought. *Out with the truth.*

"See to it that your husband gets better and finds himself a more restful job," he said.

"It's been a dreadful time."

"I understand."

"You know . . ."

She looked confused, and was nervously rubbing her hand against her left arm.

"Yes?"

"I've just been reading about Johannes online, and all of a sudden people are being nice again, not all of them, of course, but many. It's almost unreal. It's brought home to me the nightmare we've been living through."

Blomkvist leaned forward and took her hand.

"I was the one who called *Dagens Nyheter* and told them it was a suicide attempt, even though I don't know for certain what happened, exactly. Was that a bad thing to do?" she asked.

"You had your reasons, I suppose."

"I wanted them to understand how far it had gone."

"Fair enough."

"The men from Must told me something very odd," she said, looking distraught.

"What did they tell you?" he said, trying to sound calm.

"That you had found out about Nima Rita's death here in Stockholm."

"Yes, it's really odd. Did the two of you know him?"

"I'm not sure I dare say anything. They keep badgering me all the time to keep quiet about it."

"They're on at me too," he said, and added, "but do we have to be so obedient?"

She gave a sorrowful smile.

"Maybe not."

"Well then, did you know him?"

"We did for a while at Base Camp. We liked him a lot, and I think he liked us. 'Sahib, Sahib,' he said all the time about Johannes, 'very good person.' He had a lovely wife."

"Luna."

"Luna," she repeated. "She spoiled us all, she was constantly on the go. We helped them to build a house in Pangboche afterwards."

"Good for you."

"I'm not so sure. We all felt guilty about what happened to him."

"Do you have any idea how he could have disappeared from Kathmandu, presumed dead, and then turn up in Stockholm three years later and die again?"

"It makes me sick to the stomach." She looked at him, misery in her eyes.

"Tell me," he said.

"You should have seen those little boys in Khumbu. They worshipped him. He saved lives, and he paid a terrible price."

"I suppose that was the end of his climbing career."

"His name was dragged through the mud."

"But not by everybody, surely?" Blomkvist said.

"By a lot of people."

"Who are we talking about?"

"The ones who were close to Klara Engelman."

"Her husband, for example?"

"Of course, him as well."

He could hear the change of tone in her voice.

"That's a strange way of putting it."

"Well, maybe. But you understand . . . the story is more complicated than most people realize, and many lawyers have been involved. A year or two ago, an American publisher had to withdraw a book about it."

"That was down to Engelman's lawyers, I bet."

"Right. Engelman is a real estate tycoon, ostensibly an entrepreneur, but at heart he's a gangster, a mafioso, at least that's my opinion. And I know he wasn't that happy about his wife towards the end."

"How come?"

"Because she fell in love with our guide, Viktor Grankin, and wanted to leave Stan. She said she was going to get a divorce and tell the press what a narcissistic pig he had been. That's the stuff Engelman managed to suppress, even though you can probably still find bits and pieces on the internet gossip sites."

"Got it," he said.

"It was all very acrimonious."

"Did Nima Rita know?"

"They kept it very quiet, but I'm sure he did. He was looking after her."

"And did he also keep quiet about it?"

"I think so. At least while his mind was still reasonably sound. But after his wife died, he apparently became more and more confused. It wouldn't surprise me at all if he went around and blabbed about that, and other things too."

Blomkvist looked into Rebecka Forsell's eyes, and at her tall body huddled up in the chair. Somewhat reluctantly he said:

"In his last days he was talking about your husband too."

Rebecka could feel her anger rising, but she was careful not to show it, and she knew she was being unfair. Blomkvist had a job to do. He had saved her husband's life. But his words brought to mind her worst suspicions, that Johannes was keeping from her something to do with Everest and Nima Rita. In her heart she had never believed it was the hate campaign which had broken him.

Johannes was a fighter, a warrior, an overoptimistic fool who stormed on ahead, however lousy the odds. The only times she had seen him beaten were now, out on Sandön, and after his Everest ascent. She had already worked out for herself that there must be a connection. And this must be what had made her so angry, not Blomkvist. He was just the messenger.

"I don't understand that," she said.

"Not at all?"

She was silent. Then she said, "You ought to have a word with Svante," and immediately regretted it.

"Svante Lindberg?"

"That's right."

She and Johannes had had a huge row at home on the day he appointed Lindberg his undersecretary. On the face of it Lindberg was a carbon copy of Johannes, with the same energy and military heartiness. But in fact he was something quite different. While Forsell thought well of everything and everybody—until the opposite proved true—Lindberg was always calculating and manipulative.

"What can Svante tell me?" Blomkvist said.

Whatever suits his interests, she thought.

"What happened on Everest," she said, wondering if she was betraying Johannes with those words. But Johannes had failed her by not telling her everything that had taken place on the mountain. She got up, gave Blomkvist a hug and thanked him once more, and went back to the intensive care unit.

CHAPTER 18

August 26–27, Night

Chief Inspector Ulrike Jensen was conducting a first interview with the complainant, Thomas Müller, at Rigshospitalet in Copenhagen. He had been admitted at 11:10 at night with burns to his arms and upper chest. Jensen was forty-four and a mother of small children, and had spent many years dealing with sexual offences. She had lately been transferred to the violent crimes squad and often worked the night shift—it was what functioned best for her family at that point—so had had her fair share of confused and drunken witness statements. But what she was hearing now took the prize.

"I appreciate that you're in a lot of pain, and the morphine will be affecting you," she said. "But can we try to keep to the facts and concentrate on an accurate description."

"I've never seen eyes like that," he mumbled.

"So you've said. But you need to be more specific. Did this woman have any distinguishing features?"

"She was young and short with black hair, and she talked like a ghost."

"And how do ghosts talk?"

"Without any feeling, or rather . . . as if her mind was on something else. She wasn't really there."

"What did she say? Can you please repeat it so we can get a clearer idea of what actually happened?"

"She said that she never ironed her own clothes, so she wasn't very good at it and it was important for me to lie still."

"That's pretty harsh."

"It was insane."

"Is that all?"

"She said she would come for me again if I didn't . . ."

"If you didn't what?"

Müller squirmed in his hospital bed and gave her a help-less look.

"If you didn't what?" she repeated.

"Leave my wife alone. I was not to see her again. I was to get a divorce."

"Your wife is travelling, you said?"

"Yes, she . . ." He was muttering inaudibly.

"Have you done something to her?" Jensen said.

"I haven't done a thing. She's the one who . . ."

"What?"

"Left me."

"Why has she left you, do you suppose?"

"She's a fucking . . ."

He was on the point of saying something terrible, but was

smart enough not to, and Jensen could tell there was a history which would not be very pretty either. But she put it aside for the time being.

"Do you recall anything else that might help us?" she said.

"The woman said I was 'out of luck.'"

"What did she mean by that, do you think?"

"That she'd been keeping a whole load of shit bottled up inside her all summer long and had gone more or less crazy as a result."

"That doesn't tell us much, does it?"

"How am I supposed to know what the fuck she meant?"

"And how did it end?"

"She tore the tape off my mouth and repeated everything again."

"That you should stay away from your wife?"

"And I will too. I never want to see her again."

"OK," she said. "That sounds like a plan for now. So you haven't spoken to your wife this evening either?"

"I don't even know where she is, I told you. But for God's sake . . ."

"Yes?"

"You've got to get a move on and do something. This person is completely insane. She's lethal. She's going to kill someone next."

"We'll do our best," Jensen said. "But it looks as if—"

"As if what?"

"As if all the surveillance cameras in the neighbourhood were out of action just then, so we've got very little to go on," she continued, suddenly feeling very tired of her job.

· · ·

It was just after midnight and Salander was in a taxi on her way in from Arlanda airport, reading up on a divorce lawyer recommended by Annika Giannini, when she received an encrypted message from Blomkvist. She was too tired and out of sorts to want to look at it, and she stared vacantly out of the window. What was the matter with her?

She had liked Paulina. Maybe in her own twisted way she had even loved her. And how had she gone about showing it? She had sent her home to her parents in Munich, heartbroken. She had assaulted her husband, as if taking revenge on him would somehow compensate for her own shortcomings in love. She could not bring herself to kill her own sister— who had caused so much harm—but would have put an end to Thomas Müller's life in Copenhagen without batting an eyelid.

As she was sitting on top of him, holding the iron, images of Zalachenko and Bjurman the lawyer, and Teleborian the psychiatrist and all sorts of other brutes had flashed through her mind. It was as if the floodgates had burst open. As if she wanted revenge for the whole of her life, and it had taken all the self-control she could muster to stop her from going completely off the rails.

She had to get a grip on herself. Otherwise it would just go on like this: hesitation where action was needed, and madness in the place of calm.

Some part of what had happened on Tverskoy Boulevard had knocked her off balance. It was a fresh realization from her past. Not just the fact that she had lain there powerless when Zala came to fetch Camilla at night. There was her mother, too. What had she known? Had she too shut her eyes to the truth? This thought was constantly chafing at her, so much so that it made her frightened of herself—frightened by her indecision, frightened that she would be a useless warrior in what inevitably awaited: her life's crucial battle.

She had known that Camilla had received a visit from Svavelsjö M.C. ever since Plague helped her to hack the surveillance cameras around the apartment on Strandvägen. She was aware that her sister was pursuing her with all the means at her disposal and that, given the chance, Camilla herself would be unlikely to hesitate. So yes, goddamnit, she had to pull herself together. She had to be strong and unwavering. But first she had to find somewhere to go.

She no longer had a home in Stockholm, so she gave that some thought and weighed the alternatives. And then she quickly read Blomkvist's e-mail after all. It was to do with Forsell and the Sherpa, and was interesting in more ways than one. But she could not deal with it just then. She wrote back on impulse, and surprised even herself.

<Am in town. Shall we meet now, right away? At a hotel?>

It wasn't simply an indecent proposal, she thought, or even a reaction to having felt lonely, without hope. It was also . . . a safety precaution, because it was not unthinkable, was it, that having failed to track her down, Camilla and her henchmen would go for her close circle instead. For that reason alone it would make sense to lock Kalle Blomkvist away in a hotel room.

But then again, he was perfectly capable of locking himself up somewhere. When she got no response from him after ten, fifteen, twenty minutes, she snorted, closed her eyes and felt that she could sleep forever, and maybe she did actually drop off to sleep because when Blomkvist eventually wrote back, she jumped as if she had been attacked.

His sister Annika had brought him a change of clothes and shoes and driven him home to Bellmansgatan. He thought he would immediately collapse into bed. Instead he sat down at his computer and did some research on Stan Engelman. He was now seventy-four and had remarried, and he was under investigation for bribery and intimidation in connection with the sale of three hotels in Las Vegas. Although the situation was far from clear—he, of course, maintained the exact opposite—his empire seemed to be teetering. He was said to be seeking help from business contacts in Russia and Saudi Arabia.

Engelman had not made a single public comment about Nima Rita. He had, however, viciously attacked the late guide Viktor Grankin, who had employed Nima as Sirdar, and he had sued Grankin's company, Everest Adventure Tours. They had reached a settlement before a Moscow judge, as a result of which the company went into liquidation. The rage he felt against the expedition—of which Nima Rita had been a part—was in no doubt. But that did not explain why the Sherpa had appeared in Stockholm, of all places, and Blomkvist dropped that line of enquiry for the time being; he was too tired to delve into Engelman's many real estate transactions and love affairs and other ludicrous escapades, and instead he checked out Svante Lindberg, who was probably the person who knew best what Forsell had encountered on Everest.

Lindberg was a lieutenant general, a former coastal ranger, and presumably also an intelligence officer. He had been a close friend of Johannes Forsell since they were young. He was also an experienced mountaineer. Before Everest, he had climbed three other twenty-six-thousand-foot peaks—Broad Peak, Gasherbrum and Annapurna—and that was probably why Viktor Grankin let him and Johannes go for the summit ahead of the others when the pace of the group was slowing during the morning of May 13, 2008. But Blomkvist resolved to look more closely at the actual events on the mountain later, probably tomorrow now. For the time being he recorded that Lindberg had himself been one of the targets in the hate campaign against Forsell.

Some sources suggested that he was the real centre of power at the Defence Ministry. But he rarely gave interviews, and the closest thing Blomkvist found to anything personal was a long profile in *Runner's World* from three years ago, which he started to read. He later remembered that Lindberg was quoted as saying, "When you're completely finished, you've still got another 70 percent." But he must have nodded off then.

He woke up at his computer, shaking all over and with the image of Forsell sinking beneath the waves clearly in his mind. He realized that not only was he totally exhausted, he was also in a state of shock. So he dragged himself off to bed, expecting to fall asleep immediately. But his thoughts were racing too much, and in the end he picked up his mobile and saw that Salander had answered.

```
<Am in town. Shall we meet now, right away?
At a hotel?>
```

He was so tired that he had to read it twice. Then he felt . . . what? Embarrassed, awkward? He couldn't be sure. He knew only that he wanted to pretend not to have seen the message, though that would not work with Salander; by now she would have seen that he had read it. What to do? He could not bring himself to say no. He most definitely did not want to say yes. He closed his eyes, tried to organize his thoughts. So she was in Stockholm, and wanted to see him now, right away, at a hotel? Did it mean something more than that she wanted to see him now, right away, at a hotel?

"For Christ's sake, Lisbeth," he muttered.

He got up and wandered nervously around the apartment. She had thrown him even further out of kilter, and at some point he looked out of the window towards Bellmansgatan. There he saw a figure he recognized at once, standing over by the Bishops Arms. It was the man with the ponytail from Sandhamn, and at that he flinched as if he had been punched in the stomach. Because now there could be no doubt, could there?

He was being watched. His heart was pumping and his mouth was dry, and he thought he should contact Bublanski

THE GIRL WHO LIVED TWICE

or someone else in the police straightaway. Instead he sent an answer to Salander:

<I'm being shadowed>

<My fault. I'll help you shake them off> she wrote back.

He wanted to shout that he was too tired to shake anyone off, he just wanted some sleep and to get on with his blasted holiday and forget everything that wasn't straightforward and calm.

<OK> he wrote.

CHAPTER 19

August 27

Kira would have liked to sever her links with Svavelsjö M.C. She would have loved to get rid of those bloody bandits with their ridiculous leather vests and rivets, the balaclavas and the tattoos. But she needed them once more, and had therefore showered them with money. She also reminded them of Zalachenko, and declared it a matter of honour, in his memory.

It stuck in her craw. She would much rather have berated them for being lowlifes and losers, and packed them off to a hairdresser. But she kept her cool, even her dignity, and once again she was grateful to have Galinov with her. Today he was wearing a white linen suit and brown leather shoes, and was sitting in the red armchair opposite her, reading an article about the relationship between the Swedish language and Low German. It was as if all this were no more than a study trip for him. But he lent her calm, a connection to the past, and, best of all, he terrified the bikers.

When they stood up to her and baulked at taking orders from a woman, Galinov had only to lower his reading glasses and give them an icy-blue stare. Then they did exactly as they were told. She guessed they knew what he was capable of, so she didn't mind that he was being so inactive.

He would come into the picture later; the hunt for her sister was being handled by Bogdanov and the rest of the gang. So far they had found nothing, not a trace. It was as if they were chasing a shadow, and to make matters worse they had lost yet another lead tonight. Earlier she had summoned Marko Sandström, Svavelsjö's president, and he now walked into the living room with another of the thugs—Krille, she thought his name was—although she could hardly have cared less.

"I don't want any excuses," she said. "Just a factual account of how this could have happened."

Sandström smiled nervously, and she liked that. He was as big and threatening as all the others in Svavelsjö. But at least he had the good taste not to wear a beard and long hair, and his stomach was a normal size. His face was almost beautiful, in fact, and Camilla could imagine sinking her fingernails into his chest, just as she had in the old days.

"You're asking for the impossible," Sandström said, trying to sound authoritative, although he could not help glancing at Galinov, who did not even look up. She liked that too.

She said:

"What's impossible? I was only asking you not to let him out of your sight, that's all."

"Yes, around the clock," Sandström said. "That takes resources, and we're not talking about some nobody."

"How. Could. This. Happen?" she said again, stressing each word.

"That fucker . . ." the one she thought was called Krille said.

Sandström interrupted him:

"Let me deal with this. Camilla—"

"Kira."

"I'm sorry, Kira," he went on. "Blomkvist rushed off in his motorboat yesterday afternoon. There was no way we could have followed him, and pretty soon the situation became uncomfortable. The island was crawling with policemen and soldiers, and we had no idea where he'd gone, so we split up. Jorma stayed in Sandhamn and Krille headed off to Bellmansgatan and waited there."

"And that's where Blomkvist showed up."

"Late that evening, in a taxi. He seemed dead beat. There was nothing to suggest that he wasn't simply going home to sleep, and I think we should really applaud Krille for having stuck with him. Blomkvist turned off his lights, but then came out of the building carrying a suitcase at 1:00 a.m. and walked towards the tunnelbana by Mariatorget. He never turned around once. When he got to the platform he sat down, his head in his hands."

"It looked as if he was sick," Krille added.

"Precisely," Sandström said. "All that made us lower our guard. On the tunnelbana he leaned against the window and closed his eyes. He seemed completely knackered. But then . . ."

"Yes?"

"At Gamla Stan, just before the doors closed, he rocketed to his feet, dashed through the doors and vanished off the platform. We lost him."

Kira did not say a word, not at first. She exchanged a look with Galinov, then she looked down at her hands and sat there, immobile. One of the first things she had learned was that silence and calm are more intimidating than any outburst, and even though she wanted to scream, she simply said in a dry and matter-of-fact way:

"This woman who was with Blomkvist out in Sandhamn. Have we identified her?"

"Absolutely. She's Catrin Lindås, she lives at Nytorget 6. She's a well-known media whore."

"Does she mean anything to him?"

"Well . . ." Krille began.

Krille had a ponytail and small, watery eyes. He didn't exactly look like an expert in matters of the heart. But he seemed keen to have a go.

"They looked to me to be in love. They were all over each other, all day long in the garden."

"OK, good," she said. "Then I want you to keep tabs on her as well."

"Christ, Camilla . . . sorry, Kira. That's asking a lot. That's three addresses to keep an eye on," Sandström said.

Once again she sat there in silence, and then she thanked them. She was glad when Galinov, tall as he was, rose to his feet and saw them out. He said a few words to them which at first may have seemed courteous, but later, once they had sunk in, would scare the living daylights out of them.

He was so very good at that kind of thing, and it was needed, she thought. Once again she had lost the initiative, and she looked around angrily. The apartment was 1,800 square feet, bought through dummy companies and front men two years earlier, and still too impersonal and sparsely furnished. But it would have to do, for want of anything better. She got up, and without knocking went into the corner room to the right, where Bogdanov was sitting crouched over his computers, stinking of sweat.

"How are you getting on with Blomkvist's computer?"

"Depends."

"On what?"

"I got into his server, like I told you."

"But no further news?"

He shifted in his chair and she realized at once: He did not have any good news either.

"Yesterday Blomkvist was looking up Forsell, the Minister of Defence. That's interesting, of course, not only because Forsell is one of the GRU's targets and Galinov has had dealings with him in the past, but because yesterday the Minister tried—"

"I don't give a shit about Forsell," she snapped. "I'm only interested in the encrypted links Blomkvist received and forwarded."

"I didn't manage to crack them."

"What do you mean you 'didn't manage'? You'll just have to keep trying."

Bogdanov bit his lip and looked down at the table.

"I'm no longer in there."

"What are you talking about?"

"Last night someone chucked out my trojan."

"How the hell did that happen? I thought it was impossible to get at your trojans."

"I know, but . . ."

He chewed at his cuticles.

"So it was some sort of fucking genius, you mean?" she hissed.

"Seems like it," he agreed, and Kira was about to hit the ceiling when a completely different thought struck her. Instead of yelling and making a scene she smiled.

It had dawned on her that Lisbeth was closer than she had dared hope.

Blomkvist lay in bed in Hotel Hellsten on Luntmakargatan, while Salander sat in an armchair over by the window, looking at him absently. He had slept for barely two hours. It hadn't been such a good idea to go there. It wasn't as if it had been a romantic night, nor had they met up as old friends. The whole thing had gone off the rails from the moment they met in the doorway.

At first she had stared at him as if she could not wait to tear his clothes off, and even though he had been thinking about Catrin on the way there, he might not have been able to defend himself. But it was not him she was so keen to get her hands on, it was his computer, and his mobile. She grabbed them from him and squatted in a strange crouched position behind some black screens she unfolded and set up on the floor. There she stayed, silent and immobile, with only her fingers working at a frenzied speed. In the end he could not stand it any longer. He lost his temper and yelled at her that he had nearly drowned. That he had saved a bloody minister. Either he had to get some sleep or at least be allowed to talk and find out what she was up to.

"Shut up," she said.

"For Christ's sake!"

He was furious. He felt like walking out and never seeing her again. But in the end he turned his back on it all, got undressed, lay down on one side of the double bed and fell asleep like a sulky child. Some time towards dawn she crept in beside him and whispered in his ear, as if in some demented attempt at seduction:

"You had a trojan, smart-arse," and that ruined the rest of his night.

He was scared. He began to worry about his sources and insisted that she tell him what was going on, which reluctantly she did. Gradually the scale of the madness became clear to him, although not all of it, of course. As usual she was not very forthcoming and soon her eyelids began to droop. She put her head on the pillow and drifted off, leaving him alone and agitated in the bed, and he groaned, convinced that he would not be able to go back to sleep. But now he had woken up and Salander was back in the armchair, dressed in knickers and a black shirt which was far too long for her. She drifted in and out of sleep, while Blomkvist looked groggily at the muscles in her legs and the black rings under her eyes.

"There's breakfast out there," she said.

"Great." He went to fetch the trays and put them one by

one on the bed. He made coffee in the Nespresso machine by the window and sat cross-legged on the mattress, and she sat down opposite him. He looked at her as if she were both stranger and intimate friend and, more clearly than ever, he felt he understood her and yet did not understand her at all.

"Why did you hesitate?" he said.

She didn't like his question. She didn't like the look on his face. She wanted to get away from there or pull him down into the bed and shut him up, and she thought about Paulina and her husband and the iron in her hand, and about other far worse things from way back in her childhood. She was not at all sure she would answer him. Then she said:

"I remembered something."

Blomkvist looked at her intently and she regretted at once that she had not kept her mouth shut.

"What did you remember?"

"Nothing."

"Come on."

"I remembered my family."

"What about them?"

Leave it, she thought. *Just leave it.*

"I remembered . . ." she began, as if she could not help herself, or as if something inside her was determined to put this into words.

"Tell me," he said.

"Mamma knew that Camilla was stealing from us and lying to the police to protect Zala. She knew that Camilla said terrible things about us to the social welfare authorities and made the situation at home even more of a living hell."

"I know all this," he said. "Holger told me."

"But did you also know . . ."

"What?"

Should she just drop it? She spat it out:

"That in the end Mamma had enough and threatened to throw Camilla out?"

"I had no idea."

"It's the truth."

"But Camilla was only a child."

"She was twelve."

"Still . . ."

"Maybe she was just exasperated and didn't really mean it. But she was always on my side, I know that. She didn't like Camilla."

"That can happen in any family. One of the children becomes the favourite."

"But in this case there were consequences. It blinded us."

"To what?"

"To what was going on."

"What was that?"

Stop, she thought. *Stop.*

She wanted to scream and run away. But she continued, as if driven by a force she could no longer control:

"We thought that Camilla had Zala. That it was two against two in our war, Mamma and me against Zala and Camilla. But that's not how it was. Camilla was on her own."

"You were all on your own."

"It was worse for Camilla."

"In what way?"

She looked away.

"Zala would sometimes come into our room at night," she said. "At the time I was too young to understand why. But I didn't give it much thought either. He was evil and did whatever he wanted. That's just how it was, and at the time I only had one thing on my mind."

"You wanted to stop your mother being abused."

"I wanted to kill Zala, and of course I knew that Camilla had ganged up with him. I had no reason to worry about her."

"I can see that."

"But obviously I should have asked myself why Zala had changed."

"In what way had he changed?"

"He was staying the night more and more often, and somehow that didn't fit. He was used to luxury and having people running around after him. And now our apartment was suddenly good enough for him. That must have been because there was a new pawn in the game. On Tverskoy Boulevard the penny dropped. He was attracted to Camilla, like all other men."

"So it was *her* he was coming for at night."

"He always asked her to follow him to the living room, and listening to their voices it just sounded to me as if they were planning something against Mamma and me. But maybe I also heard something else, something I wasn't able to get my head around at the time. They often went off in the car."

"He abused her."

"He ruined her."

"You can't blame yourself for that," he said.

She wanted to scream.

"I was just answering your question. I realized that neither Mamma nor I lifted a finger to help her. That's what made me hesitate."

Blomkvist sat in silence on the bed, trying to absorb what he had heard. Then he put a hand on her shoulder. She pushed it away and looked out of the window.

"Do you know what I think?" he said.

She did not reply.

"I think you're just not the sort of person who shoots people like that."

"That's crap."

"I don't think you are, Lisbeth. I never have."

She took a croissant from the tray, and more to herself than to him she muttered:

"But I should have killed her. Now she's coming after all of us."

CHAPTER 20

August 27

Bublanski had a bottle of Grant's twelve-year-old scotch with him. It had been standing around at home for years, and doing this was clearly against his principles. But since the witness had asked him for whisky, he was not going to make an issue of it. Ever since yesterday, he had been focusing exclusively on Nima Rita's death, so he had spared no effort to get hold of the last witness known to have seen the Sherpa alive. In the end he had tracked him down here in Haninge, to a small apartment in a yellow block on Klockarleden.

Bublanski had seen worse hangouts, but this was not the coziest he had seen either. The place smelled bad, and was littered with bottles and ashtrays and the remains of food. But the witness himself exuded a sort of bohemian elegance. He wore a more or less clean white shirt and a Parisian beret.

"Herr Järvinen," Bublanski said.

"Chief Inspector."

"Will this do?"

He held up the bottle and got a little smile in return, and then the two of them sat down on some blue wooden stools in the kitchen.

"You met the man we now know to be called Nima Rita on the night of the fourteenth of August, isn't that right?" he said.

"Correct . . . yes . . . a total nutjob. I was feeling lousy and waiting for a man who usually sells drink at Norra Ban-torget, and then this tramp shows up, reeling, and I should have kept my trap shut. You could see from a mile away that he was crazy. But I'm a talkative sort and so I asked him, politely and tactfully, how he was and he started yelling at me."

"In which language?"

"English and Swedish."

"So he could speak Swedish?"

"Well, not really. But he knew some words. I couldn't make out a thing. He was shouting about having been up among the clouds, fighting with the gods and talking to the dead."

"Was he talking about Mount Everest, do you think?"

"He might have been. I wasn't listening all that carefully. I was feeling bloody awful, you see, and didn't have the stomach for his gibberish."

"So you recall nothing specific that he said?"

"He'd rescued lots of people. 'I saved many lives,' he said, and then he showed me the stumps on his hands. He was missing some fingers."

"Did he say anything about Defence Minister Forsell?"

Heikki Järvinen looked at him in surprise and poured some whisky into a glass, then knocked it back with a shaky hand.

"Funny you should say that."

"Why funny?"

"Because come to think of it he *did* mention Forsell in some way. But that's perhaps no surprise. Everybody's talking about him."

"What did he actually say?"

"That he knew him, I think. And knew all sorts of other important people. He was giving me a headache and I couldn't take it. I made a pretty stupid remark."

"Like what?"

"Well . . . nothing racist or anything like that. But it probably wasn't such a great idea. I said he looked like a bloody Chinaman or something, and he went berserk and thumped me. It took me so much by surprise that I didn't stand a chance. He beat the shit out of me, to be honest. Can you imagine?"

"I can see that it wasn't very nice."

"I bled like a pig," Järvinen went on, still in a state. "There's a cut here, it hasn't gone away. Look."

He pointed to his lip and there was indeed a scar there. But then there were cuts and bruises all over him, so Bublanski was not especially impressed.

"Then what happened?"

"He stormed off, and had a real stroke of luck, or perhaps I shouldn't say luck seeing as he died the next day. But that's what it felt like at the time. He ran into someone selling booze down on Vasagatan."

Bublanski leaned across the kitchen table.

"Someone selling booze?"

"A man stopped him on the pavement down by the hotel, you know the one I mean. At least it looked as if he was giving him a bottle. But it was quite a long way off and I may be wrong."

"What can you tell me about the man?"

"The seller?"

"Yes."

"Nothing much. He was thin, dark-haired, tall. He was wearing a black jacket and jeans. And a cap. But I didn't see his face."

"Did he look like a drunk himself?"

"He didn't walk like one."

"Meaning what?"

"He was too light on his feet, and quick."

"Like someone who exercised regularly?"

"Could be."

Bublanski observed Järvinen in silence for a while and felt that here was a man in free fall who, in spite of everything, was trying hard to keep up some sort of appearance. The fighting spirit was still there.

"Did you see where he went?"

"In the direction of Central Station. For a while I thought I'd follow him. But I had zero chance of catching up."

"So maybe he wasn't really there to sell alcohol? Maybe all he wanted to do was give a bottle to Nima Rita."

"So you're saying—?"

"I'm not saying anything. But Nima Rita was poisoned, and considering the way he lived it's not inconceivable that the poison he drank came in the form of a bottle of alcohol, so you can see why I'm interested in this man."

Järvinen had another slug of whisky and said:

"Well, in that case, there's one more thing I should mention. He did say that they'd tried to poison him before."

"Did he say how?"

"I had a hard job understanding that too. He was screaming and shouting about all the amazing things he'd done and all the fancy people he knew. All the same, I got a feeling that he'd spent time in the nut house and had refused to take his medicines. 'They tried to poison me,' he yelled. 'But I ran, I climbed down a mountain to the lake.' At least that's what I think he said. That he'd run away from some doctors."

"From a mountain, down to a lake?"

"I think so."

"Did you have the impression that he'd been in hospital in Sweden or abroad?" Bublanski said.

"In Sweden, I think. He pointed behind him, as if it was somewhere around here. But then again, he was always pointing all over the place, as if the heavens and the gods he'd been doing battle with were also here, somewhere around the corner."

"I see," Bublanski said, keen to get away as soon as possible.

At the desk in her hotel room Lisbeth noted that the men from Svavelsjö, among others their president Sandström, were leaving the Strandvägen address. She would have to think about her next steps.

She closed down her computer and saw that Blomkvist had got dressed and was sitting on the bed, reading on his mobile. She really didn't want to talk about her own life, or hear how she was actually quite nice deep down, or whatever Mikael had been trying to tell her.

"What are you up to?"

"What?"

"What are you doing?"

"I'm working on the Sherpa story," he said.

"Are you getting anywhere?"

"I'm checking out this Engelman."

"Nice guy, isn't he?"

"Absolutely. Just your type."

"And then there's Mats Sabin," she said.

"Yes, him too."

"And what do you think about him?"

"I haven't really got that far."

"I think you can forget him," she said.

He was curious and looked up.

"Why do you say that?"

"Because I'm guessing it's one of those things you pick up and get all excited about because there are so many different connections. But I don't think there's anything to it."

"Why not?"

Salander was thinking about Camilla and Svavelsjö as she walked over to the window and looked down at Luntma-kargatan through a gap in the curtains. Maybe she ought to apply some pressure after all.

"Why not?" he repeated.

"You found his name rather quickly, didn't you? Before you were even sure what exactly was said."

"True."

"You'd be better off going back in history, to colonial times."

"Why's that?"

"Isn't the whole Everest thing one big hangover from those days, with white climbers and people with a different skin colour carrying their gear?"

"Well, perhaps so."

"I think you should focus on that, and try to find out how Nima Rita would have expressed himself."

"Would you mind saying exactly what you mean, for once?"

Blomkvist sat on the bed, waiting for her to answer, but noticed how she seemed to be drifting off again, just as she had that morning when she'd been sitting in the armchair. He decided he might as well check it out himself and he began to pack. He would get going and meet up with her again later, so he put his laptop in the bag and stood up to hug her, and to tell her to take care. But she did not react even when he came close to her.

"Earth to Lisbeth," he said, feeling a little silly, and only then did her eyes begin to focus, and she looked at his bag.

It seemed to be telling her something.

"You can't go home," she said.

"In that case, I'll go somewhere else."

"I mean it," she said. "You can't go home, or to anybody else you're close to. They're watching you."

"I can look after myself."

"You can't. Give me your mobile."

"Just stop it. Not again."

"Give it to me."

He thought that she had already messed around enough with his mobile, and was about to put it in his pocket. But she snatched it from him, ignoring his protests, and was immediately hard at work with programme codes. So he let her get on with it. She had always done as she pleased with his computers. But after a few minutes he said rather testily:

"What are you doing?"

She looked up, with the shadow of a smile on her face.

"I like that," she said.

"What do you like?"

"Those words."

"Which words?"

"'What are you doing?' Can you repeat them, in the same tone of voice?"

"What are you talking about?"

"Just say it."

She held out the mobile.

"What?"

"What are you doing?"

"What are you doing?" he said.

"Great, perfect."

She fiddled some more with his mobile and then handed it back.

"What have you done?"

"I'm going to be able to see where you are, and hear what's going on around you."

"What?! So I won't have any private life at all?"

"You can have whatever private life you like, and I'm not going to listen in unnecessarily, at least not unless you say those words."

"So I can go on talking crap about you?"

"What?"

"That was a joke, Lisbeth."

"OK."

He smiled.

Maybe she smiled too. He put his mobile away, looked at her again and said, "Thank you."

"Keep a low profile now," she said.

"I will. Just as well no-one knows who I am."

"What?"

She didn't get that joke either, and then he really did hug her.

He left the hotel and tried to melt into the life of the city. Not all that successfully. He had got only as far as Tegnérgatan when a young man asked for a selfie, and he continued to Sveavägen. He should have kept his head down, but he sat on a bench not far from the Stockholm Public Library and once more looked up Nima Rita. He ended up reading a long article in *Outside* magazine from August 2008.

It was the most detailed account ever given by Nima Rita. But the quotes were nothing to get excited about, at least not at first sight. Blomkvist had read it all before, dutiful or sorrowful answers to questions about Klara Engelman. But then he saw something which made him sit up, and at first it was not clear to him why. It was contained in the simple, heartbroken message:

"I really tried to take care of her. I tried. But Mamsahib just fell, and then the storm came, and the mountain was angry and we couldn't save her. I am very, very sorry for Mamsahib."

Mamsahib.

Of course. *Mamsahib* could also be "memsahib," the feminine of "sahib," a form of address for whites in colonial India. Why had that not occurred to him? In the course of his investigations he had read that Sherpas often referred to Western climbers in that way.

I took Forsell. And I left Mamsahib.

That is what he must have said, and he was therefore presumably talking about Klara Engelman. But what did that mean? Had Nima Rita rescued Johannes Forsell instead of her? That was inconsistent with what he had read of the sequence of events.

Klara Engelman and Johannes Forsell had been in two different places on the mountain, and Engelman was probably already dead by the time Forsell got into difficulties. And yet . . . had something different happened which needed to be hushed up? It could be, and it could also be nonsense. But he definitely got a boost from the feeling that he could forget about his holiday; now he was more determined than ever to get to the bottom of the story. He immediately sent a text to Lisbeth:

```
<Why do you always have to be so bloody
clever??>
```

CHAPTER 21

August 27

Paulina Müller was sitting in pyjamas on her bed in the room where she had spent her teenage years, in Bogenhausen in Munich. She was talking on the telephone and drinking hot chocolate. Her mother had been running around looking after her as if she were ten again and, all things considered, life could be worse.

That is what she wanted, to be a child again, and to have no responsibilities. She wanted to be able to cry her eyes out. What is more, she had been wrong. Her parents had known all too well what Thomas Müller was about. There had been not the slightest disbelief in their eyes when she told them what he had done to her. But now she had locked her bedroom door, saying that she did not want to be disturbed for the moment.

"So you have no idea who this woman could be," Chief

Inspector Jensen said on the phone, sounding as if she did not believe one word of what Paulina was telling her.

Not only had it been instantly obvious to Paulina who the woman with the iron was. She even saw some kind of dark logic in it, and was terrified that somehow she had sanctioned what had happened. Countless times during the trip home she had said: "I can't see him again, I just can't. I'd rather die."

"No," she said. "It doesn't sound like anyone I know."

"Your husband told me that you'd met a woman and fallen in love," Jensen said.

"I only wrote that to annoy him."

"Yet he got the impression that there was some kind of emotional connection between the perpetrator and you. It even seemed as if the message was all about you. Your husband had to swear never to bother you again."

"That's odd."

"Is it really so strange? The neighbours have said you were wearing a bandage on your arm the last few days before you left. That you told them you'd burned yourself with the iron."

"That's correct."

"Not everybody believed you, Paulina. They heard screams from your apartment. Screams and the sound of people fighting."

She hesitated before answering.

"Is that really so?" she said.

"So maybe it was Thomas who burned you?"

"Maybe."

"You'll understand, then, that we suspect this may be an act of revenge—by someone who's close to you."

"I don't know."

"You don't know . . ."

That is how it went on, back and forth, until Jensen's tone suddenly changed and she said:

"By the way . . ."

"Yes?"

"I don't think you need to worry about him."

"What do you mean?"

"Your husband seems terrified of this woman. I think he'll be staying away from you."

Paulina hesitated, then said: "Is that all?"

"For the time being, yes."

"Well, I suppose I should be saying thank you, then."

"To whom?"

"I don't know," she said, adding—because it seemed like the right thing to say—that she hoped Thomas would be better soon.

She certainly did not mean a word of it, and as she was sitting there on her bed after hanging up, trying to absorb the information, her mobile rang again. It was a divorce lawyer called Stephanie Erdmann. Paulina had read about her in the newspapers. Erdmann wanted to represent her, and she said Paulina did not have to worry about paying her fees. That had already been taken care of.

Inspector Modig met Bublanski in the corridor of police headquarters and was shaking her head. He guessed that meant they had found no trace of Nima Rita in the county council registers either. But they had at least been given permission to search, and that alone had been a minor victory, given that there had been no shortage of obstructions. Their contact with military intelligence had so far consisted of one-way communication only, and he was growing increasingly irritated. He gave Modig a meaningful look and said:

"We may have a suspect."

"We may?"

"But no name, hardly even a description."

"And you call that a suspect?"

"Well, let's call it a lead."

He told her about the man Heikki Järvinen had seen from where he was standing on Norra Bantorget, some time between one and two on the morning of Saturday, August 15, who may have given Nima Rita a bottle of moonshine.

Modig was taking notes as they walked into his office and sat down opposite each other, at first in silence. Bublanski was shifting in his chair. He was trying to pin down something that was stirring in his subconscious.

"So there are no indications to suggest that he's used our health-care system?" he said.

"Not so far," she said. "But I haven't given up. He could have registered under a different name, don't you think? We've applied for a court order to be allowed to conduct a broader search based on his physical characteristics."

"Do we have any idea how long he was seen around the city?"

"It's always tricky when you're dealing with people's perception of time, but there's nothing to suggest he was in the neighbourhood for more than a couple of weeks."

"Could he have come from another part of the city, or from another town?"

"I don't think so. That's my gut feeling."

Bublanski leaned back in his chair and looked out of the window towards Bergsgatan, and in an instant it became clear to him what he had been looking for.

"The South Wing," he said.

"What?"

"The closed psychiatric unit at Södra Flygeln—the South Wing. I think he may have been committed there."

"What makes you say so?"

"It fits. It's exactly the sort of place you'd put someone you wanted to hide. The South Wing doesn't even report to the county council. It's an independent foundation and I know from old that there's a working relationship between the military authorities and the clinic. Do you remember Andersson, that crazy UN soldier from Congo who attacked people in the city? He was a patient there."

"I do remember him," Modig said. "But this sounds like a bit of a long shot to me."

"I haven't finished yet."

"In that case, Chief Inspector, please continue."

"According to Järvinen, Nima said that he had climbed down from a mountain to get away, down to a lake, and that tallies too, doesn't it? The South Wing is in a rather dramatic position on the edge of a cliff, above Årstaviken Bay. Besides, it's not that far from Mariatorget."

"Good thinking," Modig said.

"It may just be a wild guess."

"I'll check it out right away, in case."

"Excellent, although . . ."

"What?"

"It still wouldn't explain how Nima Rita turned up in Sweden and managed to get through all the passport checks without having his name registered."

"No, it wouldn't," Modig said. "But it's something to be getting on with."

"And it would also be a useful start if we could talk to Rebecka Forsell, although it seems we're not allowed to do that either."

"No," she said, looking at him thoughtfully.

"What is it?"

"There's supposed to be another woman in Stockholm, someone who knew Nima Rita and Klara Engelman."

"Who's that?"

Modig told him.

Catrin Lindås was walking along Götgatan and tried again to call Blomkvist, but he was still not answering, infuriatingly, even though sometimes his line was busy. What did she care? She had more important things to think about. She had just finished recording her podcast—a discussion about the media campaign against Forsell with Alicia Frankel, the Minister of Culture, and Jörgen Vrigstad, professor of journalism—but it had not made her any more relaxed. She felt off kilter, as she often did after a recording session.

There was always some retort or question which niggled at her, and now she worried that she might have taken too

tough a line, or been as partisan as the media she was criti-
cizing; that she had demanded nuance from others without
living up to that herself. But then she never shrank from
being self-critical, and she was well aware that the hyste-
ria over Forsell had got under her skin. Maybe it was more
about her than about him.

She knew only too well how such hatred and lies could
destroy a person and, although she had never considered
taking her own life, she did sometimes lose her footing and
self-harm—just as she had when she was a teenager—by
cutting herself. She had felt out of sorts ever since she woke
up at dawn that day and prepared for her recording, as if
something dark from the past were trying to come back. But
she dismissed it. Götgatan was full of people. There was a
group of day-care children milling about with balloons on
the pavement in front of her, and she turned into Bonde-
gatan and found her way to Nytorget, where she breathed a
little easier.

Nytorget was considered one of the most stylish addresses
in Söder and, although to some it was almost a dirty word,
it was a synonym for the in-crowd among the media elite.
She felt safe in the neighbourhood, as if she had found both
a home and place of refuge. It was true that she had over-
mortgaged herself in buying the apartment. But since her
programme had become such a success—it was Sweden's
most-listened-to media podcast—she felt reasonably secure,
and could in any case always sell the place and move to the
suburbs if necessary. She never doubted that everything
could be taken away from her at a moment's notice.

She stepped up her pace. Were those footsteps behind

her? No, she was just imagining it, silly old fears. Yet she wanted to get home as quickly as possible. She wanted to forget the world and lose herself in a romantic comedy, or anything that was not part of her own life.

Blomkvist was sitting on a balcony in Östermalm, interviewing the woman Modig had spoken about. He had come from Kungliga Biblioteket, the National Library, where he had spent the whole day reading. He was now beginning to see the chain of events more clearly, or at least where there were gaps and what else he needed to find out.

He had therefore invited himself to Elin's home on Jungfrugatan. She was now thirty-nine years old, an elegant woman with distinctive features, very slim and somewhat distant. Felke was her married name, but in 2008 she had been called Malmgård and she was quite a celebrity in the fitness world—with her own advice column in *Aftonbladet*—and had been a member of the Everest expedition led by the American, Greg Dolson.

Dolson's group made their summit bid on the same day as Viktor Grankin's climbers: May 13. During their acclimatization period, the two expeditions had lived side by side at Base Camp, and Elin had grown close to her countrymen Johannes Forsell and Svante Lindberg. She had also made friends with Klara Engelman.

"Thanks for agreeing to see me," Blomkvist said.

"It's not a problem, but as you can imagine I'm rather tired of this story. I've given almost two hundred talks about it."

"Sounds like good money to me," he said.

"There was a financial crisis then too, if you recall, so it's never been that lucrative."

"I'm sorry to hear that. But tell me about Klara Engelman. I know she and Grankin were an item, so there's no need to tiptoe around that."

"Are you going to quote me?"

"Not if you don't want me to. I only need to understand what happened."

"OK. They did have an affair. But they were discreet about it. Even at Base Camp not many people knew about it."

"But you did?"

"Because Klara told me."

"Isn't it a bit odd that Klara was a member of Viktor Grankin's expedition? With all her money and connections, why didn't she choose one of the American leaders, Dolson, for example, who was better known?"

"Grankin had a good reputation too, but there was also a link of sorts between Viktor and Stan Engelman. They knew each other somehow."

"Yet Grankin went after his wife?"

"Yes, that must have been unbearable for Stan."

"I read that you thought Klara had been unhappy at first, when she was at Base Camp?"

"No, I didn't," she said. "I saw her as the ultimate stuck-up bitch. But then gradually I came to realize how sad she was and understood that, for her, the whole Everest adventure was about freedom. She hoped it would give her the courage to get a divorce. One evening, when we were drinking wine in her tent, she told me she'd got herself a lawyer."

"Charles Mesterton, right?"

"Maybe, I don't remember his name. And she'd also been in touch with a publisher. She said she wanted to write not only about climbing the mountain but also about Stan's affairs with prostitutes and porn stars, and all his criminal contacts."

"You would have expected Engelman to feel threatened by that."

"I find that difficult to imagine. If Klara had one lawyer, then he had twenty, and I know she was scared. 'He's going to destroy me,' she said."

"But then something happened."

"Our hero set his sights on her."

"Grankin."

"Precisely."

"How did he do it?"

"I have no idea. But it was easy to be charmed by Viktor. He exuded such wonderful calm in the face of any practical difficulties. Just one look at him and we all felt: *Viktor will fix it.* He had a big, bear-like presence and dismissed all our worries with a glorious laugh. I remember envying the other group, I wished we had him as our leader too."

"And Klara fell for him."

"Hook, line and sinker."

"Why, do you suppose?"

"Afterwards I wondered if it wasn't something to do with Stan. I think Klara imagined that she could defeat her husband if she had Viktor by her side. He looked as if he could stand in a hail of bullets and simply smile."

"But then something changed."

"Yes. Even Viktor began to seem nervous, and that threw us all. It was a bit like, you know, when the flight attendant suddenly starts to look worried halfway through the flight. Then you really do begin to think that the plane is going to go down."

"What do you think had happened?"

"I've no idea. It's possible he was beginning to worry about his little escapade. Realized that Stan wasn't to be trifled with, and that there would be consequences, and to be honest . . ."

"Yes?"

"He was right to worry. I was so young at the time, and I thought the romance was pretty cool. It was as if the world's biggest secret had been entrusted to me. But with hindsight I realize it was bloody irresponsible. I'm not thinking so much about Stan or about Viktor's wife, but the climbers on the expedition. Viktor was supposed to look after all of them and not favour anybody. He let them down by becoming so fixated on Klara, and I think that's one of the reasons it all went horribly wrong. He wanted to get her up onto the summit, come what may."

"He should have sent her down."

"Definitely, but he couldn't bring himself to do it. Not just because she had such huge PR value. He was also upset that she had had to take all that crap in the press. He wanted to show the world she could do it."

"There's some suggestion that Grankin wasn't really himself during the climb up from Camp Four?"

"I've heard that too. Maybe he just exhausted himself trying to keep the group together."

"How did he get on with Nima Rita?"

"Viktor had tremendous respect for him."

"And what about the relationship between Klara and Nima?"

"Different . . . it was a bit special. They weren't on the same planet."

"Did she treat him badly?"

"He was very superstitious, you see."

"Did she tease him about it?"

"A bit, maybe, but I don't think that bothered him. He just got on with his job. It was something totally different that destroyed their relationship."

"And what was that . . . ?"

"He had a wife."

"Luna."

"That's it, her name was Luna. She meant everything to him, and I honestly think you could have said anything you liked to him. Treated him like dirt, as if he didn't exist. He didn't care. But one bad word about his wife and he became like thunder. One morning Luna came up to Base Camp with fresh bread and cheese, and mangoes and lychees and all sorts of other things in a decorated basket. She went around the tents, handing things out, and faces lit up and everyone thanked her. But as she was walking past Klara's tent she tripped over a pair of crampons, I think, or a handbag or something else that Klara definitely didn't need up there. Everything flew all over the gravel and Luna grazed her hands. There was actually no great drama, but Klara was sitting right there and instead of helping she just snapped,

'Look where you're going,' and made a fuss. Basically she behaved like a stupid prima donna, and Nima was about to explode, I could see. I was afraid that he would lose his temper. But before anything could happen, Forsell appeared and helped Luna to her feet again and picked up the bread and fruit."

"So Forsell was friendly with them?"

"He was friendly with everyone. Have you met him? Before everyone started to hate him, that is."

"I interviewed him just when he'd been made Minister of Defence."

"In that case you certainly won't get what's going on now. At that time, you see, everybody loved him. He was like a whirlwind. He stormed ahead, giving his thumbs-up sign, and he never stopped smiling. But you could be right, he may have had a particular relationship with Nima. He kept saying 'Let me bow to the mountain legend,' that sort of stuff, and would exclaim: 'What a wife you have! What a beautiful woman,' and of course that delighted Nima."

"Did Nima then reciprocate in any way?"

"How do you mean?"

Mikael did not know how to put it, nor did he want to make any baseless accusations.

"Is it conceivable that Nima might have helped Forsell on the mountain, at the expense of Klara Engelman?"

Elin gave him a bewildered look.

"How on earth would that have worked?" she said. "Nima was with Viktor and Klara, wasn't he, and Svante and Johannes went on ahead towards the summit on their own."

"I know. But later? What happened then? It says every-where that Klara was beyond rescue. But was she really?" he said, and then something unexpected happened.

Elin lost her temper.

"Too bloody right she was," she said. "I get so fed up with this. A bunch of idiots who've never been anywhere near those altitudes, they think they know it all. But I can tell you . . ." She was almost lost for words. "Do you have the slightest idea what it's like up there? You're barely able to think, and it's excruciatingly cold and tough, and if you're really lucky you've just about got enough strength to look after yourself. To take one step at a time. No-one, not even a Nima Rita, can get a person down when they're lying lifeless in the snow with their face frozen solid at twenty-seven thou-sand feet, and that's how she was. We saw them ourselves on the way down, you know that, don't you? She and Viktor with their arms around each other in the snow."

"I do know."

"And there was nothing to be done. Not a hope in hell of anybody being able to help her. She was dead."

"I'm just double-checking the facts," he said.

"Bullshit, I don't believe that for one second. You were trying to imply something, weren't you? You're out to get Forsell, just like everyone else."

I'm not, he wanted to shout, *I'm not!* But instead he took a deep breath.

"I apologize," he said. "I just think . . ."

"*What* do you think?"

"That there's something about this story that doesn't add up."

"Like what?"

"Like the fact that later Klara was no longer lying with Viktor. I know that wasn't discovered until the following year, and that any number of things could have happened in between, avalanches and terrible storms. But still—"

"Still what?"

"I don't like what I've read of Svante Lindberg's account either. I can't help feeling that he hasn't told the whole story."

Elin calmed down and looked out at the garden.

"I'm inclined to agree with you," she said.

"And why would you say so?"

"Because Svante was the big riddle at Base Camp."

CHAPTER 22

August 27

Catrin Lindås was curled up with her cat on the sofa at home on Nytorget, looking at her mobile. She had made far too many attempts to contact Blomkvist, and was both furious and embarrassed about it. She had laid herself bare, and all she had got back was one cryptic text message:

```
<I think the beggar said 'Mamsahib' to you,
as in Mamsahib Klara Engelman. Anything
else you remember? Even one word could be
helpful>
```

Mamsahib, she thought, and looked it up: "A respectful form of address for a white woman in colonial India, usually written Memsahib." That may well have been what he said, but who cared anyway, and who was Klara Engelman?

She couldn't be less interested, and she couldn't give a damn about Blomkvist either for that matter. Surely he

could have added a polite little note, like "Hi, how's things?"
But no, and certainly not an "I miss you," as she herself had
unaccountably written in a moment of weakness. He could
get stuffed.

She went into the kitchen to find something to eat. But
she realized she wasn't hungry after all, so she slammed the
refrigerator door shut and took an apple from a bowl on the
dining table, which she didn't eat either, maybe because at
that very moment a bell went off in the recesses of her mind.
Klara Engelman? It did sound familiar. Even glamorous in
some way, and she googled it. Then the whole story came
back to her.

She had read all about it in *Vanity Fair* some time ago,
but now she could only find some images of Klara Engelman, a series of posed photographs from one of the Everest
base camps, and also pictures of Viktor Grankin, the guide
who died with her. Klara was good-looking in a slightly
vulgar way, but she also seemed sad, or as if she were pretending to look happy, as if she needed to keep smiling to
ward off depression, whereas Grankin seemed . . . well, what
about him?

He was an engineer and also a professional climber,
another article said, and a former consultant to adventure
travel companies, but she thought he looked more like a soldier, special forces, especially when she saw him in another
photograph from Everest, standing next to . . . "Johannes
Forsell!" she exclaimed aloud, and even forgot to be angry
with Blomkvist. She wrote back:

<What have you found out?>

. . .

A moment earlier, Elin Felke had been indignant and angry. Now she looked uncertain and thoughtful, as if she had gone from one extreme to the other in no time at all.

"Well, my God, what can I say about Svante? What incredible self-confidence. Crazy, really. He could persuade people to do just about anything. We all even began to drink his bloody blueberry soup in the camp. He should have been a salesman or something. But I suspect that in the end things didn't turn out quite as he wanted on Everest."

"How's that?"

"Svante had also worked out that Viktor and Klara had something going, and that seemed to trouble him in some way. I can't explain it, it just felt like that. Maybe he was jealous, what do I know, and I think Viktor noticed. I even think it was one of the reasons he became more and more nervous."

"Why should it have affected him?"

"Something did rattle him, as I said. From having been the solid rock in camp he became increasingly fearful, and sometimes I wondered if he wasn't a little scared of Svante."

"Why would he be, do you think?"

"If I were to guess, I'd say he was frightened that Svante would tell Stan Engelman."

"Was there anything to suggest they were in contact?"

"Maybe not, but . . . there was something insidious about Svante, that became ever clearer to me, and occasionally he would speak about Engelman as if he knew him. The way he called him 'Stan' made it sound somehow . . . familiar. But I may be imagining it. It's hard to remember things like that now. All I know is that even Svante appeared less and less cocky towards the end. So he was treading very carefully indeed."

"You mean he too was nervous about something?"

"We all were."

"That's natural, in those circumstances," Blomkvist said. "But you referred to Lindberg as the big riddle at Base Camp."

"That's exactly how it was. Most of the time he was self-assurance personified, yet he could also be hesitant and suspicious. Extravagant and generous, but also mean. He could flatter the shirt off your back one moment, needle you the next."

"What about his relationship with Forsell?"

"Pretty much the same, I think. There was a part of him that loved Johannes."

"But another . . ."

". . . that kept tabs on him. Tried to get some hold over him."

"Why do you say that?"

"I'm not sure. But I guess I'm just influenced by all this crap in the media against Forsell."

"Influenced in what way?"

"It all seems so unfair, and sometimes I wonder if Johannes isn't paying for something that Svante did. But now I really am being indiscreet."

Blomkvist gave a careful laugh.

"Maybe you are. But I'm glad you're helping me to think,

and you don't have to worry about my story, as I said. I too love to speculate, but in my articles I have no choice but to stick to the facts."

"Sad."

"Ha, yes, perhaps. It's a bit like mountaineering, I imagine. You can't just take a guess at where the next rock ledge is going to be. You have to *know*. Otherwise you're in trouble."

"True."

He glanced at his mobile and saw that Catrin had replied. She had answered with another question, and that was as good a reason as any to end the conversation. He said a friendly goodbye to Elin Felke and walked out into the street with his suitcase, but without any clue where to go.

Fredrika Nyman got back to her house in Trångsund late in the afternoon, and saw that she had got a long e-mail from a psychiatrist called Farzad Mansoor, senior physician at the closed psychiatric unit at the South Wing. Both she and the police had sent him detailed reports along with an enquiry as to whether Nima Rita had been a patient there.

Nyman had not been expecting much to come of it. The Sherpa had been in too shabby a state to have been institutionalized, she thought, even if the traces of antipsychotic drugs in his blood suggested the opposite. She was therefore eager to see what Dr. Mansoor had written—and not only because of the investigation.

Dr. Mansoor had spoken in a soft, pleasant tone on the telephone, and she liked what she saw of him online, the glint in his eye and the warmth of his smile, and even his interest in gliding, which he had written about on Facebook. But the e-mail he had sent to her and Chief Inspector Bublanski was a passionate statement, seething with anger, a clear attempt to justify the clinic's treatment of the Sherpa.

> <We are shocked and saddened, and let me say
> right away that the event occurred at the
> most unfortunate time of the year, the only
> week in July when neither I nor Henrik Alm,
> the head of our clinic, was present. Sadly
> the case fell between the cracks.>

Which event? Which case? Which cracks? she wanted to know, as if cross that her mild-mannered glider pilot had so completely lost his composure. But after skimming the e-mail, which was long and meandering, she gathered that Nima Rita had indeed been a patient at the South Wing, but under another name, and that he had absconded during the evening of July 27 that year. Initially his absence had not been reported, for several good reasons, most of them to do with the people in charge not having been on duty. But there had also been a special classified procedure for this patient, which had been ignored—maybe out of fear, or guilt.

Farzad Mansoor wrote:

> <As you may know, Henrik and I took over
> the running of the South Wing in March this
> year. At the time, we discovered a number
> of unsatisfactory situations, including the

fact that several patients had been kept
locked up and subjected to coercive measures which, in our view, had had no ben-
eficial effects. One patient was a man who
had been admitted in October 2017, under
the name of Nihar Rawal. He had no identity documents but, according to his medical records, he was fifty-four years old
and suffering from paranoid schizophrenia
and neurological damage that was hard to
assess. He was apparently from Nepal, from
the mountain regions.>

Nyman looked at her daughters, who were as usual sitting on the sofa with their mobiles. Dr. Mansoor went on:

<The patient had received no dental care,
nor had he been seen by a cardiologist,
which should have happened as a matter of
priority. Instead he had been heavily medi-
cated and at times even been strapped down.
This was totally unjustified. There was
information—which I am unfortunately not at
liberty to disclose—suggesting that he was
vulnerable to threats. Perhaps we did not
fully appreciate how serious this was, and
we are in no way denying our responsibility.
But you have to understand that, for Henrik
and myself, the patient's best interests
were of paramount importance. We wanted to

show him a little human kindness and try to build some trust. The patient was disoriented. He never really knew where he was. At the same time, there was a rage inside him, a fury at the fact that no-one had wanted to listen to his story, and so we markedly reduced his medication and started therapy. I'm afraid this was not particularly successful either.

His delusions were too severe and, however keen he was to talk, he had developed a strong suspicion of our entire unit. But we were at least able to rectify some misunderstandings. We began to call him Nima, for example, and that was important to him. We addressed him as Sirdar Nima.

We could see that he had an obsessive fixation about his late wife, Luna. In the evenings he would walk through the hospital corridors, calling her name. He said he could hear her cries for help. He would also launch into wild, incomprehensible outbursts where he talked about a Madam—or a Mam Sahib. Both Henrik and I took this to be another way in which he referred to his wife, for there were strong similarities between the stories. But now that we read your reports, we suspect that we're not dealing with one trauma, as we thought, but two.

You may think us incompetent for not having been able to come up with a clearer
picture of his case. But we were working
in difficult circumstances from the start. I
think it is fair to say that we did make some
progress. At the end of June he was given
back his down jacket, which he had been asking for, and that seemed to make him feel
secure. It's true that he was always asking
for alcohol—probably because he was getting
fewer sedatives—but there were some nights
when he no longer seemed to hear voices, and
his night terrors also improved.

I recall that both Henrik and I left for
our respective holidays feeling reasonably
confident. We felt that we were on the right
track, both with him and the clinic generally.>

I'm sure you did, Nyman thought. But it still led to the death
of Nima Rita, and it was absolutely clear that the manage-
ment at the clinic had underestimated his determination
to get away. It was reasonable for him to be allowed on the
terrace. But it must have been against all the rules that he
should be there alone, with no staff present.

During the afternoon of July 27, he disappeared. The evidence was a small scrap of material torn from his trousers
when he squeezed through the narrow gap between the roof
and the terrace's tall railings. After that we can only assume
he climbed down the steep cliffs beyond and vanished from

Årstaviken. He must then have found somewhere to live in the area around Mariatorget.

Yet the most shocking thing of all was that no-one reported it until Henrik Alm returned from his holiday on August 4, and even then no-one alerted the police because, as Dr. Mansoor also wrote, "It had been very clearly laid down that any new developments and incidents involving the patient were to be reported to the stipulated contact person." What a load of gobbledygook, she thought, it positively reeked of classified information. In any event, it was patently obvious that something significant was being withheld. Once she had done a little more research on the South Wing clinic, and having had a long conversation with Chief Inspector Bublanski, she did precisely the same as before.

She rang Blomkvist.

Blomkvist had not yet answered Catrin's question. He was having a Guinness at the Tudor Arms on Grevgatan and trying to draw up a plan of action. He should get hold of Svante Lindberg. Blomkvist was increasingly convinced that he was a key person in the drama. But something told him that before he did so he needed more to go on. Forsell himself would be the best source, but Blomkvist had no idea what sort of condition he was in, and in any event he could not get hold of either him, or Rebecka Forsell, or even his press secretary, Niklas Keller. In the end he decided to take a break to organize somewhere to stay. He had to find a place where he could work and sleep and not endanger his host. Then he could continue. But just then his mobile rang.

It was Nyman, saying that she had discovered something interesting. He asked her to hang up, and sent a text message telling her to install the Signal app, which would allow them to talk on a secure line.

<Can't. Don't understand. Hate apps> she answered. <They drive me nuts>

<Don't you have teenagers in the house who
spend all their time on their mobiles?>
<Is the Pope a Catholic?>
<Get them to do it for you. Tell them to
help Mamma become an undercover detective>
<Ha! I'll give it a go> she wrote.

There was a pause and he sipped his Guinness and kept an eye on the street where two women passed with prams, and he let his thoughts drift until he got a text in a new language.

<R u Mikael Blomkvist, I mean 4 real?>

He decided to show what a techie he was and sent a selfie of him giving a thumbs-up.

<Cool>
<Actually not that cool>
<And Mamma's gonna be a secret agent?>

<For sure> he answered, and got a smiley back. Maybe he wasn't so bad at this after all, he thought, careful not to send a red heart this time. That would land him on the *Expressen* breaking-news posters. Instead he began to explain to the girl, the one called Amanda, what she needed to do. Fifteen minutes later, Nyman called on the app, and he went out into the street to speak to her.

"I've just gone way up in my daughters' estimation," she said.

"Well, at least I've done one useful thing today. What did you want to tell me?"

Nyman poured herself a glass of white wine and told Blomkvist what she had discovered.

"So nobody has yet said how or why he ended up there in the first place," he said.

"There's some kind of confidentiality around the whole thing. Military secrecy, I think."

"As if it had something to do with national security?"

"I don't know."

"Or else it's designed to protect certain individuals, rather than the country."

"It could be that," Nyman said.

"Isn't it all a bit strange?"

"Certainly is," she answered slowly, "and a huge scandal too. He seems to have been locked up in a small room there for several years, without even seeing a dentist, or anybody else as far as I can tell. I'm not sure if you know the place."

"I read Gustav Stavsjö's manifesto once upon a time," he said.

"It all sounded great, didn't it? The sickest of us would get the best care. The dignity of a society is defined by the way it looks after its weakest members."

"He felt very strongly about his cause, didn't he?"

"But those were different times, and his faith in dialogue

and therapy was naïve, at least for patients with such severe symptoms, and psychiatry generally was also moving in a different direction, wasn't it, towards more medication and coercive measures. The clinic, which is so beautifully located by the water and looks like some sort of mansion, became more and more of a depository for hopeless cases, especially refugees traumatized by war, and it grew increasingly difficult to recruit people to work there. The clinic got a lousy reputation."

"So I've gathered."

"There were ambitious plans to close it down and integrate the patients into the county council's health-care system. But the sons who ran the Gustav Stavsjö Foundation managed to prevent it by persuading Professor Alm, who had a good reputation, to take over. He began to modernize the clinic and rebuild the organization, and it was in that context that he and his colleague became aware of Nima, or Nihar Rawal, as he was known in his medical records."

"At least he got to keep his initials."

"He did. But there's something fishy about it. There was a particular contact person for him, whose identity the clinic has refused to disclose, who was supposed to have direct access to all information about him before anyone else. I don't know, but I got the impression it's a big name, someone important who the staff were in awe of."

"Like Undersecretary Lindberg, for example."

"Or Defence Minister Forsell."

"It's hopeless."

"What do you mean?"

"There are too many questions."

"Far too many."

"Did you find out whether Nima named Forsell during the clinic's attempts at therapy with him?" he said.

"No, I don't know that either. But Bublanski may be right in thinking that his obsession with Forsell began after he saw him on TV in the shop on Hornsgatan. He probably also got hold of your number while he was there."

"I'll have to look into that."

"Good luck," she said.

"Thanks, I'm going to need it."

"Can I ask you something totally different?" she said.

"Sure."

"That DNA researcher you put me in touch with, who was it?"

"Just someone I know," he said.

"She's got one hell of an attitude."

"There's a good reason for that," he said.

Then they said goodbye and good night, and Nyman was left sitting alone, looking out at the lake and the swans, which she could just make out over on the far side.

CHAPTER 23

August 27

Salander got an encrypted text from Blomkvist. She was busy with other things, so she ignored it. Over the course of the day she had not only acquired a new weapon—a Beretta 87 Cheetah like the one she had had in Moscow—and an IMSI-catcher; she had also collected her motorcycle, her Kawasaki Ninja, from the garage on Fiskargatan.

She had exchanged her suit for a hoodie, jeans and sneakers, and was now in a room at the Nobis Hotel in Norrmalmstorg, not far from Strandvägen, where she was keeping an eye on a bank of surveillance cameras and trying to work up the same thirst for revenge she had felt earlier in the summer. But the past kept intruding. And she had no time for the old.

She had to be focused, the more so now that Galinov was around. He was ruthless. Not that she knew all that much about him beyond the rumours buzzing about on the dark web. But some things had been confirmed to her, and that was more than enough: Galinov had been connected to her father, was a disciple of his and an ally at the GRU.

He had often worked undercover with rebel movements and with arms smugglers. He was said to possess an indefinite quality: He blended in everywhere, not because he was so good at adapting himself or had any acting talent. On the contrary, he was always his own man, and that apparently inspired trust.

He was fluent, it was said, in a number of languages, and was receptive and erudite. Because of his height and bearing, and his distinguished features, he took over every room he entered, and that too spoke in his favour. Nobody could believe that the Russians would have used a person with such a noticeable profile as a spy and an infiltrator, and he was unwavering in his loyalty. He found it just as easy to be brutal as to be tender and fatherly.

He became best friends with people whom he later had no difficulty in torturing. His days as an intelligence officer or undercover agent were long past, and nowadays he would simply call himself a businessman or an interpreter, euphemisms of sorts for gangster. But although he was heavily involved with the Zvezda Bratva, the "Star Mob" crime syndicate, he often worked with Camilla, and was extremely useful to her. His name alone was an asset.

The one thing that really worried Salander was Galinov's network of contacts and his links to the GRU. He had resources behind him which would sooner or later encircle her, so she could no longer afford to be indecisive. Standing by her hotel window facing Norrmalmstorg, she was now

set to do what she had been preparing for all day: Put them
under pressure. Try to force them to make a mistake. But
first she glanced at Blomkvist's message:

```
<Worried about you. I know you hate me say-
ing it. But I think you should ask the
police for protection. Bublanski will take
care of it. I've had a word with him. Btw,
Nima Rita was admitted to the South Wing
psychiatric clinic under a false name. I get
the feeling that the military were party to
that decision.>
```

She did not answer. She forgot the message in a second
and put her weapon in her grey shoulder bag. She then
pulled her hood over her head, put on sunglasses and left
the room, taking the lift down and striding purposefully into
the square.

It looked as if it was going to cloud over. There were
lots of people out and about and the open-air restaurants
and shops were full. She turned right into Smålandsgatan,
emerging into Birger Jarlsgatan and dropping down into
Östermalmstorg station, where she took the tunnelbana to
Södermalm.

Rebecka Forsell was sitting at her husband's bedside at the
Karolinska hospital when Blomkvist called again. She was
just about to answer when Johannes made a sudden movement, as if he were having a nightmare, so she stroked his

hair and let her mobile ring. Three soldiers were sitting outside the room, looking in at her through the glass in the door.

She was very conscious of being under surveillance. It intruded on her need to watch over him and she resented that. How could they treat them like this? They had even frisked Johannes's mother. It was scandalous, and the worst was Klas Berg, head of Must, and of course also Svante Lindberg, who had claimed to be so goddamn sympathetic and upset.

He had come with chocolates and flowers and tears in his eyes, and he commiserated and hugged her. But he had not fooled her. He was sweating too much, and his eyes were darting back and forth. At least twice he asked if Johannes had said anything out on Sandön he needed to know about, and all she had wanted to do was scream: "What are you hiding from me?" But she said nothing. She just thanked him for his support, then told him she couldn't face visitors and asked him to leave. He left reluctantly, and that was lucky because shortly afterwards Johannes came to, and told her he was sorry. His apology seemed sincere, and they talked briefly about their sons and how he was feeling, but when she asked, "Why, Johannes, why?" he gave no answer.

Perhaps he was not strong enough. Perhaps he simply wanted to escape from everything. Now he was asleep again, or just dozing. He looked anything but relaxed, however, and she took his hand. It was then that a text came through from Blomkvist. He apologized for disturbing her but said that they needed to talk, either on an encrypted line or face-to-face, in private. But she couldn't, not now, and she looked in despair at her husband who was murmuring in his dreams.

. . .

Forsell was back on Everest. In his mind he was staggering ahead in the lashing snowstorm, it was cold and unbearable, and he could hardly think any longer. He just tramped on and could hear his crampons creak, and the thunder in the skies and the wide-open spaces. He wondered how much longer he could take it.

Often he was conscious only of his rasping breath in the oxygen mask and the indistinct shape of Lindberg next to him, and sometimes not even of that.

At times he was surrounded by darkness, maybe because in those moments he was walking with his eyes shut, and if there had been a precipice he would have stepped right into it and fallen without even a scream or a care. Then even the jet streams seemed to quiet. He was heading into a black and soundless oblivion, and yet not long before he had recalled his father standing by the ski tracks, yelling encouragement: *There's more in you, my boy. There's more in you.* For a long time, when fear had him in its claws, he had clung to those words. If you dug deep enough, there was always a little extra. But no longer.

Now there was nothing left, and he looked down at the snow swirling around his boots and thought that this might be the moment he would finally collapse, and that was when he heard the shouts, the wailing carried along by the winds, which at first sounded inhuman, as if the mountain itself were crying out its distress.

. . .

Johannes said something now, quite clearly, but Rebecka did not know if it was in his sleep or he was speaking to her.

"Can you hear?"

She heard only what she had been hearing all day, the roar from the highway outside, the hum of the hospital equipment and the steps and voices in the corridor, and she did not answer. She just wiped a drop of sweat from his forehead and straightened his hair. That made him open his eyes and she felt a sudden surge of hope and longing. *Talk to me,* she thought. *Tell me what happened.*

He looked at her with such fear in his eyes that it frightened her.

"Were you dreaming?" she said.

"It was those cries again."

"Cries?"

"On Everest."

In the past they had often discussed the events on the mountain. But she had no recollection of any cries, and she considered letting it go. She could tell by the look in his eyes that his thoughts were not entirely lucid.

"I don't really know what you mean," she said.

"I thought it was the storm, don't you remember? The winds which sounded almost human."

"No, darling, I don't. I was never with you up there. I was at Base Camp the whole time, you know that."

"But I must have told you."

She shook her head and wanted to change the subject, and not only because he seemed delirious. Her heart sank, as if she could tell there was something fateful about those cries.

"Shouldn't you rest a little?" she said.

"Then I thought they were wild dogs."

"What?"

"Wild dogs at twenty-six thousand feet. Imagine that."

"We can talk about Everest later," she said. "But first, Johannes, you must help me to understand. What made you run off like that?"

"When?"

"Just now, on Sandön. You swam out into the bay."

She saw from his look that it was coming back to him, and it was obvious at once that this did not make things any better. He seemed more at home with his wild dogs on Everest.

"Who pulled me out? Was it Erik?"

"It wasn't one of the bodyguards."

"So who was it?"

She wondered how he would take it. "It was Mikael Blomkvist."

"The writer?"

"The same."

"That's strange," he said, and it was indeed incredibly strange, but his reaction did not reflect that. He sounded listless and sad, and he looked down at his hands with an indifference that frightened her. She waited for him to come back with a question. But when it did come, there was no curiosity in his voice.

"How come?"

"He called when I was at my most hysterical. He said he was working on an article."

"About what?"

"You're never going to believe me," she said, although she suspected that he would believe her only too well.

Salander got off at Zinkensdamm station and walked along Ringvägen into Brännkyrkagatan, as the memories welled up once more. Maybe because she was back in the neighbourhood where she had lived as a child, or because her mind was alive again as she prepared a new operation.

She looked up at the sky. It had turned dark. It would probably start raining soon, just like in Moscow. The air felt heavy, as if a storm was brewing, and some way off she saw a young man on the pavement, doubled up as if he were being sick. She could see drunk people everywhere, maybe there was some kind of party going on. Perhaps it was pay day, or a public holiday.

She turned left up the steps and as she approached Blomkvist's home from Tavastgatan, slowly her focus returned, absolute and complete, and she registered every detail and figure around her. Yet . . . it was not what she was expecting to find. Had she been mistaken? There was nothing suspicious, only more drunks. But no, wait, over there by the crossroads . . .

It was nothing more than a back, the broad back of a man wearing a corduroy jacket. He held a book in his hand, and criminals did not usually wear corduroy jackets or read books. He was tall and slightly overweight, and there was something about him that put her on edge, his posture or the way he looked up, and she passed him unnoticed, giving him only the briefest glance. Immediately she saw that she had been right. The jacket and book had been no more than a pathetic disguise, a clumsy attempt to masquerade as a hipster from Söder, and she realized that she not only knew *what* he was. She even knew *who* he was.

His name was Conny Andersson, and not that long ago he had been a hanger-on, a gofer. Unsurprisingly he was not a major figure in the club. He had been given a shitty assignment: to stand and wait for some man who was probably not going to show up. Yet Salander knew he was no innocent for all that. He was more than six feet tall and a debt-collection enforcer, and she walked on with her head down, as if she had not seen him.

She then turned and scanned the other side of the street. There were two young drunks of about twenty wandering a little way off, and ahead of them a lady in her sixties, ambling along much too slowly, and that was not good. But Salander did not have time to wait. The minute Conny Andersson spotted her, she would be in trouble, so she carried calmly on, straight ahead.

Then she took a sharp turn to the right and went straight at him, and he looked up and fumbled for his gun. But that was as far as he got. She kneed him in the groin and, as his body folded, she headbutted him twice. He lost his balance, and at that moment she heard the lady call out:

"Hey, what are you doing?"

Salander had to ignore her. There was no time to reassure old ladies and she was reasonably sure that she would not dare to come closer. Besides, the woman could call the police all she wanted. They would never make it in time, not now that Salander hurled herself at Andersson so that he crashed onto the road. Quick as a flash she sat on top of him, took off her sunglasses and pulled her pistol out of the bag, pressing the muzzle against his Adam's apple. He looked up at her in terror.

"I'm going to kill you," she said.

He no longer seemed so hard after all and he mumbled something as she continued in her coldest voice:

"I'm going to kill you. I'm going to kill you and all the others in your shitty little club if you so much as lay a finger on Mikael Blomkvist. It's me you want, so come for me, no-one else. Do you hear?"

"I hear you," he said.

"Or actually . . . tell Sandström I don't care whether you touch Blomkvist or not. I'm going to get you all anyway. Until there's nothing left of you except your terrified girl-friends and wives."

There was no answer from Andersson, so she pressed the muzzle of her pistol harder against his throat.

"So what's it to be?"

"I'll tell him," Andersson stammered.

"Excellent. And by the way . . . there's a woman staring at us, so I'm not going to throw away your pistol or do some other shit. I'm just going to kick you in the head, and if you so much as reach for your gun I'm going to shoot you. Because it's like this you see . . ."

She frisked him quickly with her left hand and pulled his mobile out of his jeans, a new iPhone with face recognition.

". . . I'm going to get my message out anyway. Even if you happen to die."

She pushed her pistol up under his chin.

"So, Conny, let's have a nice big smile from you now."

She held the mobile over him and unlocked it, and in no time at all headbutted him again and took a photograph. Then she put her sunglasses back on and disappeared down towards Slussen and Gamla Stan, scrolling through Andersson's contacts list. There were a few names there which surprised her, a well-known actor, two politicians and an officer in the drugs squad who was presumably corrupt. But she didn't care about them.

She pulled out the names of the other members of Svavelsjö M.C. and sent off her picture of their buddy Andersson looking terrified and bewildered. Having copied the contents of his mobile she wrote:

```
<Your little friend has something to tell
you>
```

Then she threw his mobile into Riddarfjärden.

CHAPTER 24

August 27

Forsell wanted only to withdraw into his shell, into the shelter of his dreams and memories. But hearing Nima Rita's name mentioned in such stark relief, and the restrained anger in his wife's voice, he was brought abruptly back to reality.

"How can he just show up in Sweden, out of the blue? I thought he was dead."

"Who's been here to see me?" he said.

He could see that she was irritated by his attempt to change the subject.

"I've already told you," she said.

"I've forgotten."

"The boys, of course, and your mother. She's looking after them for the moment."

"How have they taken it all?"

"What can I say, Johannes? What do you expect me to say?"

"I'm sorry."

"Thank you," she said, and then she tried to compose herself, tried to become good old robust Becka again. But she was only half successful. Forsell glanced at the soldiers out in the corridor, with escape, evasion, threats, choices and risks fluttering like restless birds through his mind.

"I can't talk about Nima now," he said.

"Whatever you say."

She had to force herself to give him a loving smile, and again she smoothed his hair. He shrugged off her caress.

"So what will you talk about?"

"I don't know."

"At least you've managed to do one thing," she said.

"What's that?"

"Look around you. At all these flowers. We've only been able to accept some of them. All that hate has turned to love."

"I find that hard to believe."

She held out her mobile. "Go online and you'll see."

He waved vaguely, dismissively. "I bet they've been busy writing obituaries."

"No, it's good stuff—really."

"Has anyone come from Must?" he said.

"Svante came, and Klas and Sten Siegler, and a few others, so the answer I guess is yes a thousand times over. Why do you ask?"

Why did he ask?

He knew the answer perfectly well, of course they had been to see him, and he saw the suspicion in Becka's eyes. He remembered the feeling of that hand grabbing his hair deep in the water. And all of a sudden it hit him with unexpected force: He wanted to speak out, but he knew that would not be possible.

Their conversation was bound to be monitored and he thought it through, weighing the arguments for and against once more. He remembered his own desperate will to live as he was sinking through the currents.

"Do you have a pen and paper?" he said.

"What? Yes, I'm sure I have somewhere."

She dug around in her handbag and took out a ballpoint pen and a small yellow block of Post-it notes and gave them to him.

We have to get out of here, he wrote.

Rebecka read what he had written and cast a fearful look at the guards through the glass in the door. Luckily they seemed bored and absorbed by their mobiles, and she answered in a nervous scribble:

Now?

He replied:

Now. Disconnect me from the machines and leave your mobile and handbag, we'll pretend we're going down to the hospital shop.

Pretend?

We're leaving.

Are you crazy?

I want to tell you everything—and I can't here.

Tell me what?

Everything.

They had been writing quickly, taking turns with the same pen. Now Johannes hesitated and looked at her with the same sad and bewildered look as before, but it also showed a streak of what she had been missing for so long, his fighting spirit, and that made her feel more than just fear.

She had no intention of running away with him, still less of leaving the hospital with all the guards and soldiers, and the paranoia surrounding him. But it would be wonderful if he really did want to talk, and it would do him good to get some exercise. His pulse was higher than normal but stable, and he was strong. They would surely be able to sneak off and find a corner, somewhere they could talk and not be overheard.

At the same time she knew they would gain nothing if she simply unplugged him from his drip and the hospital equipment and they fled, so instead she wrote:

I'll call the staff and explain.

She rang the bell and he wrote:

We'll find a place where no-one will disturb us.

Stop it, she thought. *Just stop it.*

What are you running from? she wrote.

The people at Must.

Is it Svante?

He nodded, or at least she thought he nodded. She wanted to shout: *I knew it,* and when she wrote again her hand was shaking. Her heart was pounding and her mouth was dry.

Has he done something?

He neither answered nor nodded. He just looked out of

the window towards the motorway, and she took that as a yes. She wrote:

You have to report him.

He gave her a pitying look which said, *You don't under-stand.*

Or go to the media. Mikael Blomkvist just called. He's on your side.

"My side," he muttered, and pulled a face. He reached for the pen and scribbled a couple of illegible lines on the pad. She stared at the words.

Can't read, she wrote, even though she probably could, so he clarified:

Not sure that's a good side to be on.

That triggered a new urge for self-preservation, as if Johannes were distancing himself from her with those words. As if they were no longer an obvious couple, a *we*, but two people who no longer necessarily belonged together. She wondered if she should not be running from him instead.

She glanced at the guards outside the room and tried to come up with a plan. But just then she heard steps in the corridor and the doctor, the one with the red beard, came in and asked what they wanted. She said—it was all she could think of—that Johannes was feeling a little better now, and was strong enough to take a walk.

"We're going down to the shop to buy a newspaper and a book," she said in a voice which did not sound like her own, but which carried a surprising note of authority.

·   ·   ·

It was half past seven in the evening and Bublanski should have gone home long ago. But he was still in his office, staring into a young face brimming with a kind of angry idealism. He could see some people might find it irritating, but he actually liked the attitude, and maybe he had been the same at that age; had perhaps felt that the older generation was not taking life as seriously as it deserved to be taken. He gave the young woman a warm smile.

She smiled stiffly in return, and he suspected that humour was not her strongest suit, but that her fervour would certainly stand the world in good stead. She was twenty-five years old and her name was Else Sandberg. Her hair was cut in a bob and she wore round spectacles, and worked as a medical intern at St. Göran's hospital.

"Thanks for taking the time."

"Don't mention it," she said.

It was Modig who had found the woman, after getting a tip-off that the Sherpa had put up papers at the Södra station bus stop. She had then assigned colleagues to talk to pretty much everyone who regularly caught their bus from there.

"I understand you don't remember much, but every single thing you do recall would be valuable to us," he said.

"It was hard to read. There was very little space between the lines and basically it looked like paranoid delusion."

"The signs are that it was just that," he said. "But I'd be grateful if you could try to remember."

"It was very guilt-ridden."

Dear, sweet child, please don't try to interpret it for me, he thought.

"What did it say?"

"That he went up a mountain. 'One more time,' he wrote. But that he couldn't see. There was a snowstorm and he was in pain and freezing. He thought he was lost. But he heard cries that guided him."

"What sort of cries?"

"Cries of the dead, I think."

"What was that supposed to mean?"

"It was hard to understand, but he wrote that there were spirits accompanying him all the time, two spirits I think, one good and one evil, a little . . ."

She giggled, and Bublanski was delighted that Else Sandberg had suddenly revealed a human side.

"Like Captain Haddock in the Tintin books, you know? He has a devil and an angel hovering above his shoulders when he's longing for a drink."

"Exactly," he said. "That's a great metaphor."

"It didn't seem like a metaphor to me. I got the impression that for him it was real."

"I only meant to say that it sounded familiar. Good and evil voices whispering to me when I'm tempted by something." He looked embarrassed. "What did the evil spirit say?" he said.

"That he should leave her up there."

"Her?"

"Yes, I think that's what he wrote. It was a she, a madam, or a mam-something who'd been left on the mountain. But then there was something about the valley of rainbows, Rainbow Valley, where the dead hold out their hands and beg for food. It really was all very strange. Then it clearly said that Johannes Forsell appeared. Very weird. That's as far as I got, to be honest. The bus came, and there was some bloke arguing with the driver, and I had my mind on other things. In any case I'd already guessed by then that the man was a paranoid schizophrenic. He wrote that he never stopped hearing those cries in his head."

"You probably don't need to be a schizophrenic to feel like that."

"What do you mean?"

What was he trying to say now?

"I mean . . ." he said. "That I recognize that too. There are certain things you never get rid of. They gnaw and clamour inside you, year after year."

"Yes," she said, more hesitant now. "That's true."

"Can you hang on a moment while I do a quick search?"

Else Sandberg nodded and Bublanski logged onto his computer and put three words into Google. He turned the screen to face her.

"Do you see this?"

"That's awful," she said.

"Isn't it? It's Rainbow Valley on Mount Everest. I never knew anything about this world before. But I've been reading up on it these last few days, and I recognized it as soon as you mentioned it. Rainbow Valley's just a bit of slang of course. But it does come up quite a lot, and it's easy to see why. Have a look."

He pointed at the screen and wondered if he was being unnecessarily brutal. But he wanted her to understand how serious this was. Image after image showed dead climbers in the snow above twenty-six thousand feet, and even though many had been lying up there for years, maybe even decades, they still looked muscular and strong. They were frozen in time, and all were dressed in brightly coloured clothes— reds, greens, yellows and blues—and strewn around them were oxygen cylinders, remains of tents or Buddhist prayer flags, also in brilliant hues. It really did look like a rainbow landscape, a macabre testimony to human folly.

"You see," he said. "The man who wrote the screed was once a porter and guide on Mount Everest."

"So he really was?"

"He was a Sherpa, and probably he shouldn't have called it that. Rainbow Valley is a Western invention, a stupid piece of gallows humour. But it seems to have stuck all the same, and it became mixed up with his religious representations of spirits and gods. By now, more than four thousand people have climbed the mountain, and three hundred and thirty of them have died up there. It's been impossible to bring all the bodies down, and I can really understand it if this man, who had climbed the mountain eleven times, felt that the dead were speaking to him."

"But—" she began.

"There's more," he interrupted her. "Life up there is dreadful. The risks are significant. You can get HACE, for example, High-Altitude Cerebral Edema."

"The brain swells up. I know."

"It does, exactly," he said. "You'll know more about this than I do. The brain does swell up, and rational thought and speech become a problem. You're liable to make terrible mistakes, and often you have hallucinations and lose contact with reality. Many perfectly sensible people, like you or me—well, certainly fitter and more reckless than me—have seen spirits or felt a mysterious presence up there. This man, he always climbed without oxygen, and that eats up your strength, both mentally and physically. During this dramatic event he was trying to describe, he had worked incredibly hard and gone up and down the mountain and saved many people. He must have been completely worn out, exhausted beyond imagination, and it's not at all surprising that he saw angels and demons, like Captain Haddock, not in the least bit strange."

"I'm sorry, I didn't mean to be disrespectful," Else Sandberg said, apologetic now.

"You weren't, and I'm sure you're right," Bublanski said. "The man was very sick, quite simply a schizophrenic. But he may still have had something important to tell us, so I'm asking you one last time: Is there anything else you remember?"

"Nothing really, I'm sorry."

"Anything more about what he wrote about Forsell?"

"Well, maybe."

"What?"

"You said that the man rescued people, didn't you? I think he wrote that Forsell didn't want to be rescued."

"What could that have meant?"

"I don't know, and it's only just occurred to me. But I'm not totally sure about it either. The bus came, and the next day the papers were gone."

Afterwards, when the woman had left, Bublanski stayed in his office with a strange feeling that he was having to interpret a dream. He spent a long time staring at the pictures of

Klara Engelman's body, which the jet stream had torn from Viktor Grankin higher up on the mountain, and which an American expedition had photographed a year later. Klara was lying on her back with her arms frozen in a beseeching gesture, as if she were still reaching out for Grankin, or perhaps, he thought, like a child wanting to be picked up by its mother.

What had happened up there? Probably only what had already been described a hundred times. But one could not know for sure. New layers in the story were constantly coming to light. It would now seem, for example, that there was some military connection to the Sherpa, which the doctors at the South Wing were forbidden to talk about, and Bublanski had been trying to get hold of Klas Berg at Must all afternoon and evening, hoping to follow that up.

Berg had promised the police a full account the next morning, but had qualified this by saying that he too had some unanswered questions. Bublanski did not like the sound of that. He hated having to depend on the intelligence services. Not because he worried one little bit about prestige or matters of status, but because he knew that it would have a negative effect on the police investigation. He was determined to regain the upper hand.

He closed down the pictures of Klara Engelman on his computer and tried once more to phone Undersecretary Lindberg. But again Lindberg did not answer. Bublanski got up and decided to take a walk, to see if that would help clear his head.

· · ·

Lindberg walked in through the hospital entrance. He had already been there that day and Rebecka had not made him feel welcome, so there was really no reason for him to return. But now that he knew Johannes was conscious, he had to talk to him and say . . . something . . . he was not really sure what, only that he had to get him to keep his mouth shut, come what may. He turned off his mobile because he did not want to make the chaos any worse.

He had no intention whatsoever of speaking to Mikael Blomkvist, who had been trying to reach him, or even to Chief Inspector Bublanski, who had just rung his number for the third time. He had to keep a cool head.

In his briefcase he had a bundle of classified papers about the Russian disinformation campaign. They were not especially important, at least not compared to everything else, but they would give him a pretext for a private conversation with Johannes, and he had to make sure that no-one saw him. No-one at all. He had to be strong, as always. It would all sort itself out. So he told himself.

What was that smell? Ammonia perhaps, disinfectant? He looked around the lobby, afraid that the paparazzi would be hanging about down there, afraid that Blomkvist might suddenly appear, knowing his darkest secrets. But all he could see were patients and their families and hospital staff in their white coats. An ashen-faced man who looked as if he were dying was wheeled past on a trolley bed. Lindberg barely noticed him.

He looked down at the floor, shutting out the world around him. Yet he still detected something out of the corner of his eye and turned to see the back of a tall, slender woman in a grey jacket over by the ATM next to the pharmacist's.

Wasn't that Becka? It definitely was Rebecka. He recognized her posture, the way she leaned forward. Should he go up and say a few words? No, no, he thought. This was an opportunity to snatch a few words with Johannes in private, without all the rigmarole about classified information, and he walked towards the lifts. He took a quick look back, having had the impression that she was not alone. But she was gone.

Had he been mistaken? Perhaps he had, and he was just about to step into the lift when he noticed the large column beside the ATM. Surely she wasn't hiding from him? How crazy would that be? He could not help feeling uneasy and began to walk towards the pillar, a little hesitantly at first, then more quickly. There really was something sticking out, and it looked like Rebecka's grey jacket.

He thought about what he should say to her, he even got angry—how silly to try to hide—when suddenly he tripped and fell. Before he had time to realize what had happened he sensed a movement nearby and heard footsteps running away. He cursed, picked himself up and hurried after them.

PART III

SERVING TWO MASTERS

AUGUST 27–SEPTEMBER 9

Secret agents, double agents, spies: sometimes their mission from the start is to infiltrate the enemy and to contrive smokescreens. Not infrequently they are turned politically, or submit to threats or inducements.

In some cases, their ultimate allegiance is not crystal clear. Sometimes even *they* do not know where they stand.

CHAPTER 25

August 27

Catrin Lindås had still had nothing to eat, she had only drunk some tea and read up on Forsell and the Everest expedition, and time and again she cast her mind back to her encounter with the beggar in Mariatorget, as if it were a riddle she needed to solve. Each time his outbursts sounded more and more desperate.

She remembered other things too, painful memories, the end of her childhood journey to India and Nepal when things went from bad to worse and eventually they left Kathmandu for the Khumbu. They did not get very far. Pappa's withdrawal symptoms became too severe. They did manage to make friends among the local population up there and, after going over Blomkvist's text message several times in her mind, she began to wonder if she had not recognized the beggar from the Khumbu Valley as much as from Freak

Street. She sent Blomkvist one more question, even though
he had not answered her first:

<Was the beggar a Sherpa?>

The answer came right back:

<Shouldn't be talking to you. ☺ You're
with the competition>

<Well, your latest text was pretty revealing>
she wrote.

<I'm an idiot>

<And I'm the enemy>

<Quite. You should be focusing on
skewering me in your editorials>

<I'm sharpening my sword>

<Miss you> he wrote.

Stop it, she thought. *Stop it.* Then, reluctantly, she smiled.
At last. But she was not going to go there, definitely not.
Instead she went into the kitchen to tidy up, and put on
Emmylou Harris so loudly that her cat raced into the bed-
room. When she got back to the sitting room and picked up
her mobile, she saw another text from Blomkvist.

<Let's meet up>

No way, she thought. *No way.*

<Where?> she wrote.

<Let's do this on Signal>

They went onto Signal.

<What about Hotel Lydmar?> he suggested.

<OK> she replied. Not "Hey, great idea, nice place!" noth-
ing like that, only "OK."

Then she changed and asked the neighbour to look after
the cat, and began to pack.

Camilla was standing on the balcony and felt the rain falling on her shoulders and hands. Still, she was glad to be outside. Along Strandvägen and on the boats out there in the bay, a life was going on that should by rights have been hers, but now reminded her only of how much had been stolen from her. *This cannot go on,* she thought. *It has to end.*

She closed her eyes and tipped her head back, and raindrops fell on her forehead and lips, and as she tried to escape into her dreams, she kept being drawn back to Lundagatan, and Agneta shouting at her to go away, and Lisbeth shutting up like a clam as if she wanted to kill them all with her silence, her grim rage.

She felt a hand on her shoulder. Galinov had joined her on the terrace and she turned to look at him, at his gentle smile and his beautiful face. He drew her to him.

"My girl," he said. "How are you?"

"I'm fine."

"I don't believe you."

She looked down at the quay.

"Don't worry, everything'll be OK," he said.

She searched his eyes.

"Has something happened?"

"We have visitors."

"Who?"

"Your charming bandits."

She nodded and went back into the apartment and saw Sandström and some other pathetic creature in jeans and a cheap brown jacket. The creature looked bruised, as if he had been given a beating. He was at least six-six and disgustingly bloated, and he turned out to be called Conny.

"Conny has something to tell us," Sandström said.

"So, get on with it then?"

"I was watching Blomkvist's apartment," Andersson said.

"That obviously went well."

"He was attacked," Sandström said.

She looked at his split lip.

"Was he now?"

"By Salander."

In Russian she said:

"Ivan, Conny here is taller than you, right?"

"He's certainly heavier," Galinov said. "And not quite as well dressed."

She continued in Swedish. "My sister is just five feet tall and as thin as a rake, and she . . . beat the shit out of you."

"She took me by surprise."

"She got hold of his mobile," Sandström said, "and sent a text to all of us in the club."

"What did it say?"

"That we should listen to Conny."

"I'm listening, Conny," Camilla said.

"Salander said she'd come after all of us if we didn't stop following Mikael Blomkvist."

"Then she said something else," Sandström added.

"And that was . . . ?"

"That she'd come after us anyway and destroy our entire business."

"Great," she said, and somehow managed to stay calm.

"And then . . ." Sandström said. "Well, there was a lot of

sensitive stuff on that mobile she nicked. We're actually quite worried."

"And so you should be," she said. "But not about Lisbeth, right, Ivan?"

On the outside Camilla looked sarcastic and menacing. But inside she was falling apart. Eventually she told Galinov to take over the conversation and went into her room, and there she let the past wash over her like dirty, black water.

Rebecka Forsell could not believe what she had done. She had heard Johannes whisper, "He mustn't see me," and, on an impulse she would never fully understand, she tripped Lindberg. Then they raced through the swing doors to the taxis waiting in the rain.

Forsell chose one that looked like it didn't belong to any taxi firm.

"Drive," he said, and at that the driver, a dark-skinned young man with curly hair and sleepy eyes, turned to him. He showed no surprise at seeing a man still in his pyjamas.

"Where to?" he said.

Forsell did not say a word.

"Just cross Solnabron and head into town," Rebecka said, thinking that they could take it from there. But she also noted—and it came as an unexpected relief—that the driver had not shown any sign of recognition. That may have been what Johannes had been hoping for when he picked this taxi—someone whose life was so remote from the Swedish establishment that he did not know what Sweden's most hated man looked like. But this would get them only so far, and as they swung past Solna cemetery she tried to assess the potential impact of what they had done.

She persuaded herself that it need not be all that dramatic. Her husband was going through a crisis, and she was a doctor and could perfectly well have come to the conclusion that he needed some peace and quiet away from the busy hospital. She just had to let them know, before panic broke out.

"You've got to tell me what's going on. I can't handle this sort of madness," she whispered.

"Do you remember that professor of international relations we met at the French Embassy?" he said.

"Janek Kowalski?"

He nodded and she looked at him, puzzled. Kowalski was not a part of their lives. She would not have remembered his name had she not recently read an article by him, on the limits to freedom of expression.

"That's right," he answered. "He lives in Dalagatan, up near Odenplan. We can spend the night there."

"Why on earth . . . ? We don't even know him."

"I do," he said, and she was not happy about that either.

She remembered them greeting each other almost like strangers at the embassy reception, and making polite conversation. Were they only pretending, was it all an act?

"I'll stay the night anywhere you say," she said softly, "as long as you promise to tell me everything."

He looked at her. "I will. After that it's up to you to decide what you want to do," he said.

"What do you mean, decide?"

"If you still want me."

She did not answer. She looked ahead across Solnabron and said, "Dalagatan. We'd like to go to Dalagatan," while she thought about limits, perhaps even about the limits to freedom of expression, but first and foremost about the limits to love.

What would it take for her to leave him?

What would he have to have done for her to stop loving him? Was there even such a thing?

Lindås set off along Götgatan, and was beginning to feel that life might, after all, be worth living. But my goodness, the rain. It was bucketing down and she hurried along with her suitcase. She had of course packed too much, as if she would be gone for weeks. Then again, she had no idea how long they would be staying at the hotel, only that Blomkvist could not go back to his place and had a lot of work to do, unfortunately. But then so did she.

It was half past nine in the evening and she realized how hungry she was. She had scarcely eaten since breakfast. She walked past the Victoria cinema and Göta Lejon theatre and, although she was definitely in a better mood, that uncomfortable feeling would not leave her. She looked out across Medborgarplatsen.

A long line of youngsters were waiting in the rain for tickets to some concert or other, and she was about to hurry down into the tunnelbana when she gave a sudden start and turned, looking right and left. She saw nothing out of the ordinary; no shadow from the past, nothing, and she hurried down the stairs with her case, past the ticket gates and onto the platform, trying to reassure herself that all was well.

Not until she got off the tunnelbana at Central Station and bustled along in the rain down Hamngatan, past Kungsträdgården and out onto Blasieholmen did she begin to worry again, and she quickened her pace. She was almost running and out of breath as she burst into the hotel lobby and went up the curved staircase to the reception. A young woman, hardly more than twenty years old, gave her a welcoming smile and she responded with "Good evening," but then she heard footsteps behind her and that put her off completely. What was the name in which Mikael had booked the room? She knew it began with a B . . . Boman, Brodin, Brodén . . . Bromberg?

"We have a reservation in the name of . . ." and then she hesitated. She would have to check her mobile, and that was going to seem odd, she thought—and certainly sleazy. When she saw that it actually was Boman, she said the name so quietly that the receptionist did not hear and she had to repeat it, more loudly this time. At that point she remembered the footsteps behind her on the stairs and turned to look.

But there was no-one. A man with long hair in a denim jacket was, however, just leaving the hotel and she wondered about that as she checked in. Had the man been up there only briefly? That was strange, surely. Maybe the hotel looked too expensive. She put it out of her mind.

Or she tried to, at least. She took her key card, went up in the lift and opened the door to the room, where she studied the double bed with the pale-blue sheets and wondered briefly what to do next. She decided to have a bath, and took a small bottle of red wine from the minibar and ordered a hamburger and fries from room service. But nothing helped. Not the food, not the alcohol or the bath. Nothing brought down her pulse, and now she was wondering what was keeping Blomkvist.

Janek Kowalski did not actually live on Dalagatan. But they did gain access from there and, after crossing an inner courtyard, emerged on Västeråsgatan, where they slipped in through another street entrance and took a lift to the fifth floor. His was a large apartment, not unpleasant but chaotic, the home of a bachelor, an old-fashioned intellectual who lacked neither money nor taste but could no longer be bothered to keep the place tidy and uncluttered.

There was too much of everything—too many bowls and knick-knacks and paintings, and too many books and folders. They were lying around all over the place. Kowalski himself was unshaven and dishevelled, a bohemian, especially without the suit he had been wearing at the embassy. He must have been about seventy-five and was wearing a thin cashmere sweater with a few moth holes.

"My dear friends. I've been so worried for you," he said, and he hugged Forsell and kissed Rebecka on both cheeks.

There was no doubt that the two knew each other well. Kowalski had laid out a pair of corduroys, a shirt and a V-neck sweater, and when Forsell had changed he joined Kowalski in the kitchen, where they whispered together for twenty minutes before emerging with a tray of tea, a plate of assorted sandwiches and a bottle of white wine. Both of them looked at her with grave faces.

"My dear Rebecka," Kowalski said. "Your husband has asked me to be perfectly frank and I have agreed, albeit with some reluctance. I have to confess that I'm not very good at this sort of thing. But I'll do my best to talk openly and I beg your forgiveness in advance, should I fail to live up to my commitment."

She did not like his tone; it sounded both apologetic and pretentious at the same time. Perhaps he was nervous. Certainly his hand was shaking as he poured the tea.

"I should begin by telling you what I really do," he said. "It's thanks to me that the two of you met."

She looked at him in surprise. "What do you mean?"

"It was I who sent Johannes off to Everest. I know that sounds awful, but Johannes was willing. He even insisted. He's a man who's at home in the wilds, is he not?"

"Now I'm lost," she said.

"Johannes and I met in Russia in a professional capacity and became friends. I realized early on that he was a man of exceptional ability."

"In what respect?"

"In every respect, Rebecka. He may sometimes have been a little hasty and too eager, but he was, in fact, a superlative officer."

"So you too were in the military?"

"I was"—he seemed to struggle—"a Pole who became British as a child. My parents were political refugees and old England was good to them, so that is perhaps why I saw it as my duty to join the Foreign Office."

"MI6?"

"Well, let's say no more than is strictly necessary. In any case, I settled here after retiring, not just out of love for the country, but because of one or two complications which are, in a way, connected to the business we were involved in back then. You should know, my dear, that Johannes and I had a common interest at the time which was risky enough, even without Everest."

"And what was that?"

"It was to do with GRU defectors and moles, both actual and in the pipeline, and also, I should probably add, imaginary ones, to which we decided to apply our combined wisdom. My group was made aware that a small unit within the Swedish Security Police had got hold of a major asset from the GRU, a man who became far too well known after his death because of somebody you have recently had dealings with."

"You're speaking in riddles."

"I did warn you. I do not find this easy. I'm talking about Mikael Blomkvist, who broke the story of the so-called Zalachenko affair. There has been too much said about that except, perhaps, the most important thing of all, the thing that was being discreetly whispered in our ears at the time."

"And what was that?"

"Well, um . . . how should I put this? I need to give you a bit of background first. There was a department in Säpo which protected Alexander Zalachenko—the GRU agent who defected—using any means available, because he was supplying them with what they believed to be unique information on the Russian military intelligence services."

"That's right," she exclaimed. "And he had a daughter, didn't he, Lisbeth Salander? She had a dreadful time of it."

"Correct. Zalachenko was given pretty much a free rein. He could do whatever he wanted—mistreat his family and build up a crime empire—as long as he delivered the secrets. It was decency sacrificed for a greater good."

"National security."

"I wouldn't call it anything as noble as that. Rather a sense of exclusivity, of possessing information no-one else had, which a number of gentlemen at Säpo found incredibly exciting. But it's possible—and this is what my group suspected—that they didn't even have that."

"What are you saying?"

"We had reports to the effect that Zalachenko remained loyal to Russia. That he was a double agent until the day he died, and passed back much more to the GRU than he ever let on to Säpo."

"Oh, my God," she said.

"That's exactly how we felt. But at first all we had were suspicions, and we tried to find ways of getting them confirmed. After a time we heard about a man, a lieutenant colonel who was officially a civilian acting as a consultant to the travel industry, but who had in fact worked undercover for GRU internal security and had picked up on a massive case of corruption."

"To do with what?"

"The links between a number of intelligence agents and the Zvezda Bratva crime syndicate. He was apparently furious that the collaboration should have been allowed to continue, and was said to have resigned his position at the GRU in protest, and in order to pursue his great passion—high-altitude climbing."

"Are we talking about Viktor Grankin?" Rebecka said.

"We are indeed talking about the late Grankin. An extremely interesting person, don't you think?"

"Oh yes, absolutely, but—"

"You were his expedition doctor. That surprised us, in fact."

"It surprised me too," she said thoughtfully. "But I too had a crazy urge for adventure at the time. I'd been told about Grankin at a conference in Oslo."

"We know."

"So go on."

"Grankin gave the impression of being very down to earth, didn't he? Straightforward and uncomplicated. But he was, in fact, unbelievably intelligent and complex, a man of deep feeling. He was torn by divided loyalties—between his love of his country and his sense of honour and decency. In February 2008 we began to be fairly certain not only that he knew about Zalachenko's double-dealing and his cooperation with the mafia, but also that he himself was in danger. That he was frightened of the GRU and in need of protection and new friends. That is what gave me the idea to send Johannes on his expedition to Everest. We thought that an adventure of that calibre would foster camaraderie and closeness."

"Oh, my God," she said again, turning to Johannes. "So you were there to recruit him to the West?"

"That was the dream scenario, of course," Kowalski said.

"But what about Svante Lindberg?"

"Lindberg is the unhappy part of this story," Kowalski said. "But we didn't know that then. At the time, his recruitment seemed like a very reasonable request from Johannes. Of course, we would have preferred him to take one of our people instead. But Lindberg knew his Russia, had worked closely with Johannes at Must and, above all, he was an experienced climber. On the face of it he was the perfect companion. Luckily—and we're very grateful for that now—we didn't give him the full picture. He never found out my name, or even that it was more of a British than a Swedish operation."

"I can't believe it," she said, as it all began to sink in. "So the whole expedition was an intelligence operation?"

"It turned into an awful lot more, my dear Rebecka. Johannes met you, after all. But yes . . . he went in the line of duty and we kept a very close eye on it."

"That's crazy. I had absolutely no idea."

"I'm sorry that you should have to hear about it in these circumstances."

"Well, how did it go?" she said. "I mean . . . before it all went wrong?"

Forsell shrugged, and once again it was Kowalski who answered.

"Johannes and I have a slightly different view on that. In my opinion, he did an excellent job. He managed to build trust and early on it looked promising. But it's true that the situation grew more and more tense and we had to put a lot of pressure on Viktor. We took advantage of him at a critical stage, before the climb started. So yes, Johannes is probably right. There was too much at stake. But above all—"

"We were missing some crucial information," Forsell said.

"Yes, unfortunately," Kowalski said. "But how could we have known? Nobody in the West suspected it at the time, not even the FBI."

"What are you talking about?" she said.

"Stan Engelman."

"What about him?"

"He had been connected to Zvezda Bratva since he started to build hotels in Moscow in the nineties. Viktor was aware of this, but we were not."

"How come he knew?"

"It was one of the things he had ferreted out in the course of his work at the GRU, but, as I said, double-dealing was part of his job so he pretended to be close to Stan. Secretly he thought he was despicable."

"And stole his wife."

"I think the romance was more of a bonus."

"Or else it was the trigger factor," Forsell said.

"Could you please speak in plain English?" Rebecka said.

"I think Johannes is saying that it was the love affair, and the things Klara told him, that prompted Viktor to act," Kowalski said.

"Meaning?"

"If he wasn't going to be able to squeeze his colleagues in the GRU, he could at least damage a massively corrupt American."

CHAPTER 26

August 27

Sometimes Galinov would ask her: "What does he mean to you today? What are your thoughts about him?" Most of the time she did not answer, but once she said: "I remember feeling like I had been chosen," and it really was true.

There had been a time when her father's lies were the best thing in her life, and she was long convinced that it was she who wielded the power, that she enchanted him, and not the other way around. It was an illusion that was inevitably snatched from her and replaced by a gaping abyss. And yet . . . the memory of that special feeling lingered on, and sometimes she would forgive Zala the way you might forgive a wild animal. The only thing that never went away was her hatred of Lisbeth and Agneta, and now, lying in her bed on Strandvägen, she used it to brace herself, the way she had as a teenager, when she was forced to reinvent herself and create a new Camilla, free of all constraints.

The rain was beating down on Strandvägen. Sirens were howling and she could hear footsteps coming closer, rhythmic, confident footsteps. It was Galinov, and she got up and opened the door. He smiled at her. She knew that the two of them shared the hatred and the feeling of being special.

"We may have some encouraging news after all," he said. She did not answer.

"Not a big deal in itself," he said, "but it could be an opening. The woman Blomkvist was seen with out at Sandhamn has just checked in to Hotel Lydmar."

"And?"

"Well, she lives here in the city, doesn't she? So why would she go to a hotel unless she wants to meet someone who'd rather not be seen at her place, or in their own home?"

"Such as Blomkvist?"

"Spot on."

"What do you think we should do?"

Galinov ran his fingers through his hair.

"The location isn't great. There are outdoor cafés and bars, and too many people around in the evening. But Sandström—"

"Is he being difficult?"

"No, no, on the contrary, I've got him toeing the line. He says he can have a car waiting around the corner, even the ambulance one of his minions had the bright idea to steal, and I—"

"And you, Ivan?"

"There may be a part for me to play too. It would appear that Blomkvist and I have a common concern, if Bogdanov is to be trusted."

"What does that mean?"

"We share an interest in the Swedish Minister of Defence and some of his past dealings."

Camilla felt her energy returning. "Good," she said. "Then I suggest you get moving."

Rebecka had not yet managed to digest the information, but she did not allow herself time to do so. She could see that there was worse to come.

"We've now understood that Engelman deliberately chose Grankin's expedition for his wife because he was convinced that Viktor was one of them," Kowalski went on. "But Grankin had been investigating the syndicate and was by now an angry man. I believe that Johannes, with his talent for building trust, had got him to the point where he wanted to talk: He had sowed the seed, so to speak. I think Klara simply carried on where Johannes left off."

"What do you mean?"

"Klara got Viktor to share what was on his mind. I think they egged each other on. She told him what a swine her husband was behind closed doors, and Viktor contributed accounts of Stan's activities in Zvezda Bratva."

"Love made them want to share," she said.

"Yes, maybe that's how it was. At least, that is Johannes's theory. But it doesn't in the end matter so much. What was important was that it leaked out and made its way to Manhattan—however careful they tried to be."

"Did someone spill the beans?"

"Your poor unfortunate Sherpa."

"Don't tell me."

"I'm afraid so."

"Nima would surely never have betrayed them?"

"I don't think he saw it that way," Kowalski said. "He'd been paid extra to look after Klara and report what she got up to at Base Camp. He probably felt he was doing his job."

"How much had he found out?"

"We don't know for sure, but it was enough to put him in danger later on. I'll get to that. We do know that Engelman somehow heard about the love affair, and that alone aroused a great deal of anger and suspicion, and there were others who obliged with more information so that, in the end, Stan knew exactly what was at stake. Not only his marriage, but also his future as a businessman. Possibly even his days as a free man."

"Who was responsible for the other leaks?"

"I'm sure you can guess," Kowalski said. "But you asked about Nima Rita and how he could possibly have passed anything on. Don't forget that he was worried and angry, like so many other Sherpas that year."

"Was it to do with his religious beliefs?" she said.

"Yes, and also his wife, Luna. Klara had treated her badly, hadn't she? Nima had his own reasons for not feeling any loyalty towards her."

"That's not fair to him, Janek," Forsell said. "Nima didn't have it in for anyone. He was like Viktor. He had divided loyalties. People told him: Do this, do that. He ended up carrying everything on his shoulders and was given orders and counterorders, and in the end it broke him. He had much too heavy a load, and yet it was he and none of the others who suffered pangs of conscience."

"Sorry, Johannes, I only experienced it at a distance, so to speak. It's perhaps better if you take over now," Kowalski said.

"I'm not sure that I want to," Forsell said, sounding cross.

"You promised," Rebecka said.

"I did. But I'll be extremely upset if Nima is made to take the blame for this. He had more than his fair share of pain."

"There you are, Rebecka. Johannes is a good man, don't let anyone tell you anything different. He'll always stand up for the weak," Kowalski said.

"So your relationship with Nima was really as good as it seemed?" she said.

She could hear how apprehensive she sounded.

"Maybe even too good when it came to the crunch," he said.

"What do you mean by that?"

"Let me explain," Forsell said, and he fell silent.

"Well, tell us then."

"I will," he said, "and you know most of it already. Maybe I ought to begin by saying that Viktor's and my relationship had deteriorated by the time we set off for the summit, and I'm pretty sure it had to do with Stan Engelman. I think Viktor was afraid that, by some roundabout route, the connection between us would be leaked to the GRU and Zvezda Bratva. His days would then be numbered for sure, so I kept myself to myself. The last thing I wanted was to worry anybody. We were to be a safe haven, nothing else, and, as you

know, Becka, we all set out from Camp Four just after midnight on May 13. The conditions looked perfect."

"But you were slowed down."

"Yes, Klara began to struggle and so did Mads Larsen,
and maybe Viktor was not a hundred percent either. But that
wasn't really on my mind then. I noticed that Svante was irri-
table and was pushing me. He wanted us to make for the
summit on our own. Otherwise we'd miss our chance, he
said, and in the end Viktor let us do it. Maybe he was thankful to be rid of me. We set off, so were unaware of the catastrophe that engulfed our expedition. We simply tramped
on and made the summit in good time. But on the climb
down from the Hillary Step, I began to have trouble. The sky
was still clear then, and there was not too much of a wind.
We had plenty of oxygen and fluid. But time was ticking by,
and—"

"And suddenly you heard a rumble, a bang."

"We heard thunder out of a clear blue sky. Then the
storm hit us from the north, like a tsunami. We lost visibility
in an instant. The temperature plummeted. It was unbear-
ably cold and we staggered along. Several times I sank to
my knees, and often Svante came over, reached out a hand
and helped me to my feet. But our progress became slower
and slower and the hours raced by. It was late afternoon and
then evening, and we worried about darkness falling, and I
remember collapsing again and thinking it was all over. But
just then I saw . . . something blue and red in front of me,
indistinct shapes, and I prayed that it would be the tents in
Camp Four, or at least some other climbers who could help
us. That gave me hope, and as I got to my feet I saw that it

wasn't anything good, quite the contrary. It was two bodies lying close together in the snow, one smaller than the other."

"You never told me this."

"No, Becka, I haven't, and this is where the nightmare begins. I still find it hard to describe. I was so exhausted. I simply could not go on. I just wanted to lie down and die and that's why I had the feeling I was staring at my own fate. But my own fear was more real than what I saw before me, and it never crossed my mind that they might be people I knew, I just assumed they were some of those hundreds of dead lying up there. I stood up, tore off my oxygen mask and said that we had to hurry down, get away, and I started walking, or at least I took a step. But then I was overcome by a strange feeling."

"What do you mean?"

"It was hundreds of things in a way. We had picked up information on the radio about an emergency in our expedition and perhaps my mind was on that. Then I must have recognized the clothes and other details. But above all, there was something eerie about the smaller of the bodies. I remember bending down and looking into the face, and there wasn't much you could see. The hood was pulled over the hat and forehead. The sunglasses were still in place. The cheeks, nose and mouth were coated in ice. The whole face was buried under a layer of snow. And yet I knew."

"It was Klara, right?"

"It was Klara and Viktor. She was half turned on her side, with her arm around his waist, and there was no doubt in my mind that I would be leaving them like that. But that uncanny feeling would not go away. She seemed to be frozen through and through. And yet I thought I detected something about her which was not altogether lifeless, so I pushed her away from Viktor and tried to get the snow off her face. I couldn't do it. It was too frozen, too hard, and I had no strength in my hands, so in the end I got out my ice axe. It must have looked absurd. I lifted off her sunglasses and hacked at her face. The ice chips went flying and Svante yelled at me to stop and get on down the mountain. But I kept at it manically, and I did try to be careful. But my fingers were frostbitten and I didn't have proper control. I injured her. I opened up a gash in her lip and chin, and there was a twitch in her face which I took to be movement caused by my hacking, but no sign of life. Still, I took my oxygen mask and put it on her and held it in place for a long time, even though I myself was fighting for breath and not at all hopeful. But suddenly there was an intake of breath. I could see it from the tube and the mask, and I stood up and started yelling at Svante. But he only shook his head and he was right, of course. It didn't matter that she was breathing. She was as close to death as one can be, and we were at twenty-seven thousand feet. There was no hope. She was beyond rescue. We would never be able to get her down and our own lives were at risk too."

"But you were shouting for help."

"We'd been calling out so many times that we'd lost all hope. I just remember putting my oxygen mask back on and then we carried on downhill. We struggled along and slowly I began to lose my grip on reality. I had hallucinations. I saw my father in a bathtub, and my mother in the sauna in Åre. I had all sorts of visions, I've told you that, Becka."

"Yes," she said.

"But I never told you, did I, how I saw monks too, the same Buddhist monks as in Tengboche, and then another figure who reminded me of them but was somehow completely different. He was walking up the mountain instead of downhill and, unlike the monks, he really existed. It was Nima Rita trudging towards us through the snow."

Blomkvist was running late and regretted having lured Catrin to Hotel Lydmar. He should have picked another day. But it was not always easy to be rational, especially with women like her, and now he was walking along Drottninggatan in the rain, heading for the hotel on Blasieholmen. He was on the point of sending a text saying "There in ten" when two things happened.

Someone texted him, but he didn't have time to read it before his mobile rang. He had been trying to get hold of so many people that day—even Svante Lindberg—and he hoped every minute that someone would get back to him. But no such luck; the voice at the other end of the line was that of an elderly man who did not even introduce himself. Blomkvist considered simply hanging up. But it was a friendly voice, speaking Swedish with an English accent.

"Could you repeat that?" he said.

"I'm sitting in my apartment, having tea with a married couple who are in the middle of telling me the most shocking story. They would very much like to share it with you. Preferably as early as tomorrow morning."

"Do I know this couple?" Blomkvist said.

"You've done them a huge favour."

"Recently?"

"Very recently, out at sea."

He looked up at the sky and at the rain coming down.

"I'd love to meet them," he said. "Where?"

"Let's run through the details on another line, if you don't mind, a mobile that's not connected to you and has the appropriate functions."

Blomkvist thought it over. It would have to be Catrin's mobile and her Signal app.

"I can send you a different number on an encrypted link," he said. "But first I need confirmation that this couple really are at your place and that they're doing well."

"I wouldn't say they're well," the man said. "But they're here, and of their own free will. You can have a word with the husband."

Blomkvist closed his eyes and stopped. He was standing on the slope of Lejonbacken, right next to Slottet, the Royal Palace, looking across the water to the Grand Hôtel and the Nationalmuseum. He probably waited for no more than twenty or thirty seconds, but it felt like an eternity.

"Mikael," a voice eventually said. "I owe you a huge debt of gratitude."

"How are you?" he said.

"Better than back then."

"Back when?"

"When I was about to drown."

It was Forsell.

"You want to talk?" Blomkvist said.

"Not really,"

"You don't?"

"But my wife, Rebecka, who will soon have heard it all, insists that I do. So I don't see how I can get out of it."

"I understand," Blomkvist said.

"I'm not sure that you do. But dare I ask if I can read what you write before you publish?"

Blomkvist set off towards the bridge across to Kungsträdgården, turning the words over in his mind.

"You can alter your quotes until you feel comfortable with them, and you can check my facts. You're even welcome to try and persuade me that I should be writing my article differently. But I don't promise to do as you say."

"That sounds reasonable."

"Good."

"We'll stand by, then."

"Right you are."

Forsell thanked him again and handed the phone back to the other man. He and Blomkvist agreed what to do next. Then Blomkvist sent over Catrin Lindås's number and quickened his pace. His heart was pounding. His thoughts were racing. What was going on? He should have asked more questions. Why was Forsell no longer at the Karolinska? Surely it was unwise of him to leave the hospital so soon, seeing that he had been in such a bad way—and who was the Englishman who had called?

Blomkvist knew nothing except that it was probably all to do with Nima Rita and Everest, but he was certain there were other cards in play that he had no idea about, maybe a Russian trail—the whole of Forsell's life suggested Russia—or connections to Engelman in Manhattan?

Time would tell. He would no doubt find out soon and he

felt a tremendous excitement. *This is big,* he thought, *really big.* But in truth he was not even sure about that. He needed to keep a cool head. He took out his mobile to send Catrin a message via Signal:

```
<Sorry, had a foul day, but I'll be there
any moment now and btw, sorry again, you've
got to help me with something else too.
You'll get information soon. I'll explain.
Can't wait. Hugs, M>
```

Then he remembered the message that had come in just before the telephone call. He read it and thought, this is odd. It was almost like an answer to his questions, and he wondered if it had anything to do with the conversation he had just ended or if, on the contrary, it might be something from the other side, if indeed there were sides in this affair.

```
<A little bird has told me you're interested
in what happened on Everest in May 2008. I
suggest you take a look at Viktor Grankin,
the expedition guide, who died on the moun-
tain. His background is a lot more inter-
esting than people realize. That is where
you'll find the key to all this. Grankin was
the reason Johannes Forsell was expelled
from Russia in the autumn of 2008.
    There are no official sources, but with
your experience I'm sure you'll have no
trouble finding out that his CV is a fake, no
```

more than a façade. I happen to be in Stock-
holm right now, staying at the Grand Hôtel.
I'd be happy to meet you and tell you what
I know, I have documentary evidence.

I stay up late, a bad habit of mine, I'm
afraid. Plus jet lag.

Charles>

Charles? Who the hell was Charles? This smacked of U.S.
intelligence. But equally it could be something wildly different, a trap even. It was troubling that the man should be
staying at the Grand Hôtel, just across the water from where
he was standing, and very close to the Lydmar. Then again,
nearly all rich or important foreigners stay at the Grand—Ed
the Ned from the NSA was a case in point, so perhaps there
was nothing suspicious about that coincidence.

But still he did not feel comfortable about it. No, Mr.
Charles would have to wait. What had happened was more
than enough for him to deal with and he felt bad about
Catrin, so he hurried past the Grand to the Lydmar and
raced up the stairs.

CHAPTER 27

August 27–28, Night

Rebecka Forsell had no idea what she had set in motion or what the consequences would be for her and the boys, but she saw no other way forward. It was no longer possible to remain silent, not about this.

Now she was sitting with a glass of wine in the brown armchair, deep in contemplation, aware of her husband and Kowalski whispering away in the kitchen. Was more that was crucial being kept from her? She was pretty sure it was, and she even doubted whether all that she had heard was true. But she did feel that she now understood what had happened on Everest. There was an irrefutable logic to the story and she thought about how little they had really known, not only then at Base Camp but also afterwards, when the witness statements were collected.

She knew that Nima Rita had climbed up twice to bring

down Mads Larsen and Charlotte Richter, but not that he had gone up a third time, a fact which he never once mentioned during the interviews or the subsequent investigation. It did, however, explain why Susan Wedlock, the head of their group at Base Camp, was not able to get hold of him that evening.

According to Forsell's account, it would by then have been past eight in the evening. Darkness was not far off and the cold, ferocious conditions were soon to deteriorate further. But Nima walked straight back into it, in a desperate attempt to bring down Klara Engelman. He was himself already in a bad way. The figure Forsell saw emerging from the fog and the snow was stumbling along with his head bent against the storm, as ever without an oxygen mask; all he had was a headlamp whose light darted about in the snow. His cheeks were frostbitten. He did not see Forsell and Lindberg until he was almost upon them. To them he was a godsend, once it dawned on them that it really was him in the flesh. Forsell could hardly stand upright. He was about to become the third victim on the mountain that evening. But Nima Rita paid no attention to that. "Must get Mamsahib" is all he said. "Must get Mamsahib." Lindberg shouted to him that it was pointless, that she was dead. But Nima would not listen, not even when Lindberg bellowed:

"Then you'll be killing us. You're saving a dead person instead of us—we're alive!"

Nima just walked on, up the face. He vanished into the storm with his down jacket flapping, and that was what did it. Forsell collapsed and was unable to get up, either by himself or with Lindberg's help. He had no idea what happened next or how long it took, only that darkness fell and he was freezing, and Lindberg was yelling:

"For Christ's sake, Johannes, I don't want to leave you. But I have to, I'm sorry, otherwise we'll both die."

Lindberg laid a hand on his head, and stood up. Forsell realized that he was going to be abandoned. He would freeze to death. But then he heard the shouts, those inhuman howls. As he told her this, Rebecka thought, *It's not so bad after all.* It was not pretty, but it was a human response and the usual rules did not apply up there. There were different standards on the mountain and Forsell had done nothing wrong, not then.

He had been too exhausted even to grasp what was going on, and that was why, regardless of what happened later, she wanted him to talk to a reporter like Blomkvist, someone who was capable of burrowing deep into the story, following all of its meandering paths and plumbing its psychological depths. But maybe that was a mistake. Maybe there were things which she was not aware of yet, things which were even worse.

She could not rule it out, especially with Johannes whispering so agitatedly in the kitchen and Kowalski shaking his head and throwing his arms out. Christ, what an idiot she had been. Perhaps they should try to bury the whole affair, keep their mouths shut—for the sake of the boys. For her sake. Oh, God help them, and she cursed her husband.

How could he have got them into this predicament?
How could he?

. . .

Blomkvist listened to Catrin muttering in her sleep. It was late and he was dead tired, but it was impossible to drift off. His head was filled with thoughts and his heart was pounding. *What the hell's the matter,* he thought. *I'm not exactly new to this game.* And yet he was as excited as a cub reporter working on his very first scoop. As he tossed and turned he thought back to what Catrin had said to him:

"Don't you think Grankin was a soldier too?"

"Why do you say so?"

"He looked like one," she said, and, thinking back, that really did seem right.

There was something about the way he held himself that suggested a senior officer, and normally Blomkvist would not have given it a second thought. People can give an impression of being one thing and then turn out to be something quite different. But now he had received that message from the mysterious "Charles," and it pointed in the same direction. Grankin would also seem to be one of the reasons for Forsell's expulsion from Russia. He would need to follow up on that.

It was what Blomkvist had believed all along, and he had been planning to follow it up in the morning, before his meeting with the Forsells. But since he couldn't sleep anyway, why not just get up? So long as he did not wake Catrin. He was already feeling guilty on that front. He got up slowly and carefully and tiptoed into the bathroom with his mobile. *Grankin,* he thought. *Viktor Grankin.*

He had been a fool not to run a more thorough check on him before now. But then it had never occurred to him that Grankin was anything other than an Everest guide, and that that was where his part in the story ended; just a poor bastard who had fallen in love with a married woman and made some bad decisions on the mountain, and lost his life as a result. But yes indeed, the background information on him was a little too tidy and unspecific.

He had without doubt been a distinguished climber who had conquered many of the toughest summits in the world—K2, the Eiger, Annapurna, Denali, Cerro Torre . . . and then, of course, Everest. But there was little else in the way of hard information, only over and again the fact that he had worked as a consultant for adventure holidays. What exactly did that entail? Blomkvist did not find much, but eventually came across an old picture of Grankin together with the Russian businessman Andrei Koskov. Didn't that name ring a bell?

Yes, of course, damn it. Koskov was a businessman and whistle-blower in exile who in November 2011 had exposed connections between the Russian intelligence services and organized crime. Not long after that, in March 2012, he dropped dead while out walking in Camden, in London, and at first the police found nothing suspicious. Three months later, however, traces of *Gelsemium elegans* were detected in samples taken from his blood. Blomkvist found that this Asian dicotyledon plant is sometimes known as heartbreak grass—in concentrated form it can make the heart stop—and it was by no means an unknown poison. In 1879, none other than Arthur Conan Doyle had written about it in the *British Medical Journal*. But for a long time there was no mention of the plant in historical records or on the news until it shot to prominence again in 2012 when it was detected in the body of a defector, a GRU agent by the name of Igor Popov, in Baltimore, Maryland. Now Blomkvist was on the alert. Military intelligence, suspected deaths through poisoning, claims that Forsell had systematically investigated the activities of the GRU and been thrown out of the country . . .

Was this another misleading coincidence, like the one with Mats Sabin, the military historian? After all, it was nothing more than a picture of Grankin posing with someone who had died in mysterious circumstances. But still . . . there could be no harm in checking with the confounded "Charles" and asking him what he knew. He sent off a text:

<So who was Grankin really?>

It was ten minutes before he got an answer:

<Military policeman at the GRU Lieutenant
colonel. Internal investigations>

Jesus, he thought. *Jesus.* Not that he took this at face value for one second. Nor would he until he knew who he was communicating with.

<And who are you?>

The reply came right back.

<I'm a former official>

<MI6, CIA?>

<No comment, as they say>

<Nationality, at least?>

<American, for my sins>

<How did you find out I'm digging into this
story?>

<It's the sort of thing I'm supposed to
know about>

<Why would you want to leak this to the
press?>

<Maybe I'm old-fashioned>

<In what way?>

<Happen to believe that crime needs to be
seen and punished>

<Is it that simple?>

<I may have my own reasons as well. But
does that really matter? You and I have
common interests, Mikael>

<Give me something, in that case. So I
know I'm not wasting my time>

Within five minutes a photograph arrived showing an
ID card for none other than Lieutenant Colonel Viktor
Alexeievich Grankin, bearing the emblem used by the GRU
at the time, the red five-leaf clover on a black background. It
seemed like solid information, for all that Blomkvist could
tell.

<Did Grankin and Forsell have any common
interest other than Everest?> he wrote.

<Forsell was there to recruit Grankin. But
it went horribly wrong>

"Bloody hell," Blomkvist muttered out loud. <And you
want to give me that story?>

<Discreetly and with source protection,
yes>

<Agreed>

<In that case, get a taxi here right away.
I'll meet you in the lobby. After that, even
a night owl like me will need some sleep>

<OK> Blomkvist replied.

Was he being careless? He knew nothing about this man, save that he was well informed, and Blomkvist would need as many facts as possible before the meeting tomorrow morning. Surely a one-minute walk to the Grand Hôtel was a risk worth taking? It was 1:58 a.m. and there were still voices out in the street. The city was awake. There were always taxis waiting outside the Grand at night, as far as he could recall, and no doubt there were doormen too. No, surely, there could be no danger. He dressed quietly, left the room and took the lift to the lobby, then the curved stairs down to ground level. The street outside was wet from the downpour, but the dark sky was clearing.

It was good to get out. Lights were shining in the Royal Palace across the water and further away, in Kungsträdgården, there was life still and pockets of people. He was relieved to see a few individuals on the quay too, a young couple walking by. A waitress was clearing glasses from the outside tables, and a man in a white linen suit was still seated on a chair on the far side of the terrace bar, looking out at the water. All clear, he thought, and he set off. But then he heard a voice:

"Blomkvist?"

He turned and saw that it was the man in the white suit who had hailed him, a gentleman in his sixties with grey-white hair, handsome features and a cautious smile, perhaps even a smirk. What had amused him? Was it a quip about Blomkvist's journalism, or character? If so, it was a quip he never got to share.

He heard steps behind him and felt his body jerk, as if

electricity had shot through it. He collapsed and hit his head on the pavement, and the strange thing was, his first reaction was not one of fear or pain, but of anger. And not even anger at his assailant but at himself: How could he have been so bloody stupid? How could he? He tried to move. But another shock made him twitch as if he were having a seizure.

"My God, what's the matter with him?"

This could have been the waitress.

"Looks like an epileptic fit. We need to call an ambulance."

The man in the white suit spoke in a perfectly calm voice, and the footsteps faded away. Other people approached and Blomkvist heard the sound of a car engine. Then it all happened very quickly. He was rolled over onto a stretcher and lifted in. A door was shut, the vehicle moved away and he fell off the stretcher onto the floor. He tried to shout, but he was so stunned that he could only groan and not until the vehicle had crossed Hamngatan did he manage to utter the words that now came back to him.

"What are you doing? What are you doing?"

Salander was woken by sounds she could not identify and she fumbled drowsily for her weapon on the bedside table. But as she got hold of the pistol and swept the hotel room with its muzzle, she realized that the sound was coming from her mobile. Had she heard someone calling out?

Oddly it was a second or two before she came to the conclusion that it could only have been Blomkvist, and she closed her eyes, took a deep breath and tried to put her thoughts in some order. "Come on now," she whispered. "Tell me you only happened to say those words. Come *on*."

She turned up the volume on her mobile and listened to the banging and crackling. It could be nothing, just noises from a car or a train. But then she heard him groan, followed by heavy, pained breathing. Was he losing consciousness? She leaped out of bed, cursing, and sat at the desk.

Salander was still at the Nobis Hotel in Norrmalmstorg and had been keeping an eye on the address on Strandvägen all evening, ever since her attack on Conny Andersson. There had been a certain amount of activity and she had seen Galinov leave the building. But she had not been especially worried and had gone to sleep at around one—very recently, it would seem—hoping to have gained another day's respite. She had been wrong.

On her computer she could see that Blomkvist was being taken north, out of Stockholm, and any minute now they would search his pockets and get rid of his mobile. If Galinov and Bogdanov were involved, they would know exactly how to cover their tracks, so she couldn't afford to sit there like a fool and follow their progress on the map. She had to act. She rewound the tape and heard Blomkvist call out:

"What are you doing?"

He repeated the words twice and was definitely in a bad way, in shock. All she could hear was his breathing. Had they drugged him? She banged her fist on the desk and registered that the vehicle had been on Norrlandsgatan, not far from where she was now. But that was unlikely to be where they had picked him up, so she wound the recording further back and heard his footsteps and his breathing, and a voice saying "Blomkvist?"—the voice of an older man, she thought. And after that a yelp, an exhalation of breath, and a woman shouting, "My God, what's the matter with him?"

Where had all this taken place?

Blasieholmen, by the look of it. She could not determine the exact spot, but it must have been outside the Grand Hôtel or the Nationalmuseum, somewhere around there. She rang the emergency services and reported that the journalist, Mikael Blomkvist, had been assaulted in that neighbourhood. The young man who took the call recognized the name and asked for more details in an excited voice. But before Salander had time to add anything, someone in the background could be heard saying that an alert had already come in from that area: a man had collapsed, apparently having had some kind of fit outside Hotel Lydmar, and had been taken away.

"How?" she said.

There was confusion at the other end of the line, voices talking to each other.

"An ambulance fetched him?"

"An ambulance?"

For a split second she was relieved, but then she checked herself.

"Did you dispatch it?"

"I expect we did."

"You 'expect' you did?"

"Let me check."

Again, voices in the background, but it was difficult to catch what they were saying. Then the man was back on the line, clearly nervous.

"Who's asking?"

"Salander," she said. "Lisbeth Salander."

"No, apparently we didn't."

"Well, have it stopped then," she spat out. *"Now."*

She yelled a stream of abuse, hung up and listened to the recording in real time. It was too quiet, she thought. Only the rumble of the vehicle and Blomkvist's laboured breathing. There was nothing else to be heard, no other voices, but then . . . if it really was an ambulance that was a lead of sorts, and she considered ringing the police and raising hell. But no, unless the emergency centre was staffed by idiots, they must already be after it.

It was vital she acted before the tracking signals disappeared, and just then—in case she doubted the information she had received—a siren began to howl, and then something more: a scratching sound, hands searching through Blomkvist's pockets, she thought, followed by movement and heavy breathing. Then a loud noise, a crunching crash, not a mobile being thrown away, but one being smashed to bits, and then the transmission died. It ended as suddenly as a gunshot, a power cut, and she kicked her chair. She grabbed her whisky glass from the table and hurled it at the wall where it broke into a thousand pieces. "Fucking hell . . . *Fuck!*"

She shook her head, pulled herself together and checked where Camilla was. Still at Strandvägen, of course. She wouldn't get her hands dirty. Fuck her! She rang Plague and shouted at him as she pulled on her clothes and packed a backpack with her laptop, her pistol and her IMSI-catcher. Then she kicked over a lamp, put on her helmet and Google Glass and rushed out to her motorcycle in the square.

Rebecka Forsell had asked to sleep on her own. She thought Kowalski and Johannes could perfectly well share a room. But now she was lying awake in a narrow bed, in a small study crammed with books, reading the news on her mobile. Not a word about Johannes disappearing from the hospital. She was glad she had called the hospital staff to say that she was looking after Johannes herself, as well as Klas Berg on a secure line. She had subsequently ignored his admonitions and threats. To be fair, Berg had no idea what a marginal player he was in the overall scheme of things.

She could not have cared less about him or any of the others at military high command. All she wanted was to be able to process the full implications of what she had heard, and maybe also to understand why she had not suspected anything earlier. There had been no shortage of signs, that much was clear to her now. For example, the crisis Johannes had gone through at Base Camp afterwards. She had cried tears of relief that he was alive, and safe—despite the tragedy that had befallen the others—and she could barely take in the enormity of his achievement. But he had not wanted to talk about it. All the snippets that had not meant anything at the time but which could now be pieced together to form a new whole. Like that evening in October almost three years ago, when the boys had gone to sleep and Johannes had just been appointed Minister of Defence. They were sitting

on the sofa at home in Stocksund, and he mentioned Klara
Engelman in a new, disturbing tone of voice.

"I keep wondering what she was thinking," he said.

"When?"

"When she was abandoned."

She answered that in all likelihood Klara was not thinking at all—that she was probably already dead. But now, in
the night, Rebecka understood what Johannes had meant,
and it was more than she could bear.

CHAPTER 28

May 13, 2008

Klara Engelman was not thinking anything the first time she was abandoned. Her body temperature had dropped to eighty-two degrees and her heartbeat was by then slow and irregular. She heard neither the disappearing footsteps nor the howling storm.

She was deeply unconscious, not aware that she had put an arm around Viktor or even that the body she was holding on to was his. Her organs were shutting down as a last form of defence, and she would soon be dead. By then there was no doubt, and that was perhaps, in a way, what she had wanted.

Her husband, Stan, made no secret of his contempt and cheated on her quite openly, their twelve-year-old, Juliette, was going through a crisis too, and Klara had run away from it all, taken herself off to Everest and put on a cheerful face, just as she always did. She was, in fact, suffering from severe depression, and it was only in the last week that she had found a reason to live again. It was not just her love for Viktor. She had also begun to hope that she could bring Stan down, once and for all.

She was feeling strong again, even as she headed towards the summit, and she had drunk plenty of that blueberry soup which she had heard was so good for one. But before long her body began to feel strangely heavy and her eyelids kept closing, and she felt colder and colder until finally she collapsed. She slipped away and was oblivious to the storm which now came raging in from the north, endangering the whole expedition. For her, the hours simply vanished into darkness, and silence, and she heard nothing until an ice axe started picking away at her face.

Not that she really grasped what was going on. There was just this hacking right by her, close to her and yet still remote, as if in another world. But then . . . her airways had become freer and the footsteps had disappeared, and she opened her eyes. It was a miracle, in a way. Klara, who had been given up for dead, looked around and had no idea what was going on. Except that she found herself in some sort of hell. But little by little things came back to her, and she looked at her legs and her boots and then at an arm, without quite being able to understand whose arm it was. It was frozen stiff above her hip in the air. Then she realized it was hers, and tried to move it. But it would not budge. Her body was frozen. Then something happened which got her to her feet.

She saw her daughter in front of her. She saw her as clearly as if she could reach out and touch her, and after four or five attempts she stood up and began to stumble downhill, like a sleepwalker with hands stretched in front of her, and even though she barely knew which was left and which was right, she was guided by howls, inhuman screams which seemed to be showing her the way. It was a long time before she realized that the screams were her own.

Nima Rita was in a landscape he had always believed to be inhabited by spirits and ghosts, so he took no notice of the screams. *Go on,* he thought, *scream as much as you like.* Why on earth had he come back up here? He could not believe it himself. He had seen her and said his goodbyes. All hope was lost. But he also knew that he had listened too much to the others and had left behind the one person he should not have abandoned. Maybe he no longer cared whether he too went under or not. All that mattered was for him to show that he had not given up. If he died, he would die with dignity.

His exhaustion had taken him beyond all reason, he had frostbite and he could hardly see. He heard only the blizzard and the howling in the snowy fog. But he did not for even a second connect them to Mamsahib, and he was about to pause for a breath when the sound of creaking footsteps in the snow came ever closer.

Then he saw a ghost with its arms held out, as if beseeching the living to give it something, a piece of bread, some comfort, a prayer, and he approached the ghost. The next moment the figure fell into his arms with a surprising weight. They collapsed in the snow and rolled over, and he banged his head.

"Help me, help me, I have to get to my daughter," the figure said, and then he knew.

He did not understand, it dawned on him gradually and in some confusion, and then a stab of joy shot through his exhausted body. It was her. It really was her, and that could only be because the mountain goddess was smiling on him. She must have seen how he had struggled, and with what pain. It would all be all right, he thought, so he gathered his remaining strength and put his arms around her waist and got her back onto her feet, and then they stumbled down together while she screamed and he increasingly lost his grip on reality.

His face was so strangely stiff. It was as if he were in another world, yet he was holding her up, wasn't he? And he was battling. It was clear from the sound of his breathing that he was fighting furiously. She prayed to God that she would be allowed to go home to her daughter, and all the time she promised herself not to give up, not to collapse. Not now and not later. It would all work out, she thought.

With every step she took she told herself: Once I have come out of this alive, I will be able to cope with anything, and then, further down the mountain, she made out two other figures, and that gave her more hope.

Now I am safe.

Now, at last, I must be safe.

CHAPTER 29

August 28

Catrin Lindås woke at 8:30 in the double bed at Hotel Lydmar and reached over to pull Mikael closer to her. But he was not there, so she called out:

"Bloombells?"

It was a silly nickname she had given him the night before, when he had not listened to a word she was saying—"You've got nothing but bluebells in your head, Bloombells"—and at least it had made him smile. Otherwise she found him impenetrable. Which was, after all, understandable. He was going to do an exclusive interview with the Minister of Defence, and it was all very hush-hush with encrypted instructions being sent to her mobile. The only way to get anything out of the man was to discuss his interview, and then he was not quite so remote. And at one point he tried to recruit her to *Millennium*. Straight after that she managed to undo his shirt buttons, then all the other ones as well, and they made love. Then she must have fallen asleep.

"Bloombells?" she called again. "Mikael?"

She looked at her watch. It was later than she thought. He must have left a long time ago, was probably doing the interview by now. She did wonder why she had not woken up. But sometimes her sleep was strangely deep, and it was quiet outside, you could hardly hear the traffic. She lay there until her mobile rang.

"Catrin Lindås," she said.

"My name is Rebecka Forsell," a voice said. "We're beginning to get a little worried."

"Isn't Mikael with you?"

"He's half an hour late and his mobile is switched off."

"That's odd," she said.

It was very odd. She didn't know Blomkvist that well, but surely he wouldn't turn up half an hour late for such a crucial meeting.

"You don't know where he could be?" Rebecka Forsell said.

"He'd already left by the time I woke up."

"Had he now?"

Lindås detected a note of fear in the woman's voice.

"I'm beginning to get worried," Catrin said. Or *cold*, is that what she should have said? Stone cold.

"Do you have any particular reason to worry? Apart from the fact that he's late?" Rebecka Forsell said.

"Well . . ." Her thoughts were racing. "For the past few days he's not wanted to stay in his own home. He thought he was being watched," she said.

"Is it because of this business with Johannes?"

"No, I don't think so." Lindås was not sure how much she should say, but then decided to be completely open. "It's to do with his friend, Lisbeth Salander. That's all I know."

"Oh, my God."

"Why do you say that?"

"It's a long story. But you know . . ." She sounded emotional. "I liked what you wrote about Johannes."

"Thank you."

"And I can see why Mikael trusts you."

Lindås did not mention how many times that night she had sworn by all she held dear that she would not breathe a word about the story to anyone, and every time it had seemed that he did not believe her.

"Could you hang on a moment?"

Lindås waited, but regretted it at once. She couldn't just sit around, she had to call the police and maybe also Erika Berger. By the time Rebecka Forsell was back on the line, she was about to hang up.

"We're wondering if you couldn't come over here yourself," Rebecka said.

"I'm thinking I ought to call the police."

"You probably should. But we . . . that is, our host here . . . we also have people who can investigate this matter."

"I don't know . . ." she said.

"In fact we think it would be safest if you came over here now. We'll send a car, if you give us the address."

Lindås bit her lip and remembered the man she had seen down in reception. She recalled the sensation of being followed on the way to the hotel.

"OK," she said, and gave the address.

Moments later there was a knock at the door of her hotel room.

Bublanski had just called the TT news bureau, hoping that a bulletin would bring in some leads from the public. Although they had been hard at work since early that morning, they still had no idea where Blomkvist was. They knew he had spent the latter part of the evening at the Lydmar without anybody, including the receptionists, having seen him.

He had left the hotel just after 2:00 a.m. There was a short CCTV sequence which was anything but clear, but it did, beyond doubt, show Blomkvist in good shape—probably sober, a little excited, his hand drumming against his thigh. But then something ominous happened: The surveillance cameras stopped working. They simply died. Fortunately there were other witnesses—a young woman by the name of Agnes Sohlberg, for example, who was clearing up on the terrace.

Agnes had seen a middle-aged man come out of the hotel. She had not recognized him as Mikael Blomkvist, but then she had heard an older, slim gentleman in a light-coloured suit address him. The man had been sitting at the far end of the bar, with his back to her. Shortly afterwards she heard rapid footsteps, and maybe also the sound of someone crying out. When she turned she saw another man, a younger, sturdier fellow in a leather jacket and jeans.

At first she took him to be some kind person who had come rushing over to help. She had seen Blomkvist—or the man she later understood to be Blomkvist—collapse in the street, and she heard a voice refer to "an epileptic fit" in English. Since she did not have her mobile with her, she had run inside to call the emergency services.

After that they had to rely on other witnesses, including a married couple by the name of Kristofferson who reported having seen an ambulance coming out of Hovslagargatan. Blomkvist was lifted into the ambulance on a stretcher, and the couple would probably not have given it a second thought had they not been struck by the careless way in which his body was handled. And the way the men had jumped into the vehicle did not seem to them "natural."

The ambulance, which turned out to have been stolen six days earlier in Norsborg, was later caught on camera on Klarabergsleden, heading north on the E4 motorway with sirens blaring. But then it disappeared from sight. Bublanski and his team were convinced the perpetrators had switched cars after that. Nothing was known for sure, however, except that Salander herself had alerted the emergency services. Bublanski was not happy with that.

How could Salander have known about the incident so soon? It made him suspicious that she was somehow connected with the assault, and he felt no better about it even after he'd spoken to her. He was glad, of course, that she had called; he was grateful for every piece of information. But he did not like what he heard in her voice—the rage, the pounding fury, and no matter how many times he said, "Keep out of this, let us handle it," the words didn't seem to get through. And he was certain she had not told him everything. He was convinced she was in the middle of an operation of her own, and he cursed when they hung up and cursed again now as he sat in the conference room with his colleagues Sonja Modig, Jerker Holmberg, Curt Svensson and Amanda Flod.

"What was that?" he said.

"I was wondering how Salander could have known so quickly about Blomkvist having been attacked," Holmberg said.

"I thought I told you."

"You said she'd done something to his mobile."

"That's right, she'd messed about with it—with his consent. So she could eavesdrop on him and see where he was, at least until they shut his mobile down."

"What I really meant was, how was she able to react so fast," Holmberg said. "It sounds . . . I don't know, as if she'd just been hanging about, waiting for something like this to happen."

"She said she'd been afraid it would," Bublanski said. "Like a worst-case scenario. Svavelsjö M.C. had been keeping Blomkvist under observation, both at Bellmansgatan and out at Sandhamn."

"And we still don't have anything on the club?"

"We woke up the president, Marko Sandström, this morning. But he just laughed at us. Said that you needed to be suicidal to go after Blomkvist. We're trying to track down the other members and we'll watch them. So far, we've not been able to link any of them to the incident, other than to note that several of them have been impossible to reach."

"And we don't know why Blomkvist was at the Lydmar in the first place?" Flod said.

"No, we've no idea. We've got people there now. But Blom-kvist appears to have been very cagey of late. Even his col-leagues at *Millennium* had no idea what he was up to. Erika Berger says he's taking some sort of holiday. Apparently he's mainly been working on his story about the Sherpa."

"Which may have something to do with Forsell."

"It may indeed, and that's given Must the jitters, and Säpo too."

"Could it be a foreign operation?" Svensson said.

"The fact that the surveillance cameras were hacked would suggest it. And I don't like the way they used a sto-len ambulance, that really feels like a provocation, but in all likelihood—"

"—there's a link to Salander," Modig concluded.

"That's what we all think," Holmberg said.

"Perhaps we do," Bublanski said, and he sank deep in thought. *What was Salander hiding from him?*

Salander had not told Bublanski about the Strandvägen apartment. She was hoping Camilla would lead her to Blom-kvist, and she did not want the police to mess that up for her. But for now, Camilla was staying put. Maybe she was wait-ing for the same thing as Salander, the thing that Salander dreaded: images of Blomkvist being tortured and a demand for an exchange, her for him, or, worse, pictures of Blomkvist dead and threats to kill others close to her unless she gave herself up to them.

During the night, Salander had been in touch with Annika Giannini, Dragan Armansky, Miriam Wu and a couple of others—even Paulina, who presumably nobody knew about—and had told them to go somewhere they would be safe. It hadn't been pleasant, but she had done what she had to do.

She did not have a clue where they had taken Blomkvist, except that it appeared to be northwards, which is why she was staying at the Clarion Hotel at Arlanda airport, in the same direction at least. But she was as unaware of the room she was in or of the hotel as she was of everything else, and she had not slept a wink.

She had spent hours at the desk trying to find some trace, some opening, and it was not until now, when finally she got a signal, that she sat up in her chair. Camilla was leaving the apartment at Strandvägen. *That's my girl,* she thought. *Please be a little careless now, and take me to him.* But that was hoping for too much. Camilla had Bogdanov, and Bogdanov was in the same league as Plague.

So even if her sister did show her the way to some place, it wouldn't necessarily be a breakthrough. It could equally well be a trap. An attempt to draw her off. She had to be prepared for everything, but now . . . her eyes were fixed on the map. The car carrying Camilla was taking the same route as the ambulance had yesterday, heading north on the E4 motorway. That was promising. It had to be. Salander packed her things and went down to check out, before tearing off on her Kawasaki.

Catrin Lindås wrapped herself in a bathrobe and went to open the door. She found a uniformed policeman standing outside, a young man with blond, neatly parted hair, and she stammered a nervous "Good morning."

"We want to speak to people in this hotel who may have seen or been in contact with the journalist Mikael Blomkvist," the police officer said, and immediately she felt that he was suspicious, maybe even hostile.

His eyes beamed with confidence and he stood very straight, as if to show how tall and powerful he was.

"What's happened?" she said, and the fear was plain in her voice.

The policeman came closer and looked her up and down in a way she recognized only too well. She had encountered it so many times when walking around town, the look that wanted both to undress her and do her harm.

"What is your name?"

That was part of the provocation. She could see that he knew perfectly well who she was.

"Catrin Lindås," she said.

He wrote it down in a notebook. "You've been with him here, haven't you? Did you spend the night together?"

What's that got to do with it? she wanted to shout. But she was frightened, and she stepped back into the room and explained that Blomkvist had already left by the time she woke that morning.

"Did you check in using a false name?"

She tried to breathe calmly and wondered if it would even be possible to have a rational conversation with him, especially now that he had high-handedly marched into the room.

"And do you have a name?" she said.

"What?"

"I don't seem to remember you introducing yourself."

"Inspector Carl Wernersson, from Norrmalm police."

"Good, Carl," she said. "In that case you can perhaps begin by telling me what's going on?"

"Mikael Blomkvist was attacked outside this hotel during the night and abducted, so you'll appreciate that we're taking this very seriously indeed."

She felt as if the walls were closing in on her. "My God," she said.

"So it's of the utmost importance that you give us a truthful account of what happened before that."

She sat down on the bed. "Is he hurt?"

"We don't know. You haven't answered my question," he said.

Her heart was pounding and she fumbled for words. "He was going to an important meeting this morning, but I've just found out that he never showed up."

"What sort of meeting?"

She closed her eyes. Why was she being such an idiot? She had sworn not to tell anyone about it. But she was terrified and confused, her brain was not functioning properly. "I can't tell you, I'm protecting a source," she said.

"So you're refusing to cooperate?"

She was struggling to breathe and looked out of the window, groping for a way out of the situation. But then Wernersson inadvertently helped her by staring at her breasts, and that made her livid.

"I'd be happy to cooperate. But before I do, I want to speak to a person with a rudimentary knowledge of the law on informant protection, and who at least tries to show some respect for people who've received shocking news about someone they're close to."

"What are you talking about?"

"I'm telling you to contact your superiors and get the hell out of here."

Wernersson looked as if he wanted to arrest her right away.

"*Now,*" she said, angrier by the second, and he did actually mutter "OK," although he could not resist adding:

"But you're staying here."

Without answering, she opened the door to show him out, then sat on the bed in stunned silence. A buzzing from her mobile jerked her back to life. It was a news flash from *Svenska Dagbladet*:

CELEBRATED JOURNALIST ASSAULTED AND ABDUCTED

OUTSIDE HOTEL LYDMAR IN STOCKHOLM

For a few minutes she was absorbed by the reports. There were banner headlines everywhere but precious little substance in the stories themselves, only the information that he was said to have been taken away in an ambulance, an ambulance no-one had called. It sounded . . . unbelievable. What the hell should she do? She wanted to scream. Then something came back to her, something she had heard in the night: a sound from the bathroom, a whispering, she thought, an exclamation from Mikael. She may even have whispered back: "What are you up to?"

Or had she been dreaming? It didn't matter. The whispering could have had something to do with his leaving their room. The reports said that he had been abducted outside the hotel at around 2:00 a.m., which would mean—she was trying to think clearly—that something had been worrying him. He had gone off, leaving her alone, and had immediately been attacked. Had it all been a trap, a trick to get him to go out? Shit, shit. What was going on? What had happened?

She thought of the beggar, and of Rebecka Forsell and the desperate sound of her voice, and Mikael's excitement last night about the interview. To hell with that moron of a policeman. Resolute, she dressed and packed her belongings, then went down and paid the bill at reception before being spirited away in a black diplomatic car from the British Embassy that was waiting for her. There had been no further sign of the odious policeman.

CHAPTER 30

August 28

It was hot in the high-ceilinged room, a fire was burning in a large gas furnace. No daylight penetrated the building, which was lit only by a few spotlights. The large glass windows were tinted or covered in soot, and Blomkvist let his eyes dart around the building, making out the concrete beams and iron structures, the shattered glass on the floor and the gleaming metal edges of the furnace in which he saw his own reflection.

He had ended up at some abandoned industrial site, possibly an old glassworks which must be some distance from Stockholm, but he had not the slightest idea where. The journey had not been short, he thought. They had changed cars once or twice, although he had been so heavily drugged he had only fragmentary memories of the night and the morning. And now he was here, strapped to a camp bed or stretcher, not far from the furnace.

"Help! For Christ's sake, is anybody there?!" he shouted out.

Not that he believed it would do him any good. But he had to do something other than writhe and sweat under the leather straps, feeling the heat of the fire on his feet. Otherwise he would go mad. The furnace hissed like a snake and he was terrified. His shirt was soaked in sweat and his mouth was dry, and now . . . What was that? He could hear a crunching, the sound of glass shards being crushed. Footsteps were approaching, and he sensed at once that they brought no hope of relief. On the contrary, they seemed to be ambling along with an exaggerated slowness, accompanied by whistling.

What sort of person would whistle now?

"Good morning, Mikael."

It was the same English voice that had addressed him on the terrace the evening before. But still he could not see anyone. Perhaps that was deliberate, perhaps they did not want to show their faces. He answered in English:

"Good morning."

The footsteps stopped and so did the whistling, and Blomkvist picked up the sound of breathing, the faint scent of aftershave, and he steeled himself for whatever might come, a blow, a stab, a shove of the stretcher—which seemed to be resting on some sort of trolley on rails—which would push his feet into the furnace. But nothing happened.

"I wasn't expecting such a cheerful greeting," the man said.

Blomkvist said nothing.

"That's how I was brought up," the voice said.

"How do you mean?" he managed to stutter.

"Always pretend to be calm, whatever happens. But that really isn't necessary here. I prefer honesty, and I don't mind admitting that I feel somewhat . . . ill at ease. A sort of inner resistance."

"How come?" Blomkvist said.

"I like you, Mikael. I respect your attitude to the truth, and this business . . ."

A pause for effect.

". . . should have been a simple family matter. But as is often the case with blood feuds, other people get drawn in."

Blomkvist noticed that he had begun to tremble. "You're talking about Zala," he said with a groan.

"Yes, indeed, Comrade Zalachenko. But you never met him, did you?"

"No."

"I think you should be congratulated on that. It was an impressive experience, but it left its marks."

"You knew him?"

"I loved him. But sadly it was a little like loving a god. You got nothing back. Only a radiance that dazzled, and made you foolish and blind."

"Blind?" Blomkvist repeated, hardly knowing what he was saying.

"That's right, blind and mad. I'm afraid I may be still a bit of both. It wasn't possible to cut my ties to Zalachenko, and I have a tendency to take unnecessary risks. Neither you nor I ought to be here, Mikael."

"So why are we then?"

"The simple answer is revenge. Your friend could tell you a bit about its destructive force."

"Lisbeth," he said.

"That's right."

"Where is she?"

"Where indeed? That's precisely what we're wondering."

There was another pause, long enough for Blomkvist to fear that the man would show just how blind and mad he still was. Instead the figure stepped forward, and the first thing Blomkvist noticed was the white linen suit, the same the man had been wearing the evening before. To his horror Blomkvist could imagine his own blood staining the jacket.

Then he saw the face. It was harmonious and clean-cut, with slightly asymmetrical eyes and a pale scar running down the right cheek. The man had thick grey hair with snow-white streaks. He was tall, slim and fine-limbed. In a different context he could have been taken for an eccentric intellectual, a kind of Tom Wolfe character. But right now, there was something icily unpleasant about him, and an unnatural slowness in his movements.

"I don't suppose you're alone," Blomkvist said.

"There are a few thugs here too, young men who for some unfathomable reason don't want to show their faces. And we have a camera up there." The man pointed at the ceiling.

"So you're going to film me?"

"Don't you worry about that, Mikael," the man said, inexplicably switching to Swedish. "Just see this as something entirely between you and me, a kind of intimacy."

Blomkvist's body was shaking more and more. "You speak Swedish," he said, terrified.

It was as if the man's ability to go from one language to another confirmed the impression of him as the very devil.

"I'm a linguist, Mikael."

"Really?"

"I am indeed. But you and I are going to travel beyond language."

He unfolded a black cloth he had been holding in his right hand and set out some shiny objects on the steel table next to him.

"What do you mean by that?" Blomkvist was growing increasingly desperate as he twisted on the stretcher and stared into the hissing fire and the reflection of his own contorted face just visible in the metal frame of the furnace.

"There are plenty of splendid words for most things in life," the man went on. "Especially for love, I'm sure you'd agree. You must have read Keats and Byron and all that as a young man, and I'd say they did a pretty good job of capturing love. But infinite pain, Mikael, is beyond words. No-one has been able to describe it, not even the greatest artists, and that is where we are heading, Mikael. To the wordless."

Jurij Bogdanov was sitting in the backseat of a black Mercedes driving north towards Märsta, and showing Kira the film sequence. She was watching it through narrowed eyes and Bogdanov could not wait to see the excitement that never failed to light up her face when she saw her enemies suffer.

But there was no sign of it, only an expression of long-suffering impatience, and that did not bode well. He did not trust Galinov and was convinced that it had all gone too far. Nothing good would come of going after Blomkvist. There were too many impassioned emotions involved, and he did not like Kira's determined look.

"How are you feeling?" he said.

"Are you going to send it to her?"

"First I have to secure the link. But honestly, Kira . . ." He hesitated. He knew she would not like it and avoided her eyes.

"You ought to stay away from that place," he went on. "We should fly you home now, at once."

"I'm not flying anywhere until she's dead."

"I think . . ." he began.

. . . *that she won't let herself be captured so easily,* is what he wanted to say. *That you're underestimating her.* But he said no more. He must not allow a word or a look to betray the fact that he actually admired Salander, or Wasp, as he had come to know her. There were good hackers, there were geniuses and then there was Wasp. That is how he saw it, and instead of speaking he bent forward and pulled out a blue metal box.

"What's that?" she said.

"A noisebox. A Faraday cage. For your mobile. We mustn't leave any tracks."

Kira looked out of the window and put her phone in the box. Then they sat in silence, looking fixedly ahead at the driver and the passing landscape until Kira demanded to see more of what was going on within the industrial building at Morgonsala, so Bogdanov showed her.

They were images he could have done without.

Salander was just passing Norrviken when the signal on her Google Glass disappeared, and she swore and hit the handlebar with her right hand. She had been expecting it, though, and slowed down until she spotted a small patch of woodland by a roadside rest area with a wooden bench and a table. She settled there with her laptop and hoped she would now reap the rewards from all those hours spent charting Camilla's circle of helpers that summer.

The operation would have been impossible without the services of members of Svavelsjö M.C., and even though Salander assumed they only had prepaid mobiles with them, she still wanted to believe that one or another of them would have made a small mistake along the way. She tried again to check the men who had been to see Kira at Strandvägen: Marko, Jorma, Conny, Krille and Miro. Once again she drew a blank, in spite of the fact that she had hacked their operator and could access the base stations. She slammed her fist on the wooden table in fury and was ready to give up and look for another solution when suddenly she remembered Peter Kovic.

Of everyone in the club, Kovic had the worst criminal record, and was said to have a problem with alcohol and women, and discipline. She had not seen him anywhere near Strandvägen, but he was one of the men who had been at Fiskargatan that summer, so she tried his mobile as well. A short time later she exclaimed in triumph. Early that morning, Kovic had followed the same route as Camilla was now travelling, only he had carried on further north towards

Uppsala, past Storvreta and Björklinge. She was just about to have a closer look when her phone rang.

At first she had no intention of answering, but it was Erika Berger from *Millennium*. All she could hear was Erika yelling and the only words she could make out were:

"He's burning . . . he's burning!"

She began to grasp what was happening.

"They've shoved him into a huge furnace. He's screaming, he's in excruciating pain, and they say . . . they've written—"

"What?"

"That they'll burn him alive unless you, Lisbeth, meet them in the woods outside Sunnersta. They say that if they see any police in the area, or anything suspicious, Mikael will die a terrible death . . . and then they'll go after others who are close to you and Mikael, they won't stop until you give yourself up. My God, Lisbeth, it's so awful. His feet—"

"I'll find him, do you hear? I'll find him!"

"They told me to send you the film, and an e-mail address to communicate with them. Lisbeth, you've got to tell me what's going on!"

Salander hung up. She had no time. She needed to get back to Peter Kovic. Last night he had taken the same route as Camilla now, but had gone further north on the E4 towards Tierp and Gävle, and that was encouraging. In fact it was beginning to look promising, and as she drummed her fingers on the table, she muttered:

"Go on, you bloody drunk. Lead me to them."

But the trail ended in Månkarbo. Salander stared blankly at the road, and looked so full of rage that a young man who had just pulled into the rest area in a Renault got a fright and drove off again. She did not even register him. With jaws clenched she watched the film Berger had sent, and saw a close-up of Blomkvist.

His eyes were open wide, and so white it was as if the pupils had disappeared into the sockets, and his whole face was so tense and disfigured that he was hardly recognizable. Sweat was pouring off him, off his chin, his lips, and the front of his shirt was soaked, while the camera moved down his body to his jeans and feet. He was wearing red socks which were slowly being fed into a large brown-brick furnace with a raging, hissing fire. The socks and the bottoms of his trouser legs caught fire and, after an extraordinary time lag, as if Blomkvist was holding it back for as long as he could, there was a crazed, heartrending scream.

Salander did not say a word, she hardly moved a muscle. But her hand, at that moment like a claw, scratched three deep furrows into the table in front of her. Then she read the message they had sent, checked the e-mail address—it was some fucking encrypted crap—and forwarded the lot to Plague together with some brief instructions, a picture of Peter Kovic and a map of the E4 and northern Uppland.

Then she picked up her computer and her weapon, put on her Google Glass and set off for Tierp.

"Lisbeth, you've got to tell me what's going on!" Erika Berger yelled into the telephone.

But the only people who could hear her were her colleagues gathered in the magazine's offices on Götgatan, and they could tell she was beside herself. Sofie Melker, who was standing closest to her, was afraid that Erika was about to collapse and rushed over to put an arm around her. Berger was desperately trying to concentrate on coming up with a plan of action. They had written that she was absolutely not to call the police, not under any circumstances. But was that really an option? Not only was this the worst thing she had ever seen, it was Blomkvist, her oldest friend and great love, and she had been totally unprepared. She had checked her e-mails in the casual way you do when you're not even aware that you're doing it. You just go in as a matter of reflex and then, all of a sudden, this . . .

When she rang Salander, she had still not taken it in, nor ruled out the possibility that it might just be some macabre joke, a fake film sequence. But any such thoughts were immediately dispelled when she heard her voice and understood that this was pretty much what Salander had been anticipating: absolute evil.

It was indescribable, she swore loudly and incoherently, and only then realized, as if she had been in an entirely different dimension, that Sofie was hugging her. For a brief moment she considered telling the team exactly what was going on, but then she shook herself free and muttered:

"Sorry, but I need to be alone. I'll explain later."

Then she went into her office and slammed the door, and there was no need even to say it: She would not survive if anything she did were to cost Blomkvist his life. But that didn't mean she could sit around and do nothing, still less simply follow the bandits' instructions. She needed to . . . well, what? . . . think! Focus, of course, and wasn't that always the pattern with this kind of crime?

The perpetrators do not want the police involved. But when they're caught, it's always because the police have, in fact, been secretly informed. She had better ring Bublanski on a secure line, hadn't she? But when she called, after a moment's hesitation, she couldn't get through, he was busy on another line. She began to shake uncontrollably.

"Goddamn fucking Lisbeth," she hissed. "How could you drag Mikael into this? How *could* you?"

Chief Inspector Bublanski had spoken at length to Catrin Lindås. Now the receiver had been handed to a man who introduced himself as Janek Kowalski, who said he was connected to the British Embassy. Bublanski reckoned he would have to take his word for it.

"I'm a little worried," the man said, which made Bublanski reflect briefly on the British fondness for understatement.

"In what way?" he said drily.

"We have two disparate stories running together rather neatly here, and that may be a coincidence. Or not. There are links between Blomkvist and Lisbeth Salander, are there not, and Johannes Forsell—"

"Yes?" Bublanski said impatiently.

"Towards the end of his time in Moscow, in 2008, Forsell was working on an investigation into Salander's father, Alexander Zalachenko, and his defection to Sweden."

"I was under the impression that only the Säpo group knew about it at the time."

"Nothing, Chief Inspector, is ever as secret as people like to think. The interesting thing is that Camilla, the other daughter, later formed a bond with the man at the GRU who was closest to Zalachenko, and who then stayed in touch with him even after his treason."

"And who is that?"

"His name is Ivan Galinov and, for reasons we can't quite understand, he's remained loyal . . . how shall I put it? . . . beyond the grave. He has targeted Zalachenko's old enemies even after his death, and silenced people who hold damaging information in their possession. He is ruthless and dangerous, and we believe that he's in Sweden right now and involved in Blomkvist's abduction. It would mean an enormous amount to us if he could be arrested, and we are therefore offering you help, especially since Defence Minister Forsell has his own plans, which I have somewhat rashly blessed."

"I'm afraid I don't understand."

"In due course you will, I assure you. We're sending over some material, and pictures of Galinov which are anything but recent, unfortunately. Goodbye, Chief Inspector."

Bublanski nodded to himself. It was unusual for him to be offered assistance by an official like that, because by now he had worked out exactly what sort of person Kowalski was, and his mind was on that and all sorts of other matters. He got up and was about to go see Sonja Modig and put her in the picture when the telephone rang. It was Erika Berger.

Catrin Lindås was sitting in a brown armchair in Kowalski's sitting room, opposite Johannes Forsell and next to Rebecka. She was having trouble concentrating, she couldn't stop thinking about Blomkvist. She had been able to borrow a tape recorder, having had to put away her mobile, and thought that would allow her to keep working. And little by little she became more absorbed, in spite of everything.

"So you couldn't take another step?" she asked.

"No," Forsell continued. "Darkness had fallen and it was icy cold. I was literally freezing, and hoping it would be over quickly. That I would lapse into that last state of lethargy when the body loses its heat and apparently you feel well again. But just then I heard the cries and looked up, and at first I didn't see anything. Then Nima Rita appeared again out of the storm, but this time he had two heads and four arms, like a Hindu deity."

"What are you saying?"

"That's how he looked to me. But in fact he was dragging someone along. It was a while before I registered this, and even longer before I understood who it was. I was too tired to think. Too tired to even hope for rescue. Maybe even too tired to *want* to be rescued, and I must have lost consciousness. I came to when I felt a body lying right next to me, a woman with her arms stiffly stretched out as if she wanted to embrace me. She was mumbling about her daughter."

"What was she saying?"

"I never understood. All I remember is that we looked at each other, completely desperate, of course, but astonished. I think we recognized each other. It was Klara, and I patted her on the head and shoulder, and remember thinking that she would never again be beautiful. Her face had been destroyed by the cold. I saw the cut my ice axe had left in her lip and perhaps I said a few words. Maybe she replied.

I don't know. As the storm crashed around us, Svante and
Nima were having a row above our heads. They were snarl-
ing and shoving at each other. It was all very peculiar and the
only thing I heard was something so absurd and unpleasant
that I thought I must have got it wrong. I heard those ugly
English words 'slut' and 'whore.' Why were those expressions
being used when the crisis was at its worst? I simply could
not understand it."

CHAPTER 31

August 28

Blomkvist had never wanted to die, not in the way Forsell longed for death on Everest. He had never even been in a major crisis. But now as he lay on that stretcher, with severe burns to his legs and feet, he wanted to fade away and disappear. Nothing existed but his pain, and he was not even able to scream. His body was in shock and his jaw was clenched, and he could not conceive that things could get any worse. But they could.

The man in the white suit, who had introduced himself as Ivan, picked up a scalpel lying on the table beside him and cut into Blomkvist's burns, and then he arched his back and screamed. He howled and screamed until he was drawn back into the conscious world. But it was a while before he realized what had happened, and he was only vaguely aware of more footsteps approaching, the click of heels this time. He twisted his head and saw a woman with strawberry-blond hair and a face of unearthly beauty. She smiled, and that should perhaps have given him hope of some sort of relief. Instead he felt only a greater terror.

"You . . ." he forced out.

"Me," she said.

Camilla stroked his forehead and hair. Blomkvist flinched at her touch.

"Hello," she said.

Blomkvist did not answer. His whole being was one screaming wound. And yet . . . his thoughts raced, as if he had something important to tell her.

"Lisbeth worries me," she said. "You should be worried about her too, Mikael. The clock is ticking. Tick, tock. But you've probably lost track of time, haven't you? I can tell you that it's already gone eleven, and Lisbeth would have been in touch by now if she wanted to help you. But we haven't heard a word."

She smiled again.

"Maybe she's not all that keen on you after all, Mikael. Perhaps she's jealous of all your other women. Of your little Catrin."

He shuddered. "What have you done to her?"

"Nothing, my dear, nothing. Nothing yet. But it looks as if Lisbeth would rather see you dead than cooperate with us. She's sacrificing you—the same way she's sacrificed so many others."

Blomkvist closed his eyes and tried to trawl his mind for something he knew he wanted to say, but all that was there was his pain. "It's *you* who are sacrificing me," he said. "Not Lisbeth."

"Us? No, no, Lisbeth was made an offer which she did not accept, and I have nothing against that. I'll be happy for her to discover what it feels like to lose someone you're close to. Weren't you important to her once?"

Again she ran her hand over his hair, and in that second he saw something unexpected in Camilla's face. He saw a similarity to Salander, not in appearance maybe, rather the speechless rage in her eyes, and he managed to stammer:

"The ones . . ."

He struggled to master the pain.

"What, Mikael?"

". . . who mattered to her were her mother, and Holger, and she's already lost them," he said, and in that moment he realized what he had been searching for.

"What are you trying to say?"

"That Lisbeth knows perfectly well what it is to lose someone close, while you, Camilla—"

"While I . . ."

". . . lost something worse."

"And what would that be?"

He spat it out through gritted teeth:

"A piece of yourself."

"What do you mean?" Fury flashed in her eyes.

"You lost both your mother and your father. A mother who did not want to see what was being done to you, and a father . . . you loved . . . but who took advantage of you, and I believe—"

"What the hell do you believe?"

He shut his eyes and tried grimly to focus. "That you became the biggest victim in the family. Everyone let you down."

Camilla grabbed him by the throat:

"What has Lisbeth put into your head?"

He was having trouble breathing, not only because of Camilla's hand. It felt as if the fire was creeping closer and he was sure that he had made a mistake. He had wanted to awaken something inside her. But he had only managed to provoke her fury.

"Answer me!" she yelled.

"Lisbeth has said that . . ." He gasped for breath.

"What?"

"That she should have understood why Zala came to you at night, but she was so focused on protecting her mother that it didn't register."

Camilla took her hands from his throat and kicked the stretcher so that his feet hit the side of the furnace.

"Is that what she told you?"

His pulse was racing. "She didn't understand."

"Bullshit! She knew all along, of course she did," Camilla shouted.

"Calm down, Kira," Galinov said.

"Never," she hissed. "Lisbeth's been telling him barefaced lies."

"She didn't know," Mikael stuttered.

"So that's what she's saying? Do you want to know what really happened with Zala? Do you? Zala made me a woman. That's what he always said." Camilla hesitated and seemed to be searching for words. "He made me a woman, just as I'm making a man of you now, Mikael," she said, leaning forward and looking straight at him, and if at first there had been only rage and revenge in her eyes, now they changed.

There was a glimpse of something vulnerable there, and he imagined that a connection had formed between them, perhaps she recognized something of herself in his defence-lessness. But he could have been mistaken. The very next second she turned and walked out, shouting something in Russian that sounded like an order.

Now Blomkvist was alone with the man whom he knew only as Ivan, and all he could do was try to endure, and not look into the flames.

IIIII

MAY 13, 2008

When Klara saw the climbers in the snowy fog, she collapsed and rolled down the slope, away from Nima Rita, and fell against a body lying there, a man. Was he dead? No, no, he was alive, he moved. He looked at her, and shook his head. He was wearing an oxygen mask. She could not see who it was. But he patted her shoulder.

Then he took off his mask and sunglasses and when his eyes smiled at her, she smiled back, or at least she tried to. But not for long—soon she heard an argument going on over their heads. She caught only fragments. It was to do with everything Johannes—did they really say Johannes?—had done for Nima, and still would do. Build a house. Take care of Luna. But she could make no sense of this.

She was in so much pain. She just lay there in the snow, helpless, she could not get up and she prayed to God that Nima would help her again and yes, there he now was, bending over her, and it felt as if the whole world were reaching down. She was going to be safe. She would go home, see her daughter again. But Nima did not pull her to her feet.

It was the other man, and at first she was not unduly worried. They were just picking him up first. She looked up to see the man draped over Nima, just as she had been hanging over his back before, and she thought that the other person there would help her, the one who had been shouting at Nima. But the minutes went by and then something deeply worrying happened. They staggered away from her. They couldn't be leaving her behind, could they?

"No," she screamed. "Don't leave me, please!"

But they did leave, without looking back, and she stared at their backs disappearing into the storm, and only once she was left with nothing but the sound of their creaking footsteps did the sheer terror of it strike her, and she shrieked until she had no more strength and all she could do was sob quietly, in a despair that she had never imagined possible.

Jurij Bogdanov was sitting in a newly built annexe opposite Kira, who had settled into a leather armchair and was nervously sipping an exquisite white Burgundy which had been sent for her benefit.

Bogdanov's eyes were fixed on his computer. He had to keep track of a whole series of video sequences, not only the one showing Blomkvist writhing in pain, but also coverage of the surrounding countryside.

The building was a glassworks, now disused, which had produced high-quality vases and bowls until it went bust a few years ago, when Kira bought it. It was in an isolated spot far from any built-up area, close to the edge of the forest, and even though the windows were large and tall, it was impossible to see through them; Bogdanov had been obsessive in ensuring they took every precaution. They ought to be safe here. But he was nevertheless not entirely confident, and his thoughts went to Wasp and what he had heard about her. She was said to have got into the NSA's intranet and read things that not even the President had been allowed to see. She had succeeded in doing what was considered impossible, and in his world she was a legend, whereas Kira . . . well, what about Kira?

Bogdanov looked over to where she was sitting, beautiful Kira who had picked him out of the gutter and made him rich. He should be feeling nothing but gratitude towards her, and yet—and he felt it like a sudden weight in his body—he was tired of her. He was fed up with her threats and blows, her thirst for revenge, and so, without quite knowing why, he went to the e-mail address he had created and paused for a few seconds, feeling a strange sense of excitement in his body.

Then he typed in the GPS coordinates.

If they couldn't track down Wasp, she would have to come to them.

Salander had pulled into another rest area, not far from Eskesta on the E4, and was sitting there with her laptop when a car stopped by the side of the road. It was a black Volvo V90 and that made her start and reach for the weapon under her jacket. But it was only a middle-aged couple with a small boy who needed to get out to pee.

Salander went back to her screen. Plague had just sent her a message containing . . . well, it was nothing like a break-through, not remotely, but still, a new direction, to the east.

Just as she had been hoping, that idiot from Svavelsjö, Peter Kovic, had screwed up and got caught on a surveillance camera at a service station on Industrigatan in Rocknö, north of Tierp, at 3:37 that morning. He looked like shit. Big and wet and bloated. In the video footage he could be seen removing his helmet and drinking from a silver-coloured water bottle, before he poured the rest over his hair and face. Probably trying to recover from the mother of all hangovers. She wrote back:

```
<Have you been able to follow him
further?>
```

Plague answered:

```
<After that, nada>
<What about any signals from his mobile?>
<Stone dead>
```

That drunk buffoon could have gone anywhere. Either

inland, into the depths of Norrland, or up towards the coast. And she had no fucking clue where they had taken Blomkvist. She felt like screaming and hitting out. But she controlled herself and sat there wondering if it would be worth contacting the bastards, seeing if that would help her work something out. She went into the e-mail account she had been given and discovered something new: two lines of numbers and letters she could not make sense of at first. Then she saw that they were GPS coordinates, of a place in the Uppland parish of Morgonsala:

Morgonsala.

What did that mean? Last time they had summoned her to a place outside Sunnersta, with incredibly detailed instructions on how to get there. Now, no directions, not a single word, just a reference to a position located ... where? ... she had a closer look—somewhere in the sticks, in the middle of a field. She saw that Morgonsala was a small community with sixty-eight inhabitants, northeast of Tierp, consisting mainly of forest and plains. There was a church, of course, and some ancient ruins as well as a few abandoned industrial sites from the '70s and '80s, when the district was humming with entrepreneurial spirit. She thought that looked quite promising, and when she put the coordinates into Google Earth she discovered a long, rectangular brick building with large glass windows standing in the middle of a field, not far from the forest.

Just about any building in Sweden could be a hiding place for criminals, there was a whole country to search through. Why point straight at that one? Why send her any coordinates at all? Was it a red herring? A trap?

She looked again at the map and saw that Rocknö, where Kovic had stopped at the service station, was right by the turnoff to Morgonsala.

Had one of Camilla's lot squealed? Was that conceivable? Admittedly, it couldn't have been a popular move to order the Svavelsjö crew to go after someone like Blomkvist. It would have seemed too risky, but why leak the information to her? What were they hoping for in return?

It made no sense. She wrote to Plague:

<May have a lead in Morgonsala>

<Tell me>

She sent him the GPS coordinates and wrote:

<Going there now. Could you create some havoc in the neighbourhood?>

<Always happy to stir up shit. How?>

<Electricity, multiple mobile messaging>

<Got you>

<Keep in touch>

Then she got on her motorcycle and rode at a reckless speed to Morgonsala. Before long she noticed the wind growing stronger. The sky was clouding over and she gripped the handlebars so tightly that her fingers whitened inside her gloves.

CHAPTER 32

August 28

Ivan Galinov looked down at the journalist on the stretcher.
What a fighter. He had not for a long time seen anyone go
through this level of pain with such stoicism. But that did
not help now. Time was passing and they could wait no longer. The journalist had to die—perhaps in vain, but it no
longer mattered. For better or for worse, Galinov thought,
here he now was, driven by the shadows of the past. By the
fire itself, one could say.

Unlike so many of his colleagues at the GRU, Galinov had
not applauded when Zalachenko's twelve-year-old daughter
threw a Molotov cocktail into his car and watched him burn.
Instead he had withdrawn, and sworn to go after that girl
one day. There was no denying that he had been floored all
those years ago when he heard that Zalachenko, his closest
friend and mentor, had defected and become the worst of
the worst, a traitor to his country.

But later he realized it was not that simple, and they had reconnected, picking up more or less where they left off. They met in secret to exchange information, and they built up Zvezda Bratva together. Nobody, not even his own father, had meant as much to him as Zalachenko. Galinov would always honour his memory, in spite of the fact that he knew Zala had been the author of so much evil, not only in his profession but in other ways too, against his own flesh and blood, for instance. And that was another aspect of the drama that had brought him here.

He would do anything for Kira. He saw in her both Zala and himself, both the traitor and the betrayed, both the victim and the one inflicting the pain, and he had never seen her as distraught as she was after speaking to Blomkvist on the stretcher.

Galinov drew himself up. It was afternoon by now, his body was tired and his eyes were stinging. But here he was and he had to finish off the job. He had never enjoyed this kind of work, not like Kira or Zala. For him it was only a duty.

"Let's get this over with, Mikael," he said. "You'll manage just fine."

Blomkvist did not reply. He just clenched his jaw and steeled himself. The stretcher he was lying on was soaked in sweat. His feet were badly burned and gashed and there was a steady blaze in the furnace, like a gaping monster in front of him. Galinov had no trouble imagining himself in Blomkvist's position.

He had himself been tortured and at one point was certain that he was going to be executed. As some sort of comfort both for him and for Blomkvist, he believed there must be a limit to extreme pain, a moment when the body closes down. There was no evolutionary point in limitless suffering, especially when all hope was gone.

"Are you ready?" he said.

"I . . . have . . ." the journalist said, but he had evidently reached that limit because nothing more was heard.

Galinov checked that the stretcher would still roll freely and wiped the sweat from his cheeks. He caught a glimpse of himself in the metal frame of the furnace and readied himself.

Blomkvist would have liked to say just about anything, if only to buy himself some respite. But his strength was gone and now memories and thoughts washed over him like a tidal wave. He saw his daughter before him, and his parents and Lisbeth and Erika, it was far more than he could take in, and he felt his back arching. His legs and hips were shaking and he realized, this is it, I am going to burn alive, and he tried to look up at Galinov but everything was blurred.

The whole room seemed hazy, he couldn't tell if the lights really were starting to blink and go out, or if he was hallucinating. For a while he thought that the darkness was a part of his mortal terror. But then he heard footsteps and voices, and saw Galinov turn and say in Swedish:

"What the hell's going on?"

Several agitated voices answered. What was it? Blomkvist only knew that there was a sudden commotion in the building, that the electricity seemed to have failed. Everything had gone out except the furnace, which still burned with the same menacing intensity, leaving him one push away from an agonizing death. But all this uproar must mean . . . that there was hope, surely. He looked around and saw shadowy figures moving in the dark.

Perhaps the police had arrived, and he tried to think and to rise above the pain. Was there anything he could do to frighten them more? Tell them they were surrounded? But no, that might make them shove him into the oven even faster. His throat tightened. He could barely breathe. He looked down at the leather straps across his legs. The heat of the furnace had scorched them, searing them into his skin. A savage pain cut through his throbbing calves. His skin was in shreds, and yet . . . maybe he could tear himself free? It would be excruciatingly painful. But there was no time to think about that now. He closed his eyes and with difficulty said:

"Holy shit, the ceiling's coming down!"

Galinov looked up, and Blomkvist took a deep breath and yanked his legs out of the straps with a monumental bellow that cut through the air. Without even thinking, he swung the lower half of his body and kicked the man in the stomach, and then everything went skewed and blurry. The last thing he remembered before he blacked out was the sound of voices shouting:

"We need to kill him."

|||||

MAY 14, 2008

It all came back to him the next day, on his way down to Base Camp, those words that had sounded so faint through the storm and the driving snow, the last they heard from Klara, the desperate cries:

"Don't leave me, please!"

It was more than he could bear, and he knew then that those words would echo within him for the rest of his life. Yet beyond that he was alive, and it was intoxicating. Time and again he prayed to God that he might make it all the way down, so he could fall into Rebecka's arms once more. He was weighed down by guilt but he also wanted to live, and he felt gratitude too, not only towards Nima Rita but also to Lindberg. Without him he would have died up there. Still, he could not bring himself to look him in the eye, and he concentrated instead on Nima. It turned out that he was not the only one; they were all worried about him.

Nima was a wreck. There was talk of taking him to hospital by helicopter, but he refused to accept any help, least of all from Lindberg and Forsell. He was a potential source of trouble, there was no denying it. What would he have to say once he regained his strength? It worried Forsell. It appeared to worry Lindberg even more, and the atmosphere grew increasingly tense. In the end Forsell decided to let it be. Things would just have to run their course. As he grew weaker and they headed down towards the safety of Base Camp, apathy replaced his will to live, and when finally he did get to take Rebecka in his arms, the feelings he had dreamed of were not there. No sense of security, no sense of achievement in having reached the summit, no yearning for her . . . only a heavy heart.

He barely wanted to eat and drink. He just slept, for fourteen hours, and when he woke up, he was all but mute. It was as if the whole dizzying mountain landscape had been cloaked in ash and he could not find solace anywhere, not even in Rebecka's smile. Everything seemed dead. Only one thought filled his mind: he had to say what had happened. But he kept putting it off, and not only because of Lindberg and his anguished looks. Word had gone around camp that Nima Rita's career as a climber was over. Would he be the one who put the final nail in that coffin? Would he be the one to reveal that the man, who in every other way had been the great hero on the mountain, had left a woman to die in the storm in order to save his, Johannes Forsell's, life?

It was all but unthinkable. Yet that is probably what would have happened had Lindberg not approached him on the trek down from Base Camp. They were level with Namche Bazaar, not far from a ravine with a brook rippling through it. He was walking on his own. Rebecka was further ahead, looking after Charlotte Richter, who was concerned about the frostbite on her toes. Lindberg put his arm around Forsell's shoulders and said:

"We can't say anything about this, not ever, you get that, don't you?"

"I'm sorry, Svante. I've got to say something. I can't live with myself otherwise."

"I do understand, my friend. Of course I do. But we're in a bit of a tight spot here," he said, and in his most obliging voice went on to tell him what the Russians had on them, at which Forsell replied that he might just wait and see, after all.

Perhaps he even saw it as a means of escape, a way out when his inner voice was telling him he had a duty to tell the truth about what happened.

IIIII

The geography was not obvious. Salander had decided to avoid taking the road, assuming she had identified the right building. She had come skidding along a woodland path and was now standing by her motorcycle in the midst of a clump of blueberry bushes behind a tall fir tree, looking across a field at the building.

At first, she had detected no signs of life, and been convinced that it was all a smokescreen, a way of throwing her off the scent. The brick and stone building was long, like a stable, and showed signs of disrepair. The huge windows looked like they hadn't been cleaned for a decade. The roof needed mending, the paint was peeling away from the short end wall, and from where she was standing she could not see any cars or motorcycles. But then she noticed smoke coming from the chimney and gave Plague instructions to start their operation.

Soon after that someone looked out the door of the building, a long-haired man wearing dark clothes. She caught only a glimpse of him, but she registered his nervous expression as he scanned the surroundings, and that was good enough for her.

She set up her IMSI-catcher and her mobile base station, and moments later another man peered out, looking very worried too. It had to be them, she was now certain of it. There were probably a number of others as well. Bound to be if they had Blomkvist in there, so she photographed the building and sent the GPS coordinates to Chief Inspector Bublanski in an encrypted message, hoping that would get the police there quickly. Then she approached the house.

Although it was windy and the sky was dark, it was a big risk: There was nowhere to hide in the open area. But she wanted to look in through the tall windows on the long side of the building, which extended all the way to the ground. She moved forward in a crouch, her weapon drawn, but the windows were tinted, she could not see a thing. Sensing danger, she began to back away. She had come too close. Turning abruptly, she checked her phone. An intercepted text:

<We need to finish him and get out of here>

Looking back on events later, it was difficult to say exactly what happened. To Salander it felt as if she had hesitated, just as she had on Tverskoy Boulevard. But Conny Andersson, who picked her up on the cameras at that very moment, got the impression instead of a fiercely determined figure racing up towards the forest.

. . .

Bogdanov spotted her on his screen but, unlike Andersson, he did not raise the alarm. He only looked on in grudging fascination as she disappeared among the trees. For some seconds she was invisible. Then there was the sound of an accelerating engine and he saw it on his screen: She was riding a motorcycle straight at them, at high speed. The bike bounced as it flew across the open space, and he assumed that was the last he would see of her.

He heard gunshots and the sound of breaking glass, and the motorcycle swerved out there in the field. But Bogdanov did not wait to see how it would end. He grabbed the car keys lying on the table next to him and hurried out, feeling an irresistible urge to break free at last, to escape from something that could not possibly end well, either for them or for Wasp.

Blomkvist opened his eyes and saw the blurry figure of a man right in front of him, a bloated, unshaven guy in his forties with long hair, a square jaw and bloodshot eyes. The man's hands were shaking and he was holding a pistol that was also shaking as he looked nervously at Galinov, who was still trying to catch his breath.

"Do I shoot him?" the man shouted.

"Shoot him," Galinov said. "We have to get out of here," and at that Blomkvist began to kick wildly as if he could fend off the bullets with his wounded feet. He had time to see the man's eyes narrow and the muscles tense in his forearm. He had just shouted, "No, for God's sake, no!" when he heard the roar of a vehicle approaching at top speed. Then the man spun around.

There was shooting all around, maybe from machine guns, it was impossible to tell. The only certainty was that the vehicle was heading straight for them. There was a crash, and a shower of broken glass flew across the factory floor. A motorcycle came thundering in through a window, and on it sat a skinny figure dressed in black. She drove right into one of the men standing there and was thrown against the wall in the collision.

The gunfire continued and the flabby man with the square jaw was aiming his pistol not at him now, he was aiming it at the figure who had been thrown from her bike. But she was already up and moving. Frantic, hurried footsteps came charging towards him and Blomkvist saw Galinov's face stiffen with fear or concentration. He heard more shooting and screams before pain and nausea overwhelmed him and he lost consciousness again.

Lindås, Kowalski and the Forsells had eaten an Indian takeaway, having broken off from their work. Now they were sitting in the living room and Lindås was trying to gather her wits once more. She was anxious to get a better understanding of what Lindberg had said to Forsell while they were trekking down from Base Camp.

"I thought that he had my best interests at heart," Forsell said. "He told me he was worried we'd be hit with other accusations if we told people what had happened, and that it was already touch and go as it was."

"What did he mean by that?"

"The top people at the GRU knew who we were, obviously. They would be asking themselves if there was some connection between Grankin's death and our presence on the mountain. Svante went on in the same friendly tone: 'They've been wanting to get you for some time, as I'm sure you know,' and it's true, I did know that. The GRU considered me dangerous and an aggravation. Then, in the same damn understanding voice, he reminded me that they probably had *kompromat* on me."

"*Kompromat?*"

"Compromising material."

"What was he referring to?"

"An incident with a government minister called Antonsson."

"The Minister for Trade?"

"That's it. At the time, in early 2000, Sten Antonsson was recently divorced and feeling a bit lost, and he fell in love with a young Russian woman called Alisa. The poor man was on cloud nine. But during a visit to Saint Petersburg—and I was in the city then—the two of them drank buckets of champagne in his hotel room. In the middle of all the fun, Alisa started fishing for sensitive information, and I think that's when the penny dropped. Not true love after all, just a good old-fashioned honey trap, and he totally lost it. Started raising hell and his bodyguards came rushing in, and there was complete pandemonium. Someone had the idiotic idea that I should question the woman, so I was summoned up to the room."

"What happened?"

"In I went as swiftly as I could and the first thing I saw was Alisa, wearing lacy knickers and garters and the whole shebang. She was hysterical and I tried to calm her. Then she started yelling that she wanted money, or she'd sue Antonsson for assault. I was caught off guard and, since I had a wad of rubles on me, I gave them to her. Not all that elegant. But it was the only solution I could come up with on the spur of the moment."

"And you were worried there might be pictures?"

"I was, yes, and Lindberg reminding me of the incident made everything that much more complicated. I thought of Becka and of how much I loved her, and I was terrified that she would think that I was some kind of sleazebag."

"So you kept quiet about what had happened?"

"I made up my mind to wait, and when I saw that Nima wasn't talking either, I put it to one side. Anyway, we then started having other problems."

"What sort of problems?"

Kowalski answered:

"Someone leaked to the GRU that Johannes had tried to recruit Grankin."

"How could they do that?"

"We thought it was Stan Engelman," Kowalski said. "That summer and autumn we were getting convincing reports suggesting that he was also a member of Zvezda Bratva. We suspected Engelman of having a mole on the expedition

who had told him about the friendship between Johannes
and Viktor. We even thought it might be Nima Rita."

"But it wasn't?"

"No, yet there was no doubt that the GRU had somehow
been informed, even if we didn't think they knew anything
for certain. Nonetheless . . . a formal complaint was lodged
with the Swedish government. It was suggested that pressure
from Johannes had aggravated the stress Grankin was suffering on Everest and had cost him his life. As you know,
Johannes was deported from Russia."

"So that's why?" Lindås said.

"Partly. In fact the Russians were kicking out a great
number of diplomats at that time. But yes, that was part of
the picture, and it was a tremendous loss for us all."

"But not for me," Forsell said. "For me, it was the start
of something new and better. I left the military and felt an
enormous sense of relief. I was in love and we were married,
and I built up my father's business and had children. I felt
life was wonderful again."

"And that's dangerous," Kowalski said.

"Don't be such a cynic," Rebecka said.

"But it's true. A happy man lowers his guard."

"I grew careless and didn't put two and two together as
I should have," Forsell said. "In my eyes, Lindberg remained
a trusted friend and supporter. I even made him my parliamentary undersecretary."

"And you think now that was a mistake?" Catrin said.

"To put it mildly—almost immediately after that, things
began to catch up with me."

"You were the victim of a disinformation campaign."

"That too, but above all, I had a visit from Janek."

"And what did he want?"

"I wanted to talk about Nima Rita," Kowalski said.

"Do explain."

"Certainly," Forsell said. "You see, I had stayed in touch with Nima for a long time. I helped him with money and built a house for him in Khumbu. But in the end it made no difference what I did. After Luna died, his entire life collapsed and he became seriously ill. I managed to reach him a few times on the telephone, but I could hardly understand him. He was just rambling. His head was one big mess and no-one could be bothered to listen to him anymore. He was seen as harmless—even by Lindberg. But by the autumn of 2017, the situation had changed. A journalist with *The Atlantic*, Lilian Henderson, was writing a book about the events on Everest. It was due to be published the year after, to mark the tenth anniversary of the drama. Lilian was exceedingly well informed; not only did she know about the romance between Viktor Grankin and Klara, but also about Stan Engelman's links to Zvezda Bratva. She had even looked into the rumour that Engelman had wanted to see both his wife and Grankin dead on the mountain."

"My God."

"Exactly. And she conducted a hard-hitting interview with Stan Engelman in New York. Stan denied all the accusations, of course, and there were no guarantees that Lilian would be able to produce evidence to back up what she had uncovered. In spite of that, it must have been clear to Engelman that he was in serious trouble."

"So what happened?" Lindås said.

"Lilian Henderson made the mistake of mentioning that she was going to Nepal to speak to Nima Rita. As I said, under normal circumstances Nima was perfectly harmless, but maybe not in the face of an investigative journalist with enough background knowledge to be able to sort the facts from the madness."

"And what were the facts?"

"The very ones Lilian was interested in, among others," Kowalski said.

"What do you mean?"

"One of our people at the embassy in Kathmandu read Nima's manifesto. In among everything else was the information that Engelman had asked Nima to kill Mamsahib on the mountain, although it seems Nima talked about an Angelman, making it sound as if the instructions had been issued by a dark angel from heaven."

"And you think that's true?" Lindås asked.

"Yes, we do," Kowalski continued. "We believe that Engelman had been toying for some time with the idea of using Nima Rita."

"Is that even possible?"

"Don't forget that Engelman would have been desperate when he understood that Klara and Grankin were scheming to get him."

"How did Nima react? Do we know anything about that?"

"He was deeply shaken, as you can imagine," Forsell said. "Everything he had done, his entire career, had been designed to help people, not take lives, and he refused to listen. But afterwards, when he saw that he had in the end contributed to her death, it simply would not let him go. You can just imagine. He was devastated by guilt and paranoia, and in the autumn of 2017, when Janek came to see me, Nima was desperately trying to confess his sins in Kathmandu. He wanted to tell the whole world."

"That's certainly what it looked like," Kowalski said, "and I told Johannes that the prospect of Nima's meeting with Lilian Henderson would put him in danger. There was a risk that Engelman and Zvezda Bratva would want to get rid of him, and Johannes said immediately that it was our duty to look after him and give him protection."

"And you did?"

"Yes."

"How did you go about it?"

"We informed Klas Berg at Must and flew him over here on a British diplomatic flight. We had him admitted to the South Wing in Årstaviken Bay, where sadly . . ."

"What?" Lindås said.

"He was not particularly well looked after and I . . ." Johannes faltered.

"And you . . ."

"I didn't go to see him as often as I had intended. Not only because I was so busy . . . it was just too painful to see him in that state."

"So you went on being happy?"

"I suppose I did, but that didn't last so long either."

CHAPTER 33

August 28

Salander lowered her head as her motorcycle crashed through the window, and when she raised it again she saw that a man in a leather vest was aiming a pistol at her. She rode straight into him. The impact was so violent that she was thrown from the bike and hit the wall with her body, then landed painfully on an iron beam on the floor. She was on her feet in a second and leaped behind a metal column while her eyes registered the details of the building, the number of people and their weapons, the distances, the obstacles and, further away, the furnace she had seen in the film sequence.

A man in a white suit was standing right next to Blomkvist, wiping his face with a handkerchief, and she realized that she was already hurtling towards them, driven by an irrepressible inner force. A bullet glanced against her helmet. Others whistled around her. She shot back and one of the men by the furnace crumpled and fell, which was something. But she did not really have a plan.

She just charged on ahead and saw that the man in the white suit had taken hold of the stretcher to push Blomkvist into the flames. She fired another shot, but missed, so she ran straight at the man and both of them went crashing to the floor. What happened afterwards was not at all clear.

She only knew that she headbutted him, crushing his nose, then got back on her feet and shot at another shadowy figure. She fumbled to undo the leather strap around one of Blomkvist's arms, which was a stupid mistake. Yet it seemed necessary to her. He was on a stretcher that was laid on a kind of trolley on rails. One push would have put him inside the furnace, and although it had taken only a few seconds to release the buckle, she had been distracted.

She felt a blow to her back and a bullet hit her arm and she fell forward, unable to parry a kick to her hand that sent her gun flying. Disaster. Before she had time to get up she was surrounded, and was certain they would shoot her right away. But there was confusion and tension, perhaps they were waiting for orders.

She was the one they had been after all along, and she cast about for a means of escape, knowing that two men were down and a third wounded but still standing. That left her alone against three men. And Blomkvist was not going to be able to help. He seemed dazed, and his legs . . .

She turned away and looked at the thugs again. Her old friends Jorma and Krille from Svavelsjö M.C., and also Peter Kovic, he was the one who had been injured. He was the weak link, and Krille wasn't in very good shape either. Was he the one she had ridden into?

A little further away there was a blue door leading into an annexe. *There'll be more of them in there,* she thought, and she could hear the man she had headbutted groaning behind her. That must be Galinov. He hadn't been put out of action either, and now blood was pumping out of her arm. It became increasingly clear that she was done for. One careless movement and they would shoot her. But she refused to give up. Her brain went into overdrive. What sort of electronics did they have in the place? A camera, of course, and a computer and an internet connection, and maybe also an alarm system. But no . . . she had no access to all that right now. In any case there was no power.

Her only option was to play for time, and she looked at Blomkvist again. She needed him. She needed all the help she could get, and she needed to think positively now. At least she had saved Blomkvist, even if it was only temporarily. Everything else had been a monumental failure. Ever since her hesitation on Tverskoy Boulevard, she had caused nothing but trouble and suffering, and she berated herself even as her brain searched for solutions.

She studied the men's body language and measured the distance to the hole in the window and her motorcycle and an iron rod, a glassblowing tool which was lying on the floor. She considered and rejected various plans of action. It was as if she were photographing every detail of the building, and she listened for sounds and anything that stood out, but also felt a strange premonition. A moment later, the blue door flew open and an all-too-familiar figure came towards

her, footsteps resounding with triumph, but also with hope-
lessness. Tension and gravity filled the air, and behind her a
weary voice said in Russian:

"For Christ's sake, Kira, are you still here?"

||||

SEPTEMBER 30, 2017, KATHMANDU

Nima Rita was squatting on his haunches in a backstreet not
far from the Bagmati River, where the dead are cremated,
and he was sweating in his down jacket, the same one he had
worn the last time he saw Luna in the crevasse up on Cho
Oyu. He could see her there in front of him; how she had
been lying on her stomach with arms spread wide as if she
were flying, calling from beyond the world of the living:

"Please, please don't leave me!"

Her cry sounded the same as Mamsahib's. She was just as
desperate, and the thought of it was unbearable. Nima Rita
downed his beer. Not that the alcohol silenced the cries—
nothing could—but it did dampen them, and the world
would sing a softer tune. Looking down, he saw that he had
three bottles left and that was good. He would drink them.
And then go back to the hospital to meet Lilian Henderson,
who had travelled all the way from the United States to see
him, and that was something really big, probably the only
thing in ages that had given him hope, although of course

he was afraid that she too would end up turning away from him.

He had been struck by a curse. Nobody listened to him now. His words just whirled away, as the ash is blown from the riverside. He was like a disease people shunned. Someone stricken by the plague. Yet he prayed to the gods on the mountain that someone like Lilian would understand. And he knew exactly what he wanted to tell her. He was going to say that he had been wrong, Mamsahib was not a bad person. The bad people were those who had said that she was, Sahib Engelman and Sahib Lindberg, the ones who wanted her dead, who had tricked him and whispered terrible words in his ears. It was they who were evil, not she, that is what he was going to say—but would he be able to? He was ill. He knew that himself.

It was getting muddled, all of it. It felt as if he had not only left Mamsahib to die in the snow but also his Luna, and therefore he had to grieve for and love Mamsahib in the same way that he grieved for and loved Luna, every day, and that made his unhappiness twice as great. A hundred times greater. But he would steel himself and try to distinguish between the voices and not get them all mixed up and risk frightening Lilian, the way he had frightened off the others, and so he drank his beer, quickly and methodically and with his eyes shut. The smell of spices and sweat was all around him. Crowds of people were milling about, but now he could hear footsteps coming very close and he looked up. He saw two men, an older and a younger one. And they said, in English with a British accent:

"We are here to help you."

"Have to tell Mamsahib Lilian," he said.

"You'll have your chance to talk," they said.

He was not sure what happened after that, only that he found himself in a car on the way to the airport, and that he never did meet Lilian Henderson. Nobody found out what really happened, and it did not matter how many times he prayed to the gods for forgiveness. He was lost.

He would die a doomed man.

‖‖‖‖

Catrin Lindås leaned forward and looked Forsell in the eye.

"If Nima wanted to speak to journalists, how come he wasn't allowed to?"

"It was decided that his condition was too poor."

"You said that he got lousy care. That he spent most of his time locked up. Why didn't somebody help him sort out his story?"

Forsell looked down. His lips moved nervously. "Because—"

"—because you didn't really want him to," she interrupted, sounding sharper than she had intended. "You didn't want anything to spoil your happiness, did you?"

"For heaven's sake," Kowalski said. "Have some mercy. Johannes is not the villain in this piece and, as we know, his happiness did not last all that long."

"You're right, I'm sorry," she said. "Keep going."

"You don't have to apologize," Forsell said. "It's true that my behaviour was deplorable. I put Nima out of my mind, and I had my hands full dealing with my own life and my work."

"That whole wave of hatred?"

"It never affected me all that badly. I saw it for what it was—bluff and disinformation. No, the disaster came only a few weeks ago."

"What happened?"

"I was in my office at the Ministry. I had known for some days that Nima Rita had disappeared from the South Wing, and I was worried and thinking about it when Lindberg came in. Something was obviously wrong. You see, I had never told him that we brought Nima over here. Never mentioned it. Those were the orders from Janek here, and his group. But then I just couldn't contain myself. Even though I knew perfectly well how manipulative he could be, in times of crisis I relied on him for support. It was something I had taken with me from Everest, and so I told him everything. It just came out."

"What was his reaction?"

"Calm, collected. He was surprised, to be sure. But I didn't notice anything alarming. He just nodded and left, and I thought everything would be all right. By then I had already been in touch with Klas Berg, who had promised he would find Nima and take him back to the hospital. But nothing happened. It wasn't until Sunday, August 16, that Lindberg called. He was in his car outside our home in Stocksund and needed to talk. He said not to bring my mobile, so I gathered it was something sensitive. He had loud music playing inside the car."

"So what did he say?"

"That he'd found Nima Rita and discovered he'd been putting up his screed describing what had happened on Everest. He'd been trying to contact journalists. 'We can't afford to let that sort of information get out now,' Lindberg said, 'not now that we're in such a precarious position.'"

"What was your answer?"

"I don't honestly know. I just remember him saying he'd taken care of things, and I didn't need to worry any longer. I hit the roof and demanded that he tell me exactly what he had done, to which he calmly replied: 'I'd be happy to talk about it, but then you'd also be involved. That would make two of us,' and I screamed at him. 'I don't give a fuck,' I said. 'I want to know what you've been up to.' And then the bastard gave me the whole story."

"What did he tell you?"

"That he'd found Nima Rita at Norra Bantorget and handed over a doctored bottle without Nima recognizing him, and that he died peacefully in his sleep the next day. Those were his words, 'died peacefully in his sleep,' to which he added that no-one would ever imagine it had been anything other than a natural death or an overdose. 'The guy looked like shit,' he said, 'shit.' And then I got mad, I really lost it. I said I would report him and get him locked up for life. But he just looked at me calmly, and that's when I understood it all. It all became clear, as if I'd been hit by a bolt of lightning. Who he was and what he was capable of. So much became obvious that I hardly know where to begin. But I remember thinking about the blueberry soup on Everest."

"Blueberry soup?" Catrin Lindås sounded surprised.

"Lindberg had got himself sponsored by a company in Dalarna which produced a particularly nourishing blueberry soup, and of course you know that's very Swedish. But on Everest he spoke so warmly of the soup that everyone on our expedition was drinking it, and as we sat there in the car it came back to me how in Camp Four he had handed out bottles just before we set out for the summit. Our Sherpas had carried them up there. I remember him giving Viktor and Klara one each, and I was thinking about how lethargic they became afterwards, and then I realized—"

"That he'd doctored bottles before."

"It's not something I can prove, and he certainly didn't admit to it. But I realized that's the way it was done. He put something into their drink that weakened them, and possibly also a sleeping drug. He must have planned it with Engelman. The two of them were working to protect themselves and Zvezda Bratva."

"But you didn't dare to report them?"

"No, and that's what really broke me."

"What did Lindberg have on you?"

"He had the pictures of me giving the money to Antonsson's mistress for a start. That was bad enough, but it was by no means everything. There were various reports that I'd hired prostitutes and been violent with women. He claimed there was a whole file on me, and it was so absurd that I just sat there gasping for breath. I've never laid a finger on a woman in that way, as you know, Becka. But it was written all over him, and it was as if I were seeing it for the first time."

"What?"

"That to him it didn't matter one little bit that it was

all trumped up. And our friendship was of no importance either. He would destroy me if it suited him, and I'll never forget that he even threatened to nail me for murdering Nima Rita if I picked a fight with him. I was terrified, frankly. I could see us facing disaster, Becka, and I couldn't cope. Instead of doing something, I took a week's leave and went out to Sandön and the rest you know. I couldn't live with it, and I ran into the sea."

"What an evil swine," Lindås said.

"Unspeakable," Rebecka said.

"What about the file Lindberg mentioned? Does it exist, or was he bluffing?"

"It does exist, unfortunately," Kowalski said with a new depth to his voice. "But maybe you'd better deal with that too, Johannes, and I'll fill in if you need me to."

Kira was about to enjoy what she had been looking forward to for her entire adult life, yet it felt . . . what? . . . in truth, mostly anticlimactic. Not just because then it would all be over, and she would no longer be able to dream of it. But because the triumph was not quite as glorious as she had imagined. Because the hurry and the worry in the air had taken the shine off this great moment. Above all, because of Salander herself.

Salander looked nothing like what she had been hoping for—neither crushed nor frightened. She was indescribably dirty and skinny as she lay there on her stomach, with blood running from her arm. Yet somehow she still managed to look like a feline about to pounce. She was propped on her elbows, as if getting ready for an attack. Her black eyes looked straight past them all towards the door leading out of the building, and that alone—the feeling of not even being registered—made Kira furious. *Look at me, sister,* she wanted to shout. *Look at me.* But she must not show any sign of weakness.

"So we've finally got you here," she said.

Salander was silent. She only looked around the room and saw Blomkvist and his badly burned legs and the furnace beyond. She seemed to be searching for her own reflection in the shiny metal, and that gave Kira a small boost. Perhaps Salander was a little scared after all.

"You're going to burn, just like Zala," Kira said, and finally her sister responded.

"Will it feel better afterwards, do you think?"

"You ought to know."

"It doesn't feel better."

"For me it will."

"Do you know what I regret, Camilla?"

"I couldn't care less."

"I regret that I didn't see."

"That's crap."

"I regret that we didn't stick together, against him."

"It would never . . ." Kira began, but then she stopped, either because she had no idea what she wanted to say, or because she knew that whatever she said would be wrong. Instead she yelled:

"Shoot her in the legs and take her over to the furnace," and that did send a shiver of excitement through her chest.

Those bloody idiots did open fire, but they must have

hesitated for one second too long. Salander managed to roll over and Blomkvist was suddenly on his feet, though God knows how he did it. Kira backed away, seeing that her sister had grabbed a rusty iron rod that was lying on the floor.

With all the attention now fixed on Salander, Blomkvist had been able to pull his hands out of the leather straps and had tried to stand up. His legs could scarcely carry him, but the adrenaline rush enabled him to stay upright and grasp hold of one of the knives on the nearby table.

A few yards away, Salander had rolled across the floor holding an iron rod and managed to make it over to her motorcycle. With one sudden and violent wrench, she pulled it up on its wheels, and for a second or two used it as a shield against the bullets. Then she jumped up onto it and started the engine, and rode out through the window and disappeared across the field. It was so unexpected that the gang even stopped shooting. Was she fleeing?

It seemed inconceivable. But the engine noise really did grow fainter and eventually die away. Blomkvist felt as if a cold wind was sweeping through him.

He looked into the burning furnace and down at his horribly wounded legs, and felt that the knife in his hand was pathetic, like a wooden stick in a battle to the death, and he collapsed on the floor in excruciating pain.

Everything had come to a sudden stop. There was disbelief in the air, and heavy breathing and grunting, and the sound of his tormentor, Galinov, getting to his feet. His nose was bloodied and smashed, he had bloodstains and ash all over his white suit, and he was muttering that they ought to get out of there immediately. Camilla met his eyes and made an indeterminate movement with her head, which could have meant yes or no or nothing at all. She seemed as shocked as everyone else. She swore under her breath and kicked one of the men lying wounded on the floor. Further off a man was calling out something about Bogdanov.

At that precise moment Blomkvist heard a new sound, an engine racing, accelerating towards the building. It had to be Salander. What was she doing? She was heading towards them again, but not so fast this time, and she was not making for the hole she had smashed through the window. She was riding towards him and the furnace, and the thugs started shooting again, wildly and recklessly now. But the engine noise kept coming closer and now the motorcycle came thundering through the window straight ahead of him.

Once again, Salander made her entrance in a vast spray of broken glass, which cascaded over the floor and hit Galinov's head and shoulders, and made him jump as if he'd seen a ghost. It was easy to understand why. Salander was deathly pale and looked completely crazed, and this time she was not holding on to the handlebars. Wielding the iron rod, she knocked a gun out of the hands of one of the men before ramming into the stretcher and falling over Blomkvist, straight into the wall. But she was back on her feet in a trice, and she grabbed the weapon which had slid along the floor and began to shoot.

There were flashes all around the building, and Blomkvist could no longer grasp what was going on. He heard only the shots and the yelling, the footsteps and breathing, the grunting and the falling bodies. When the noise finally died down, at least for a moment, he decided to act, to do something . . . anything.

He realized that he was still holding the knife and tried to get up. But the pain was extreme. He took a deep breath and tried again, and made it up onto his feet this time. Dazed, he looked around, and saw that now only three people remained standing: Salander, Galinov and Camilla.

Only Salander held a weapon. The situation had swung in her favour and it was time to wrap it all up. But she remained strangely still, as if her movements had frozen. Even her eyes were immobile, she hardly blinked. There was something wrong. Blomkvist felt it as a stab of fear in the chest, and now he saw it too: Salander's hand was shaking.

She could not shoot, and Galinov and Camilla dared to move forward, each from a different direction, Galinov bleeding and stunned and Camilla shaking with fury. For a few seconds Camilla glared at Salander, her eyes full of hatred and something like madness. Then suddenly, as if wanting to be shot, she ran straight at her sister. But Salander did not fire at her—not this time either.

Instead she fell backwards and banged her head on the bricks close to the furnace. Galinov ran to her, took hold of her. A man lying further away lumbered to his feet. Once again, it looked to be the end for them.

CHAPTER 34

August 28

"I was growing more and more desperate at the time, and it wasn't just fear," Forsell said. "It was also the self-contempt. Lindberg was not only threatening me. He also managed to distort my whole perception of myself. The accusations he claimed to have against me seeped into my veins, and I started to feel like someone who doesn't deserve to live. I mentioned all the hate in the media a little while ago. I never paid much attention to it. But after the exchange with Lindberg in his car, everything that had been said seemed true and real, as if in fact it were a part of me, and I couldn't handle it anymore. I just lay in bed on Sandön, paralyzed."

"And yet I heard you yelling into the telephone," Rebecka said. "You still seemed prepared to fight."

"That's true, I did want to fight. I had rung Janek here, and told him, and often I had the telephone in my hand and was on the point of calling the prime minister and the head of police. I was getting ready to take some sort of action. At least that's what I'd like to believe. And it must have worried Lindberg when I took time off. He came out to Sandön. Looking back on it, I wonder if he didn't do that just to keep an eye on me."

"Why do you say that?" Lindås said.

"Because one morning, when Becka had gone shopping, he turned up unannounced and we stood on the beach and talked. That's when he showed me the dossier. It was all fake, but it was quite uncanny how well it had been put together, with pictures of women who'd been beaten black and blue and witness statements, copies of reports to the police and supporting evidence, certificates which looked like proper scientific or technical proof. It was a comprehensive set of documents, clearly the work of professionals, and I realized at once that enough people would be taken in by it for long enough to cause irreparable damage. I remember walking back into the house and looking around. Every object in there—every kitchen knife, the upstairs windows, the electric sockets—had turned into something with which to injure myself. At that moment, I wanted only to die."

"Not quite, I don't think, Johannes," Kowalski said. "You still had some fight left in you. You called me again and told me everything."

"That's true, I did."

"And you provided enough information for us to be able to confirm that Svante Lindberg had been recruited by Zvezda Bratva early in the 2000s. Not only did we realize that he was corrupt through and through, we also finally understood what had really happened."

"That he drugged Grankin and Klara Engelman?"

"We knew exactly what his motives were all along. Just like Stan Engelman, he was deeply concerned about what Klara and Viktor could reveal. We don't believe that Grankin knew about Lindberg's role in the syndicate, but that's not so important. Once you've been sucked into an organization like that, you do as you're told. By this time, Zvezda Bratva had every reason to get rid of Viktor and Klara."

"I'm beginning to understand," Lindås said.

"Then you'll appreciate that Lindberg had more than one reason to leave Klara up there to die—it wasn't only to help a friend."

"He wanted to silence her."

"Her rising from the dead meant that the syndicate was once again in danger. But the sad thing was that we were so focused on the material we had, we forgot to keep Johannes in the picture."

"You left him in the lurch," Rebecka said.

"We forgot to give him the support he deserved, and that pains me deeply."

"I should hope so."

"You're absolutely right. It was very regrettable and unfair, and I hope that's what you think too, Catrin, having listened to all this."

"What?" she said.

"That all along, Johannes was only trying to do the right thing."

Lindås did not answer. She was staring at a news flash on her mobile.

"Has something happened?" Rebecka said.

"There's a police operation going on in Morgonsala, it may be something to do with Mikael," she said.

Salander's head banged against the brick wall, and she could feel the rush of heat from the furnace. She knew she had to get a grip on herself, and not only for her own sake. What the hell was her problem? She could burn men with irons. She could tattoo words onto their bellies. She could go completely wild. But she could not shoot her sister—not if her own life depended on it.

She had hesitated once more, and now, in the midst of the whirling madness around them, Camilla grabbed hold of her injured arm and tried to drag her towards the furnace. Her hair hissed as the fire singed it, and she was close to falling into the flames. But she stayed upright and saw how one man, Jorma she thought it was, was aiming a pistol at her from across the room. She shot back and hit him in the chest. There was movement and danger on all sides, and now Galinov bent to pick a weapon off the floor, and she was about to shoot him as well. But she did not have time.

Blomkvist collapsed, grimacing with pain, but in his fall he managed to grab hold of Galinov's shoulder. Just then Camilla took a step back and stared at Salander with a hatred that knew no bounds. Her whole body was shaking as she braced herself. She rushed forward to shove her into the furnace. But Salander stepped to one side, and Camilla's own momentum carried her forward. It was over in no time at all.

Yet it seemed to take forever. Not just the movement itself and the fall and the flailing hands. It was also the crashing sound, the noise of her body landing in the flames, the sizzle of scorched skin and her hair catching fire, and the screaming that followed and was stifled by the blaze and her desperate effort to get out, and then the first staggering steps back onto the floor, her hair and blouse ablaze.

Camilla howled and shook her head, writhing in agony, while Salander just stood there motionless, observing the scene. For a brief moment she wondered if she should help her sister. But she remained immobile, and something else happened instead. Camilla fell silent, paralyzed. She must have caught sight of her own reflection in the metal frame of the furnace, because suddenly she started screaming again:

"My face, my face!"

It was as if she had lost something more precious than life itself. Yet somehow she was still able to act. She bent down, picked up the weapon Galinov had dropped and aimed it at her sister, and that galvanized Salander. Now she was prepared to shoot back.

Camilla's hair was still burning, which had to be affecting her vision. She stumbled around with the pistol held high, and Salander had her finger on the trigger of her gun, ready to fire. For a split second she thought she had. A shot went off. But it was not from her own pistol.

It was from Camilla's. She had shot herself in the head and, without realizing what she was doing, Salander held out a hand and was about to say something. But whatever it was, it remained unsaid. Camilla crumpled and Salander stood and looked down at her sister while a whole world flashed by in her thoughts, a world engulfed by fire and destruction.

She thought of her mother, and of Zala burning in his

Mercedes, and soon after that the hammering of a helicopter's blades could be heard overhead and she looked down at Blomkvist, still lying on the floor, not far from Camilla and Galinov.

"Is it over?" he mumbled.

"It's over," she said, and at the same moment she heard the police shouting outside as they approached the building.

CHAPTER 35

August 28

Bublanski—or Officer Bubble as he was sometimes known—was walking in the field in front of the old glassworks. There were policemen and medical personnel all over the place. A TV crew was broadcasting live, and he was informed that Blomkvist and many of the injured had already been taken away. But to his surprise he caught sight of a familiar outline sitting inside an ambulance a little way off.

The doors were open and the figure was covered in cuts and dirt, and had singed hair and a bandaged arm. She was staring blankly at a stretcher being carried away from the building, on it a body wrapped in a grey blanket. Bublanski approached hesitantly.

"Lisbeth . . . how are you?" he said.

She did not answer. She did not even look at him, and so he continued:

"We have you to thank. Without you—"

"This wouldn't have happened," she cut in.

"Don't be hard on yourself. Dare I ask you to promise—"

"I'm not promising anything," she said in a voice which frightened him. He thought again of the fallen angel in paradise: *Serves nobody, belongs to nobody*, and he smiled self-consciously and urged the ambulance crew to take her to hospital as quickly as possible.

He turned to Sonja Modig, who was walking across the field towards him, and for the thousandth time he thought that he was too old for this sort of madness. He longed for the sea, or for anywhere at all which was peaceful and lay far away.

They sat there glued to their mobiles. Someone was reporting live on national television that Blomkvist and Salander had been carried out of the building, injured but conscious, and Lindås felt the tears welling up in her eyes. Her hands shook and she stared emptily ahead. She felt a hand on her shoulder.

"It looks as if they're going to make it," Kowalski said.

"Let's hope so," she said, wondering if she had not better leave at once.

But then she realized that she would not be able to help at all at this stage. She might as well finish what she had started, and there was still one question which needed to be answered.

"I should imagine that people will sympathize with your predicament, Johannes, at least those who want to understand," she said.

"There aren't usually too many of those," Rebecka said.

"Nothing I can do about that now," Forsell said. "Can we drop you off somewhere, Catrin?"

"I'll be all right, thanks," she said. "But there's one more thing I'd like to ask you. You said you didn't visit Nima Rita all that often at the South Wing. But you went there a few times, didn't you, and surely you must have noticed that he wasn't doing well?"

"I did."

"So why didn't you ask for something to be done? Why didn't you see to it that he was moved to a better place?"

"I insisted on all sorts of things. I even yelled at the people there. But not enough, I suppose, and perhaps I gave up too easily. I ran away from it. Maybe it was more than I could handle."

"In what way?"

"We all have things we can't deal with," he said. "In the end you just look away and pretend they're not happening."

"Was it that bad?"

"To begin with, I was there quite often. Then I waited for almost a year. It just turned out that way, and I remember feeling nervous and uncomfortable when I went back. He came shuffling towards me, wearing grey clothes. He looked like a prisoner who had been crushed. I got to my feet and put my arms around him, but his body was stiff and lifeless. I tried to talk. I asked him endless questions. His answers were monosyllabic. He seemed to have given up, and I had a violent reaction. I felt this tremendous rage."

"Towards the clinic?"

"Towards him."

"I don't understand."

"That's how it was, quite simply, guilt can do that to you. It ends up breeding a load of anger. Nima was like . . . the flip side of me. He was the price I had paid for having such a happy life."

"Can you explain that?" Lindås said.

"Don't you understand? I owed him a debt I could never repay. I couldn't even thank him without going back to the very thing that had torn him apart. I was alive because Klara had been sacrificed. Because *he* had been sacrificed, and in the end his wife too, and I couldn't bear it. I never went back to the South Wing. I looked away."

CHAPTER 36

September 9

Berger shook her head again. No, she said, she had no idea how it had all happened, but she made it clear that she did not like their choice of words. She's not some Little Miss Perfect or tone-deaf moralist. She's actually damned good. She writes with passion and power, and you should be proud instead of complaining, so get out of here and do some work.

"Now," she said.

"Yes, yes," they mumbled. "We just thought—"

"What did you think?"

"Oh, forget it."

The two young reporters, Sten Åström and Freddie Welander, slunk out of her office and she sent them on their way with a few more angry words. But sometimes she wondered too, there was no denying it. How the hell had it come about? It was the unexpected consequence of a romance, a night at a hotel, that much she knew, but still . . . Catrin Lindås.

She was the last person on earth Berger would have expected to find writing for *Millennium*. But Lindås had delivered a staggering disclosure, her story borne along by a raw fervour, and before it had even been published, Defence Minister Forsell had resigned and his undersecretary, Svante Lindberg, had been arrested, there being reasonable grounds to suspect him of murder, blackmail and aggravated espionage. Yet none of the information that had already trickled out into the media and caused banner headlines, day after day, hour by hour, had robbed the magazine of its kudos or dampened eager expectations for the latest edition.

"In view of the revelations to be published in the next issue of *Millennium*, I will be resigning my position in the government," Forsell had vouchsafed in his press release.

It was nothing short of fantastic, and the fact that some of her own staff were unable to rejoice at their success, but felt it necessary to bad-mouth the person who had delivered the scoop, only went to show how envious journalists can be. They also complained about having to cooperate with the German magazine *Geo*, in which a Paulina Müller, a writer none of them had ever heard of, had written an article about the scientific work which had helped to identify the Sherpa Nima Rita.

Blomkvist himself had not written a single line, although he had of course done the groundwork. He had spent most of the time lying in a daze of morphine, coping with the pain and a series of operations. The doctors had been reassuring: He would probably be able to walk normally again within half a year, and that was a great relief. Yet he remained taciturn and downhearted and only occasionally, as when they were discussing her divorce, did he sound like his old self again. He had laughed when she told him that she was having a romance with a man called Mikael.

"How convenient," he had said. But he did not want to talk about himself or his ordeal.

He was bottling up his suffering and she worried about him. With any luck he would open up a little today. He was going to be allowed home, and she thought she would visit him that evening. But first she was going to look through his story about troll factories, which he had not wanted to publish and had only reluctantly sent her. She put on her spectacles and started reading. OK, not a bad beginning, all things considered, she thought. He did know how to write an introduction, but then . . . she could understand why he had not been happy with it.

It sagged. He was being too complicated. He was trying to say too much at once, and she went to get herself some coffee before crossing out a sentence here and there. But then . . . what on earth was this? Towards the end of the article there was a clumsy addition which said that a man called Vladimir Kuznetsov not only owned troll factories in Russia, but was ultimately responsible for them. He was also the man behind the hate campaign which had preceded the murders of LGBTQ people in Chechnya, and that was not previously known.

She checked. No, all she could find online about Kuznetsov was almost . . . endearing. He was apparently a restaurateur and a bit of a character, an ice-hockey fan who also specialized in cooking bear steak and organizing lavish parties for the ruling elite. But Blomkvist's article said something very different. It identified him as the person who had launched the disinformation and hacker attacks that triggered the stock market crash that summer. He was the driving force behind a large proportion of the lies and hatred spreading across the world. How sensational was that? And what the hell was Blomkvist playing at? How could he hide that kind of revelation deep inside the story, and dish it up without a shred of evidence?

Berger read the piece again and saw that Kuznetsov's name contained a link to a number of documents in Russian and so she called over Irina, their editor and researcher who had helped Blomkvist earlier that summer. Irina was stocky, with large horn-rimmed spectacles and a crooked, warm smile. Immediately she settled down on Berger's chair and immersed herself in the material, translating it aloud, and at the end they looked at each other and murmured:

"Bloody hell."

Blomkvist had just made it back to his apartment on Bellmansgatan on crutches, and could not understand what Berger was going on about on the telephone. But then he was not particularly alert. He was full of morphine and his head was heavy, and he was haunted by flashbacks.

At first Salander had been there with him at the hospital, which had lent him a degree of calm; perhaps he felt better with a person by his side who knew exactly what he had been through. But just as he was getting used to having her around, she left without a word of goodbye. There was uproar, of course. The doctors and nurses ran around looking for her, as did Bublanski and Modig, who had not finished questioning her as a witness. As if that made any difference to her.

Salander was gone, and he took it badly. *Bloody hell, Lisbeth, why are you always running away from me? Can't you see that I need you?* But he would just have to live with it, and he compensated for her absence by cursing with rage and increasing his intake of painkillers.

At times, in that no-man's-land between night and day, he was driven to the edge of madness and, if he did manage to drop off during those hours, he would dream about the furnace in Morgonsala. How his body was gradually pushed into that sea of fire and consumed by the flames, and then, when he woke with a start or a scream, he would look down at his legs in bewilderment, to make sure that they were not burning.

He was most calm in the afternoons, when he had visitors, and sometimes he almost forgot about himself; or at least he managed to keep the memories of the glassworks at bay. And he was altogether taken by surprise when a black woman with sparkling eyes appeared, a bouquet of flowers in her arms. She was wearing a bright-blue suit with flared trousers and her hair was neatly braided. She looked like a runner or dancer and moved almost soundlessly. At first he could not think why she looked familiar, and then it dawned on him: It was Kadi Linder, the boardroom professional and psychologist whom he had met in the doorway of what was now her apartment at Fiskargatan.

Kadi had come to see if there was anything she could do to help, she said, deeply moved by what she had read about him in the newspapers, but she seemed also to want to tell him something else. Seeing her fidget and look somewhat awkward, he asked what was troubling her.

"I got an e-mail," she said. "Actually, e-mail isn't the right word. My screen blinked, and as if by magic there was this file about Freddy Carlsson at Formea Bank. You know, that guy who's been getting at me and bad-mouthing me for years because I said he was dishonest in *Veckans Affärer*."

"I vaguely remember that," he said.

"Well, that file contained unequivocal proof that, when he was in charge of the bank's business in the Baltic, Freddy had engaged in sophisticated money-laundering activities, and I saw that he wasn't just casually dishonest but actually a criminal through and through."

"Good grief."

"But that wasn't what surprised me the most. It was the message just below the link to the file."

"What did it say?"

"Something like 'I've been keeping an eye on the security cameras in case someone hasn't realized I've moved.' That was all, and at first I had no idea what it meant. There was no sender and no name. But then I thought of your visit and the dramatic events at Morgonsala. And the penny dropped: I'd bought Lisbeth Salander's apartment, and that made me—"

"You don't need to be worried," he interrupted her.

"Worried? Oh no, my God, not at all, I was starstruck! I could see that the file on Freddy Carlsson was Salander's way of making up for any hassle I might have because of her.

Frankly, I was overwhelmed, and it made me want to help the two of you even more."

"That's not at all necessary," he said. "It's already good of you to come to see me."

In a move so inspired that he surprised himself, Blomkvist then asked Kadi if she might consider becoming chair of the magazine's board of directors, bearing in mind *Millennium*'s exposed position in the media market and all the aggressive attempts to buy them up. She lit up at that and at once said yes, and the very next day he got Erika and the others to agree to the idea.

Catrin had of course been his most frequent visitor at the hospital, not just because they were virtually a couple now, but also because he was working with her on her report. He read successive drafts and they discussed the story over and over. Both Lindberg and Engelman had been arrested, and so had Ivan Galinov. Annika Giannini, who paid the occasional sisterly visit to Blomkvist's bedside, told him that Lindberg would in all likelihood receive a life sentence for his treason and certainly faced confiscation of his illicit gains. It looked like the end for Svavelsjö M.C., although perhaps not for Zvezda Bratva, whose protectors were too powerful.

Forsell, however, looked as if he would come out of it reasonably well, and at times Blomkvist thought that Catrin was being too easy on him. But Forsell had, after all, given them the scoop. And besides, he liked the man, so he supposed it was a concession he would have to live with. In any case it was bound to be a relief for Rebecka and the boys.

It was particularly heartening that Nima Rita had been cremated according to Buddhist custom back home in Teng-boche, Nepal. There was also to be a memorial service, and Bob Carson was coming over from Denver. Fredrika Nyman would be there too. Everything seemed to be falling into place. Yet somehow none of it made him really happy. He felt that he was on the sidelines, especially now that Erika was babbling excitedly at him over the telephone. What on earth was she talking about?

"Who's Kuznetsov?" he said.

"Have you completely lost your marbles?"

"What do you mean, my marbles?"

"You've hung him out to dry."

"I have?"

"What drugs are they giving you?"

"Nowhere near enough."

"And it's a lousy piece of writing too."

"I did warn you."

"But in your usual lousy style you've emphasized very clearly that it was Vladimir Kuznetsov who set off this summer's stock market crash. He was also one of the people behind the murders of homosexuals in Chechnya."

He had no idea what she was talking about. He hobbled over to his computer and opened up his old article.

"That sounds pretty crazy."

"Not half as crazy as your reaction to my questions."

"It must be . . ." He did not finish his sentence, but then he did not have to either. The same thought had occurred to Erika.

"Is this something to do with Lisbeth?"

"I honestly don't know, Erika," he said, shocked. "But tell me now. Kuznetsov, you say."

"You'll have to read it yourself. Irina is busy translating the documents and the evidence that was attached. But it's an absolutely mind-boggling story. Kuznetsov's the one the Crazy Sisters sing about in 'Killing the World with Lies.'"

"In what?"

"Sorry, I keep forgetting that you lost touch somewhere around Tina Turner."

"Pack it in."

"I'll do my best."

"At least give me a chance to look into it."

"I'll pop over this evening and we can talk about it."

He thought about Catrin, who was meant to be coming over late that afternoon.

"Let's meet up tomorrow, that'll give me time to get my head around a bit more of this."

"OK. And how are you feeling, by the way?"

He gave it some thought. And decided that she deserved a serious answer.

"It's been pretty tough."

"I can imagine."

"But now . . ."

"What?"

"I've just begun to feel alive again."

He was in a hurry to hang up.

"I have to . . ." he went on.

"Get in touch with a certain person."

"Something like that."

"Take care then," she said.

He ended the call and tried again what he had tried to do countless times from hospital—get hold of Salander. He had not seen a single sign of life since she had vanished, had heard nothing at all of her except that she had sent that message to Kadi Linder, and he was worried. It was part of his general anxiety, a creeping unease which was always worst at night and early in the morning. He was afraid that she was unable to stop; that she would seek out new shadows from her past, and that eventually she would run out of luck. It was—he could not get the thought out of his mind—as if she were predestined for a violent end, and he could not bear the thought.

He picked up his mobile. What would he write this time? The clouds were rolling in outside. The wind was picking up and rattling the windowpanes and he felt his heart beat in his chest. Memories of the gaping furnace in Morgonsala washed over him and he toyed with the idea of making his message sound quite strict: She must get in touch. Otherwise, he would go mad.

But in the end it was lighthearted—as if he were afraid to show how worried he was.

```
<So giving me a scoop wasn't enough? You
had to hand me Kuznetsov's head on a plat-
ter too>
```

But there was no answer. The hours passed and day turned to night and Catrin came. They kissed and shared a bottle of wine, and for a while he forgot his troubles. They didn't stop talking until they both fell asleep at around eleven, entwined in each other's arms. He woke up three hours later with a feeling of impending doom and nervously picked up his mobile. But there was nothing from Salander. He reached for his crutches, limped into the kitchen and sat there until dawn, thinking about her.

EPILOGUE

The sky was heavy with a gathering storm when Inspector Artur Delov parked on the gravel road outside the charred remains of a house in Gorodishche, northwest of Volgograd. He simply could not understand why the fire had caused such a commotion.

No-one had been injured and it had not been much of a house. The whole neighbourhood was poor and run-down and nobody had even laid claim to the building. Yet there were VIPs out there, intelligence people, gangsters too, he thought, and also a number of small boys who should really be in school or at home with their mothers. He shooed them away and surveyed the ruins. About the only thing left was an old iron stove and a toppled chimney. Everything else had been destroyed and burned to the ground, there were not even any glowing embers. The entire plot was a black, desolate scene, and there was a gaping hole in the middle of it all, like a hatch leading down into the underworld. Some scorched, ghost-like trees were standing next to the site, their branches sticking out like charred fingers.

Gusts of wind whipped up ashes and soot from the ground and made it hard to breathe. There was a feeling of poison in the air, and Artur's chest tightened. But he shook it off and turned to his colleague Anna Mazurova, who was standing there, looking down at the debris from the fire.

"What's this all about?" he said.

Anna had flakes of soot in her hair. "We think it's a statement."

"What do you mean?"

"The house was bought a week ago through a law firm in Stockholm," she said. "The family who lived here moved to new and better accommodation in Volgograd. And yesterday evening, when the last of the furniture had been carried out, explosions were heard from inside. The house burst into flames and burned to the ground."

"And why are people concerned about that?" he said.

"Alexander Zalachenko, the man who created Zvezda Bratva—the 'Star Mob' syndicate—spent the first years of his life here. After his parents died, he was moved to a children's home in Sverdlovsk in the Urals. That property burned down the day before yesterday, which seemed to worry some of the bigwigs, especially since it coincides with a number of other setbacks for the syndicate."

"So it looks as if there's someone who's determined to put the very roots of evil to the torch," he said, looking pensive.

There was a rumbling in the sky. A squall swept by, pulling with it ashes and soot from the ruins and carrying them past the trees and away from the neighbourhood. Soon the rain began to fall, a liberating shower which seemed to purify the air, and Artur Delov felt the pressure release across his chest.

Not long after that, Salander landed in Munich, and in the taxi going into town she looked at her mobile and saw a series of text messages from Blomkvist. She decided at last to answer.

<I've put a full stop> she wrote.

The reply came back straightaway.

<Full stop?>

<Time to begin again>

Then she smiled and, although she did not know it, Blomkvist also smiled, at home on Bellmansgatan. It felt like it was time for something new.

ACKNOWLEDGMENTS

My heartfelt thanks go to my publisher, Eva Gedin, and my agents, Magdalena Hedlund and Jessica Bab Bonde. A big thank-you to Peter Karlsson, publisher at Norstedts, and my editor, Ingemar Karlsson. Thanks to Erland and Joakim Larsson, father and brother to Stieg Larsson. Thanks to journalist and author Karin Bojs, who tipped me off about the Sherpa gene, and Marie Allen, professor of forensic medicine, who helped me with my research into it. Thanks too to David Jacoby, senior security researcher at Kaspersky Lab; Christopher MacLehose, my British publisher; George Goulding, my translator into English; Henrik Druid, professor of forensic medicine; Petra Råsten-Almqvist, head of the Stockholm department of the National Board of Forensic Medicine; Johan Norberg, guitarist and writer; Jakob Norstedt, DNA consultant; Peter Wittboldt, Inspector in the Swedish police; and Linda Altrov Berg, Catherine Mörk and Kajsa Loord at Norstedts—and also to my first and most important reader, my Anne.

ALSO AVAILABLE FROM

THE MILLENNIUM SERIES

THE GIRL WITH THE DRAGON TATTOO
by Stieg Larsson

Harriet Vanger, a scion of one of Sweden's wealthiest families, disappeared over forty years ago. All these years later, her aged uncle continues to seek the truth. He hires Mikael Blomkvist, a crusading journalist recently trapped by a libel conviction, to investigate. He is aided by the pierced and tattooed punk prodigy Lisbeth Salander. Together they tap into a vein of unfathomable iniquity and astonishing corruption.

Crime Fiction

THE GIRL WHO PLAYED WITH FIRE
by Stieg Larsson

Mikael Blomkvist, crusading publisher of the magazine *Millennium*, has decided to run a story that will expose an extensive sex trafficking operation. On the eve of its publication, the two reporters responsible for the article are murdered, and the fingerprints found on the murder weapon belong to his friend, the troubled genius hacker Lisbeth Salander. Blomkvist, convinced of Salander's innocence, plunges into an investigation.

Crime Fiction

THE GIRL WHO KICKED THE HORNET'S NEST
by Stieg Larsson

Lisbeth Salander, in the ICU of a Swedish city hospital, is fighting for her life in more ways than one: when she's well enough, she'll stand trial for three murders. With the help of Mikael Blomkvist, she will have to prove her innocence. And, on her own, she will plot her revenge—against the man who tried to kill her and the corrupt government institutions that very nearly destroyed her life.

Crime Fiction

THE GIRL IN THE SPIDER'S WEB
by David Lagercrantz

One night, Mikael Blomkvist receives a call from a source who claims to have been given information vital to the United States by a young female hacker. Blomkvist, always on the lookout for a story, reaches out to Salander for help. She, as usual, has plans of her own. Together they are drawn into a ruthless underworld of spies, cybercriminals, and government operatives—some willing to kill to protect their secrets.

Crime Fiction

THE GIRL WHO TAKES AN EYE FOR AN EYE
by David Lagercrantz

Lisbeth Salander is serving time in Flodberga Prison. When a sadistic gang leader nicknamed Benito starts to torture Faria, a young Bangladeshi prisoner, Salander finds it impossible not to intervene. Now a target of Benito and her gang, Salander's time in prison is further complicated by news from her old guardian, who tells her she may have been a subject in a secret experiment known as the Registry. She enlists her friend Mikael Blomkvist, the crusading publisher of *Millennium* magazine, to help her look into it. Once Salander is released, she devotes her time to uncovering the truth in the case that landed Faria in prison, and Blomkvist continues his search into Salander's background. But when the two cases start to dovetail, Salander and Blomkvist must join together to fight for justice and their lives.

Crime Fiction

VINTAGE CRIME / BLACK LIZARD
Available wherever books are sold.
www.vintagebooks.com